"Hello, Cole.
It's been a long time."

"Maggie!"

Shocked, he stared in disbelief. Somehow his brain had no control over his gaping mouth.

When she moved toward him with feline grace and confidence, Cole began to feel like a bowl of cream about to be consumed. Maggie extended a gloved hand to him, and he didn't know whether to kiss it or shake it, so he squeezed it and then pulled her into his arms and hugged her. From the feel of the curves pressed against him, she sure as hell wasn't a kid anymore.

Other **AVON ROMANCES**

THE MACKENZIES
COLE

ANA LEIGH

AVON BOOKS
An Imprint of HarperCollins*Publishers*

This is a work of fiction. Names, characters, places, and incidents are products of the author's imagination or are used fictitiously and are not to be construed as real. Any resemblance to actual events, locales, organizations, or persons, living or dead, is entirely coincidental.

AVON BOOKS
An Imprint of HarperCollins*Publishers*
10 East 53rd Street
New York, New York 10022-5299

Copyright © 2002 by Ana Leigh
ISBN: 0-380-82009-9
www.avonromance.com

First Avon Books paperback printing: December 2002

Avon Trademark Reg. U.S. Pat. Off. and in Other Countries, Marca Registrada, Hecho en U.S.A.
HarperCollins ® is a registered trademark of HarperCollins Publishers Inc.

Printed in the U.S.A.

10 9 8 7 6 5 4 3 2 1

Prologue

Alaska
1896

The sudden pop of a log on the campfire jarred Maggie's attention away from the conversation between Cole and her father. His announcement that he was leaving Alaska had been a shock. She hugged her knees to her chin as thoughts of the past two years and the three of them panning for gold swirled through her head.

How could Cole just up and leave them? He had been so much of her life in these past years that she couldn't imagine a day without him. Except for an occasional trip into Dawson City for supplies, the three of them had been together every day and night since she was fourteen, when he had strayed into their camp and joined them.

A sudden burst of laughter caused her to look over at him. With his head flung back, his black hair glistened with carmine streaks from the glow of the fire, and his teeth gleamed whitely against the dark beard that shadowed his cheeks and jaw.

How well her young heart had memorized that face: the olive luster of his maternal Spanish blood, the chiseled jaw and incredible sapphire eyes of his father's lineage.

She was so in love with Cole MacKenzie that thoughts of him monopolized her every waking hour. How could he now speak—and even laugh about it—of leaving? Couldn't he see how much she loved him? Why didn't he look at her or kiss her, as he did the cheap whores in Dawson City? Couldn't he see that despite the fact she was only sixteen, despite the boy's trousers her father made her wear, the oversized shirts that concealed her breasts, and her hair cropped short and shoved under a battered hat, the undeniable truth was that inside she was a woman—with all a woman's yearning for the man she loved.

And that man was Cole MacKenzie.

Unable to bear the thought of never seeing him again, Maggie jumped to her feet. "No! No! You can't leave. You can't leave."

Sobbing, she ran into the cabin and flung herself down on her bunk.

For a long moment after Maggie's outburst the two men remained speechless. Then Pop O'Shea shook his head.

"Poor Maggie. It's time we left, too. Growing up like a lad in these wilds is no life for a gal. Time she got some education."

"You've done a good job of educating her, Pop."

"Just book learning, Cole. My little jewel needs some polishing, the company of young folks her own age. Time I sent her to one of those finishing schools where she can learn the proper way of young ladies. Besides, there's a lot more unsavory characters arriving daily, and it'll soon be too hard to keep her identity a secret. Yeah, it's time for us to leave, too."

"I bet the kid's not going to like that, Pop."

"I don't much care. She needs it."

"I think you're right." Cole had had mixed feelings about leaving the two in these wilds. If something happened to Pop, what would become of the kid?

"Anyway, we've got enough gold to live comfortably for a while. I never was a greedy man," Pop said. "And I'd bet my last ounce of gold you aren't either. We'll pack up and get out of here in the morning. I'll go tell Maggie. 'Night, Cole."

"Good night, Pop."

Long after Pop left, Cole remained at the fire. For the past month he'd been fighting the restlessness that had plagued him as long as he could remember. In his twenty-three years there wasn't too much he hadn't tried. He had laid railroad track, worked as a lumberjack, and served as a deputy sheriff in Tombstone.

For a short time he'd even ridden with a gang of outlaws. Cole grinned, thinking about that experience. When Zach tracked him down, his cousin had almost kicked his ass back to Texas.

One thing he knew for certain: he'd had enough of being a lawman after he'd done his stint with the Texas Rangers like the rest of the MacKenzie men.

His grin stretched into a wide smile as he thought

about his cousins Josh and Zach. Growing up together, they sure had shared some good times, but the restlessness in him had always caused him to move on and see what was over the horizon. And as much as he loved his family and the Triple M, he was not ready to settle down to a life of ranching. One day he'd meet the right woman and settle in the way his cousins had done—but that day hadn't dawned yet.

He dug a battered envelope out of his pocket and reread the letter from his mother. It had taken almost a year to reach him. So his cousin Kitty had remarried. Good for her. She'd taken the death of her husband, Ted Drummond, real hard. He and Kitty had always been close, and he missed her as much as he did his folks.

Yeah, he re-resolved, just like his cousins, one day he'd meet the right gal, and then he'd go back to the Triple M for good.

Bright and early the next morning they packed up the mules and for the last time closed the door of the crude cabin that had been their home for two years. They retraced their trail across the White Pass, following the dangerous twists and turns bordered by a hill on one side and a drop of hundreds of feet down the other side.

At times the trail narrowed to not much more than two feet, and they would unpack the mules and carry the heavy pokes of gold by hand, which required a dozen trips back and forth, in fear that the mules would slip and go over the side. And when the trail widened, they would repack the gold until the next narrow stretch. It was a tiresome and slow process, but they finally reached Skagway, traded in their gold and mules, and then left on a packet to Juneau, where they then boarded a steamer to Seattle.

Once in Seattle, Cole said a sad good-bye to Pop, who was returning to his hometown of Lawford, New Mexico. Cole promised to write to him as soon as he got settled in California. Turning to Maggie, he tapped her chin lightly with his fist.

"Take care of yourself, kid."

She glared belligerently at him. "I'm not a *kid*, Cole MacKenzie."

Then with five thousand dollars in his wallet, Cole boarded the steamer for San Francisco.

Chapter 1

San Francisco
1898

Cole was bored with the poker game. He was a bet-ter than average player but never had acquired his father's love for the game.

And he was bored with the idleness he'd been living in for the past two years as well. Restlessness and idleness were two different things. He suffered with the first, but not the second.

"Deal me out." He shoved back his chair, picked up his money, and left the barroom. The desk clerk stopped him when he entered the hotel.

"This telegram just came for you, Cole."

"Thanks, Joe." A worried frown creased his brow as he ripped the envelope open. Who would send him a telegram unless it was bad news? Had something happened to Jeb?

NEED YOUR HELP STOP SITUATION DESPERATE STOP
CAN YOU COME AT ONCE STOP POP O'SHEA

At least it wasn't the news he feared about his brother, but Pop had to be in serious trouble to send such a message. Cole thought of his friend's last letter to him. After returning to his hometown, Pop had started a stagecoach line and appeared to have been settled into a life of contentment. What could have happened to cause him to sound so desperate?

Cole purchased a ticket for the next eastbound train out of there, then went to the Western Union office and sent a return telegram to Pop. After withdrawing his money from the bank, he hurried back to his room and packed up his clothes.

Bright and early the following morning he boarded the train bound for New Mexico. He glanced across the aisle at the young couple holding hands and looking cow-eyed at each other. They had to be honeymooners. That wasn't for him. At least he was footloose and fancy-free. Nothing and no one to keep him in San Francisco.

His dad had said that he, too, had always had the same kind of restlessness until he'd met Mom, taken one look at her, and known she was the one. Well, maybe if he'd ever meet a woman like his mom, he'd do the same thing. But he hadn't met a woman yet he'd want to be tied down with for the rest of his life.

Glancing again at the honeymooners, he saw the new bride now had her head on her husband's shoulder. Those two would have been better off in a private compartment.

Cole leaned back, stretched out his long legs, and propped his feet on the empty seat opposite him. Then he closed his eyes. No-siree-bob, not for him! No wife. No children. No responsibility. What better way to live your life?

Three days later Cole climbed down from a creaking wagon.

"Thanks, Gus," Cole said to the driver, who'd been nice enough to give him a ride from Noches.

The old timer nodded and flicked the reins of his team, and the wagon rolled away, kicking up a cloud of dust.

Cole put down his traveling bag and glanced around in disgust. Between delays resulting in four train changes and a bumpy, twenty-five-mile ride on the wagon, because the stage wasn't running, it had taken three days to get there.

He glanced around in disbelief at the town of Lawford, New Mexico. The country was on the brink of the twentieth century, but apparently no one had told the local residents. If the town had been painted in a sepia tone, Lawford could have been a page out of an almanac of the old West. From what he could see, the roads were unpaved, the only brick building was the bank, and the business section wasn't much longer than a block.

The streets were deserted, but the sound of voices raised in the hymn "Rock of Ages" caused him to glance up to where a crowd was gathered on a nearby hillside.

He picked up his suitcase and headed for a building with the sign—O'SHEA STAGELINE COMPANY—hanging above the front door. He tried to enter, but the door was locked. Peering through the window, he saw the office was deserted. Rather than tote his bag around with him, he crossed the street to the Lawford Hotel.

The lobby of the two-story structure was neat and clean. A red couch and several chairs were set invitingly in a group in the corner.

"This town always this quiet?" he asked the desk clerk, who was so young he hadn't sprouted his first whisker.

"Most of the folks are at Pop O'Shea's funeral."

The unexpected reply felt like a blow to the gut. "Pop's dead!"

"They ain't plantin' him alive, mister."

Dammit, he'd just heard a dear friend was dead, and he didn't want to hear any shit from this snot-nosed kid. He loved that old man, and he had all he could do to keep from pulling this smart-ass over the counter.

"How did he die?"

"Fell and broke his neck in an old mine."

"A mine? Pop ran a stageline, didn't he?"

Somehow his withering glance must have conveyed his mounting irritation.

The lad nodded. "Yeah, but he liked to explore old mines. Heard tell he used to pan gold in Alaska."

Situation desperate. Can you come at once? The cryptic message echoed over and over in his head. "When was he killed?"

"They found his body yesterday. Guess he'd been missing a couple of days."

Sonofabitch! Cole clenched his hands in frustration.

If only he'd gotten here sooner, Pop might still have been alive. *Situation desperate. Can you come at once?* Was it really an accident or was it foul play? He sure as hell wasn't leaving until he got to the bottom of it.

"Did you know Pop well?"

"Heck, yes. Everybody in town knew Pop. We all loved him."

"He was easy to love."

"Sure was. Didn't have an enemy. He got along with everybody, 'cept maybe Ben Lawford. Now and then they'd have a go at it, but I wouldn't call 'em enemies."

"What did they find to argue about?"

"Mostly about the stageline. Ben wanted to buy it, but Pop wouldn't sell it to him."

"Why did this Lawford want it?"

"Reckon because he owns everything else in town."

Cole signed the register, and the clerk slipped the key across the desk. "That's two dollars in advance, mister. How long you plannin' on stayin'?"

Cole tossed a sawbuck on the desk and picked up the key. "Until I'm ready to leave."

By the time Cole had unpacked his clothes and gone back downstairs, the funeral had ended, and people were returning to their businesses.

Cole figured the best place to pick up any more gossip was the local saloon, and in Lawford that appeared to be a place called Dallas's. He liked the name anyway.

There were a half-dozen men in the bar—the usual variety. Towns could change, but saloons and the people in them never seemed to. Cole bellied up to the bar, and the bartender, who looked more like a bouncer, came over to him.

"Whiskey or beer?"

"A double and chase it with a beer."

Cole raised the whiskey in a silent toast to Pop and quaffed the liquor. He waited for the whiskey to kick in, then he picked up the glass of beer and drank it down. When he motioned toward the whiskey glass, the bartender refilled it.

"Leave the bottle."

"Looks like you plan on doing some serious drinking, stranger."

"Name's MacKenzie, not stranger." After another drink he could feel the whiskey, beer, and Pop's death blending together, only this time he was chasing it down with anger and frustration.

"Don't recall seeing you before, Mr. MacKenzie."

"Could be because I've never been here before."

"You don't look like any drummer. What brought you to Lawford?"

"Pop O'Shea."

"Yeah, sorry about his passing. He was a good man."

Right answer! "Pour yourself one, ah . . ."

"Vic Chance."

"To Pop, Vic," Cole said, raising his glass.

"To Pop," Vic echoed. The bartender downed the drink then asked, "You kin or friend?"

"Friend. We were partners in Alaska."

"MacKenzie! Sure, that's why the name sounded familiar. Pop spoke of you. Loved you like a son."

Pay dirt. "Pop was easy to love."

"Hell, yes."

Since he'd already been down that road with the desk clerk, Cole pursued a different line.

"Pop sure knew his way around mines. Seems strange he'd be careless enough to fall in one and break his neck."

"Accidents happen."

"I can't see why he'd even be poking around in a mine. He owned the stageline, didn't he?"

"Yeah." Vic had suddenly turned reticent.

"That surprises me, too. I thought Ben Lawford owned everything in town."

"Practically."

"Everything except the stageline," Cole said.

"And Dallas's. Nobody owns Dallas."

The speaker stood at his side. She was a blond woman—an incredibly attractive blonde. She was probably twenty years his senior, but she lacked the tough veneer of the women of her age and profession that he'd met previously. There was a soft vulnerability about her that made her very appealing sexually and added to her attractiveness. He liked her on sight.

"And I bet my best pair of boots that you're Dallas."

Her light laughter was pleasant to the ears. "Dallas Donovan."

Cole doffed his hat. "Pleasure to meet you, ma'am. Name's Cole MacKenzie."

She picked up the whiskey bottle and grabbed a couple of glasses.

"Let's sit down, Cole. I get homesick every time I hear one of you Texas boys." Once seated at a corner table, she asked, "What part of Texas are you from?"

"My family's got a spread northwest of Fort Worth, up near the Red."

She leaned back in her chair and made no attempt to disguise her perusal of him. "You're a handsome one all right, Texas. That dark skin and those blue eyes. Looks like your ma must be Mex or Indian."

Cole grinned. "Actually Spanish, but born and bred in Texas, same as I."

Dallas gave him a lopsided smile. "I bet you've left a trail of broken hearts as long as the Rio Grande."

He cringed in mock pain. "Dallas, you do me an injustice. I *love* women."

"Is that right? I'd bet my best bustle no gal's been able to rope and hog-tie you."

"Who says one hasn't?"

She laughed in response. "Texas, you've got that bachelor look, if I ever saw one. You look like another MacKenzie I met once by the name of Josh. You wouldn't be kin by any chance?"

Cole grinned. "Cousins."

"Well, I'll be damned. Must be ten years since I last saw him. How's that good-looking buck doing? He was riding with the Rangers then."

"He's back on the Triple M now with a wife and a couple of kids."

"The Triple M! Is *that* your family's spread?"

Cole was surprised to see her astonishment. "Yeah, you heard of it?"

"Honey, anyone between here and the Mexican border has heard of the Triple M. So you must be the MacKenzie who prospected with Pop in Alaska. I tell you, this world is getting smaller every day."

"You'd never know by the looks of this town. It belongs back in the Dark Ages. I was surprised to discover there's running water in the hotel. Dallas, there's paved streets, trains, electricity, telephone, even horseless carriages out there."

"Now, no complaining, Cole. We love our little town just the way it is. It's a good place to live in."

"Or die in," Cole said, remembering his purpose for being there. "Pop found that out."

Her eyes narrowed in wariness. "What's that supposed to mean? Hope you're not thinking Pop's death was foul play, Cole MacKenzie. No one in this town would hurt Pop. We all loved him."

"Yeah, so I've been told."

A tall man entered the saloon and made a straight line to their table. He appeared to be in his early forties, with a mustache as well trimmed as his lithe body. And the suit he was wearing sure hadn't come from any rack in Lawford's general store. The same could be said for his Stetson and boots.

"Howdy, Keith," Dallas said. "Keith, this is Cole MacKenzie, a friend of Pop O'Shea's."

"I suspected as much," Lawford said, extending his hand. "How do you do, Mr. MacKenzie. I'm Keith Lawford. I've been expecting you. I'm Mr. O'Shea's attorney and handle all his legal affairs. I was given the wire you sent him and regret you had to be greeted with such unfortunate news. But I'm glad you're here. There are some matters that involve you and, of course, Margaret."

"Margaret?" Cole asked, perplexed.

"Mr. O'Shea's daughter."

"Oh, yeah. The kid."

In his shock over the unexpected news of Pop's death, Cole had completely forgotten about Maggie. What would the kid do without the old man? He remembered Pop telling him he and Maggie had no other family—just each other. Now the poor kid didn't even have Pop. What would happen to her? He knew his folks would take her in, but what he remembered of the girl, she was very stubborn and ornery as hell.

"Mr. MacKenzie, I was hoping I could set up an appointment with you and Margaret."

"Where's the kid . . . ah, Margaret—now?"

"Needless to say, she's very stricken and went home after her father was laid to rest."

"Alone?"

"No, of course not. The O'Sheas have a housekeeper."

Cole started to get up. "I should go and see her."

"Margaret has indicated she does not wish any visitors."

Lawford's patronizing tone pissed the hell out of Cole. He sat back down. "Let's get something straight, Lawford. Drop all this formality crap. Pop is Pop. He hated to be called Mister anything. Same goes for me. It can be Cole or MacKenzie."

"As you wish . . . Cole. Will ten o'clock tomorrow morning be convenient for you?"

"No problem, Lawford."

The corners of the attorney's mouth lifted in a suggestion of a smile. "It's Keith or *Mister* Lawford." He stood up and extended his hand. "It's been a pleasure meeting you. I wish it could have been under more pleasant circumstances."

"Same here."

"Good afternoon, Dallas," Lawford said, tipping his hat. He departed.

The prick. "What a stuffed shirt," Cole said.

"Keith's not so bad once you get to know him," Dallas said. "But his father can be a real pain in the rear end." She stood up. "Hope you'll be around for a while, Texas."

Oh, he was going to be around, all right. He wasn't leaving until he got to the bottom of Pop's death.

Cole watched Dallas walk over to the bar, speak to Vic in a whispered tone, and then climb the stairway. As much as he liked her, he could tell she knew a damn sight more than she was saying. In all probability, so did Vic. And if he was any judge of people, Cole figured the bartender had just got the word from his boss to clam up.

Cole decided to take a closer look at the town. He nodded to Vic and then at Dallas, who was standing at the top of the stairway. As he walked to the door, he could feel their stares smack between his shoulder blades.

After three shots of whiskey and a beer chaser, Lawford still didn't look any better to him than it had when he arrived. He walked down to the stagecoach office, and this time his gut wrenched when he read Pop's name on the sign over the door. Observing the big barn connected to the office, he entered the building.

There were six horses in stalls. Upon checking, he saw the stalls had been mucked out and there was fresh grain and hay in each of them. Someone had the presence of mind to remember the horses. With Maggie in a state of mourning, he doubted it would have been her.

At the sound of scurrying behind him, Cole spun around and saw a young boy peering over the top of a barrel. The youngster couldn't have been more than nine or ten years old.

"¡Hola, pequeño! ¿Habla usted inglés?"

"Sí, señor."

"What's your name, son?"

"Juan Morales, señor."

"I'm Cole MacKenzie, Juan. Are you the one who took care of the horses?"

"*Sí*, Señor MacKenzie. Every morning Abuelo give Juan twenty-five centavos to clean the stalls and feed the horses."

Cole nodded. "You do a good job. Did you always call Pop O'Shea 'Grandfather,' Juan?"

"It gave Abuelo much pleasure, Señor MacKenzie."

"I'm sure it did," Cole said sadly, remembering the beloved old man's fondness for young children. What a pity Pop hadn't lived to have grandchildren of his own.

"You are a friend of Abuelo's?" Juan asked.

"Yes."

"He was a good man. Juan's heart held much love for him."

"Mine did, too, Juan." Cole could feel the sorrow pressing in on him again. He slipped a coin into the youngster's hand. "Take care, son."

Juan smiled broadly. "*Gracias,* Señor MacKenzie," the youngster said, staring in awe at the dollar.

"*De nada, Juan. Adiós.*"

By the time Cole left the barn, dusk had descended on the small town, closeting its deserted streets in stretches of purple shadows, except for a patch of sunlight that seemed to hang above the hillside like a beacon.

He entered the Lawford Diner. Since becoming aware that Ben Lawford owned most everything in town, Cole couldn't help wondering if the name Lawford—branded on practically every building— referred more to the owner's name than to the town's.

Personally, from what he'd seen of Lawford, New Mexico, if Lawford and that prick Keith—who most likely was his son—did own most of the town, it sure as hell was nothing to swell their heads. But it did make Ben Lawford high man on the totem pole.

Just how much of a thorn could Pop O'Shea have been in Lawford's rear end?

After a tasteless meal, Cole returned to the saloon and played poker. He was into the game for fifty bucks when he decided to call it quits. Until he knew all the players in the town, he wasn't about to flash a wad of money around. On the other hand, he had no intentions of depositing it in the Lawford Bank and Trust Company either.

Cole stepped out of Dallas's. All day he had put off the obvious thing he still had to do. Moonlight had now become the beacon over the hill, and he paused at a sign printed Boot Hill with an arrow pointing to the top.

Boot Hill. Cole shook his head. *Good God, couldn't they even give the cemetery a respectable name?* How did a town that was twenty-five miles away from the nearest modern transportation, lacked paved streets, rejected every modern convenience and any attempt at urbanization keep from becoming extinct like so many other towns in the West? Any moment he suspected a war party of Apaches to come charging down the hill.

He followed the path up the hillside. Even in the dark it was not difficult to find the fresh mound of dirt. Shoulders slumped, hat in hand, he gazed down at the final resting place of one of the finest men he'd ever known.

"Talk to me, Pop. Tell me what happened? Was your death really an accident, or did it have something to do with that telegram you sent me? I swear I won't leave this damn town until I have the answer."

Cole lost track of how long he stood at the graveside before he became aware that he was being watched. He turned his head and peered into the darkness surrounding him. Tombstones and carved markers formed grim silhouettes in the moonlight, but he saw no one.

Cautiously he approached the clump of tall shrubbery at the top of the hill. It was the only place a person might possibly conceal himself. Not a leaf rustled, not a limb stirred as he passed, but the feeling remained at the nape of his neck as he walked back down the hill.

To satisfy his own curiosity, he went back to Dallas's. Nothing had changed except that she was now working the bar.

"Thought you left for the night, Texas." She poured him a whiskey.

"Thought so, too. Reckon the night air chased the sleep out of me. You tending bar now, Dallas? Where's Vic?"

"He went out back for a smoke and some fresh air." She looked away and suddenly became real busy wiping up the bar.

"Speak of the devil," Cole said, when Vic slipped back in looking harried and winded. "You look like you've just run a mile, Vic."

"Wind's stirring up outside," Vic mumbled, and moved down to the other end of the bar.

Cole figured he'd solved who was lurking in the shadows. Question was, why was Vic spying on him?

Yep, Pop, I ain't leaving Lawford until I get some answers.

He downed his drink and left.

Chapter 2

Maggie finally gave up trying to sleep, got out of bed and dressed, then went down to the office. She paused in the entrance. Maybe it was a mistake to come back so soon. There were so many reminders of Pop that she felt her heart would burst. She looked through her tears at the framed photograph on the wall of Pop with his arms around her and Cole. It had been taken the day they left Skagway. Turning away, she moved to his desk and tenderly touched the pipe and tobacco pouch lying there, and then she sat down in his chair and picked up the worn deck of cards that he used to play solitaire.

Why, Pop? You said you wanted to live out the rest of your life in peace and tranquillity. Why did you have to go poking around in mines?

Slamming down the cards in despair, Maggie moved to the window. Her tear-filled gaze swept the deserted street. Suddenly she stiffened in shock when she saw the lone man on the balcony of the Lawford Hotel. She recognized him at once, and her heart leaped to her throat.

Naked except for the pair of jeans that hugged his slim hips and long legs, he hadn't changed. Somehow she'd hoped his shoulders weren't as broad, the crisp hair on his chest so sensually appealing, as her girlish infatuation had remembered. And she was certain that if she were near enough to see, his sapphire eyes would be like deep-blue pools. Those same eyes that had failed to recognize her love for him.

A mixture of poignant memories and bitterness flashed through her head as she relived those years in Alaska and the heartache of parting. What had hurt the most—the actual good-bye, or his obliviousness to her feelings for him?

The one thing she knew for certain was that despite her having met dozens of young bachelors in the past two years, Cole MacKenzie remained the one man— the one image—her heart would not forget.

And now at the height of despair over Pop's death, she would have to face him again. Her face hardened with the bitterness that overwhelmed her. At least she was no longer that naïve sixteen-year-old girl.

Maggie sat down at the desk and cradled her head in her hands. Pop's death and now Cole. Did she have the fortitude to face both crises together? She felt the sting on her cheeks from the hot slide of tears and wiped them away with a handkerchief.

A life of indolence for the past two years had not changed Cole's sleeping habits. Raised on a ranch, he was an early riser, and regrettably at this hour there wasn't much in Lawford to observe from the balcony of the hotel except for a mutt meandering from one side of the street to the other, sniffing at the discarded cigar butts and whatever else might have ended up there.

A light breeze tickled the dust on the road, and the rising sun had begun to cut a hazy gold through the gray horizon. In another hour there'd be no breeze and the blasted heat would roll in.

Cole leaned back against the dilapidated wall of the building. Sunrise and sunset were his favorite times of the day: the stillness of dawn and the serenity of a setting sun. As the English poet wrote, "God's in His heaven—all's right with the world."

He moved to the railing, and from the balcony his roving glance fell on the stagecoach office. The sight brought an instant reminder of Pop's death, and Cole frowned. *Maybe the rest of the world, Mr. Browning, but not Lawford, New Mexico.*

Deciding it might be a good idea to get into the office and check it out, Cole climbed back through the window to get dressed.

The stage office was unlocked, and Cole smelled the faint scent of jasmine as soon as he entered. The flowery fragrance was noticeable in an office that was so masculine, from its battered oak desk to a tarnished brass cuspidor in the corner. For a long moment he studied the photograph on the wall of Pop, Maggie, and himself. It resurrected the memory of that bygone day. He turned away, poignancy replaced by the bitterness of the day's grim reality: Pop was dead.

Sitting down at the desk, Cole aimlessly read a stagecoach schedule and then moved a pipe and tobacco pouch off several invoices that lay under them. He was relieved to see the balances were current. At least Pop had kept his head above water. A dainty white handkerchief trimmed with lace lay on the corner of the desk. He picked it up and discovered the source of the jasmine fragrance. Dallas wore the same perfume, and despite his melancholy, he grinned. Could there have been something between Pop and Dallas? He couldn't figure out why that thought pleased him.

Then his grin slipped into a grimace. Maybe whatever was between them is what had gotten Pop killed.

No, she wasn't that good an actress. Dallas Donovan came across as genuinely liking Pop. But it still didn't make her above suspicion.

Cole quickly perused the contents of the drawers. Nothing unusual. What did he expect to find—a signed confession from Pop's killer?

He slammed the last drawer and got up to leave. Halting at the door, he looked back, his gaze sweeping the office in a final perusal. Something wasn't right. He could feel it. The clue was right before him, but he wasn't recognizing it.

Returning to his room, Cole tossed aside his hat and pulled off his boots. After plumping up the pillows, he stretched out on the bed and tucked his hands under his head. He had to think. Something he'd seen or heard since his arrival in Lawford continued to tickle his mind like an itch he couldn't quite reach to scratch, just beyond his fingertips.

He lay deep in thought. Time and time again he

went over his conversations with Vic, Dallas, and Keith Lawford. He conjured up the image of the stage office. Was it the handkerchief? Just what was the connection between Pop and Dallas? Business or pleasure? Whichever one, Dallas sure as hell didn't look devastated yesterday. And he needed to meet this Ben Lawford for sure. Sounded like the town marched to his tune.

Frustrated, he stood up. He had to get out of there. He couldn't think straight cooped up in the small room.

As he descended the stairway, a clock in the lobby chimed out the hour. He had time to eat breakfast before his appointment with Keith Lawford.

Normally Maggie gave little consideration to what she wore, but after leaving the stagecoach office that morning, she had gone back home and taken particular pains in dressing, not out of vanity, but a need to show Cole MacKenzie just what he had so blatantly tossed aside for greener pastures.

Her contemplation over her wardrobe had given her a temporary respite from her grief, because as soon as she was finished, although satisfied with the result, she had been overcome with misery. In reality, what did it really matter anymore how she appeared to Cole MacKenzie?

Now, as she waited in Keith's office, Maggie nervously drummed her gloved fingers on the desktop.

"He's only ten minutes late, Margaret," Keith said.

"Obviously he hasn't changed one bit. Cole MacKenzie ignores time. He doesn't even carry a watch. Knowing him, he'll probably be late for his own funeral."

"Just how well do you know the man, Margaret?"

"Well enough to know he's the most exasperating person I've ever met. The man is impossible." She rose to her feet and moved to the window.

Keith's question carried more than just idle curiosity. She knew he wanted to marry her. He had told Pop, and Pop had told her. But she wasn't ready for marriage. As much as she liked Keith, she didn't love him. And now with Pop's death, marriage was the furthest thing from her mind.

Dozens of butterflies began to dance in her stomach to the rhythm of her pounding heart when she saw the tall figure striding toward the office. She would have recognized that walk if he'd been in the midst of a mob.

"Here he comes now."

When she turned and saw the ambiguous look in Keith's eyes, Maggie became aware her hand had moved to her breast to still her quickened heartbeat. She dropped it quickly to her side and was saved from having to say anything when Keith crossed the room in response to the knock on the door.

Maggie turned away and glanced aimlessly out of the window. She surely had the grit to get through this. Cole MacKenzie might have been the handsomest man that ever walked this good, green earth, but he was a mere mortal, no Greek god. And she, Margaret Mary O'Shea, was no longer any love-struck, sixteen-year-old with the backbone of a jellyfish.

She closed her eyes when she heard his voice as he greeted Keith. The warmth of his chuckle rippled her spine. *Please, Lord, I'll need Your help, too.*

Maggie drew another deep breath, forced her lips into a smile, and turned slowly to face her nemesis.

* * *

As he shook hands with Lawford, Cole became aware of the woman standing at the window. If the front of her was as attractive as the rear, the sights of Lawford had just improved. From her stiff stance at the window, he figured she must be Lawford's girlfriend and he probably had walked in on a lovers' quarrel.

"I'm sorry if I'm interrupting. I must have misunderstood the time of our appointment," he said to Lawford.

Then the woman turned and spoke.

"Hello, Cole. It's been a long time."

"Maggie!"

Shocked, he stared in disbelief. Somehow his brain had no control over his gaping mouth.

When she moved toward him with feline grace and confidence, Cole began to feel like a bowl of cream about to be consumed. Maggie extended a gloved hand to him, and he didn't know whether to kiss it or shake it, so he squeezed it and then pulled her into his arms and hugged her. From the feel of the curves pressed against him, she sure as hell wasn't a kid anymore.

She smelled delicious. Jasmine. So it must have been her perfume he had smelled in Pop's office. *Sorry, Pop.*

Stepping back, he grasped her shoulders and grinned at her. "Little Maggie O'Shea."

"I prefer Margaret," she replied, with a soft modulation intended to take the sting out of the words.

"I can't believe it. You're all grown up."

"That's right, Cole. I'm all grown up. I see you haven't changed." This time the tone was less velvety.

"The world has, though, hasn't it, kid? I don't have to tell you how badly I feel about Pop's death."

"I know you loved him, too."

Her eyes had become misty, and he had the urge to hold her and kiss away her sorrow. Then, to his disgust, he wondered if those full lips tasted as luscious as they looked.

What in hell was he thinking? Pop had been laid to rest only the day before, and here he was entertaining carnal thoughts about the old man's daughter, now left alone and vulnerable to the likes of lechers like him.

"Shall we get seated and get on with the business at hand," Keith Lawford said.

The lawyer's timely reminder came as a godsend to Cole. As soon as Maggie was seated, he sat down on the chair next to her.

"Just what is the business at hand, Lawford?"

"Mr. O'Shea's last will and testament."

"Why does it concern me?"

"I really don't know, Mr. MacKenzie," Lawford said, extracting a thick envelope from his desk drawer.

"I thought you handled Pop's legal affairs."

"I did, but shortly before his death, Mr. O'Shea went to the legal office of Barnes and Patton in Albuquerque and drew up a will with specific instructions for it to remain sealed until his death. I have no knowledge of what it contains, but my instructions are to see that the will is properly executed. Had you not arrived on your own cognizance, I would have had to inform you to attend."

Once again the lawyer's officiousness had begun to irritate Cole. "I came here, Lawford, because Pop wired me to come. I didn't expect this."

Keith Lawford remained placid. "For whatever reason, Mr. MacKenzie, the important thing is that you are here." He tore open the envelope, cleared his throat, and began to read aloud Pop's will.

Cole sat stunned throughout the reading. Occasionally he glanced at Maggie. Her sorrowful expression had changed to horrified disbelief, becoming more appalled with every passage of the document.

When he finished, Keith Lawford put aside the will and flattened his palms on the desk. "Well, I have to say this is an interesting turn of events."

"No! No! No! I won't stand for it," Maggie declared. "Surely, Keith, we can go to court and have the will nullified."

"On what grounds, Margaret?"

"Maybe Pop wasn't of sound mind at the time."

"Margaret, you know as well as I your father was of sound mind. There isn't a person in Lawford who would testify to the contrary."

Maggie jumped to her feet. "He would have to have been to write such a will." Her voice rose almost to a screech. "You've got to do something, Keith."

In a blink of an eye Lawford was around his desk and attempting to calm her rising hysteria. "I understand how you feel, Margaret, but try to remain calm."

Maggie shrugged aside his hands. "If you don't try to do something, I'll find a lawyer who will."

Lawford succeeded in getting her to sit down again and returned to his chair. He took time to recenter the inkwell and pen that had been dislodged, neatly stacked the papers relating to Pop's will and assets, and then cleared his throat.

"Of course I'll see what I can do, Margaret, but the will appears in order." For the first time since finishing the reading, he looked at Cole. "What do you think of the whole situation, Mr. MacKenzie?"

Cole was just as shocked as Maggie by the conditions of the will. They were the last things in the world he had expected to hear. What in hell was Pop thinking of?

"I'm not any happier with this than Maggie."

"Margaret! I told you my name is Margaret," she railed at him.

"You could have fooled me. You sure as hell sound like the Maggie I remember," he retorted.

"Please, we're all adults here. Let's not resort to a shouting match," Keith Lawford implored them with a pained expression. "Can't we discuss this calmly?"

"There's nothing to discuss," Maggie declared. "I have no intention of holding myself accountable to an irresponsible, skirt-chasing vagabond like Cole MacKenzie."

"Margaret, I'm sorry, but you're a minor. Your father not only has made Mr. MacKenzie your legal guardian, but the trustee of his estate as well."

"What does *that* mean?" Her glare at Cole could have frozen the perspiration that dotted his brow.

The damn room was as stuffy as Lawford.

"It puts him in control of all your father's assets until you are of legal age, with the exception of the half interest in Dallas's. Your father willed that outright to Mr. MacKenzie. As for any remaining capital, the house, the stagecoach line, and the property known as Timberline, Mr. MacKenzie is free to buy or sell as he deems it in your best interests, as well as control the distribution of any funds to you."

"Are you saying until I'm twenty-one I have to ask him for every dollar I spend, but he is free to buy or sell what is rightfully mine?"

"Basically yes. You could take him to court if there was a lack of discretion on his part, and of course, he can't deny you a reasonable standard of living. As for Mr. MacKenzie's legal guardianship of you, it equates to any parent's right to approve of your conduct or any educational or matrimonial choices you may wish to make."

"You mean I can't even get married without *his* approval?"

"I'm afraid not, Margaret," Lawford said. He looked almost as miserable as she did.

The way they were discussing him and his intentions made Cole feel like the villain in a melodrama.

Maggie turned her full wrath on him. "I hate you, Cole MacKenzie. Why did you come back to interfere in my life?" Sobbing, she ran out the door.

Cole had been thrust into a situation not of his choosing—much less his liking—and already she blamed him, branded him like some kind of Simon Legree. Next he'd be accused of turning Little Eva out in the snow.

"I'm sure Margaret didn't mean what she said," Lawford said. "This has all been a shock to her. After all, she just buried her father yesterday."

"Yeah, I understand," Cole said. "It's a shock to me, too." But he was perplexed by her outburst. Did Maggie actually hate him as she said, or was it just a reaction to everything piling on her at one time?

"I'd like to go over Mr. O'Shea's assets with you. Do

you want me to remain as legal counsel with regard to the O'Shea will?" Lawford asked.

"Later," Cole said. Right now he needed some fresh air. "I need some time to think this all out. We'll discuss it later."

He left the office in time to see Maggie running up Boot Hill, but rather than follow, he went back to his hotel room and stretched out on the bed. He had a lot to think about, and he'd rather do it in private than with that damn Lawford. Maybe it would have been wiser to go over Pop's assets, since he was responsible for them. If that stagecoach line was any example, it wouldn't take too much thought. Who in hell ever came to Lawford to make running a stagecoach line worthwhile? The cost of feeding the horses was enough to bankrupt it. That certainly would be the first thing that he'd get rid of if he didn't see any profit from it.

And what was he going to do about Maggie? The poor girl was mourning her father, and the conditions of Pop's will were enough to put her over the edge. He should have been more considerate, sided with her, and straightened it all out later. Instead, he had taunted her. And she sure hated him. He had no idea what in hell he'd ever done to the kid, but she sure was bearing a grudge. Her father's will must have only added fuel to the fire.

He needed to have a quiet talk with her—just the two of them without Lawford taking in every word. He'd seen her head up Boot Hill. Maybe by now she'd have calmed down enough for him to try. Grabbing his hat, he hurried out the door.

Cole crested the hill and saw Maggie kneeling at

Pop's grave, only to discover Lawford was with her. Since they hadn't spotted him, rather than intrude on the private moment, he concealed himself in the bushes. His private talk with Maggie would have to wait.

Chapter 3

S obbing, Maggie continued to kneel at her father's grave. Desperation and a sense of betrayal warred with her feelings of despair and sense of loss.

"Why, Pop? Why did you do this to me? Didn't you trust me to take care of myself? I wish I could understand, but it hurts, Pop. It hurts so much. And why Cole of all people? Wasn't losing you enough heartache to try and bear? Oh, why, Pop, why?" Her voice broke in such intense sobbing that she could no longer choke out words. With bowed head, she remained at the grave, engulfed in an insurmountable feeling of wretchedness and despair.

"Margaret, it's time to leave."

Maggie turned her head to the speaker, and Keith Lawford stepped forward.

"I'm sorry. I didn't realize you were here."

"I have been for the past half hour," he said gently. "I didn't want to disturb you."

He was right. She was sinking deeper and deeper into depression. No matter how she felt, Maggie knew Pop wouldn't want her to give in to it.

"Let me help you," he said, when she started to rise.

His hand on her arm felt comforting as he helped her to her feet, then he withdrew a clean, white hand-kerchief from his pocket and began to brush the dirt off her skirt and hands.

Embarrassed by her earlier outburst, she said, "I'm sorry about the scene in your office, Keith. You must think I'm an awful baby." If only she had maintained her composure instead of giving in to anger—and her deep resentment of Cole MacKenzie.

"Not at all. I think you're a very courageous young woman, Margaret. I admire you for it, and I'll do whatever I can to help you resolve this situation with MacKenzie."

She grasped his hands in gratitude. "Thank you, Keith. With Pop gone, you and Ellie are the only real friends I have."

"Weren't you and Cole MacKenzie friends in Alaska?"

The memory of those two years of her secret, unrequited love for Cole MacKenzie seared the edges of her mind. "Cole tolerated me because I was Pop's daughter, but we were never close. The only thing we had in common was our mutual love for Pop. Cole considered me quarrelsome and spoiled. I think he regarded me the same way he would have if I'd been Pop's pet dog." She managed a weak smile. "Probably better, if I had been."

She smiled up at him. "I'm grateful for your support, Keith."

"I don't want your gratitude, Margaret. I want . . . These past few days have been traumatic for you, Margaret. You should go home and rest, but not until you eat some lunch, young lady. How about it? Then I'll take you back to your house."

Maggie wondered what he had cut himself off from saying. She wasn't hungry, but he was trying so hard to be considerate, she couldn't refuse the luncheon invitation.

"I'd like that, Keith."

He took her arm, and they walked down the hill.

As soon as they disappeared, Cole shoved up his hat and rocked back on his heels. Maggie and Lawford. Was it possible they were sweethearts? Could Maggie actually be in love with that stiffneck? Good Lord, he had to be over twice her age. Not that it was any of his business, but . . . Hell, yes, it was his business. Pop's will had made it his business.

He wasn't the type to lurk in bushes eavesdropping, but when he heard his name mentioned, he hadn't been able to help himself. And he sure as hell had gotten an earful. Had he really treated her that badly in Alaska? He couldn't have been *that* much of a bastard. Granted he wasn't as charming as his dad, but who was? His dad had turned affability into an art form.

Well, he'd show Miss Margaret Mary O'Shea just how nice he could be.

But as he started down the hill, Maggie's words still disturbed him.

Pet dog, indeed. Besides, if he'd been as bad as she claimed, Pop would have said something.

As soon as Cole saw Maggie and Lawford enter the diner, he went back to the lawyer's office. Just as he hoped, the legal papers were still on the desk. Cole began to read them.

From what he could see, the bank balance was nearly busted. Probably just enough cash to get through next week. As far as he was concerned, the stagecoach had made its last run.

The property called Timberline that Pop had bought was a mystery, though. He had strapped himself financially to buy it. What had he intended to do with it? Obviously he had something in mind, since it was a recent purchase. Maybe Maggie knew. Well, it was too late now. Maybe he could find a buyer for it. Maggie could use the money. The only possible source of revenue he could see was the half interest in Dallas's, and Pop had willed that to him. But Maggie needed that income to exist, so he'd give it to her. What it boiled down to was that she needed a husband to take care of her. It would take a big load off his shoulders if she married. What in hell did he know about raising a grown girl? From what he observed in the cemetery, Lawford had more than a passing fancy for her. And he appeared to be able to afford her. But could he be trusted? As far as Cole was concerned, Lawford was a suspect the same as everyone else—especially inasmuch as he was the son of Ben Lawford.

There was another solution to the Maggie problem: the Triple M. As much as he didn't want to start turning the screw on the poor girl, legally he could demand she go there. He couldn't believe she wouldn't be better off surrounded by his family. His mom and dad would be great surrogate parents, and Kitty, Emily, and Rose would be great company for her. He smiled cunningly. And, God willing, if his younger brother came home, maybe Jeb would take a shine to Maggie and marry her. That way his responsibility to Pop would be over, and he could return to being footloose and fancy-free.

Cole grinned with pleasure. Yeah, he liked that idea better than trying to marry her off to Lawford. But they couldn't leave the damn town until he got to the bottom of Pop's death.

"Mr. MacKenzie, how long have you been waiting?"

Speak of the devil. Lawford's question interrupted his thoughts. The lawyer came in and sat down behind his desk.

"Not long."

"I see you've found yourself some reading material."

"Mite careless to leave your office unlocked with important papers lying around. Anyone could walk in and read them or even steal them, if they had a mind to."

"Now, who would want to do that?" Lawford said. "Do you have a question about any of them?"

Lawford had slipped into his pompousness again, but Cole wasn't intimidated. "Curious, that's all. I don't understand why Pop broke himself buying that property. Did he give you a reason?"

"I was not consulted, Mr. MacKenzie." His mouth puckered in disapproval. "Perhaps you'd be better advised to contact the office of Barnes and Patton."

"You're right, Lawford, I think I'll do just that. Seems strange, though, that Pop wouldn't have come to you. I'd have thought he'd trust his own lawyer."

Cole folded up the papers and tucked them into his shirt pocket. "One more question, Lawford. What happened to whatever Pop had on his body when he was killed?"

"It was all destroyed."

"Too bad. He might have had a paper or note that would have given us a clue as to why he bought the property."

"If there was, it was burned. Mr. O'Shea's clothing was bloodstained and muddied. I thought it would be too difficult for Margaret to have to deal with sorting out what should be saved or destroyed, so I ordered for him to be completely stripped from head to toe and everything on him burned."

"I see. Well, from what you say, it sounds like it was probably the best thing to do. For Maggie's sake," he accentuated. Lawford looked at him peculiarly, and Cole stood up. "Thanks for your time, Lawford."

Lawford rose, and they shook hands. "If I can be of any further help, don't hesitate to ask. Miss O'Shea's welfare is of foremost interest to me."

"Reckon we have that in common, Lawford. See you around."

Figuring Maggie was now back home, Cole felt he shouldn't put off their talk any longer. The problem was that he had no idea where she lived. Fortunately he found Juan in the stable and got the directions.

The O'Shea house was located on the edge of Lawford. Set in the shade of towering oaks and pines, the two-story white building looked typical of so many built in the early part of the century.

As Cole dismounted, he recalled Pop saying he'd

been born in it. Despite its age, the house had obviously been enlarged, and its clapboard slats and black shutters appeared freshly painted.

He doffed his hat when an aged woman opened the door to his knock. "How do you do. I'm—"

"I know who you are, Cole MacKenzie," she said. "And I'm mighty peeved how you've gotten my little girl all upset." Her disapproving grimace looked as severe as her gray hair pulled back into a bun at the nape of her neck.

Cole remained unflappable. "And you must be the housekeeper, because I remember Pop said his wife died giving birth to Maggie."

"Never said I gave birth to her. Name's Ellie Masters; I'm the housekeeper."

"It's a pleasure to meet you, Mrs. Masters."

Her face remained frozen in a disapproving frown. "Never said I was *Mrs.* Masters either."

"My mistake. Would you please tell Miss O'Shea I'd like to speak to her?"

"I will when she wakes up, but the little darlin' is plumb tuckered out, and I ain't gonna wake her. She needs the rest."

He wondered if maybe it was the water that affected the personalities of the people in the town.

"If you don't mind, Miss Masters, I'd like to come in."

"What if I mind?"

"I'd come in anyway."

"Figure you would." She stepped aside. "Wipe your feet before you do, and don't you try to wake that gal."

The interior appeared homey and comfortable. There was a parlor, a small dining room, a kitchen with running water, and a back bedroom on the first floor.

"You figure on buying the place?" Ellie asked, after he finished his inspection.

"Whose bedroom is this?" Cole asked, glancing into the rear room.

"Mine. And keep your nose out of it," she ordered, closing the door of the room.

"And how many rooms are there upstairs, Miss Masters?"

"Mick's room, Mag . . . ah, Margaret's room, and a bathroom."

"Excellent. That will work out just fine."

"What will?" Ellie Masters asked.

He figured it must be difficult, but the woman managed to eye him suspiciously without disturbing the disapproving frown she wore.

"Well, Ellie, I have news for you. You're moving to an upstairs bedroom."

"No, I've got news for you, Mr. MacKenzie—"

"Call me Cole, Ellie."

"Like I was saying, I've run this household from the time Maggie was born. I kept this house in order even when Mick took off, 'cause I knew that one day he'd return. And no Johnny-come-lately like you is gonna move in and tell me what to do."

"Perish the thought, Ellie, dear," he said, slipping an arm around her shoulders. "I wouldn't think of it. There's no reason for a fine woman like you getting all hot and bothered. I've been told you make the best coffee in town, so why don't you and I sit down and have a cup while I explain everything to you."

Don't say I didn't learn anything from you, Dad. He pulled out a chair for Ellie to be seated. By instinct he went to the right cupboard, pulled out two mugs, then filled them from a pot sitting on the stove.

Once seated, he said, "Don't suppose that's freshly baked sugar cookies I smell. Sure smells like it. There's nothing like the smell of baked sugar cookies. Reminds me of home."

"Ain't saying it is, and ain't saying it ain't." She got up and came back with a plate of cookies. "I baked them for Mag—Margaret. Thought it might perk her up a bit." She leaned forward and whispered, "Between you and me, she's got a sweet tooth but won't admit it."

"That's right. I remember," he said. "When we were in Alaska, whenever I went to Dawson City, I always brought her back a bag of peppermint candy." *Pet dog, indeed. That gal has a short memory.*

"Ain't it about time you tell me what's on your mind, Cole MacKenzie?"

"I intend to move in. I don't know how long I'll have to remain, but for propriety's sake, I think it would be better if I took the downstairs bedroom and you two ladies the upstairs ones."

Ellie sucked in her lower lip and shook her head slowly. "She ain't gonna like it. We haven't packed up Mick's things yet."

"Is there an empty trunk, Ellie?"

"Yes." The frown was starting to realign itself.

"I'll pack up Pop's belongings in that while you move yours upstairs."

Ellie hesitated. "I don't know. Shouldn't we tell her before the doing of it."

"Ellie," Cole said patiently, "whatever his reason, Pop made me Maggie's guardian."

"The darlin' prefers Margaret," Ellie corrected him.

"I know. She's informed me. But I don't change horses in midstream. She'll always be Maggie to me."

"Me, too," Ellie said. A smile finally cracked her countenance, and Cole couldn't help grinning.

"And as I was saying, Ellie, much as I prefer pleasing Maggie, there are things I must do for her own good." He reached over and grasped Ellie's hand. "I need your help, Ellie. You may rest assured that whatever I do, I'll have Maggie's best interests at heart. Shall we get moving? If we have it all done before she wakes up, it might be easier." *Damn easier.* He patted her hand. "Where's the trunk?"

"In the closet across from the bathroom. Mick's room's on the left of the stairs. Maggie's is on the right."

While Ellie scurried away to begin gathering her belongings, Cole climbed the stairway and managed to move the trunk into Pop's bedroom without disturbing Maggie. In truth, since Pop had always been a man of few wants and needs, it wasn't difficult to pack up his clothing and personal keepsakes.

He was about to close the trunk's lid when he froze and stared down at the smoking jacket he'd just folded and packed. Pop loved that jacket, and even in Alaska he'd change into it at night to smoke his pipe by the campfire.

Suddenly it hit him like a lightning bolt: the itch that had been gnawing at the back of his mind from the time he'd gone to Pop's office. The pipe and tobacco.

Pop never went anywhere without that pipe and tobacco pouch.

And it hadn't been retrieved from his body, because Keith Lawford had said that Pop's clothing and everything he had with him the day he was killed had been burned.

So if Pop had left town to go off and explore mines, he sure as hell wouldn't have left his pipe behind. He hadn't been killed in any damn mine accident. He more than likely had been killed right there at the office or abducted and his death made to look like an accident.

Cole closed the trunk lid. *There isn't enough dynamite to blast me out of this town, Pop, until I find out the truth.*

He had the room stripped down to the furniture by the time Ellie arrived toting a houseplant and an arm-load of clothing.

Cole made the next trip with her, and they cleared her room of the rest of her clothing and keepsakes, as well as another houseplant. Then he went back to the hotel, packed up his bag, and checked out.

To his immense relief, Maggie was still sleeping when he returned. Ellie had changed the linens on the bed, and the room smelled of the scent of roses that floated in through the open window.

"I'm gonna miss them rose bushes," she said. "Look forward to them every spring."

"Ellie, if things work out as I'm hoping, you'll prob-ably be sniffing them next spring."

"Well, I best get to making dinner. I suspect all hell's gonna break lose when she wakes up."

He tucked his arm through hers as they returned to the parlor. "Don't worry, darlin', I can handle Maggie."

"You best hope you can," she said in warning, " 'cause she's right behind you."

Ellie scurried off to the kitchen.

Chapter 4

Cole turned with a smile. "Margaret, did you enjoy your nap?"

"My nap was fine. What did Ellie mean that all hell's going to break lose when I wake up?"

"Most likely because you've been so upset. We're both very worried about you."

Maggie eyed him skeptically. He was smooth, all right. He actually looked genuinely sincere, but he didn't fool her for a minute.

"What are you doing here, Cole?"

"Let's sit down. We have to talk. This situation is awkward for both of us. I've thought of a couple immediate measures to take, but I want to make sure you're comfortable with them, too. Fortunately we're both adults, so I'm sure we can work out any differences."

"Don't patronize me, Cole. Do you actually think I can't see through this latest attempt of yours to manipulate me? I'm not as gullible as my father was."

"Dammit, that's not fair. I loved and respected Pop. You of all people should know that. I neither lied to him nor manipulated him, Maggie."

"Margaret," she corrected him, remaining calm. "Well, get on with it, Cole. What did you come here to say?"

Maggie sat down on the couch, and Cole took the chair opposite—Pop's favorite chair. No matter what he said, she would remain calm, not lose her composure as she had done in Keith's office. She'd show Cole MacKenzie that she was no longer that tomboy he remembered, but an adult—and a lady to boot. As boring as they had been, some good had to have come out of the two years she'd spent in that St. Louis finishing school.

"Frankly, Margaret, I hate to discuss this so soon after Pop's . . . well, so soon. I know you're dealing with a lot of grief right now, but I didn't want to go ahead with what I have in mind without informing you."

"I appreciate that."

"I've read over the list of Pop's assets," he said, "and I hate to tell you it's pretty grim. Are you aware Pop was broke?"

"You mean there's no money in the bank?"

Cole nodded. "Just about enough for another week or so."

That *was* a shock. Pop had never discussed their finances in the past, and she had never forced the issue. She swallowed hard, forcing back the sudden lump in her throat.

"Of course, I'll turn over to you any income Pop has from Dallas's," he continued. "I haven't spoken to her yet, so I don't know how much it will be. Although from what I've seen of this one-horse town, I figure it can't be much."

"There's no need for me to accept your charity, Cole. There's still the stagecoach business. Surely there's enough income from that to support me."

"The stagecoach is a losing proposition. It's the first thing I intend to dump."

"Don't you dare, Cole MacKenzie," she snapped, knowing her control had begun to slip. "I don't want to sell the stagecoach."

"That's too bad, because even if it made money, there's no one to run it."

"I'll run it."

He snorted. "You going to drive it, too?"

"If I have to, but Emilio Morales has always been the driver."

"It doesn't matter. You can't run a stagecoach without passengers. And besides, it's no job for a woman."

"Why not?"

"Why, Miss Margaret, it would be improper . . . un-ladylike . . . for a proper lady like you to—"

She was on her feet at once. "Don't you dare make fun of me, Cole MacKenzie."

"What makes you think I'm making fun of you?"

"It must be because of that smirk on your face."

She had let him do it to her again. Despite all her vows to the contrary, it hadn't taken him more than a couple of sentences to rile her. Maggie took a deep breath, and with the most theatrical gracefulness she could produce, she sat down. Forcing a fake smile, she asked sweetly, "Do tell me, Cole, what do you consider a proper position for a lady?"

He arched a brow and grinned wickedly. "You really don't want me to say, do you Maggie?"

She clenched her teeth together to keep from shrieking. "I meant employment, Cole."

"A woman's place is in the home."

"Doing what?"

"Those things that a wife and mother does so well. God bless her."

"For instance like cleaning, cooking, and pleasing the lord and master she was idiot enough to marry in the first place." Her voice had risen with every word until she ended up screeching like a banshee.

"You sure as hell got that right, Miss Margaret."

"Oh, you're an impossible human being. Get out of this house before I start screaming."

"You mean louder than you are now?" He shook his head. "Not too ladylike, Miss Margaret."

"Get out of here!"

"Unfortunately that's impossible. You see, I've moved in."

"You've what?" She gasped for breath and stared, horrified, at him. At least he had enough conscience to look sheepish.

"I took Ellie's room. She moved upstairs into Pop's."

"No. No, you wouldn't do that to me, too." She raced to the kitchen. Ellie was at the stove. "Is it true, Ellie?"

The housekeeper didn't turn around or have to ask what she meant. Ellie just nodded.

Maggie stormed back into the parlor, and to her distress Cole had not budged from the chair. "I want you out of my father's chair, and I want you out of my house. Pop may have made you my guardian, but that doesn't include your moving in with me."

"Maggie, it includes whatever I judge is beneficial."

"Ha! And pray, Mr. MacKenzie, how does your presence in *my* house benefit *me*?"

"It's the practical thing to do, since there's an available bedroom here. Hotels cost money, and I don't know how long I have to remain in this town."

"Don't remain on my account."

"I have to consider Pop's other interests, too."

"Then consider them and leave me alone."

"I think you were his main interest, Maggie. So that makes you my main interest, too."

"Well, it's not proper to stay here. I have to consider my reputation."

"I'm sure with Ellie present propriety won't be an issue. She'll see that your reputation remains unblemished."

"You bet your boots, cowboy," Ellie declared, standing in the doorway with her arms folded across her chest.

Maggie had seen that stance enough times to know it was an unscalable stone wall. Thank God she still had Ellie on her side.

"You have no right to do this. I refuse to let you control me. Do you understand? I won't let you."

Maggie ran out of the room and up the stairway. The slamming of her bedroom door rattled the pictures on the parlor wall.

Cole glanced at Ellie. "I guess I handled that wrong."

"Humph!" Ellie returned to the kitchen.

"Do you think I'm wrong, too?" Cole asked, following her.

"Ain't my business to say one way or t'other."

"Come on, Ellie, you probably understand Maggie better than anyone."

She spun on her heel and shook the wooden cooking spoon she'd been using at him. "That's right. Ain't nobody who knows that gal like I do, and I ain't gonna stand by and watch you hurt her."

"Ellie, I don't want to hurt Maggie, but she's got to listen to me. Pop trusted me to look after her interests, and that's what I'm trying to do."

"The poor girl just lost her pa. She's hurting right now, and you're coming at her with too much. Give her some breathing time."

"I wish I could, Ellie. Trouble is time's as scarce as the money Pop left her."

Cole went into his bedroom and unpacked his clothing. When he finished, he decided to take another look at Pop's office. As he left the room, Ellie came into the kitchen, grumbling under her breath.

"Where are *you* going?" she asked when he grabbed his hat to leave.

"Out for a while."

"I'm just putting dinner on the table."

"Go ahead. I'm not hungry." He continued on to the door.

"Dang blast it!" She slapped the spoon into the kettle. "Maggie's holed up in her room and don't want no dinner. You're leaving. If I go to the trouble of cooking another meal around this house, there best be somebody to eat it." She shoved past him and thumped back upstairs.

Shaking his head, Cole left. Good God, how in hell did he end up in the middle of this mess? Maggie was enough to handle. Now he had two temperamental females to cope with.

Why me, Lord?

Juan was in the stable with a man who appeared to be a few years older than Cole. "Señor Cole, this is my *papá*."

Cole smiled and offered a hand to the short, slightly built man. "Cole MacKenzie. You must be Emilio Morales."

"*Sí*, Señor MacKenzie."

Cole liked him immediately. Integrity gleamed in Emilio's dark eyes as they shook hands.

"I don't stand on formality, Emilio. Just call me Cole. Let's go into the office. I'd like to explain what I'm doing here."

Once seated, Cole said, "Pop made me Miss O'Shea's guardian and has put me in charge of his business. I understand you're the stage driver, and I'd like your opinion whether you think the line is profitable enough to continue with it. Without passengers it looks like a losing proposition to me."

"It is true there are few passengers, Señor Cole, but often we bring or take freight. Sometimes even mail."

"That's hardly enough to even feed the horses, isn't it?"

"That, too, is true. But if you turn it into just a freight line, you could haul much more freight."

"That's a possibility. What, Emilio?" he asked, when the driver looked perplexed.

"In the week before he died, Pop say many times he knows how to bring more passengers to town."

"How?"

"He not tell me. He just say there's a way."

This was a twist that Cole had not expected. What did Pop have in mind? Poking around in mines, could the old timer have found gold? If so, he wouldn't have announced it to everybody before working a claim himself. And there sure was no evidence in his bank balance that showed any sign of pay dirt.

"And many times I hear Señor Lawford offer to buy the stageline."

"You and the whole town, Emilio. Why do you suppose Pop didn't sell it to him?"

"I think because Pop was *más terco*— what your people call—"

"Very stubborn."

Emillo grinned. "You speak my language."

"I was born and raised in Texas, Emilio. My mother is Spanish. And you're right. Once Pop put his mind to something, there was no changing it."

"And Señor Lawford, he is the same." Shaking his head, Emillo put his hands to his cheeks. "*¡Santa María!* Two such stubborn *hombres!*"

Cole joined him in laughter, then thought of the real troubling issue at hand. "Emilio, do you know any reason why Pop's death might not have been an accident?"

The laughter left the Mexican's eyes. Frowning, he asked, "Not an accident?" He shook his head. "I think not, Señor Cole. Everyone loved him."

Cole was beginning to feel disheartened. Apparently he was the only person in Lawford who saw reason to question Pop's death. He opened the drawer and saw that the pipe and pouch had been moved from the desktop into the drawer. "I won't let you down, Pop."

As soon as Emilio left, Cole pulled out the few files

Pop had kept in the bottom drawer of the desk. Nothing he saw gave him a clue, and the simple records Pop had maintained revealed nothing more, other than grounds for his opinion that the stagecoach was a losing proposition.

He headed for Dallas's to discuss their partnership, but there was no sign of her. Where she could go in Lawford at night was a mystery to him, but he figured she sure wasn't at the church ladies' auxiliary meeting.

"Heard tell you're Dallas's new partner," Vic said when Cole bellied up to the bar.

"News travels fast," Cole said, and downed the drink Vic had poured. "So how did Dallas take the news?"

"You'd have to ask her."

"That's what I came for. Where is she anyway?"

Vic shrugged. "Can't say."

"Can't say or won't say?"

"You ready for a refill?"

"Yeah, right." End of conversation.

Since he wasn't getting anything out of Vic, he gave up and sat in on a poker game, hoping Dallas would show up. After a few hours, he headed back to the house. As he walked along the street, he once again had the feeling he was being followed, but when he looked back, he didn't see anyone.

Maggie and Ellie had already retired for the night, but his growling stomach reminded him that he hadn't eaten that evening. He rooted through the icebox and found the makings of a chicken sandwich, then finished off the snack with a glass of milk and a couple of Ellie's sugar cookies.

Once in his room, he reread Pop's legal papers. After

his talk with Morales, a new factor had been added to the mystery. How had Pop expected to turn things around for the dying stageline and town?

Cole didn't have a clue. All he knew was that things were piling up too fast: the damn will, his strained relationship with Maggie, and the truth behind Pop's death. And he couldn't rule out any of the players: Keith Lawford, Dallas Donovan, Vic Chance, and, of course, Ben Lawford, whom he had yet to meet.

Unless he was a really bad judge of people—and he'd been in enough tight places as a Ranger to have to depend on his instinct about others—the only three people above suspicion were Maggie, Ellie Masters, and Emilio Morales.

Frustrated, he tossed the papers aside and went outside to get some fresh air. He sat down on the top step of the porch and glanced up at the sky. Even the moon was lurking behind dark clouds. He'd only been in Lawford for two days, and the town had already begun to close in on him.

And so was the night.

He stood up to return to his room and go to bed when he heard a sound at the rear of the house. Someone or something was prowling around back there. Maybe he had been followed.

Dammit, MacKenzie, everything in this town puts you on edge.

He left the porch and moved stealthily to the rear of the house. It was darker than hell. He peered through the blackness but couldn't see anyone. Then suddenly he caught a glimpse of movement, so he stepped back and waited as the figure drew closer. When he recognized who it was, Cole stepped out of the shadows.

"Maggie."

She shrieked and jumped back in alarm. "Oh, it's you."

"What are you doing out here in the dark?"

"What do you think!" She started to walk past him.

"Will you answer me, please."

"I went to the . . . ah, lavatory."

He broke into laughter. "Lavatory. You're unbelievable, Miss Margaret. The Maggie I knew would call it what it is—an outhouse."

"The Maggie you knew no longer exists, Cole. I wish your pitiful excuse for a brain would accept that fact."

He moved nearer so he was close enough to see her face and smell the scent of jasmine. She was angry, all right. "I could, but Maggie keeps popping out from under those fine airs you put on, Miss Margaret."

"That's what you—" She looked riled to near bursting and sucked in a deep breath. "Good night."

When she started to leave, he grabbed her arm. If Pop had been murdered, for all he knew, Maggie might be the killer's next target. "I don't want you walking around out here alone at night. Do you understand?"

"Am I expected to get your permission? The way you're issuing orders right and left, isn't it enough you've taken over the inside of the house, must you take over the . . . the . . . *outhouse*, too?" She was so angry at this point, she couldn't speak without sputtering.

Cole couldn't help chuckling. "Well, there, Miss Margaret, you said the unmentionable. Was that so hard?"

"Oh, you're the most exasperating . . . unbearable

individual I've ever met. How I would love to smack that smirking face of yours."

"Then go ahead, if it will make you feel better."

To his surprise she did. The slap stung his cheek, and for a few seconds as she stared at him, her astonishment appeared as great as his.

"So who did that help the most, Margaret or Maggie?" he asked gently.

Maggie turned her back to him. "I can't believe I did that. I'm sorry." She ran inside.

After retiring, Cole lay in bed and listened to the creaking of springs from the room above. So Maggie couldn't sleep either. He visualized her lying in bed just above, tossing and turning much like him. To his disgust it conjured up an erotic picture. This was the second time thoughts of her had tickled his libido.

Good Lord, he was becoming more depraved by the minute.

Why did he continue to taunt her every chance he got? Despite his resolve and good intentions he always ended up upsetting her. He had to stop—tighten the cinch on his tongue.

He fell asleep, haunted by the vulnerable look on her face after she slapped him.

Maggie couldn't sleep. She flopped from one side of the bed to the other, reliving that horrendous scene in the yard. How could she have actually struck him? Why couldn't she control her emotions when they were together? It was so futile to keep plaguing herself with whys. Nothing could change the reality that for the next three years she was at his mercy. Unless . . . Cole MacKenzie was too restless to stay in one place for too long. If she could keep a hold on her emotions, maybe it would convince him she was adult enough to take care of herself and he would leave.

Beginning tomorrow, I'll show him a different Maggie . . . a different Margaret, that is.

Chapter 5

"**G**ood morning," Cole said, entering the kitchen. Ellie was at her usual station at the stove.

" 'Morning, Cole." She poured him a mug of coffee and handed it to him.

He took a sip of the hot brew. "Lord, that's good. Marry me, Ellie. I'll worship at your feet, your stove will be my altar."

Ellie preened with pleasure. "Go sit down. Breakfast is almost ready."

"I can wait for Maggie." He had hardly got the words out when she came into the kitchen."

"Good morning, Ellie." Maggie kissed the house-keeper on the cheek.

" 'Morning, honey."

"Cole." She nodded in his direction.

"Good morning, Margaret," he said. "Did you sleep well?"

"Oh, yes. Very well."

"Glad to hear it," Ellie said. "I don't think you've slept more than a couple hours since your . . . well, in the last few days. Must have finally caught up with you, honey."

"Must be."

Cole dropped his gaze. *That's a damn lie, Maggie O'Shea. You tossed most of the night, and I even heard you pacing the floor.*

"Sit down. Breakfast is ready." Ellie put a platter of flapjacks and bacon on the table. "I want to see you put some of this hot food in your stomach, young lady, and be sure to take a couple strips of that bacon, too."

"Does she always mother you like this?" Cole asked, grinning. He held the platter as Maggie put two pancakes and a strip of bacon on her plate.

"Always. It seems nobody thinks I'm capable of taking care of myself."

He knew the remark was meant for him, but he only grinned. "Must come from having such endearing qualities, Miss Margaret."

Maggie smiled sweetly. "Why, Cole, I hadn't thought you noticed." She took a bite of the bacon strip.

He returned the smile. So she was Margaret again this morning. Well, he had to give her credit. She was persistent in plugging away at that image.

Cole spent the rest of the meal admiring how pretty she looked that morning. When she didn't try to put on airs, she was a delightful combination of Maggie and Margaret.

"I intend to ride out to the site of Pop's accident. I'll need the directions."

"Pop drew me a map. I'll get it." She dashed off and was back in minutes. "Just ride south for five miles until you come to a big stretch of timberline. You'll see Pop's stake. His name's on it. The site of the accident is a mine about a quarter mile west of the stake."

"Would you like to come with me?" he asked.

She suddenly looked terrified. "No, I have something else to do." Then her expression shifted to a resentful pout. "Unless you order me to go with you."

"Of course not."

"Thank you." She excused herself and departed quickly.

"Where is she off to so early?" Cole asked.

"I didn't ask," Ellie replied. "You're her keeper, not me."

Cole went upstairs. The bathroom was just that: a bathtub and a washbowl. At least they had hot water. He shaved and brushed his teeth, then changed his clothes and said good-bye to Ellie.

Needing a mount, he went to the stage's stable, and when he saw that four of the horses were gone, he asked Juan where they were.

"Señorita Margaret, she send coach to Noches."

"She what!" he shouted.

Juan's eyes widened in alarm. "The señorita tell my *papá* to go to Noches, Señor Cole. Maybe she tell you." He scurried away.

Eyes blazing, Cole stormed into the office. Maggie was seated behind the desk. "Don't get too comfortable in that chair, lady, because I'm about to pull it out from under you."

"Did you wish to sit down, Cole?" she asked calmly. "I'll be glad to get up."

Her calmness did nothing to lessen his anger. "Maggie, I understand you sent Emilio to Noches after I told you that I'm closing down the stageline."

"You didn't say when you intended to do so."

"The *when* was *when* I told you. As usual, Maggie, you're being obstinate."

"And as usual, Cole, you're being bullheaded."

"No wonder you beat it down here to do exactly what *you* wanted to do. You're still the same spoiled brat you were in Alaska. I could never figure why Pop ever tolerated it, but he probably recognized you weren't capable of making any kind of right decision. Well, those days are over. You're dealing with me now. So enjoy your last day of sovereignty, princess, because when that stage gets back, your royal butt is getting kicked off the throne."

Cole spun on his heel and stormed out of the office. He went in to the stable, looked over the horses that remained in the stalls, and picked what appeared to be the better of the two. Saddling it, he rode out of Lawford.

The day was perfect for a ride, and it felt good to be back in the saddle. Cole hadn't realized how much he'd missed it. How much he missed the Triple M and his family.

As soon as he got around to leaving Lawford, he'd go back for a visit. Maybe he could convince Maggie to go with him. Meet his family. The little hellion sure needed a stabilizing influence in her life, and his father and mother could be just that.

Cole had no trouble finding Pop's marker and veered off in the direction Maggie had indicated. From what he could observe, Pop had made a wise choice. Timberline was set in the foothills of the Sangre de Cristo range. Thick stands of towering spruce, white fir, and ponderosa pine seemed to stretch to the sky. The Pecos River formed the eastern boundary of the property, the waters of the river lapping at the clumps of yucca lining the river banks. High on a rocky precipice Cole spied the remains of an abandoned Indian pueblo. He would have ridden right past the concealed cave had it not been for the hoofprints at its entrance. Dismounting, he studied the small opening.

What had Pop discovered? Gold? Silver? There were many copper and lead mines in New Mexico. Could he have been seriously considering returning to mining? If not, what was he doing poking around in a damn mine? Pop was too smart to have been searching for legendary caches of silver buried by the Spanish conquistadors.

Inside the entrance he found a kerosene lantern, matches, and a can of kerosene. He lit the lamp and looked around. It was not a particularly large cavity. He could make out the outline of the back wall from where he was standing, and there didn't appear to be any tunnels leading off it. In fact, this wasn't a mine. The interior appeared to have never been disturbed: no beams, no posts, and no sign that the rocky wall had ever been touched.

As he continued to explore the cave, he hit a patch of wet earth and almost lost his balance. Water trickled through the rocky wall and had eroded the ground beneath it. Through the years it had scooped a deep cavity in the earth.

Cole knelt down. Raising the lantern for a closer look, he peered into the hole. The pit appeared to be about twenty feet deep, and he wondered if this was where Pop had fallen and broken his neck. *Fallen or been pushed.*

Sickened, he stood up and brushed himself off and then stepped outside into the sunshine.

A man lounged against a tree holding the reins of a huge black stallion. When he straightened up, his head was almost on the same level as Cole's.

"Figure you must be Cole MacKenzie. Keith never told me you were a Mex." His voice was gruff and authoritative with no attempt at friendliness.

"Maybe he didn't think it was worth mentioning. For the record, I'm Spanish and Scot, born and bred in Texas. You've got a problem with that?"

The man snorted. "Spanish, Mex, it's all the same."

"I don't think that my Spanish hidalgo grandfather would have agreed with you."

The man wasn't young by any stretch of the imagination. His age showed in the lines of his rawboned face and the heavy shock of gray hair when he removed his Stetson and wiped the perspiration off the inside band. But his body was that of a man half his age, muscular and lean. Cole figured there wasn't an ounce of useless fat or flesh on him.

He had the compelling presence of a man used to giving orders—but more significantly, used to having them obeyed. And after one look into the man's hawk-like hazel eyes, Cole knew he'd just encountered Ben Lawford.

Cole offered his hand. "You must be Ben Lawford."

The rancher's grip was like a vise.

And it was clear to see that the rancher was sizing

him up just as intently as he was Lawford. Two war-horses priming for battle.

"My son tells me Mick O'Shea made you the ramrod of his assets. Such as they are." He made no effort to disguise his smirk.

"That's right."

"You thinking of selling 'em, MacKenzie?"

Cole shrugged. He wasn't about to show his hand to this cardsharp. "I haven't had time to go over everything yet. I intend to do what's best for Margaret."

"The old fool doesn't have that much to go over. He was broke except for that rundown stagecoach line and this property."

"I understand in the past you've expressed interest in the stagecoach line."

"Just to dress it up. Have you seen it? It's an embarrassment to the town."

"I've seen it and the town. It's a standoff which one is the worse."

"This is my town, MacKenzie. I own it. And I don't like strangers poking their noses into it."

"Not everything, Lawford. You don't own the stage-line. And I own half of Dallas's. I've been told Dallas owns the other half."

For the first time in the conversation, Lawford looked uneasy. "You planning on working that claim?"

"Are you talking about Dallas or this one?" Cole asked, nodding to the entrance of the cave.

"I didn't figure you for a fool, MacKenzie. There ain't nothing worth mining in that cave."

"I'll decide that myself. Pop O'Shea was no fool. He saw something of value here."

"There ain't nothing valuable here except the scenery. I'll give you five thousand dollars for it."

"If it's so worthless, Lawford, why are you willing to buy it?"

"It borders my ranch. I don't like strangers crowding me. And the longer it takes you to make up your mind, the less the offer will be."

He swung effortlessly into the saddle. "You see, MacKenzie, I'm holding an ace in the hole. Even if you don't sell it to me, I'll get it when my son marries O'Shea's daughter."

Cole watched Lawford ride away. One thing was for certain: Ben Lawford was a force to be reckoned with. And right now Lawford had the upper hand and knew it. But the rancher sure as hell wanted this property. Why? He didn't believe Lawford's explanation for a minute.

Mounting up, he headed back to town, convinced more than ever that Pop's death had not been an accident. The time had come to have a long talk with Dallas Donovan.

As soon as Cole had left, Maggie returned to listing the expenses in the hope of determining what could be shaved. As it was, they were already at a minimum. Cole was right that the problem lay in the need for more income, not less overhead.

After several fruitless hours, she finally tossed the pencil aside and cradled her head in her hands. She couldn't decide between screaming in frustration and crying herself into exhaustion. Cole was right. She couldn't even make a decision about that either.

What should she do? She felt helpless, adrift. No

control of her own life. Cole had the say about everything. Maybe she should get married. Keith Lawford wanted to marry her. He was a good man, and she knew he would do whatever he could to make her life happy and comfortable. And if she asked, he'd buy the stageline and let her run it. That would show Cole MacKenzie.

Trouble was, she didn't love Keith. And he was too nice a person to deceive. It wouldn't be fair to him—or any man—to marry just to gain her own ends. It would make Cole right about that, too. She'd be nothing more than a spoiled child getting her own way. Not just a brat. A deceitful, scheming brat.

Tears misted her eyes. *Oh, Pop. I feel so worthless. I miss you so much.*

Maggie lifted her head when she heard a light tap on the connecting door to the stable. "Come in," she called, dabbing at the tears in her eyes.

Juan came in and stood at the door, his straw sombrero in hand and his beautiful brown eyes rounded and sorrowful. She knew he couldn't have avoided hearing the earlier argument between her and Cole.

"My work is through, Señorita Margaret. Is there more you wish for Juan to do?"

"No, Juan, that's fine." She opened her purse and walked over and gave him a quarter. "I'm sure you've heard that Mr. MacKenzie intends to close down the stageline, so I don't know how much longer we'll be needing you."

"*Sí.*" The young boy hesitated and then said, "Señorita Margaret, my *papá* and I are very sad for you. But *Papá* say Señor Cole is a good man. He will do what is best for you. Juan thinks so, too."

Maggie smiled, then hugged him and kissed him on the cheek. "Thank you, Juan, I hope he will."

From the time she had found out that Juan had been raised motherless, as she had been, the young boy had held a special place in her heart.

"You know, Juan, Minnie always makes strawberry ice cream on Saturdays. How about you and I going to the diner for a big dish of it?"

The youngster grinned from ear to ear. "Juan thinks he would like that."

"I thought Juan would like that," she said, slipping her arm around his shoulders.

Once at the diner, they sat down at a table by the window, and as they were enjoying the treat, Keith Lawford walked by and saw them. Maggie waved to him, and he came in.

"Ah hah! Caught in the act, are you?" he said. "So this handsome chap is my competition." He grinned at Juan, and the boy hung his head as if he'd done something wrong.

"Guilty as charged, Keith."

"Actually, Margaret, I was just on my way to your house. I realize it's still soon after your father's death, but I was hoping you'd do me the honor of joining me for dinner tonight. That is, if your jailer will let you out of jail," he added, intending to be humorous.

Margaret had observed in the past that Keith's attempts at humor usually failed. This time was no exception, because the issue was so sensitive to her. The Maggie in her wanted to tell him as much, but instead Margaret tittered in response.

"Oh, Keith, you're so funny, but I doubt even Cole MacKenzie would try to carry his authority as far as determining my dining preferences, so I'll be pleased to join you."

"Wonderful. Will seven be convenient for you?"

"Yes, of course. I'm looking forward to it, Keith."

Keith put a dollar down on the table. "Permit me to pay for your refreshment."

"Thank you, Keith."

"*Gracias*, Señor Lawford," Juan said.

"Until then, Margaret." Keith tipped his hat and departed.

Juan grinned at her. "Señor Keith has the eye for you."

"You think so, Juan?"

"*Sí*, Señorita Margaret. But Juan thinks Señor Cole has the eye for you, too."

"Cole? That's ridiculous. Señorita Margaret thinks Juan must have consumed too much ice cream. His belly's fuller than his head."

Laughing, they left the diner.

After returning to the office, Maggie spent the next couple of hours with her thoughts alternating between trying to figure out how to promote business for the stageline and how to persuade Cole not to close it down. Sighing, she moved to the window in time to see Cole ride up. She listened to him moving about in the stable and knew he was unsaddling the horse.

Maggie sat down at the desk and fortified herself for Cole's entrance.

When Cole entered the office, he was surprised to see Maggie. "You still here, Maggie?"

"I've been waiting for Emilio to get back from Noches."

She was tired. It sounded in her voice and showed in the slump of her shoulders.

"What time is he due in?"

"Anytime now. Did you have any problems finding Pop's claim?"

"No. Your directions were easy to follow."

"What did you think of it?"

"I'm going to have to ride out and take another look. Your boyfriend's father showed up, so I didn't get a chance to get a good look at it."

"My boyfriend? What are you talking about?"

"That prick Lawford."

He could see she was as determined to hold on to her temper as he was and grinned when she forced back her rise of anger with a smile.

"Keith's not my boyfriend, Cole. And you're being unfair. He's a very nice man. If you knew him better, you'd realize that."

"I doubt that. He's too prissy for my tastes. Go home, Maggie. I'll wait for Emilio. I don't suppose you told him this was his last run."

"No, I didn't, because I'm hoping you and I can discuss it further."

He sighed in exasperation, shoved his hat to his forehead, and struck a familiar stance: legs apart and hands on his hips. In Alaska, she'd always called it his Wyatt Earp at the OK Corral stance. Funny how he'd begun to remember these things about her.

"Maggie, I don't want to argue. There's nothing more to discuss."

"Neither do I, Cole. Can't you just sit down so we can talk about it calmly?"

He pulled over a chair, straddled it, and then draped his arms on the back.

"All right, Maggie, we'll discuss it one more time. The stagecoach line does not make money, so we have to close it down, because there's not enough money in the bank to continue buying feed for the horses." Remarkably, he didn't raise his voice once, but he couldn't disguise his exasperation. "I wish you would try to understand that and accept my decision without resentment."

Maggie looked up, her eyes imploring. "Please, Cole, you can't do it. You don't understand. This isn't just an issue between you and me. I'll promise you anything if you at least give me a chance to try and make a profit. You don't understand how much this stageline meant to Pop. If you close it down, you're burying his dreams along with him."

"Dammit, Maggie, don't look at me like that. What in hell do you expect of me? Pop trusted me to consider your best interests. You ask me to keep Pop's dream alive. It's impossible to do both."

"Just give me a chance, Cole," Maggie pleaded.

This was the Maggie he'd glimpsed last night. Vulnerable. Sensitive. Effective arguments against ordinary common sense. He couldn't believe he was losing his, but what choice did he have?

"All right, Maggie. My dad always told me the decisions made with the heart are easier on your conscience than those made with the head. You've got thirty days to turn this line around."

He got out of there before he could change his mind.

Actually, allowing Maggie to keep the office open did fall in with his scheme. While appearing to humor her, it gave him the excuse to hang around town without raising suspicion while he investigated Pop's death. *And why try to kid yourself, MacKenzie? Maggie got to you with that plea to keep Pop's dream alive.*

Cole went back to the house, got two hundred dollars of his money. He'd deposit it in Pop's checking account to keep the account in the black for a while.

But spend it wisely, Maggie, because I'm not throwing any more good money after bad.

Maggie felt she'd been given a new lease on life. She now had thirty days to resolve the problem. Feeling considerably more hopeful, she put the files back in order while awaiting Emilio's return from Noches. Her step was lighter as she went to the window, hoping to see some sign of the stagecoach. Cole was walking down the street.

She had always loved watching him when he wasn't aware of it. His every movement, from his long-legged stride to the way he shoved his hat to his forehead, had always fascinated her. Still did.

Damn you, Cole, why can't I hate you? Why do I still feel the same excitement I've always experienced when I'm around you? Despite how much I resent your interference in my life, it's useless to try and deny that I'm not still drawn to you.

Will I ever be able to ignore that underlying element when I'm with you? Stop comparing every man I meet to you? If only you could see me as a woman, as Keith Lawford does. If only Juan's youthful observation was correct. If only you could see that I'm Maggie the woman—not Maggie the kid you remember.

If I'm to ever get you out of my heart and mind, Cole MacKenzie, it will only happen when we're on equal ground and face the issue as man and woman.

Maggie turned away from the window when he entered the bank. *Stop hoping for the impossible, Maggie. These "if only" yearnings are useless—he never will.*

The rumble of the returning stage jarred her out of her musings. She went into the stable to greet Emilio as he climbed down from the box.

"Any problems, Emilio?"

"No, Señorita Margaret, but I think we'll have to replace the right front wheel. I was lucky to make it back. I brought back the usual two passengers and some freight."

Another blow to the expenses. If she hadn't trusted Emilio's loyalty, she'd swear he was in cahoots with Cole. "Some freight! That's good. Let's hope it will be enough to pay for a new wheel. Who's it for?"

"Señor Hanson," Emilio said as he unhitched the team. Maggie helped him get the harnesses off the horses and the horses into stalls.

Emilio climbed back onto the stage to unload the freight. As soon as he lifted up one of the crates, she heard clucking.

"Is that what I think it is?"

Emilio grinned. "*Sí,* señorita, chickens. Two crates of them." He lowered them to the box seat.

"Oh, well, every little bit helps. Let me help you with those."

Maggie stepped up on the wheel. Just as he started to hand her down one of the wooden crates, she heard a loud cracking sound as one of the spokes broke. The wheel rolled off, and the stagecoach listed to the right. Then the front end collapsed. The crate of chickens fell through her hands as she toppled backward. The other crate slipped off the seat and, like the first one, crashed to the ground and broke open. Fluttering and squawking like angry fishwives, the dozen chickens scattered in all directions.

Emilio jumped down and helped Maggie to her feet. "Are you hurt, Señorita Margaret?"

"Only my dignity," she said. "Let's gather up these cackling chickens before they spook the horses."

"Where should we put them when we do catch them? The crates are broken."

Maggie looked around in desperation and spied some empty burlap bags. "We'll stuff them in those bags then take them over to Clem Hanson's right away."

She never knew chickens could move so fast. They always managed to flap their way out of her grasp. And it seemed as if they were actually taunting her. They'd perch on a bale of hay or the edge of a horse stall, then the instant she'd grab for one, they'd flutter away.

Maggie stalked one that kept moving by inches out of her reach. She made a daring lurch for it, tripped over another one of the elusive fowl, but as she fell she managed to grab it. The captured chicken flapped and squawked as it tried to escape, but Maggie held firm to the devious creature's skinny leg.

Flat on her stomach, with her arm outstretched holding the chicken, Maggie lay breathless, celebrating her victory. A pair of boots stepped into her vision. Slowly she raised her head. Cole MacKenzie lounged against the open office door, his arms folded across his chest.

"Well, Miz Margaret, as long as you insisted upon running this chicken feed operation, it was inevitable the chickens would come home to roost."

Chapter 6

After capturing and delivering all the chickens, a very reserved Maggie went home to dress for her dinner date with Keith, only to find Cole in her father's chair in the parlor reading legal documents. She couldn't bear to look him in the eye after the fiasco in the stable but felt since he had relented and agreed to keep the stageline operating, she should try to make polite conversation. Trouble was, any time their gazes met even accidentally, he'd return to reading the document he held.

Oh, he was irritating. But she didn't want to fight with him.

Smiling, she asked, "You mentioned you met Ben Lawford today. What did you think of him?"

"We didn't have much to say to each other." He hadn't bothered to even look up.

"Did he tell you Keith is his son?"

His eyes appeared over the top of the document. "He made a point of informing me of that." He returned to reading.

"Why do I detect the meeting wasn't all that cordial?" She grinned slyly. "I'd even venture to guess it was more likely downright hostile."

This time she drew his attention. "Now, why would you think that, Miz Margaret?"

"I remember in Alaska you always used that aloof tone of annoyance whenever you were displeased. Did you find Ben annoying, Cole?"

"Not as annoying as you are right now."

"Now I'm convinced of it. You met your match, didn't you, MacKenzie?"

He lowered the paper to his lap. "You know, Miz Margaret, you just can't help being annoying little Maggie, can you?"

"I'm not certain I understand what you mean." She clamped her lips together to keep from giggling.

"The same simpering grin you're wearing now. In Alaska you always made a point of smirking at me every time you succeeded in manipulating Pop into giving in to you."

"Whatever you might have thought, Cole, I never manipulated Pop. I loved him too much to deceive him."

"Okay. You were just a kid, so I'll give you the benefit of the doubt." He returned to reading.

She felt like a child who had just been reprimanded. "I was only teasing you about Ben, Cole. I didn't mean anything by it. I think both of us carry too many unpleasant memories of Alaska. I guess that's why we can never be friends."

He folded the document and looked at her. She saw a glint of sadness in his sapphire eyes. "I hope you're wrong, Maggie." He stood up. "If you'll excuse me, I have some business to attend to."

"Wait, Cole. What *was* your opinion of Ben Lawford?"

"My opinion doesn't matter, Maggie. It's yours that'll count." He departed quickly.

The conversation had disturbed her, but she couldn't put her finger on why. Entering the kitchen, she asked, "Ellie, what kind of business do you suppose Cole has on a Saturday night?"

"Most likely the same kind those other cowboys come to town for. But why ask me? Between the two of you, there's been a lot of those mysterious business errands lately."

Maggie moved to the window. Cole was almost out of sight. "I think you're right. I bet that business is at Dallas's."

"It's no skin off your teeth, honey," Ellie said. She looked askance at her. "Or is it?"

"What do you mean by that?" Maggie began to fidget nervously with the top button on her blouse.

"You aren't falling for that rogue, are you?"

I fell for him four years ago. I'm trying to pick myself up now.

"Don't talk so foolish, Ellie. I'll be relieved when he leaves town for good." Ellie was too canny at reading between the lines, so Maggie rushed up the stairway before she could reveal any more.

The cowboys from the surrounding ranches were in town for the start of the weekend, and Dallas's was clearly the attraction for them. The tavern was bustling with noise and activity. Cole spied Dallas holding court at the end of the bar.

"Well, howdy, Texas," she said in greeting.

"Dallas, I need to talk to you."

"So long, fellows, see you later," she said to a couple of old-timers at the bar. "What's the problem, partner?"

"So you've heard," Cole said. "Who told you?"

"Keith Lawford."

"I was surprised to find that Pop held an interest in this place. That's what I came to discuss."

"No time like the present. Vic, pour the man a drink."

Cole grimaced. "How about some place less noisy. Have you had dinner?"

"Not yet."

"Good. I'll take you to dinner where we can sit down. I need some answers."

"Texas, I've got a business to run here."

"I'm sure Vic can handle it. Right, Vic?" Cole said as the bartender poured him a drink.

"No problem. You want a chaser with this?"

"Not right now."

"I'll be back in an hour, Vic," Dallas said, after Cole had downed the shot of whiskey.

Once outside, he took her arm, and Dallas smiled up at him. "You're a real gentleman, Texas. Your ma must be real proud of you."

"Comes naturally, I guess. My dad adores women. Treats every one of them like royalty."

"So he's got a roving eye, huh?"

"Nothing like that. It's safe to say it's never occurred to him to look at another woman from the time he met my mother. Dad simply respects women. He says they're the most remarkable creatures on earth."

They entered the diner and took a corner table.

"I can't remember the last time a gentleman took me out to dinner," Dallas said. "This is real nice of you, Cole."

"Their loss is my gain."

"You are a charmer, Texas. If I weren't old enough to be your mother, your smooth talk would be enough to turn my head."

"I think it would take more than a smooth line to turn your head. Looks like it's on your shoulders pretty solidly."

After the waiter had taken their order, he asked, "Where are you from, Dallas?"

"My name says it all."

At that moment Cole saw Maggie and Keith Lawford enter the restaurant. After seating her, Keith came over to their table, said hello to Dallas, then turned to Cole.

"My father said he ran into you at the O'Shea property today."

"That's right."

"What did you think of it?"

Intentionally pretending to misunderstand the question, Cole replied, "Didn't know what to think. I couldn't quite figure out what he was doing there. You have any idea, Lawford?"

Lawford wasn't amused. "I don't question my father's actions, Mr. MacKenzie. You'd be wise not to either. My pleasure, Dallas." He nodded to her and left.

"What have you got against Keith?" Dallas asked when the attorney had returned to his table.

Cole glanced over to see Maggie smiling at Lawford. "I didn't come here to discuss Keith Lawford. So what made you leave Texas, Dallas?" he asked, returning to their interrupted conversation.

"Not what, who. His name was Johnny Donovan. I was sixteen when he married me." She smiled. "Lord, he was a handsome devil. But he couldn't remain in one place. We moved around a lot. Johnny was always looking for the big break, promising that one day we'd settle down in a big mansion where I could live the life of milk and honey." She shook her head. "It never happened. But how I loved that man."

"How long were you married?"

"Ten years," she said, pensively.

"What happened to him?"

"Apaches. They attacked the stage we were on. We made it this far, but Johnny was killed."

He reached over and clasped her hand. "I'm sorry, Dallas."

"It was a long time ago."

"So how did you and Pop happen to go into business together?"

"Lawford was nothing much more than a relay station at the time. The town grew out of it."

"It didn't grow too far," Cole said derisively.

"I had no money, no place to go, so I ended up staying here. Mick and his wife, Rachel, took me in, and then Mick staked me and I opened the tavern. They'd been trying to have children for years, and two years later, when Rachel finally got pregnant, they were so happy."

Dallas's eyes misted. "Rachel died giving birth to Maggie. It took the heart out of Mick, until he got interested in mining." A tender smile softened her face. "Mick reminded me of Johnny in a lot of ways: kind, generous, and always looking for that pot at the end of the rainbow. Oh, he'd hit a small claim now and then, but never the big one. Maggie was about four or five when he left with her. He finally came back two years ago. I think you know the rest."

"How come he never married you?"

"I don't think it occurred to either of us. Mick and I were good friends, and Rachel was the best friend I ever had."

Deep in reflection, Dallas smiled. "Besides, MacKenzie, even if it had occurred to me, it wouldn't have done me much good. Rachel O'Shea was the only woman Mick could ever have loved. Maggie is the spitting image of her."

Well, MacKenzie, so much for your theory that Pop and Dallas might have been carrying on. Coincidental that she and Maggie wear the same perfume, though.

Cole's gaze wandered back to where the couple sat deep in conversation. For a long moment he took in the vision of the young girl. Hell, young woman. Maggie was no girl anymore. It was time he stopped thinking of her as one. She was a woman, all right—a damn beautiful woman.

And as much as it would stick in his craw, maybe the best thing he could do for her and Pop was get her married off to Lawford.

But not until he was sure the prig had nothing to do with Pop's death.

"Dallas, how much money does the tavern take in? From what I see, this is Maggie's only source of income."

"I thought Mick left his half to you."

"He did. But Maggie needs the income."

"And Prince Charming is riding to her rescue. You're something, Texas."

"Hey, we didn't come here to talk about me either."

"Well, I have to say it's not worth keeping the doors open during the week. We make our money on Saturday nights. Particularly the one right after the hands draw their pay. We take in a couple hundred dollars then, but then it peters out the rest of the month to just twenty or thirty dollars a week. By the time I pay off Vic and the whores—"

"The what?" Cole almost choked on the bite of beef he'd just taken.

"The whores. Every Saturday night I bring in two of them from Noches. Mick never charged me for their passage because they meant money in his pocket, too."

"Pop running prostitutes. What does Maggie think of it?"

Dallas laughed. "Mick told her they're my nieces who come to visit me every weekend."

Cole never felt so stupefied in his life. "Pop . . . running prostitutes." He shook his head. "I can't believe it."

"Well, if it's any consolation to you, it was my idea. But why is that such a surprise to you? You're no schoolboy, Texas, and you've been around enough to know which end is up. So don't expect me to believe you've never used a whore out of necessity."

"I'm not denying that. It just surprises me, that's all."

"It's a simple business decision. If I don't bring them in, the boys will go to a different town. It's been my experience that a man can do without a full belly or a bath, but he can't do without a woman. As a man you should understand that."

"And as a woman you shouldn't condone it."

"Mick didn't like it either. As soon as I could afford it, we agreed that I was going to buy him out. I'm willing to make you the same offer, Cole."

"Dallas, I have no desire to run a whorehouse, but right now for Maggie's sake I have no choice but to let you make the call. As soon as things are settled here, you can buy her out."

Pouting, she leaned forward. "Does this mean the end of our friendship, Texas?"

"Not at all, Dallas. You're one great lady, and you can run your business as you see fit. One favor: as long as I remain involved, just keep it honest."

Dallas broke into laughter. "You know, Texas, I liked you the moment I met you. Now I adore you. Confidentially, I don't like using women that way any more than you do, but it's a business, honey, and I've got to get back to mine. So eat up, partner."

He squeezed her hand. "I'm glad we understand each other, Dallas. I think this is the start of a good partnership."

At the sound of Dallas's burst of laughter, Maggie cast a resentful glance at the corner table. So that was his important business. They looked to be pretty intimate for two people who barely knew each other.

Of course, Cole always could get friendly with women he barely knew. It was a woman who put up with his domination, bad moods, sarcastic mouth, and being downright ignored by him that he couldn't get intimate with—a woman like herself for instance.

"I'm sorry, what did you say, Keith?" she asked, becoming aware that he had spoken to her.

"I said you aren't listening to me, Margaret."

"I'm sorry, Keith. I guess I shouldn't have accepted your invitation tonight. I'm just not good company."

"It's my fault, Margaret. It was very inconsiderate of me. I should have allowed you more time to mourn before asking you to dinner."

Allow. She didn't like that word. It sounded too controlling—too much like something Cole MacKenzie would say.

Her stomach leaped to her throat when she saw Cole reach over and grasp Dallas's hand. "I didn't realize Cole and Dallas were so friendly."

"I have no idea, Margaret. Eat your dinner, you've barely touched your food."

Now he sounded like a parent reprimanding a child. She took a bite of the roll on her plate.

"Margaret, as I've mentioned before, since your return to Lawford one thing has become obvious to me: I have developed a deep feeling for you."

"That's very kind of you, Keith. I can't tell you what a comfort your friendship means to me."

He reached over with his napkin and dabbed at the corner of her mouth.

At her questioning look, he said, "Just a crumb, my dear."

"Oh, thank you, Keith."

"I have something I wish to discuss with you, but you seem preoccupied. Has it got something to do with MacKenzie?"

"Why do you say that?"

"You keep looking in his direction."

"I'm sorry, Keith. You know how much the man upsets me."

"Yes, I've noticed. Would you like to leave?"

"No, of course not. I'd never give him that satisfaction. I'll have to learn to live with it. At least for three more years."

"Well, that's what I want to discuss with you."

Keith adjusted the knife he'd already placed exactly across his plate. She'd noticed he had a fetish for such petty details, and she was beginning to find the habit annoying to the point of being . . . prissy.

Her angry gaze swung back to the corner table. *Damn you, Cole, now you've got me thinking it!*

"What is it, Keith?"

"I want to marry you, Margaret."

The proposal didn't come as a surprise. She knew he eventually would get around to asking her, but she'd already made the decision that she couldn't marry him—at least at this time. She simply didn't love him.

"Keith, you do me a great honor. And I don't wish to appear ungrateful for all your kindness. But I'm just not ready to get married."

"I understand why, Margaret. I didn't mean at the moment. I certainly would expect you to need time to mourn your loss. But I would hope that you would consider marriage in the future."

"Then you understand why I cannot accept your proposal at this time."

"I would like us to have an understanding that you will when the time comes."

"I can't do that, Keith. It would be the same as accepting your proposal now. Do you understand what I mean?"

His lips pinched in disapproval. "I suppose I do,

Margaret, but I intend to pursue the issue in the future."

She smiled in gratitude. "Thank you for your understanding, Keith. You're a wonderful person, and I appreciate your patience."

"You have that. Now finish your dinner, Margaret. Your food's getting cold."

She obediently picked up her fork.

On their way out, Cole and Dallas stopped and said good-bye to Maggie and Lawford.

"And, Lawford," Cole added, "don't keep Margaret out too late." He took Dallas's arm, and whispered, "Let's get out of here before she throws a glass at me."

Returning to the tavern, Cole saw there was no room at the poker table, so he headed for the bar.

"Usual?" Vic asked.

"Just leave the bottle," Cole replied.

Vic arched a brow. "That must have been one hell of a dinner." He put down the bottle and walked away.

Don't be so cocky, Vic. I suspect you as much as anyone. What have you gotten yourself into, MacKenzie? Wasn't it bad enough you agreed to let Maggie keep that worthless stageline operating? Now you're in the business of procuring prostitutes. You've become a damn pimp!

He reached for the whiskey bottle.

Chapter 7

By the time he'd poured himself the second shot, Cole knew he couldn't drink away his troubles. They'd still be there in the morning along with a headache if he tried. So he left and went back to the house.

Once stretched out on the bed, he found himself in the same fix. He tossed restlessly. Unable to sleep, he got out of bed, pulled on his jeans, and padded barefoot into the kitchen. A parlor light was still burning, which indicated that Maggie was still out with Lawford. What in hell were they up to at this late hour?

Cole turned off the lamp and sat down in the darkened room. A summer breeze swept through the open window, stirring the drapery and carrying the pleasant fragrance of roses into the house. It was a restful moment for a man with a lot on his mind. No noise. No distractions. Just plain peaceful.

When the low murmur of voices intruded on this solitude, Cole moved to the window and saw that Maggie and Lawford were on the porch. He remained at the window and found himself watching them from concealment for the second time in as many days.

Normally it would not have been enough to hold his attention, but there was an intimacy in the way they stood together: Lawford with his hands on her shoulders, Maggie looking up into his eyes. It was a pose of lovers.

Cole knew he shouldn't watch when Lawford took her in his arms and kissed her. He felt a rise of resentment when she failed to protest and yielded submissively. But what the hell, hadn't it crossed his mind to marry her off to Lawford? So why did he have the urge to go out there now and punch the bastard in the face?

"Good night, my dear," Lawford said.

"Good night, Keith."

Her voice sounded throaty, sensual. It bothered the hell out of him. Rather than have her discover he'd been lurking in the dark, Cole hurried back to his room.

After the restless night Cole decided the wisest thing to do was try to keep Maggie and Keith Lawford apart as much as he could until he was certain Lawford had nothing to do with Pop's death. He needed to go back to Timberline but didn't want to leave her alone all day for Lawford to work on her, so the situation called for a little manipulation.

"Maggie, do you feel like a ride this morning?" Cole asked, when they finished breakfast.

"Where to?"

"Timberline."

The very mention of the word turned Maggie to ice. "You were just there yesterday," she said sharply.

"I was interrupted yesterday. I intend to take a longer and harder look at it. Forget it. I'm sorry I asked," Cole said.

Maggie knew her tone had given him the wrong impression. Her objection had nothing to do with the tension between them. The truth was she could not face seeing the spot where Pop had died. Would Cole understand if she tried to tell him or think she was just being childish again?

She was grateful to Cole for letting her keep the stageline open, and the time had come to bite the bullet and give some concession on her part, too—as well as show some maturity. But her heart was still so full of sorrow over Pop that it was hard to keep her control. She just wished Cole would go away.

But other people's lives still went on, no matter how much she was grieving. And she'd been acting like a child since Cole arrived in Lawford. She had to start showing him she was just as capable of concession as he was, no matter what her problems were.

"I think I'd enjoy a ride, Cole."

He grinned in pleasure. "The trail's too steep in spots for a buggy. We'll have to take horses."

"That's fine. Give me a few minutes to change my clothes."

Once upstairs, Maggie pulled off her gown and petticoat. As she changed into a split skirt and white blouse, she reconsidered her motives for agreeing to go with him. Until now she had intentionally avoided going to the site where Pop had been killed. Even Cole would understand her aversion to it. There could be other ways to convince him that she was grateful and willing to cooperate.

Nevertheless, despite her internal struggle, she pulled on her boots, slapped on a hat, and went down to join him.

Ellie had just finished packing a picnic basket when Maggie returned to the kitchen.

"Where's Cole?"

"He went to saddle the horses. Said he'll come back with them." Ellie glanced askance at her. "I know how you feel about Timberline, honey; I'm surprised you're even going."

"I thought it was the least I could do since Cole's been so cooperative."

"Sure that's your only reason?"

"What do you mean by that? What other reason could I possibly have?"

"He's a good-looking fella. The idea of spending some time alone with him can't be too displeasin'."

That was the furthest thought from her mind. The idea was ludicrous. "You're talking nonsense, Ellie."

"I ain't blind, gal. You've got feelin' for that fella that you ain't admittin' to."

"I'm only trying to be more cooperative. You're the one who always said you can catch more flies with honey than you can with vinegar." Relieved to see that Cole had returned, Maggie grabbed the picnic basket, kissed Ellie on the cheek, and hurried outside.

Cole grinned with pleasure when he saw how she was dressed. "Miz Margaret's looking like Maggie again. I'm glad you dressed lightly. This day's gonna be a hot one," he said, rolling up his shirtsleeves to the elbows. He took the picnic basket, and while he tied it to the back of his saddle, Maggie climbed onto her mount.

Cole came over to adjust her stirrup straps. She tried to pretend his nearness didn't bother her, but Cole MacKenzie was not an easy man for her senses to ignore: his flashing grin, the dark hair that dusted his forearms, the male essence of him, along with the strength in his hand when he grasped her ankle and anchored her foot in the stirrup were all sensory assaults on her feminine sensitivities.

He looked up at her, and for a long moment she struggled with the sensual potency of his sapphire eyes as their gazes locked.

"Feel okay?"

"I feel fine," she replied.

His lips curved at the corners, but his gaze never altered. "I meant the stirrups, Miz Margaret."

Maggie blushed. Surely he couldn't read her mind. But she was such a novice at this man and woman thing, and he was such a master. If he ever suspected how much he affected her, he'd always have the upper hand. She just had to get over the girlish crush she had on him, and the only way to do it was to force herself to be around him, not avoid him.

With a smile of bravado, she challenged him. "I'm ready any time you are, MacKenzie." Let him try and figure out what she meant by that.

Cole found the ride that day to be more enjoyable than the previous day's had been. He knew it was because of Maggie. Glancing over at her, he saw that she appeared to be deep in thought, so he didn't say anything. But there was a pleasant companionship in riding side by side with a beautiful woman—even one who hated him.

He'd never done much riding with any of the girls back in Calico except for his female cousins. Maybe he should have stayed around longer and given it more of a try with the local gals—he might have ended up not leaving the Triple M. Although he doubted that. He was a wanderer at heart.

He stole another glance at Maggie. In the past two years she sure had grown into a beautiful woman. The more he saw of her, the more attractive she became. Funny how he'd never noticed her beauty in Alaska. Pop had done a great job of disguising her body and that gorgeous auburn hair, but when he'd looked deeply into those haunting green eyes of hers, there was no hiding their beauty. How could he not have noticed them years ago? She was one beautiful woman, all right—and one who couldn't bear to be around him or have him so much as touch her.

And that parting jab of hers when they left Lawford was almost a challenge for him to go ahead and try if he dared. Well, he had no one to blame but himself for her dislike of him. He hoped that somehow by the time he left Lawford, they would be friends.

Cole reined up when they reached Pop's marker. "This is where we turn off. Would you like to rest before we go on?"

"Only if you want to. From what I remember of the map Pop drew, we must be pretty close to the mine, aren't we?"

"Yes, but from here on we'll have to ride single file.

There's no trail to follow, and the going gets much harder and slower. Haven't you been here before?"

"Never."

That unexpected fact astonished him. He'd just assumed that Pop would have shown her the property before he bought it.

"How good a rider are you, Maggie? We can leave the horses and walk the rest of the way, if you prefer."

"I'm no Annie Oakley, but I think I can manage to stay in the saddle, Cole. I did in Alaska, didn't I?"

"Yeah, you did. I'd forgotten," he admitted, recalling those narrow mountain passages they had traversed.

"Apparently there's a lot about Alaska you've forgotten."

"I guess you're right," he said, remorse heavy in his voice. "I just don't want anything to happen to you."

"Like it did to Pop."

His brow narrowed in grimness. "Pop's neck wasn't broken from any fall off a horse, Maggie."

Cole wheeled his mount off the trail and began to pick his way along the route. Maggie followed in silence behind him. She could handle a horse on the rough terrain, all right. It was just another reminder of how much he'd underestimated Maggie O'Shea.

Dismounting when they reached the entrance to the cave, he went over to assist Maggie, but she had already dismounted. After tying the reins to a tree, he loosened the cinches on the horses as Maggie stared, transfixed, at the gaping hole in the rock.

"So this is Pop's mine. It doesn't look worth dying for," she said bitterly.

"It's not actually a mine, Maggie. It's a cave." He lit

the lantern and they stepped inside. "You see, these are solid rock walls. There's no sign there's ever been any attempt to mine it."

"Then what was Pop doing in here?"

"I haven't figured that out."

"Whatever it was, it cost him his life." She shivered and rushed back outside.

"What's wrong, Maggie?" he asked, following her.

She folded her arms across her chest to try to control her trembling. "I'm sorry. I thought I could, but I can't bear to go in there and see where Pop died." Her eyes glistened with tears. "You said it wasn't a mine, so what could he be looking for in that horrible place?"

"Maybe whatever he was looking for had nothing to do with this cave."

"What do you mean?"

"I was wondering if you remember whether there was a storm that day?"

"I can't remember. Everything is so jumbled in my mind. It all seems so long ago when he said good-bye and left." She looked at him, wide-eyed with shock. "My God, it was only less than a week ago. Less than a week." She was close to sobbing. "And I miss him, Cole. I miss him so much."

He could see her control was breaking down fast, and he put his arms around her. "Hey, you're doing great. Just let it out, baby."

She stepped away. "I'm sorry. I guess it's this place. I'm fine now."

"Let's get away from here."

"But you said you wanted to examine it more closely. I can wait."

"It doesn't have to be now. I can always come back." He led her over to the horses.

"Why are you so interested in what the weather was like?"

"I was just kicking around some theories: if there was a storm, there's the possibility Pop might have just gone in there to stay dry. Or maybe he was chased in there by an animal. We can't just assume he was looking for something in there."

"Now I remember," she suddenly blurted, "it did rain that afternoon and into the evening. That's the reason Ellie and I weren't too concerned when Pop didn't show up for dinner. I remember now Ellie even commented that he probably was holed up somewhere to get out of the rain."

"So in truth this cave could be a red herring."

"How can you say that?" she cried, appalled. "Regardless of what Pop was doing in here, this is where they found his body."

"Yeah, I guess you're right. Well, this is as good a time as any to have lunch. Let's find a good place to do so."

After about a quarter hour, Cole could see that Maggie had calmed down, and they dismounted. She sat down, leaning back against a tree trunk. Cole untied the picnic basket and then sat down beside her.

"Bless you, Ellie. I'm hungry enough to eat a horse," she declared when he spread out the fare on a red and white checked tablecloth.

"Sorry, no horse. You're going to have to settle for cheese sandwiches, fresh strawberries, and slices of chocolate cake."

Maggie made no attempt to put on her Margaret airs. Instead, she consumed the food voraciously, licked the chocolate off her fingers, then leaned back again in satisfaction.

"That was delicious," Cole said. "I wonder what Ellie would have come up with if we'd given her more time."

"I can't remember when I've enjoyed a meal so much." Her gaze was calm now as it swept the terrain. Despite the heat of the day, the early signs of the coming fall had begun to speckle the leaves with gold and red.

"This whole area is so beautiful, but it holds a memory too painful for me to bear. Please sell it, Cole. I don't want anything to do with this property."

"I probably will, but I don't want to be hasty, Maggie."

"It's not being hasty. I never want to live up here, so what value is it to me other than what I can sell it for."

"Maggie, Pop wasn't a stupid man. There has to be a good reason why he chose this particular property. Surely he must have given you some hint."

She shook her head. "None that I know. Once he said he thought he knew of a way to save the town. He never mentioned this land, though, and I never even knew he'd bought the property until Keith read us the will. I'll bless the day I'm rid of it."

"I understand your misgivings, Maggie, but it is a beautiful property."

"I have a confession to make, Cole. I came along today to try to prove to you how mature I've become. I'm sorry I broke down. I'm afraid I've done just the opposite again."

"No, you haven't, Maggie. You're grieving. That's

natural and nothing to apologize for. Our trouble, Maggie, is that we're both too quick at misjudging each other. We should be working together to do what's best for you. Instead, we always end up at odds. I need your help, Maggie. I don't trust anyone's motives— particularly those of your friend Keith Lawford and his father."

She dropped her gaze again and stared at the ground. "You're wrong about Keith. He's asked me to marry him."

"And did you accept his proposal?"

"I haven't decided. Keith has been a wall of strength to me throughout this tragedy."

Even though the idea of her marrying the lawyer had crossed his own mind, now, faced with the actual possibility, an immediate jolt of resentment streaked through him.

"For God's sake, Maggie," he declared, jumping to his feet, "you're vulnerable right now. That's no reason to marry him. The man's old enough to be your father."

"And who are you to criticize? It's for sure no one could ever accuse you of robbing the cradle. Good heavens, the way you were fawning over Dallas last night was pathetic. Now she *is* old enough to be your mother."

"I already have a mother, thank you," he replied, sarcasm heavy in his voice.

"Well, I just lost a father, so maybe I need a replacement."

For a long moment they glared at each other.

The silence between them became deafening. Cole felt like a bastard. He knelt down in front of her. "I'm sorry, Maggie. We're doing it again to each other, aren't we? I thought the ride up here would be a good change of pace for you. A pleasant afternoon. Instead, it's turned out to be a nightmare for you. I should have left well enough alone. Reckon I've upset you as much as this place does."

"That's not true. No matter what you think, Cole, I'm glad I came. Deep down I know I have to face this and see where Pop died, but until now I was never able even to get up enough courage to come up here. At last I finally did, which is a step in the right direction. Next time maybe I can enter that cave." She grasped his hands and looked up at him with her green eyes all watery and shining with trust. "I'm very grateful to you, Cole."

"Well, ain't this a pretty sight," a voice said gruffly.

They turned their heads in surprise to see Ben Lawford astride his huge black stallion.

"Howdy, Margaret." He nodded to Cole. "MacKenzie."

"Lawford," Cole acknowledged, rising to his feet.

"Sorry to interrupt. The two of you look mighty cozy."

"What can we do for you, Lawford?" Cole asked.

"Might ask the same of you, since you're on the Lazy L."

"We are? Our mistake, Lawford. I thought we were still on Timberline."

"You must have missed the marker a few yards back."

Maggie began to pack up the basket. "We're so sorry, Ben."

"No call to rush off, gal. Ain't trying to hustle you off."

"No, that's quite all right. It's time I got back to town anyway." She handed Cole the picnic basket.

"You've got some good-looking land here, Lawford," Cole said, tying the basket to his saddle.

"Yeah, and looking is about all it's good for. I run cattle on my ranch, not mountain goats. Just the same, I don't want anybody moving in and spoiling the view."

"I'm surprised you didn't buy Timberline to avoid that possibility."

"Why buy the cow when the milk's free? Never figured any homesteader would want it. It's too damn rocky to farm."

Ben Lawford turned to Maggie. "Why don't you ride back to the house with me? Keith's home, and I'm sure he'd hate missing you, Margaret."

"Not today, Ben. I have to get back to town and see if Emilio was able to replace a wheel on the stagecoach. But say hello to Keith for me." She swung up onto the saddle.

"I'll do that, gal," Ben said.

As they rode away, Cole glanced behind. It appeared that neither Lawford nor the black stallion had moved a muscle.

Later that night, as Maggie lay in bed going over the conversation and the events of the day she'd spent with Cole, with few exceptions she realized Cole had gotten what he hoped for—it had been a pleasant afternoon. "I love you, Pop," she whispered, and with a contented smile, she closed her eyes.

Five miles away Ben Lawford slammed his fist down on the solid oak desk, hand-carved and shipped in from San Francisco, toppling several items to the floor. Then he raised the same fist in the air and glared at his son standing a few feet away.

"You hear me well, boy. Tomorrow you haul your ass out of here and get that gal to agree to marry you."

Keith Lawford picked up the humidor that had been knocked to the floor, replaced several cigars, which had fallen out of it, and then put it down carefully on the desk.

"Father, I've told you Margaret's not ready to marry yet. She's in mourning. Good grief, she buried her father less than a week ago."

"I've heard enough of that bullshit. It sure ain't stopping her from holding hands and looking doe-eyed at MacKenzie. When I rode up on them, they were closer than two flies on a mouse turd."

"Margaret has no romantic interest in Cole MacKenzie. In fact, she harbors a great deal of bitterness toward him."

"If she's convinced you of that, you're dumber than I thought."

"Thank you, Father. You always manage to personalize any argument."

Ben walked around the side of the desk, and Keith backed away reflexively. "I want Timberline, and I'll do what has to be done to get it." He shook a finger at Keith. "One week, you hear me? One week is all you've got to convince her, then we do it my way, whether you like it or not."

"You stay away from Margaret, Father. I won't stand for you threatening her."

Ben snorted. "What'll you do, sue me?" He opened

the humidor and took out a cigar, bit off the end, and spat it into a nearby brass cuspidor. "Cigar, son?"

"No, Father. You know how much I abhor them. They're untidy and malodorous."

With a sorrowful frown, Ben looked at his son. "Untidy and malodorous. This is the West, boy. If you think they make a mess and they stink, then say it. Them fancy words you learned at that dude eastern college will only get you booted out of any bunkhouse in the territory." He shook his head sadly. "You're such a prick, son." He clamped the cigar in the corner of his mouth. "You've got one week, boy."

Then he strode out of the room.

Chapter 8

The next morning, as soon as Maggie awoke, she dressed quickly and then hurried into the office. She retrieved the local letters from the drop box outside the door and had just put them in a mail pouch when Juan came into the office.

"Señorita Margaret, my *papá* he has accident and can not drive the stage today."

"An accident? Is it serious, Juan?"

"*Sí*, Señorita Margaret. The doctor he say *Papá* has broken leg."

"A broken leg! Oh, good Lord! How did he break his leg?"

"The roof of our house have big hole. So *Papá* he nail a piece of wood over the big hole."

"Yes, I understand," Maggie said. "But how did he break his leg."

"*Papá* he fall off roof."

"Oh, poor Emilio. But thank God he didn't break his neck. We can be very grateful for that."

"*Sí*, Señorita Margaret. Juan tell Father Pedro he is very grateful."

"I must go and see if I can be of any help."

"The doctor he give *Papá* the medicine to make him sleep. He say *Papá* must stay in bed."

"Is he alone now?"

"No, the Holy Sisters are there."

"Well, then, I'll wait until later."

This was the worst news Maggie could hear. Not only did she feel concern for Emilio, but she also had the stageline to consider. On Mondays Dallas's two *nieces* had to be taken back to Noches, and in as much as Lawford didn't have a post office, the stage delivered the local mail to the Noches post office to be processed.

For a moment Maggie considered her plight and made a decision. "Juan, hitch a team to the stage."

"But who will drive it, Señorita Margaret?"

"I will. Pop taught me how to handle a team. And there's only four horses, so it won't be much worse than driving a wagon."

The boy hesitated. "Juan thinks that is not a good idea. Maybe Señorita Margaret should tell Señor Cole."

"Oh, good heavens, no. He's the last person to tell. Just do as I say."

"Señor Cole will not like it, Señorita Margaret."

"Juan, if I'm to prove that I can make a success of this stageline, I've got to be able to act independently without his help. Now, get that team hitched up while I go home and change my clothes."

"*Sí*, señorita."

"You're a dear." She lifted off his hat, kissed the top of his head, and then dashed out.

The youngster replaced the hat on his head. "But Juan is thinking Señor Cole will not like it," he mumbled.

To Maggie's relief, when she returned to the house, Cole was in the bathroom, preparing to take a bath. She quickly donned a pair of trousers and a shirt that she'd worn in Alaska. Time and time again the clothing had come in handy when she helped to muck out the stalls or clean up the stable. After pulling on boots, she grabbed her hat and was in and out of the house without Ellie or Cole being the wiser.

Returning to the stage office, she found the stage's two passengers were waiting. "Just climb in, ladies. I'm in a hurry," Maggie said.

"Where's Emilio?" one of the women asked.

"He's had an accident. I'll be driving."

"Well, watch the ruts, honey," the other warned. "We've got to catch up on our sleep."

"I'm sure you do."

Maggie went into the office, wrote a short note to Ellie advising her of the situation, and asked her to take Emilio some soup. When she returned to the coach, both women were stretched out on the seats, already asleep.

Maggie felt a surge of invigorating excitement as she tossed the mail pouch up on the box and then climbed up and took the reins. She leaned down and handed Juan the letter.

"Juan, clean up the stalls and feed the horses, and when you finish, take this note to Ellie, but not before.

Then go home and take care of your father. And if Señor MacKenzie shows up before you're through, don't tell him any sooner than you have to."

"*Sí*, Señorita Margaret."

"Good-bye, *amigo*. She winked at him, and then released the brake. "Yaw," she shouted to the team, whipping the reins. "On Dasher, on Dancer, on Prancer, on Vixen."

With creaking wheels, the coach jerked forward, kicking up a cloud of dust. Foul curses emanated from within.

Juan watched sadly until the stagecoach disappeared around a bend. Shaking his head, he murmured, "But, Señorita Margaret, Juan fears that Señor Cole will be one mad *hombre*."

Whistling, Cole left his bedroom and sat down at the kitchen table. He felt good. Yesterday he'd made great strides with Maggie and their relationship. They had actually sat and talked quietly without ending up in an argument. And recalling how he had felt when he viewed the site where Pop had died, Cole realized he should have had enough sense to know how it would affect Maggie.

Perhaps today they could pick up where they left off when Lawford interrupted them. One thing he knew for certain: no matter how much Maggie disliked him, he couldn't bear to see her hurting—especially when he was at fault.

She'd had a tough life. Why hadn't he recognized that sooner? Sure, Pop adored her, but the kid had never had a mother to bring gentleness into her life, had no siblings for companionship, no home growing up except shacks in Alaska that were usually cold in winter and hot in summer. Shifting from camp to camp disguised as a boy for her own protection.

Yeah, she'd had a tough life, all right. And all things considered, she'd turned out good. Damn good. And if she married Keith Lawford, she'd have a comfortable life from now on—but would it be a happy one? That was the doubt that stuck in his craw.

Comparing his childhood to Maggie's, Cole now realized that he'd never stopped to count his blessings. Growing up on the Triple M had been a good life: the best parents any child could hope for, brothers, sisters, cousins, aunts, and uncles. Everyone looking out for everyone else. Yeah, if he ever had children, he'd want them to grow up the same way.

"What's made you so bright-eyed and bushy-tailed this morning?" Ellie asked, putting a plate of ham and eggs down in front of him. She grinned wryly. "If I didn't know you were here in bed, I'd figure that last night you paid a visit to one of Dallas's nieces."

"Ellie, I know as well as everyone else in this town that those two women aren't Dallas's nieces."

"Well, Mick didn't want Maggie to know he had anything to do with bringing in prostitutes."

"He wasted his time. I'm sure Maggie saw enough soiled doves in Alaska to recognize one on sight. Ellie, I've got some good news. I think Maggie and I have finally made our peace with each other."

"Is that so?" she said.

"Yeah. We had a good talk yesterday, and I think we understand each other much better now."

"Is that so?"

"All right, Ellie, you've got canary feathers all over your mouth. Out with it. What aren't you telling me?"

"Emilio Morales broke his leg."

"I'm sorry to hear that."

"Good thing, though, that you and Maggie had such a good talk, made your peace and all that, 'cause now you ain't gonna get upset when you read it."

"Read what?" he asked.

She reached into her apron pocket and pulled out a piece of paper. "This note she wrote." She put it down in front of him, and then returned to the stove.

Puzzled, Cole picked up the paper and read it. "*She* drove the stage to Noches!" He shoved back the chair and jumped to his feet. "How long ago did she leave?"

"About a half hour or so."

"Why didn't you tell me sooner?"

"Your door was closed."

"You ever think of knocking?"

"Don't start sassing me, boy, just because you can't control her."

Cole dashed to his room and grabbed his hat, then headed out of the house.

Ellie followed him to the front door. "You listen, Cole MacKenzie. Don't you hurt that gal when you catch up with her."

"Too late. I'm going to wring her neck," he said.

When he reached the stable, there was no sign of Juan. As he quickly saddled a horse, Cole cursed and muttered angry threats of what he'd do to Maggie.

When he galloped away, Juan Morales stepped out from behind the bale of hay where he'd been crouching. He quickly crossed himself. "*¡Santa María!* It is as Juan feared. Señor Cole is one mad *hombre*."

Maggie had covered half the distance to Noches—and doubled his anger—by the time he caught up with the stagecoach.

"Get the hell out of that box before I yank you out," he ordered when Maggie brought it to a halt.

"What's the problem, Cole?" she asked, but obeyed and climbed down.

"You! You're the problem!" he shouted in a thunderous rage. "What in hell were you thinking of, lady? It takes an experienced driver to handle a four-horse team."

"Pop taught me how to handle a team," she said defiantly.

"And how many times have you driven a stage?"

"Well . . . actually none until today."

"Lady, you shouldn't be permitted outside without supervision. If you'd lost control of the horses or even swung wide on a curve, this stage would have ended up at the bottom of this mountain."

"I know what I'm doing."

Her defiance only increased his rage. "Sure you do. You're so damn headstrong, you don't stop to think of the danger."

"Hey, will you hold down the shouting? We're trying to sleep in here."

Cole was shocked to see the blond head of the speaker poked out the window. Appalled, he turned to Maggie. "You've got passengers? Isn't it bad enough you risk getting yourself killed? Must you risk the lives of passengers, too?"

"Hey, Gladys, get a look at this. The scenery's lookin' better," the blonde said.

A brunette appeared at the opposite window. "If this is a holdup, we don't have any money. You're gonna have to take it out in trade, honey."

Under any other circumstances Cole would have found the situation humorous, but he was too angry with Maggie to be amused.

"Dammit, how many others are in there?"

"Just the two of us, Good-Looking," the blonde said. "I'm Lyla Loving and she's Gladys Divine. Climb in, honey, and we promise you'll enjoy the ride." She arched a plucked brow to drive home the double entendre.

"Ladies, I'm sure I would, but I'll have to take a rain check for now. How about the two of you going back to sleep?"

"Bet he couldn't afford us anyway," Gladys said.

"The handsome ones never can," Lyla lamented as they withdrew.

"If you're through with your pandering, Cole, I'd like to continue on my way." Maggie started to climb back on the stage, but he pulled her back.

"I'm not through with you. Take a look at this front wheel. Can't you tell it's on the verge of busting apart? The wheel's left a wobbly track all the way from Lawford."

"Oh, that wheel's just a temporary one. The other one broke, so Emilio put this old one on until I can replace it."

Frustrated, he shoved his hat to the top of his forehead. "And when did you intend to do that?"

"As soon as I get to Noches."

"Don't you mean *if* you get to Noches? You're asking for trouble. That wheel could give out any time. What condition are the other ones in?"

"They're fine."

"You will forgive me if I check," he said sarcastically. He circled the wagon, hunching down to inspect each wheel.

When he was through, he stood up. "If I turn my mount loose, will it find its way home?"

"Cupid?" She snorted. "Of course. He's been up and down this trail so often, he doesn't need your guidance."

"That makes the damn horse smarter than you are," Cole grumbled. He unsaddled the horse and sent it on its way with a whack to its flank. Then he tossed the saddle onto the coach.

"All right, climb into the coach. I'm driving."

"Why can't I ride in the box with you? There's plenty of room."

"I'm afraid I'd be too tempted to toss you off," he grumbled.

Ignoring his orders, Maggie climbed up and sat down. Cole followed, took the reins, and released the brake.

"You better start praying that we make it to Noches before that wheel collapses."

As they neared the town, Cole finally relaxed. Maggie hadn't said a word the whole time. It was just as well—the less said between them, the easier to avoid an argument. And it had given him time to think.

He was still perturbed over her foolhardy action, but his hot anger had long abated. That was typical of him. He'd get mad and then he'd get over it just as fast. In the past couple of hours he'd come to recognize that most of the anger was due to fear for her safety more than the impulsiveness of the act. In retrospect, he realized that any woman on the Triple M could handle a four-horse team competently if she had to, so he shouldn't have doubted Maggie's capability.

And hadn't he given her a chance to prove she could operate the stageline independently? So why did he get so upset and interfere?

It boiled down to the plain, simple truth that he'd been worried about her safety.

"Maggie."

"What?" Her tone was so cold it could have turned water into ice.

"I'm sorry."

He turned his head to look at her and saw she was staring at him more surprised than hostile. "You had every right to do what you did, and I was wrong for losing my temper."

"Then why did you?"

She wasn't making it any easier. "I was afraid you'd get hurt, and I guess I let it out in anger."

"I've told you I can take care of myself, Cole."

"I know. I guess I didn't believe you."

"Well, I suppose I should have had the consideration to discuss it with you, instead of just taking off the way I did."

He grinned at her. "And I probably still would have gotten mad. Friends?"

"I thought we agreed we could never be friends."

"I didn't agree. That was your theory."

She started to laugh.

"What?" he asked.

"I think we're starting a new argument."

Her words ended in a cry as the right front wheel hit a rut. For several seconds the stage rocked from side to side, then the wheel shattered, and Maggie was tossed off as the front end collapsed and the team bolted.

Cole fought to halt the team as it galloped down the road dragging the careening coach with the two screaming women trapped within. He feared that any second the axle would snap, sending the coach and passengers plunging over the side.

Exerting all his strength, he finally succeeded in halting the team and jumped down. Clinging to each other, Lyla and Gladys climbed out of the coach.

"You ladies okay?" Cole asked. They nodded. "Sit down until I get back," he yelled as he ran past them to get back to Maggie. She was about a quarter of a mile down the road, and he was relieved to see her walking toward him.

"Are you okay, Maggie?" he asked when he reached her.

"My hands are scraped a little bit, but I don't think anything's broken. How are Lyla and Gladys?"

"They're just shaken up."

"And the team?"

"They're fine."

She sighed in relief. "Thank God. I suppose the stagecoach is in pieces."

"I didn't have a chance to check it yet, but I don't think the axle cracked, so other than the wheel, it's in one piece."

When they got back to the coach, Gladys and Lyla were sitting with their backs against the granite rock that lined the inner side of the road. While Cole checked the damage to the wagon, the three women sat in silence, their gazes fixed on his every move.

As he thought, the axle hadn't cracked, and once the wheel was replaced it looked as if the coach would be serviceable.

"It's hard to believe this old pile of wood and bolts even held together," he said, unhitching the team. "Ladies, I figure it's less than a mile to town. You have several options. One, you can wait here and I'll come back with a buggy. Two, you can climb on the horses and I'll lead you in. Or three, you can walk."

"Are you sure it's less than a mile?" Lyla asked.

"Can't be much more than that, considering the sign I saw about five miles back."

Gladys stood up. "I don't care if the damn town is ten miles away. I'm keeping my feet on solid ground." Flinging a pink feather boa around her neck, she started down the road.

"Wait for me," Lyla called, and hurried after her.

"What about you, Maggie? I think you got the worst of it."

"I'll walk, too. Maybe it will keep me from getting stiff. I need the mail pouch, though."

"You go ahead with the others, and I'll bring the pouch with me as soon as I string the horses so I can lead them."

Cole unharnessed the team, then strung them together like pack mules. He saddled the lead horse, hooked the mail pouch on the saddle horn, and then mounted. By the time he caught up with the three women, they had reached the outskirts of the town.

After the harrowing experience they had shared, the three women hugged and kissed, then said tearful good-byes—at least until the following Saturday night.

Chapter 9

A performance by Lillie Langtry that evening and a horse auction scheduled for the following day had brought an unusually large crowd of people to Noches. While Cole led the horses to a livery, Maggie delivered the mail pouch to the post office, and they met at the wheelwright's shop. Unfortunately the news was bad. He didn't have any spare wheels, and it would take a couple of days to make one.

"Looks like we'll have to spend the night," Cole said. "We might as well register at the hotel and then get something to eat. I'm hungry."

The news was equally bad at the hotel when the desk clerk informed them that there were no rooms available.

"Do you know where we might find rooms?" Cole asked.

"I know the boarding house is full. Only other place

I can think of is the Widow Hallaway's house. She's got two bedrooms she rents out on special occasions like this."

"We'll give her a try," Cole said. "Where is Mrs. Hallaway's house located?"

"Two blocks down the road, then turn right and go a block down. She ain't got no sign on the lawn, but hers is the white house with green shutters on the corner."

"Appreciate your help," Cole said.

"Hey, mister, tell Josie that Pete Schneider sent you." The clerk grinned. "I've got a mind to courting her, so it don't hurt to get in her good graces."

Cole winked at him. "I understand exactly, Pete."

They had no problem locating the house. Before approaching it, Cole stopped. "Just a minute, Maggie, I've got an idea." He began to shove her hair under her hat.

"What are you doing?"

"I've got a hunch we'll have better luck getting rooms if people think you're a boy. It worked in Alaska."

"Oh, yes, Alaska. How could I ever forget?" Maggie grumbled as he continued tucking away her hair until all of it was concealed under the hat.

"Just hang back behind me, keep your head down, and don't say anything. Let me do all the talking."

"You usually do," Maggie murmured.

The woman who opened the door to his knock had long exchanged the bloom of youth for the matronliness of middle age. She wore it well and with dignity. Her smile was pleasant as she regarded Cole with a look of curiosity. He introduced himself and inquired about the rooms for rent. She peered around him and smiled at Maggie. Maggie nodded and lowered her head even more.

"Mr. MacKenzie, I see neither of you is carrying any traveling bag or saddlebags. How long are you planning on staying?"

"Just one night. We hadn't anticipated spending the night in Noches, ma'am." Cole proceeded to tell her about the accident with the stagecoach and added, "Pete Schneider advised us to come here."

"You know Pete?"

"Sure do, and confidentially, I know for a fact he's very fond of you, Mrs. Hallaway . . . or should I say Josie?"

She blushed profusely. "So you operate the stageline between here and Lawford, Mr. MacKenzie."

"Well, actually, it's the other way around, ma'am. We operate between Lawford and here." He laughed and she joined him.

Disgusted, Maggie listened to the two of them. *He's done it again. He's hooked her, and now he's reeling her in. Am I the only woman who doesn't swallow his bait?*

"I must say your credentials are satisfactory, Mr. MacKenzie. I hope I haven't offended you, but a widow has to be particular who she lets into her house."

"No offense taken, ma'am. A woman in your position can't be too cautious."

"However, there's only one room available. I've converted the smaller bedroom into a sewing room."

"That won't be a problem, Mrs. Hallaway. My brother and I can double up." Maggie started to protest and Cole snapped, "Quiet, Mag . . . got."

"Your parents named your brother Maggot?" Mrs. Hallaway asked, looking rather astonished.

"No. I just call him that. You know, it's a brotherly thing."

She shook her head. "I never did understand the reason for the strange names you men give one another. But if you and your brother have no objections to sharing the room, I'll be happy to show it to you."

"We have no objections, Mrs. Hallaway. It's merely that whenever possible I've always preferred separate rooms. You see, I hate sharing a bed with him because he talks in his sleep. It's very disturbing."

"I understand exactly," she said. "My Henry sometimes did the same when he was alive."

Ask her if her Henry still does it now that he's dead.

As quickly as it had crossed her mind, Maggie regretted the unkind thought. It was unconscionable to think so flippantly about the dead. *Forgive me, Pop. I wouldn't care what you did—awake or sleeping—if only you were still with us.*

"Come in," Mrs. Hallaway said. "If the room's to your liking, I charge two dollars each. That includes breakfast but not dinner. And there are certain rules I insist upon: no loud shouting, no liquor, and no bringing in prostitutes."

Mrs. Hallaway stepped aside for them to enter, and Cole turned to Maggie. "Be sure and wipe your feet, Maggot."

Maggie clenched her hands into fists to keep from smacking him.

Mrs. Hallaway gave Cole a pleased smile. "I can see your mother did a fine job of raising sons, Mr. MacKenzie." Amusement glinted in her eyes. "Is your brother always so reticent?"

"Only around women, ma'am."

Maggie clamped her mouth closed so tightly that she bit her lip.

The room was a pleasant surprise. Roomy and taste-fully adorned, it was an appealing blending of old and new, from the quaintness of a small fireplace still used for heating the room to the convenience of a connecting bathroom.

"This is a comfortable room, Mrs. Hallaway," Cole said.

"Thank you. This was the bedroom I shared with my husband." She glanced at a portrait of a naval offi-cer that hung above the fireplace. "But since his death, I've moved to the lower bedroom."

"Did he die in this room, ma'am?" Cole asked.

"No, he was on the *Maine* when the ship blew up in Cuba."

"I'm sorry. I have a brother serving in the cavalry there, ma'am."

"Then I'll pray for his safe return, Mr. MacKenzie." Her loving gaze swept the room. "But this room shall always hold precious, shared memories for me—about life, not death."

Maggie's heart went out to the poor woman. She knew that once Cole left and her household was back to normal, she would never consider moving into her father's bedroom, even though it was larger than her own, warmer in the winter, and offered cross-ventilation in the summer. To the living, some memo-ries remain sacrosanct when a loved one is lost.

You can forget your courting aspirations, Pete Schneider. Josie Hallaway is still grieving for her dead husband.

As soon as Mrs. Hallaway left them, Maggie turned in disgust to Cole. "How could you tell that sweet woman all those bold-faced lies?"

"I'm not any happier about it than you are. I don't make a habit of lying to people, Maggie. The trouble with telling a lie is that it begins like a spark and keeps stretching out until it becomes a blaze that can't be extinguished."

"Spare me the metaphors, Cole. You're that fire you describe. You feed on people's trust."

"We needed a room. I got us one," he said sharply. "And nothing I said could hurt the woman personally."

"And now you expect me to spend the night in here with you."

"Maggie, for two years in Alaska we lived under the same roof. What difference does one more night make?"

"The difference is that we didn't have to share the same bed," she said, with a fretful glance at the big brass bed that dominated the room.

"It's only a bed. Maggie," he said, clearly exasperated, "there are many different things people do in a bed. They nap, they convalesce, make love, and often die in bed. And Lordy, Lordy, sometimes they even *sleep* in bed. That's what we intend to do—or at least, I do. So whether we do that together or separately in the same bed doesn't make one damn difference."

"You simplify everything to suit your purpose, don't you?"

"No, you simply complicate everything. Now, let's get out of here and get something to eat."

"You go without me. I'd rather stay here and take a hot bath."

"Now you're being stubborn. You must be hungry. You haven't eaten anything all day."

"I'm not being stubborn, Cole. Truly. I'm just tired and achy. But if you don't mind, I would appreciate it if you'd bring me back a sandwich."

"Okay, if that's what you want. I thought maybe you'd enjoy going to the theater and seeing Lillie Langtry."

"Thank you, but I'm just too tired. Besides, I couldn't go dressed like this anyway."

"You wouldn't look any worse than some of the other men there."

"I'm not a man, Cole." She felt like screaming, *I'm a woman! When will you recognize that?* "But don't let me spoil your evening. Go to the theater."

"It's not that important to me. I've already seen her perform in San Francisco. I just thought you might enjoy her." He put on his hat. "I'll bring you back a sandwich."

As soon as Cole left, Maggie slumped down on the bed. Would she and Cole ever be able to be together without a quarrel? Within minutes, she became engulfed in a feeling of loneliness. Strange how she'd never felt lonely until Pop's death. Now, whenever she was alone, this feeling would overwhelm her.

Maggie lay back and closed her eyes. She just needed more time to get over this sense of despair. At least she no longer broke into tears every time she thought of him.

Maggie boggled his mind. Cole didn't know what was the answer for him and her. The least little thing seemed to set off an argument between them. He would have liked to walk away from the whole damn mess and not look back.

Trouble was, that would be running away, and his folks had never raised a son to run from any obligation. He owed it to Pop. And like it or not, he owed it to Maggie, too. He couldn't leave her to be devoured by that Lawford wolf pack.

He stopped in front of a drugstore. If Maggie was aching now, no doubt she'd be worse in the morning. Not only had she taken a bad fall from the coach, but also after driving that team, she would feel the effects in her shoulders and arms of the pull of the reins.

He went in and found a tube of unguent, then he picked up a couple of toothbrushes and tin of powder to brush their teeth and a brush and comb for Maggie to groom her hair. Since he hated the idea of whiskers, he found a cheap razor and added a bar of shaving soap.

It was still early, and he faced the prospect of a long night in the bedroom, so he selected a dime novel for Maggie, in the event she couldn't sleep, and got the daily newspaper and a deck of cards for himself.

As he was paying for his purchases, another item caught his eye. Grinning, he said to the clerk, "Add a bag of that peppermint candy, too."

Once outside, he headed for a diner, but stopped in front of a lingerie store. A skimpy black silk combination was displayed in the window. Maybe he should get Maggie a pair of underpants and stockings for her to wear tomorrow. Of course, if he presumed to buy her anything—even as hygienic as a pair of cotton underpants—it would probably send her flying through the roof.

He stared at the silky black combination and for a tantalizing moment conjured up the image of Maggie standing in it, the transparent garment clinging to her curves and her auburn hair hanging past her shoulders. Shaking aside the dangerous vision, he quickly moved on.

Make up your mind, MacKenzie. Temptress or child? If you don't settle the distinction, you're going to blow your brain apart.

Cole moved on to a diner but rather than eat dinner there, he ordered each of them hot ham sandwiches, potato salad, coleslaw, and root beer. Then he hurried back to Mrs. Hallaway's.

Maggie was sound asleep. It was evident she'd fallen asleep before she could even bathe. Trying not to wake her, he pulled off her boots and then managed to work the quilt out from under her without waking her. She stirred and rolled over on her side, and he pulled the quilt over her.

For a long moment he stared at the sleeping figure. *Make up your mind. Woman or child? She's not both.*

He moved to a chair and sat down to read the newspaper as he ate his supper. The headlines carried the news that the war in Cuba had ended. He thought of his brother Jeb, who had rushed off and joined the army, ending up in the expeditionary force that had invaded the island.

According to the letter he'd received from his mother right before he left San Francisco, she hadn't heard from Jeb for nearly a year. Cole put aside the newspaper. It was time he headed home. His folks were sick with worry over Jeb, and God forbid, if the news about his brother ended up bad, he should be there for them.

His glance swung to the bed. What should he do about Maggie? *What should I do, Dad? You taught me never to run out on a friend who depended on me.*

The only solution was to make a visit home and then return to Lawford to get to the bottom of Pop's death. The problem would be in persuading Maggie to go with him. He was sick of the hassle with her about everything he suggested.

Jeb and his folks were important to him.

As soon as they returned to Lawford, he'd break the news to her. He wasn't fool enough to tell her sooner, or he'd be in for a miserable ride back.

Cole finished reading the newspaper, then played several hands of solitaire. He heard a clock somewhere in the house chime the hour of ten. Removing his boots, he lay down on top of the quilt. *That should be proper enough for your puritan little mind, Miz Margaret.*

Grinning, he rolled over onto his side with his back to her, closed his eyes, and fell asleep.

Chapter 10

Maggie awoke, sat up, and glanced around, disoriented, at the unfamiliar room until she remembered her whereabouts. How long had she slept? There was light shining through the window, so she knew that at least it was still daylight. If she hurried, she'd probably still have time to take her bath before Cole returned with a sandwich for her.

Bolting out of bed, she gasped in pain. Her body from neck to toe felt as if she'd been tortured on a rack or someone had tried to rip her arms out of their sockets.

She needed that hot bath more than ever. Gingerly she moved to the bathroom. Opening the door, she drew up with a shriek.

Startled, Cole MacKenzie turned his head and looked over his shoulder, water dripping from his naked body.

Horrified, Maggie slammed the door and then flinched with pain from the hasty move. Her embarrassment was as great as her shock. She wanted to get out of the room as quickly as possible and struggled painfully to put on her stockings and boots.

"Maggie."

She stiffened when she heard his voice but was too embarrassed to turn around and look at him.

"I'm sorry, Cole. I didn't know you'd returned. I'm so embarrassed."

"Returned? Maggie, you've been asleep all night."

"What?" Without thinking, she now looked at him and was relieved to see he was clothed. "What did you say?"

"It's morning, Maggie. You slept last night away."

This new revelation was so surprising that it helped to diminish her embarrassment. "I don't believe it."

"It's true. When I got back here last night, you were sleeping so soundly that I didn't want to wake you, so I covered you up and let you sleep. Then this morning, since I'm an early riser, I thought I could get in a bath before you woke up. I'm sorry there wasn't a lock on the bathroom door."

She felt the hot blush sweeping through her again. "Not half as sorry as I am. Let's not discuss it any further."

"Yesterday I bought a couple of items that I figured you'd need this morning. They're in the bathroom. Tell you what, I'll go and check on what progress has been made on that new wheel." He added lightly, "If you promise not to fall asleep again, that should give you time to take your bath."

Maggie nodded. "I'd appreciate that."

When he left, Maggie hobbled over to the bathroom. As she filled the tub, she brushed her teeth and combed the snarls out of her hair. Then, with a grateful sigh, she lowered her aching body into the soothing comfort of the hot bath. She sat in the hot water until it turned tepid.

By the time Cole returned, Maggie was sitting at the desk playing solitaire. "I should have mentioned I bought you a novel to read," he said.

"I saw it, thank you, but I don't read dime novels, Cole."

"You did in Alaska."

"When I was fourteen."

"Mrs. Hallaway missed us at breakfast. I told her you were too tired to come downstairs and I had an important errand to run. I figured we could eat breakfast somewhere else."

"I already ate." He looked at her, puzzled. "A cold ham sandwich and warm root beer. I passed on the potato salad and coleslaw."

"They would have tasted much better last night."

"Too bad someone didn't wake me."

"Will that issue be the argument for today? Why don't we take an oath to get through the day without an argument?"

The corners of her mouth turned up in amusement. "What about the wheel?"

"It should be finished by five o'clock."

"Not until then," she said, disappointed. "At least we'll still have time to drive back to Lawford."

"Yeah, but that team is old, Maggie. They can't do much better than five miles an hour. If it gets any later than that, I think we'd be wiser to pull out first thing in the morning. I told Mrs. Hallaway in that event we might have to spend another night."

"You mean I'll have to continue to pretend I'm a boy?"

"Just around Mrs. Hallaway, Maggot."

She gave him a disparaging look. "Be careful, MacKenzie, or that blaze you started is liable to send you up in smoke."

After leaving their room, Maggie took off her hat and shook out her hair. It felt good. In Alaska, Pop had kept her hair cut short, but in the past two years it had become too long and thick to try to keep it shoved up under a hat. They stopped at a diner and she drank a cup of tea while Cole ate a plate of ham and eggs.

"What do you suggest we do until five o'clock?" she asked.

"Check out the town, I guess."

"I've seen this town before."

"We can go to the horse auction. They're always interesting. But that doesn't start for another two hours."

"Anything sounds better than going back to the room and reading the dime novel you bought me."

"We could always go back and play three-card monte."

"No, thank you. We did that enough in Alaska. It's another one of those Alaskan memories I'm trying to forget."

Cole chuckled. "You've got to admit it helped to pass a lot of long nights.

They left the diner, and as they were walking past a

bicycle shop, he came to a quick stop. "I have another brilliant idea."

"I hadn't been aware you made any previous ones."

He pointed to a sign in the window advertising bicycles for rent. At her appalled look, he shoved up his hat. "Don't tell me you've never ridden a bicycle."

"Just once in St. Louis. I didn't like it."

"Why?"

She looked sheepish and lowered her head. "I just didn't like it."

"You were afraid, weren't you?"

Darn him, he could read her mind. "I didn't say that."

"You don't have to. I can tell. Will you explain to me how a gal who doesn't hesitate to drive a four-horse team is afraid to climb on a bicycle?"

"I am *not* afraid." She shoved past him and marched into the store. The clerk informed them that the only model available was a bicycle built for two.

"That's perfect," Cole exclaimed.

"Why is it that no matter what, I end up having to share it with you."

"It must be destiny, Maggie. Maybe on the ride back to Lawford, we can each take a rein."

"That's very funny." She almost groaned aloud when she lifted her leg to climb on the bicycle. The stiffness was still there.

As they rode along, Cole began to sing Harry Dace's popular "Daisy Belle," substituting her name for the title's.

"Maggie, Maggie, give me your answer true. I'm half crazy, over the love of you."

Getting into the spirit of the moment, Maggie sang back, cleverly improvising on the Englishman's words, "There'll be no stylish marriage, for, frankly, I'd rather perish."

He turned around and grinned. "But you sure look sweet upon *this* seat—"

"Of a bicycle built for two," they finished together harmoniously.

The silly moment was short-lived. The bicycle crashed into the wall of an outhouse, and they landed on the ground, laughing.

When they finally controlled themselves enough to get to their feet, Maggie took the front seat.

"From now on, I'll do the driving."

By the time they went on to the horse auction, rather than whine to Cole, Maggie didn't tell him how much her body ached. And although the walk to the site helped alleviate some of the stiffness in her lower body, nothing could ease the ache in her arms and shoulders.

A section of bleacher seats had been erected for spectators to watch the event. The serious buyers were on benches near the small arena. These shrewder bidders had already looked over and examined the horses in their stalls. They now waited to make their bids. Many among them were rodeo exhibitors, others racetrack owners and ranchers looking to improve their stock.

Maggie found the auction fascinating as one after another of the horses was bid for and bought.

"If I could afford it, I'd buy a new team for the stagecoach," she said. "The team is so old, the darlings should be put out to pasture, where they could finish their lives grazing restfully."

"You need a ranch for that, Maggie."

"I know." *I could have one if I agreed to marry Keith.*

"There's a beauty," Cole murmured when the bidding began on a huge black stallion. "They saved the best for last."

"How can you tell from here? You haven't examined it."

"Look at its stance, the way it holds its head. Just the way it moves. That horse will bring a good price."

Cole was right. By the time it closed, the bidding had climbed to almost a thousand dollars.

"Good heavens," Maggie exclaimed, "why would anyone pay that kind of money for a horse they've probably never even seen run?"

"For breeding, if nothing else." His sapphire gaze fixed on her face. "It's like a man deciding on a woman to marry. He sees her beauty, her bearing, her pride and heart, and he knows she'll bring those qualities to their children."

"Cole MacKenzie, you have to be the sickest person I've ever met. Are you implying that a man regards a woman as a brood mare?"

"Of course, he has to love her, too."

"I would hope so. You may know horses, MacKenzie, but you certainly need some schooling in the fundamentals of love."

"Well, I admit I've never experienced it, but when did you become an authority on the subject, Miz Margaret?"

"I don't pretend to be. But I hope the man I marry

will regard me as more than a blue ribbon winner at a horse auction." He had succeeded in raising her dander again, and it'd been his idea not to argue today.

Cole looked at her with devilment in his eyes. "And did I mention spirit, Miz Margaret? Spirit's important, too."

Sitting in the bleachers had made her stiffen up again, and she was glad when the auction ended so she could get up and stretch her legs.

"What now?" she asked when they were on their way. "It's only three o'clock. The wheel won't be ready for another two hours."

"Well, we can eat now. That should kill some of the time. It's a long ride back to Lawford."

He suddenly peered intently at a building across the street. "That's a roller rink over there. Let's try that, and then eat."

"No, thank you. I don't know how to roller-skate. Besides, I already have bruises from falling off a stagecoach and a bicycle. I'm not about to add roller skates to the count."

"Honey, you don't know what you've been missing. All you need is a sense of balance," he assured her as they crossed the street. "You've ice-skated, haven't you?"

"Yes. I'm not very good at it, though."

"Well, roller-skating is much easier."

Maggie doubted that, but she was a good enough sport to be willing to try.

A few minutes later, as he clamped the skates on her shoes, she watched young children whiz past, couples hand in hand, some even skating with the man's arm around his partner's waist. She gasped in wonderment at a couple who were actually waltzing on the skates to the music provided by a piano and an accordion.

The first time they circled the rink, Maggie was afraid to lift her feet, so she rolled along as Cole pulled her by the hand. The second time she got more daring and propelled herself slowly and cautiously, time and time again grasping Cole's hand or clinging to him in order to keep her feet from sliding out from under her. By the third time they circled the rink, she had mastered the skill, and she and Cole were soon waltzing together like the other accomplished skaters.

On occasion they were tripped up, then, laughing, they'd cling to each other to keep from going down.

And Maggie was very proud that by the time they left she had managed to end up only once on the floor.

They cut through the park on the way to the diner. The day's festivities had now moved to that location, and the air was permeated by the smell of freshly popped corn and frying chicken. A small band on a gazebo in the middle of the park was playing Sousa marches, while vendors shouted above the music, hawking balloons and American flags.

"Smells good enough to eat," Cole said.

She grinned with pleasure. "Why don't we? We can eat right here in the park. I'm game if you are."

"You're my kind of gal, Maggie O'Shea."

Grabbing her hand, he led her over to a shady spot under a tree, and while Cole went to get them food, Maggie sat down, leaned back against the tree trunk, and watched several young boys rolling hoops along the walk, cutting in and out among the strollers.

Cole returned shortly with plates of fried chicken and potato salad, foamy mugs of root beer, and thick slices of apple pie still hot from the oven. The food was delicious, and Maggie consumed it down to the last drop and bite.

When they were through, Cole stretched out on his back and tucked his hands under his head.

"You're not going to sleep, are you? It'll soon be time for us to leave."

"No. Just relaxing."

"I enjoyed myself today, Cole."

"So did I. You're a good sport, Maggie."

"Were you in San Francisco the whole time these past two years?"

"Mainly. I looked around at a couple of the neighboring cities but always ended up back there."

"Do you have a home there?"

"No. When I'm ready to settle down, it'll be on the Triple M."

"A girlfriend, then?"

He chuckled. "No one special, if that's what you mean."

She blushed profusely. "I meant that must have been your reason for always returning to San Francisco. I imagine you intend to go back when you leave Lawford."

"No, I had enough of San Francisco. A lucky streak is what kept me there as long as I stayed."

"A lucky streak?"

"Poker. I've had a winning streak for the past two years. I've lived off the winnings and still have more than triple what I left Alaska with. What about you, Maggie? What have you been up to these past two years? I know Pop sent you to a finishing school in St. Louis."

"And it almost did finish me, all right. I hated every moment of it. I had nothing in common with any of the girls. When we weren't in classes, all they talked about was boys. I spent the better part of my free time in my room, reading."

"No school romances?"

"Occasionally some of the boys from a nearby military academy would come over for a cotillion."

Cole broke into laughter when she added, "They were skinny, pimple-faced, and arrogant. Most of them acted as if they were doing the girls a big favor by attending. They sure didn't have to come on my account."

"But I bet they did."

"What do you mean?"

"Come on your account. You're quite an eyefull, Maggie."

"I only stayed to please Pop. But I missed him. Now all I can think of is that we wasted two years when we could have been together."

"Didn't you come home the whole time?"

"Yes, but the visits were too few and too short."

"Apparently long enough to catch Lawford's eye."

"Keith? Cole, let's be realistic. You've seen the town. It's dying. Other than Dallas Donovan, I doubt that there's any other woman under the age of sixty."

Dark clouds had begun to drift across the sky. Cole eyed them warily. "I don't like the looks of that sky. There's a storm moving in. We should try and get out of here as soon as we can."

Hurrying to the wheelwright's, they were relieved to find out that the wheel was ready. They got the team, loaded the wheel, and rode back to the abandoned stage.

As Cole began to attach the wheel to the coach, the sky opened up, and the rain started to fall. By the time he had finished, their clothing was sodden and the rain had turned into a torrent, with a driving wind that made visibility difficult.

"We've got to go back to Noches, Maggie. Another hour of this, and the road will be a quagmire. Climb into the coach and I'll drive us back."

Maggie was too tired and achy to argue. Shivering, she did as he ordered.

After the team was stabled for the night, the liveryman drove them to Mrs. Hallaway's.

"Oh, you poor darlings!" she exclaimed when she saw them. "As soon as that rain began, I figured you'd be back. Get upstairs and get out of those wet clothes before you catch pneumonia. I'll bring you some extra blankets to wrap around you while your clothes dry. If I were you, I'd take a hot bath. The tank's full, so there's plenty of hot water, and there's wood in the room so you can get a fire going to dry them out."

"You first, Maggie," Cole said as soon as they were upstairs. She was too cold and miserable to worry about convention. Maggie went into the bathroom, turned on the bath water, and then shed her clothing. The hot bath was soothing, but the drenching rain had aggravated her aching shoulders and arms. Still she managed to get through shampooing her hair using the bar soap.

Cole tapped on the bathroom door. "Maggie, whenever you're ready for them, Mrs. Hallaway brought up some blankets and extra towels."

"I need a towel and blanket, and you be sure and cover your eyes, Cole."

The door opened, and he shoved in a towel and blanket. Maggie climbed out of the tub, wrapped the towel she'd used that morning around her wet hair, and then toweled herself dry. She wrung out her wet clothing in the bathtub and then drained the tub and wiped up the wet floor with the towel.

Wrapping the blanket around herself, she went into the other room. Cole had stripped off everything except his jeans and had a fire going on the hearth. It drew her like a beacon.

"The bathroom's all yours," she said.

He disappeared into the bathroom, and Maggie strung out her wet clothing on the fireplace. Then she sat down on the rug in front of the fire, stretched out her legs, and began to comb out her wet hair. The quality of her life had improved.

Barechested and barefoot, with a blanket wrapped around his waist and hips, Cole came out of the bathroom.

"That didn't take long. Didn't you take a bath?" Maggie asked as he spread out his wet clothing.

"No. I've been out in worse rains than this during roundups at home. It's a relief, though, to get out of those wet clothes." He sat down beside her.

For a long moment they sat in companionable silence, the glow of the fire casting a pleasant coziness over the darkened room.

Tightening the blanket around her, Maggie shifted her position. Hugging her bent legs, she rested her chin on her knees. "Don't you feel the love in this room, Cole?"

"I beg your pardon?" he asked.

"Love, Cole. Henry and Josie's. They must have been very happy in here."

"Why do you say that?"

"I can feel it. Can't you?"

"I'm afraid I don't have your imagination, Maggie."

He smiled tenderly at her. She'd brushed out her hair, and its auburn richness glimmered with copper from the fire's glow. In the past two days, he'd grown so accustomed to seeing her in those oversized boy's clothes that he'd forgotten how feminine and lovely she actually was.

Having warmed up, she'd pushed the blanket off her shoulders and arms, folded it, and tightened it over her breasts. He couldn't stop his mind from wandering to the tantalizing thought of how easily a simple tug would release it. He forced his roving thoughts back to what she was saying.

"Cole, remember that word game we used to play in Alaska? Pop would give us a word, and we'd say the first thing that came to mind?"

"Yeah, I remember," he replied.

"Of course, you always managed to give a sexual intimation to everything you came out with, but what would be the first thing you'd think if I said 'this room'?"

"Ah . . . warm. In fact looking at you in that blanket, it's getting warmer by the minute."

"Be serious, Cole."

"All right, I guess I'd say 'pleasing.' Yeah, the room's pleasing. So what would you say?"

"Felicitous."

"That's the same as pleasing. At least we're on the same track."

Maggie shook her head. "No, it's not the same. Felicitous has a much deeper meaning. It implies something that's not only pleasant, but appropriate."

"Appropriate? I don't get it."

"Josie and Henry." She glanced at the portrait above the fireplace. "There's an aura of Henry Hallaway in this room, his personality, the love they shared here. That's why the room's so pleasing and appropriate: a shrine with aesthetic icons, not visible ones, so to speak. Her gaze swept the room in awe. "This room has only known happiness." She nodded in conviction. "Yes, a felicitous room."

"Maggie, you're a sentimentalist. You've never met Henry Hallaway, so how do you know anything about him or his personality? Next you'll be conjuring up Henry's ghost. Furthermore, if they were so much in love, why does she leave his picture in here."

"Because this is where it belongs, the room in which they were the happiest. You won't admit I'm right because you're a cynic and don't believe in love."

"That's not true. I definitely do believe in love. My folks have set the example for me. And if they weren't enough, I've a couple of uncles and aunts and a raft of married cousins who've convinced me."

"And yet you've never been in love."

"No. I suppose when I meet the right woman, I'll want to marry and go back and settle down on the Triple M, like the rest of my family. I just haven't met her yet. Lately, though, I've been thinking a lot about the ranch. How much I miss them all. And the idea of getting married has become more appealing to me, but I'll have to wait until I meet her."

"I see."

He saw her eyes were glistening with tears. "Hey, Maggie, cheer up. I'll meet her some day."

"Oh, don't pay any attention to me."

"Why are you crying, Maggie?"

"It's, ah . . . my shoulders and arms. They've been aching all day."

"Dammit, Maggie, why didn't you say something sooner? I figured you'd be sore after yesterday, so I bought a tube of liniment. Now, where the devil did I put it?"

Cole got up to search and finally found it under the newspapers. He came back and knelt down beside her. "Let me help you."

Cole squeezed some of the salve onto his hands and rubbed it into her arm, then he did the same to the other one. She never said a word but continued to stare at him, her eyes round and liquid.

"Do they feel any better?"

"Yes, thank you," she said.

"Turn over on your stomach, Maggie."

She did as told and stretched out. Cole squeezed out more of the salve and began to massage it into her shoulders. Her skin felt like satin beneath his fingers. He rubbed her neck and the gentle slope of her shoulders. She felt good. Soft and satiny. And she felt like a woman—and that was better. Trouble was, his manhood was responding to it—and that was bad.

"Turn over on your back, Maggie."

He put some more of the salve on his hands. He could barely wait to put his hands on her. The cords of her neck felt tight, and he traced the slender column of her neck and the hollows of her shoulders.

He was unaware just when the massage turned to caresses.

His touch was as tender as it was exciting. Each stroke of his hands sent shivers of desire flowing through her. For the first time in her maiden life, she felt the sublime arousal from a man's touch—from Cole's touch. It was glorious. It was everything she had hoped for.

She hadn't been able to hold back her tears when he'd said he hadn't yet met the woman he wanted to marry. So what if he didn't love her. She'd wanted him for so long that she reveled in this moment.

His slickened fingers skimmed across the swell of her bosom, moving nearer and nearer to the tucked blanket. If she'd had any pride, she'd have told him to stop—but feared if she did, he would. Her breasts were aching for the feel of his hands, her body throbbing with this new sensation as she waited hopefully, expectantly, and shamelessly.

His gaze locked with hers, and she thrilled at the sight of the desire in his eyes. He wanted her. She'd thought of this moment for years, but her expectation had never touched on the actual exhilaration it generated.

"Maggie," he whispered in a voice so heavy with desire that it thrilled her to greater expectation. When he lowered his head, she closed her eyes and parted her lips.

His mouth was firm and warm, closing over hers as if their lips had been matched to fit. At first the kiss was slow, persuasive until she could hold nothing back and gave herself up to the breathless sensation of her first arousal.

The kiss lengthened, deepened. Pressure increased, passion soared. He broke away and covered her face and eyes with quick, rapid kisses before he reclaimed her lips. This time his tongue joined the assault on her senses with darting probes that sent currents streaking to the core of her newly discovered sensuality.

She groaned when she felt the wondrous, sensual slide of his hand as he tugged at the blanket and released it, and then she gasped with pleasure when he cupped the fullness of her breast in his warm palm. She barely had a chance to savor the tantalizing sensation before it was replaced by the exquisite feel of his mouth closing around the nipple of her breast.

It felt divine—so incredibly divine that she was near to crying with joy.

Suddenly he stopped. She wanted to shout her protest, pull him back, and press his mouth to her breast and continue the erotic play.

Opening her eyes, she saw that his head was raised alertly. Then she heard what her passion-filled mind had deafened her ears to before—the light tapping on the door.

"Mr. MacKenzie," Mrs. Hallaway called. "I've brought you some more firewood."

Cole stood up and for the briefest moment gazed down at her, regret now replacing the passion that had so recently fired his eyes.

Startled back to reality, Maggie pulled the blanket around her and jumped to her feet. She sped to the bathroom as Cole opened the door.

"Thank you, ma'am. That's most thoughtful of you," Maggie heard him say.

She wet a washcloth with cold water and put it to

her brow and then to the back of her neck. That's when she became aware she was trembling from what had just happened between her and Cole. And with that awareness came the cold shock of reality.

Surely it was Providence that had caused Mrs. Hallaway's interruption to come at such a timely moment, or they might have . . . She rinsed her flushed face again.

When Maggie finally built up enough courage to open the door, Cole was adding more logs to the fire.

"I thought it wiser if I made myself a bed on the floor tonight. You'd better get to bed now. We'll pull out early in the morning."

"Good night," she murmured, and climbed quickly into the bed.

Maggie lay awake listening to the pop of the fire and the splatter of rain on the window.

She sensed that Cole was doing the same.

Chapter 11

Toward midnight the rain slowed to a steady drizzle. Cole spent the night drifting in and out of sleep, keeping a fire going, and shifting and turning the clothes so they'd be dry by morning.

And he had time to think. Or commiserate would be more realistic. If he could kick himself, he would. The relationship between him and Maggie had been shaky enough, but this would surely put it over the top. How could he possibly justify to her what had happened between them? She was too naïve to know that it was due to proximity—the nature of the human animal. Given the same situation and conditions, the same thing would have happened between most men and women. Even with that prick Lawford.

But the fact was that it had happened between them. How could he hope to ever gain her trust again or at least clear the air between them? His misery led to a long and restless night.

In the morning, as anxious as he was to get back to Lawford, he didn't have the heart to wake Maggie. He knew she, too, had been in and out of sleep during the night, and a couple of hours delay wouldn't make that much difference one way or another. So he went downstairs and had breakfast with Mrs. Hallaway.

When he returned to the room with a breakfast tray for Maggie, she was up and dressed.

"Good morning, Maggie."

"Good morning. Where were you?"

"I had breakfast with Mrs. Hallaway. She sent you up this tray, so sit down and eat while the food is still hot, and then we'll get out of here."

She sat down without offering an argument, and while she ate, he gathered together their meager belongings in preparation for leaving.

"I thought you'd like to know I told Mrs. Hallaway the truth."

Maggie glanced up, surprised. "Really? Was she angry?"

He chuckled and shook his head. "Not at all. She said we hadn't fooled her for a moment. But she was pleased that I admitted it to her. She asked me to give you her condolences over the loss of your loved one and said she understands what you're going through."

"I'm sure she does." Maggie smiled. "And I'm glad she knows the truth."

"Uh, Maggie, about last night. I'm sorry—"

"There's nothing to apologize for, Cole. After all, all we did was kiss."

"That's right, all we did was kiss," Cole said, relieved. "I just thought that maybe you were offended."

"Of course not. To tell you the truth, I've been curious for a long time. When I was in finishing school, many of the other girls would talk about petting and letting their boyfriends fondle them. Now I know what it's like, and the best thing, Cole, is since we don't love each other, we don't have to feel there's any obligation to each other," she added lightly.

"Like what?"

"Oh, getting married or some such foolishness like that."

Cole was flabbergasted. "I have to say, Maggie, you surprise me. I really thought you'd be offended."

"Oh, heavens, no. Confidentially, Cole, I enjoyed it. In fact, so much that I now look forward to petting with Keith."

He didn't like this turn of events at all. "Maggie, as your guardian, I don't advise that."

"Why not?"

"Well, ah . . ." He cleared his throat. "There's always the possibility that it could go beyond mere petting and—"

"Oh, nonsense, Cole," she blurted quickly. "Keith is too much a gentleman to compromise me. Besides, even if it did happen, we could always get married." She smiled sweetly. "Shall we leave? I'm anxious to get back."

Maggie paused at the doorway and her gaze swept the room. She sighed deeply. "Yes, felicitous, just as I said."

Then she breezed out the door.

After a good-bye to Mrs. Hallaway and their promise to come back, they soon were on their way to Lawford.

While Maggie sat in the coach, reading the dime novel and chewing on pieces of peppermint candy, Cole sat on the box, trying to avoid muddy potholes and puddles while pondering the unpredictability of females. He'd never understand them if he lived to be a hundred. But there was one thing he did understand— the predictability of males. And as long as he was Maggie's guardian, there was no way that prick Keith Lawford would lay a hand on her.

Maggie was too pleased with herself to even notice the bumps and jolts of the ride. She could tell her plan was working. Cole's confusion was evident.

Twelve hours ago she'd cowered under a sense of humiliation and shame. She had felt a divine intervention had prevented her from becoming a sinner. And for the next several hours she had struggled with that guilt until she had come to a reckoning.

Maybe it was God or maybe the ghost of Henry Hallaway, but whoever it was, someone or something in that room had made her finally see the light.

For the past four years she had mooned over Cole MacKenzie. Indeed, had spent idle hours in reverie over how much she loved him. Had fretted over her lack of femininity to attract him and censured herself time and time again for her childishness and lack of maturity to please him.

Her misgivings had destroyed her self-esteem where he was concerned, and in her lovesick obsession, she had given him the upper hand by languishing in self-absorbed "why can'ts" until she was choking on them.

And then last night in that mystical room that embraced lovers, the truth had come to her like an epiphany.

Yes, his kiss, his touch, the feeling of arousal had been greater than her wildest fantasy. And yes, Providence had intervened, because had they continued, Cole would always have held the upper hand. Had he reached for her in love, in need—other than carnal lust—only then would they have met as equals.

Oh, she knew now beyond a doubt that she could never want any other man's kiss or touch. That was a foregone conclusion. But now, thanks to Providence, she had recognized how to gain them.

He claimed not yet to have met any woman he'd marry. Oh, yes, he had. Cole MacKenzie was not going to wed any woman but herself.

No longer would she play the lovesick lass to his indifferent lad, *No, indeed, laddie.*

From now on she'd show him the real meaning of indifference. Maybe last night he hadn't come to her in love, but the next time, he'd *crawl* to her in love.

And there would be a next time.

Smiling, Maggie put aside the novel she'd been pretending to read and popped a piece of peppermint into her mouth.

She wasn't even aware the stagecoach had come to a halt until Cole slogged past, spewing a mouthful of curses. Maggie poked her head out the window.

"What's wrong?"

"Miss Margaret, do you suppose you could put

aside your novel long enough to take the reins while I try to get us out of this mess?"

"What mess?" she asked, stepping out of the coach.

"What in hell do you think? We're stuck in the mud."

"Did somebody not get enough sleep last night?" Her sugary patronage was enough to make even her nauseated.

"Just do it, Maggie."

Maggie sloughed through the mud and climbed up on the box. Cole took hunks of the splintered wood he'd salvaged from the broken wheel and shoved them under the rear wheels of the stagecoach.

"Okay, give it a try," he yelled.

"On Dasher, Dancer, Prancer, Vixen. Giddyup."

Cole put all his weight behind the effort, and the wheels rose, than dropped back into the sludge.

"Dammit! Don't those horses have any pull? Try it again," he yelled.

"Come on, darlings, pull," Maggie called out.

At the third try the coach rolled forward.

Cole returned, and Maggie shifted over on the seat.

"This is a stagecoach, not a sleigh, Santa Claus. Four horses aren't enough horsepower to pull a stage," Cole grumbled.

"Well, after Comet and Blitzen died, Pop said there was no sense in replacing them and cut back to a four-horse team, since we never carried a full coach or any heavy freight."

"All I know is that I could make better time pushing this stage than these horses are doing pulling it."

The trip back took seven hours, and by the time they reached Lawford, Cole had almost reached boiling point.

Maggie wisely chose to avoid him and stayed in her

room while he took a bath to clean off the mud. Then he announced he was going to bed.

"You got anything to tell me, gal?" Ellie asked, after Cole had gone into his room and closed the door.

"Nothing, Ellie. Nothing at all. How's Emilio doing?"

"About as good as you can expect with a broken leg."

"I hope you told him why I haven't been over to visit him."

"Yes, as soon as I got Cole's wire about the accident. Emilio said he warned you that wheel was only temporary."

"Ellie, at the time that warning was the farthest thought from my mind."

"It was a durn fool thing to do. You could have gotten yourself killed. Don't think I'd of stood losing both you and Mick."

"Maggie hugged her. "Ellie dear, you're not going to lose me ever, I promise you."

Ellie swallowed a sob and blew her nose. "Keith Lawford's been sniffing around here the past two nights, looking for you. Wouldn't surprise me if he showed up again tonight."

"Well, I hope not. I think Cole had the right idea in going to bed."

Ellie gave her a shrewd glance. "Something beside a broken wheel keep the two of you from sleeping the last couple nights?"

"I can only speak for myself, Ellie. I had no problem."

Maggie hurried from the kitchen.

* * *

Cole woke up to the sound of voices coming from the other room. He glanced at a clock on the wall and saw that he'd only been sleeping for four hours. He stretched out again and closed his eyes. When he heard a man's laughter rise above the murmur of voices, he was intrigued enough to get out of bed and open the door.

Startled, the three people seated at the kitchen table looked up.

"Oh, Cole, I'm sorry. Did we wake you?" Maggie asked.

"Not at all. It's time for me to get up and go to bed."

Lawford looked confused. "Why wouldn't you just remain in bed, then?" he asked.

"Keith, that is an example of Cole's attempt at humor," Maggie said.

What a prick! What in hell was Lawford doing here anyway?

"Ellie, is there anything to eat? I think my empty stomach is what woke me," Cole said.

Ellie went to the icebox. "There's some rabbit stew left over from dinner. I'll warm it up. In the future, Cole MacKenzie, if you expect to be fed around here, you'll sit down with the rest of us."

"Yes, ma'am."

Keith stood up. "Shall we leave now, Margaret?"

"Where are you going?" Cole asked.

"Keith and I intend to take a walk."

"No, you're not. You're in for the night."

A nervous laugh slipped past her lips. "You're joking, of course."

"Not in the least," he said, with a fixed stare. "I told you before that I don't want you wandering around in the dark."

"Oh, Cole, that's so humorous." She flashed a smile at Lawford. "Isn't it, Keith."

"Very," he replied. "What could happen to her when I'm with her?"

Cole looked him squarely in the eye. "Practically anything, Lawford. I suggest you say good night now and get out of here."

"Cole!" Maggie declared, aghast. "Apologize to Keith. You're being exceedingly rude even for you. Whether you like or not, Keith and I are going for a walk."

Cole had had all of this conversation he intended to. "Maggie, don't press this. I'm tired. I've had very little sleep in the past week, so I don't intend waiting up while you and Lawford are off doing God knows what."

"I beg your pardon, sir," Keith declared indignantly.

"Who's asking you to wait up, Cole? Aren't you carrying your responsibilities as my guardian a little too far?"

"That's for me to decide. You heard me. Forget that stew, Ellie. I'm not hungry after all. Good night." He strode back into his room and slammed the door.

Ellie returned the dish of stew to the icebox. "I swear I don't understand what's happening around this house anymore. One minute it's do this, the next, it's don't do it." Grumbling, she went upstairs.

"Keith, I'm so sorry that you had to witness such a display of bad temper. Shall we leave for our walk now?"

"Dare you, Margaret? Mr. MacKenzie's orders to you were quite explicit."

"I don't take orders from Mr. MacKenzie, Keith. And I don't intend to take them in the future either. If you've changed your mind about our walk, I'll go alone." She spun on her heel to depart.

Keith chased after her. "Margaret, do you think it's wise of you to incur Mr. MacKenzie's wrath?"

"Oh, pishposh, Keith. I'm always incurring Mr. MacKenzie's wrath. I'm not afraid of him. I wish you weren't," she declared as they left the house.

"Margaret, my concern is for you, not myself."

"What can Cole do to me?"

"Legally he can make things quite difficult for you."

"In what way, Keith?"

"Well, for instance, he could send you off to college against your wishes or even go as far as to forbid you to have suitors."

"There isn't money to send me to college, and furthermore," she said with a secretive smile, "I've figured out exactly how to handle Cole MacKenzie."

They stopped and visited Emilio Morales. Maggie was happy to see that Juan and his father were doing well, but Emilio told her the doctor said it would probably be at least six weeks before she could hope for his return to work. That was a serious problem, and somehow she would have to come up with a solution.

"What a lovely evening, isn't it, Keith?" Maggie said when they resumed their walk.

"Margaret, as indelicate a subject as it is, I'm glad you brought up the issue of your finances earlier. Are you aware that my father made Mr. MacKenzie a very generous offer for the Timberline property."

"Cole and I have discussed the property, Keith, and I did request him to sell it. I want nothing to do with Timberline."

"Then why hasn't MacKenzie acted on your request?"

"He said he feels Pop must have bought it for a good reason so he doesn't want to be too hasty in selling it." She tittered lightly. "But my goodness, Keith, you're as impatient as Cole. I only discussed it with him a few days ago, and we've been in Noches for the past two days. I'll be sure and remind him of my wishes the next time I see him."

"And what do you intend to do about the stageline? I was very concerned when I heard of the accident, Margaret."

"It was frightening enough, but fortunately the only casualty was the wagon wheel."

"I hope you don't intend to drive that stage again, Margaret. It's dangerous and certainly not proper for a young lady to attempt."

"Et tu, Brute. At least you and Cole are in accord on that issue, Keith."

Unintentionally their random walk had led to the top of Boot Hill.

"Keith, will you excuse me for a few moments?"

"Of course, my dear." He stepped back into the shadows.

With the moon offering the only light, Maggie went over and knelt at her father's graveside.

"Pop, I know you loved Cole, and I do, too," she said softly. "And I know you would never sanction my deceiving him. But I must try, Pop. It's my only hope to win him. He says he doesn't love me, but I'm hoping I can make him come to love me. I've tried for these past two years to forget him, but I just can't. I guess it's your fault, Pop. It's in my blood. I know you were never able to forget my mother. So I'll stoop to deceiving him, because I don't know what else to try. Forgive me. I love you."

When she stood up, Keith came over to her. "My dearest, I know the pain and difficulty you're going through. If only you'd become my wife, I could ease some of that hardship for you."

"Just your support has done that, Keith. I'm so grateful to you. But if I married you now, it would be out of gratitude, not love. So let's wait until the time when we're both thinking with clear heads—and hearts—to make a decision."

She grasped his hand. "I know it's selfish of me, but for now it's comforting to know I can always depend on you."

"You can, indeed, my love," he murmured, and lowered his head and kissed her.

Cole sat in the darkened parlor and tried to get a hold on his anger. Where the hell were they? There was nothing opened in town except Dallas's and the hotel. Lawford wouldn't take Maggie to a saloon, and he damn well better not have taken her to a hotel. But she was wild enough to go—for no other reason than to defy him.

How much of what she said this morning in Noches could he believe? Was it just some more of her talk-back, or had he opened a Pandora's box last night? The

Lord only knows how it would have ended if Mrs. Hallaway hadn't knocked on the door. And this very minute the two of them could be in a hotel room—or Lawford's office.

He jumped to his feet. Yeah, that was it! Lawford took her to his office. That's something the sneaky prick would do. That way they wouldn't be seen. No one would be the wiser.

Cole sat down again. No, Maggie wasn't the type of woman to sneak around in that kind of liaison. Sure she was headstrong and reckless, but she was too spirited and honest to consider such an arrangement. With Maggie everything would have to be open and above board.

The only trouble was she was curious, too. And that could lead to trouble, especially if she was curious enough to find out what lies beyond a kiss.

He got up and began to pace the floor. The damn fool girl would be the death of him yet.

Cole stopped and listened when he heard their footsteps on the porch. He heard them exchange low murmurs—and then silence. He damn well knew what that meant, bolted to the door, and opened it. The couple stepped apart hastily.

"Inside, Maggie." His voice was as cold as a north wind sweeping across the Panhandle in winter. "You're out of here, Lawford. Get moving."

Keith Lawford hesitated as if to speak, then he turned and walked away.

Maggie glared at Cole as she stepped past him. "Must you always act like a complete boor, Cole?" She started up the stairs.

"Not so fast. I want to talk to you," he said, lighting the lamp.

Anger gleamed in her eyes when she turned to face him. "I'm not interested in anything you have to say. I'm sick of your orders, Cole, and of your prying into my personal life. I don't care what Pop's will says. I'll do what I wish. And I don't need you to tell me otherwise."

"Well, somebody should. Where in hell were you tonight?"

"None of your business."

"Lawford take you to the hotel, or did you do it in his office?"

Her face twisted in a smirk. "Do what, Cole?"

"You know damn well what?"

"Do you mean what *you* were going to do to me last night?"

"I'm not proud of it. Trouble was, last night I hadn't expected you'd act like a kid with her first taste of candy—and me as the peppermint stick."

"I suppose I did. And I liked it. What's your excuse, MacKenzie?"

"Maggie, I'm just trying to warn you. That sweet tooth of yours could get you into trouble."

"Is this where you explain the birds and the bees to me, Cole? No, thank you. We had that talk this morning. I told you then, and I'll tell you again. I liked it." She lifted her chin in defiance. "And I'll do it every chance I can. I never knew what I'd been missing."

When she started to leave, he grasped her shoulder and spun her around to face him. "Even with a man who might have killed your father?"

He might just as well have slapped her in the face. She paled and could barely get the words out. "What . . . what are you talking about?"

Damn my big mouth. "I have reason to suspect Pop's death was no accident, Maggie."

"No." Maggie shook her head in denial. "No. Don't say that, don't ever say that. I won't listen to any more. You said that horrible thing just to hurt me. To get even with me for defying you tonight." Stifling a sob, she tried to get away, but he held her firmly and pulled her into his arms.

"Maggie, I'm not trying to hurt you. I've suspected foul play from the moment I heard how Pop died."

He released her and she turned away from him. "I don't believe you. Why would you suspect such a thing?" she cried out.

"Will you sit down and listen to me?" he asked in a calmer voice. She walked over and sat down stiffly on the couch.

"Maggie, do you know of a reason why anyone would want to kill Pop?"

"Of course not. Everyone loved him. That's why anything you have to say is ludicrous. Insane. Pop didn't have an enemy, and he certainly didn't have anything worth killing him over." But somehow he must have gotten through to her, because her frantic gaze denied the faith of her words.

"Have there been any recent deaths from accidents in this area?"

"I don't know. None that I've heard of."

"What about thefts or a bank robbery. Or maybe someone tried to hold up the stage."

"No. Why are you asking these questions?"

It was too late to turn back now. "I wanted to make sure there wasn't the possibility that Pop might have witnessed a murder or theft of some kind. How about the mail? Did he ever mention it'd been tampered with?"

"For heaven's sake, no. The post box isn't even locked. Anyone could go through it if they wanted to."

"Then as far as I'm concerned, that rules out any other possibilities I can think of and narrows my suspicions down to four people: Dallas, Vic, Ben Lawford, and his son Keith. And with the little I know right now, I'd put my money on Ben Lawford."

"You're wrong, Cole. I know those people. None of them would commit a murder. And besides, they'd have nothing to gain from it."

"Ben Lawford would gain Timberline. And he sure as hell wants it. He boasted as much to me."

"How would he gain it by killing Pop?"

"When his son marries you."

She sucked in her breath. "If you're suggesting that's why Keith asked me to marry him, you're so wrong. He showed interest in me long before Pop bought Timberline. You're making these rash accusations about people you don't even know. Neither Ben nor Keith would commit murder. You simply dislike the Lawfords for reasons of your own, not for anything that happened to Pop. And what makes Dallas a suspect? She had nothing to gain from Pop's death."

"Full ownership of the saloon. According to Dallas, she had an agreement to buy him out. She just didn't have the money. Maybe she got tired of waiting and thought you'd be easier to negotiate with."

"And why Vic?"

"Vic's Dallas's stooge. And I know he's been follow-ing me. I don't doubt he'd do whatever he thought would benefit Dallas. It's for damn sure they both know more than they're saying. Maggie, do you know if Dallas and Pop were romantically involved?" She looked at him as if he were crazy. "I found a handker-chief in Pop's office that smelled of jasmine. Dallas wears that perfume."

"So do I."

"I'm aware of that."

"Does that make me a suspect, too?"

"Maggie, I thought maybe Pop might have given you each a bottle. And if Pop and Dallas were meeting in his office, Vic is so fixated on her that it's a good mo-tive for Vic to want to get rid of Pop."

"I'm sorry to disappoint you, but Keith gave it to me last Christmas. Can't you see there isn't any substantial evidence to indicate Pop's death wasn't an accident? You've just got a lot of theories and suspicions about people who have always been his friends."

"Ben Lawford a friend?" Cole snorted. "With a friend like that, who needs an enemy?"

"Ben has a lot of bluster, but he's not a murderer, Cole. Neither is his son."

"You could be right. But another thing that seems odd to me is why Pop would go to Albuquerque to have a will drawn when his own lawyer is right here in town."

"Maybe he thought Keith might reveal the contents to me—especially your involvement."

"Or maybe Pop just didn't trust your boyfriend for some other reason."

"This is all ludicrous." She put her hands over her

ears. "I don't want to hear another word. You have no evidence whatsoever, and it's cruel of you, Cole, to even make such a horrendous suggestion to me."

"Maggie, I have another reason why I suspect Pop met with foul play. He never went anywhere without his pipe and tobacco. So why did he leave them behind in his office on the day he was killed? I don't think—"

"That's your clue?" Her laughter bordered on hysteria. It worried the hell out of him. Had he pushed the issue too soon for her to handle it?

"A couple of months ago Pop misplaced his pipe and pouch, so he bought a new set. Ellie found the old one under Pop's bed, so he began to use both of them. He probably had the other one with him when he died. You see, Cole," she cried, "you're wrong, you're so wrong."

"I suppose I'm wrong about the telegram, too."

"What telegram?"

"Just a minute." He hurried to his room and returned seconds later with the wire. "I received this the day before he apparently was killed."

Maggie read it swiftly and looked up at him in bewilderment—the bewilderment of the vanquished. "I don't understand. He sounds so desperate." Tears welled up in her eyes. "If he was in danger, why didn't he say something, ask for help?"

"Maybe he thought if he did, it would put you in danger, too, Maggie," Cole said gently.

"It's hard enough to accept he's gone, but I could never bear to think he'd still be alive if someone hadn't . . . You have no right to put such a thought in my head. No right at all. Pop's death was an accident." She began to weep.

He sat down and put his arms around her. Sobbing, she leaned her head on his chest. He could feel her trembling.

"Cry it out, baby," he murmured, and hugged her tighter.

When her tears abated, Maggie leaned her head against his chest. "Cole, remember the time in Alaska when Pop found that lost child and carried her for five miles in a blizzard? The child's mother said she'd bless his name every remaining day of her life."

"I remember, honey," Cole said.

"And the time he jumped into freezing water to save Sourdough Charley? Charley said he owed his life to Pop."

"Yeah, he sure did, Maggie."

"So you see, Cole, everyone loved Pop. No one would kill Pop," she said in the singsong voice of a little girl, which ripped his gut apart.

She began to cry again, this time in quiet sobs. He held her, rocking her back and forth, until she finally cried herself to sleep. Then he got to his feet and carried her upstairs.

Cole put her gently on the bed, and then removed her shoes and covered her with a quilt. He smiled. Tucking the poor kid in bed was becoming almost a nightly ritual. For a long time, he stood at her bedside. Occasionally a sob slipped past her lips in her slumber. He wanted to comfort her. Lie beside her and hold her through the night. Bending down, he pressed a kiss to her forehead, then he left the room.

It had become another night of hell for both of them.

Chapter 12

Cole knew it would be useless to go to bed, so he headed over to Dallas's. He needed answers, and she probably had them.

The barroom was empty except for Keith Lawford and Vic Chance.

"Where's Dallas tonight, Vic?"

"Dead night. She left."

"Didn't expect to find you here, Lawford," Cole said to Keith.

"Why not?"

"It's not your cup of tea, is it?"

"How would you know what is my cup of tea, Mr. MacKenzie?"

"Just figure a dude like you might think you'd soil those fancy clothes and high-priced boots in a place like this."

Lawford downed his drink and placed the glass

carefully on the bar. "You know, MacKenzie, I've had just about enough of your insinuations."

"Now why doesn't that scare me?" Cole motioned to Vic for a refill.

"And that goes tenfold for me, MacKenzie. You don't scare me. Bathing regularly and not swaggering around with horseshit on my boots doesn't make me a dude. My western roots go beyond wearing a Stetson and boots. I was born and raised in Lawford, MacKenzie, on a working ranch, where I had to pull my own weight. I've mucked out more stalls than I care to remember, roped calves, wrestled steers, busted broncos, driven herds, and strung wire the same as any other working hand. I ate dust in the summers and froze my ass off in the winters. So I had the brains to choose a different lifestyle. Furthermore, MacKenzie, who are you to judge? I don't hear you singing 'Home on the Range' either." He shoved his shot glass across the bar. "Fill it up, Vic."

"If you two fellas aim to have a pissing contest, take it outside," Vic said. "I don't want you breaking up the joint. I'm the one who has to clean it up."

"Well, I'll be damned!" Cole said. "I didn't figure you had it in you, Lawford. Vic, give my friend here a drink and pour yourself one while you're at it."

Vic refilled all their glasses. Lawford's outburst had surprised Cole. He hadn't given him that much credit. He decided this might be a good opportunity to pry some information out of both of them.

"I admit I can be a real bastard at times," Cole said. Keith raised his glass in the air. "I'll drink to that." He and Vic clinked their glasses together.

"Where Maggie is concerned," Cole qualified, with a jaundiced glance at them.

"Margaret," Keith corrected. "This round's on me, Vic."

Two hours later after many more rounds, Cole was still lamenting the woes and tribulations of being a guardian.

"It's a tough job to have the responsibility of a young girl on my hands."

"Woman," Keith corrected him for the dozenth time.

"Yeah, woman," Cole agreed. *All woman.* He downed the drink. This one seemed to bounce off his empty stomach and make a beeline right for his head. His vision had become slightly blurred. "Vic, you got a menu?"

"For what?"

"Food. I just remember I haven't eaten since early this morning."

"This is a bar, not a restaurant," Vic said. "Couple of hard-boiled eggs left in that bowl at the end of the bar. He moved down to it and came back carrying the bowl.

"Egg?" Cole asked, offering one to Keith. When Keith declined the offer, Cole began to peel it. "My biggest problem is money."

"Isn't that everybody's?" Vic said.

"Can't figure why Pop would bust his bank account to buy that damn piece of land."

"Must be he never figured on dying that soon," Keith suggested.

"Pop ever tell you what he wanted with Timberline, Lawford?"

"Not me," Keith said.

"What about you, Vic?" The bartender shook his head.

"Sure leaves Maggie in a fix."

"Margaret," Keith declared. His speech had begun to be slurred.

"Yeah, to Margaret," Cole said, raising his glass in the air.

Keith nodded. "To Margaret."

"Margaret," Vic echoed.

Cole looked at his glass, perplexed. "Can't make a toast with an empty glass."

"This one's on me," Vic said, and filled their glasses.

"Shesh wouldn't have a problem if shesh'd marry me."

Confused, Cole tried to focus his eyes on Keith. "Who's Shesh?"

Yawning, Keith cradled his head in his hand. "Margaret. Who do you think?"

"How come you can call her Shesh but I can't call her Maggie?"

"You're not making any shenze, MacKen... MacKen... ah, Cole."

"I think it's time both of you go home," Vic suggested wisely.

"We're fine. Aren't we, pal?" Cole said, slapping Keith on the shoulder.

"Jush fine," Keith said.

Cole could feel the effects of the liquor. The egg had been too little, too late. It would help if his vision would clear. The blurriness was making him dizzy.

"Vic, why do you think Ben Lawford wants Timberline so badly?"

"Wouldn't know, Mr. MacKenzie. He don't confide in me."

"Hell, Vic, call me Cole. Pop O'Shea come in here often?"

"Often enough."

"He ever act like he was worried about anything?"

"Like what?"

"Anything. Suspicious or the like?"

"You still thinking his death was no accident?"

"No accident?" Keith spoke up. "Why would you think Mick's death washn't an accident?" He turned, bleary-eyed, to Vic. "My glassh ish empty, Vic."

Vic poured them another drink, and as Cole picked his up to drink it, the thought of Maggie and her heartache tonight hit him right between the eyes. He stared blankly into the glass. "Something wrong with the drink, Cole?" Vic asked.

"No, it's fine." He downed the whiskey.

A short time later Dallas returned. By this time Cole and Keith had their arms slung around each other's shoulders and they were singing "Home on the Range" at the top of their voices.

"How long has this been going on?" Dallas asked.

"Too long," Vic said. "I told them both to go home, but I could have saved my breath. They're too drunk to toss out of here. They'd probably end up sleeping in the street all night."

Cole peered through a drunken haze at her. "Dallas, my love, come and join us," he called out when he recognized her.

"Yesh, Dallash, join us," Keith said. Slowly lowering his head to the bar, he proceeded to pass out.

"That's a sight I never thought I'd see," she said, amused. "Ben would be so proud of him."

"Found out he's not a prick after all. But it looks like my pal can't hold his liquor."

"Your pal, Texas? Since when have you and Keith become such good pals?"

"Listen, Dallas," Cole said, shaking his finger at her, "when I'm wrong about somebody, I'll be the first to admit it." He looped his arm around her shoulders. "I was wrong about Maggie, too."

"I think you were wrong about our little town here as well, Texas."

"Dallas, do you want to know what a bastard I am?"

She winked at Vic. "You! I can't believe it."

"I make her cry all the time. And I don't want to. And tonight I really made her cry. I think I broke her brave little heart."

"Maggie?"

"Yeah, brave little Maggie O'Shea with round green eyes that touch a man's soul."

"Is that why you're sucking up whiskey like there's no tomorrow?"

"I broke her heart, Dallas. Might just as well have stuck a knife into her. You're a wise woman, Dallas. Whatta ya think I should do about it?"

"I think you should go home and sleep it off, Texas. You're gonna hate yourself in the morning."

"I hate myself now. Anyway, I can't do what you said, even if I want to," he said, his gloom increasing. "My home's way down in Texas. I miss the Triple M. Did I ever tell you how much I miss the Triple M, Dallas?"

She cringed. "You aren't going to start crying in your beer, are you, Texas?"

"No, I wouldn't do that. I'm not drinking beer." He propped his cheeks between his hands and stared into space.

Dallas shook her head. "How much have they had to drink?" she said softly.

"He and Keith's been drinking straight shots for the past couple hours. MacKenzie's been asking a lot of questions."

Dallas jerked up her head. "Questions? About what?"

"Timberline. Mick O'Shea's death."

"What did you tell him?"

"I don't know nothing."

"And keep telling him that. Maybe he'll quit asking. Well, there's no way we can get them home in their condition. Let's get them upstairs. They can sleep it off in a bed up there."

Maggie awoke, and as soon as she realized she had not changed into nightclothes, all that Cole had said about Pop's death flooded her thoughts in a torrent. She lay in the dark and went over and over their conversation calmly and as objectively as she could, without allowing her emotions to interfere with her reasoning.

As damning as the telegram appeared, there had to be a logical explanation for Pop's desperate message. Maybe it wasn't anything sinister. Maybe he just needed money. She just couldn't accept the idea that someone deliberately killed him. Cole's suspects were above suspicion in her mind.

But what if Cole was right? Would she be able to bear it? And why condemn him for his suspicions? That had been her initial reaction. His motives were sincere. Whether he was right or wrong, he believed in not letting Pop's killer go unpunished.

And if there was the remotest possibility . . . *Dear God, don't let it be true.*

She had to get it out of her mind or she'd fall apart again. But he had planted a seed of suspicion, and now she must rid herself of it.

One thing was certain: she did owe Cole an apology. He truly had her interests at heart. In lieu of this latest revelation, her scheme to turn the tables on him and make him fall in love with her by pretending indifference now seemed shallow and unimportant. The real truth of Pop's death had to be resolved in her mind above anything else.

And if she was to do that, she would have to begin by returning to Timberline and facing her demons.

Even though it was the middle of the night, Maggie got out of bed. Before she lost her courage, she'd tell Cole her intention and also admit to him how much she appreciated what he was trying to do. She went downstairs.

Maggie tappped lightly on Cole's bedroom door. When there was no answer, she opened it and peeked inside.

Moonlight gleaming through the window gave her a full view of the bed, an empty bed. Where was he at this late time of night—or—she reconsidered her choice of words—early hour of the morning?

It occurred to her that Cole might be on the porch. He hated being cooped up in a room and may have gone outside and fallen asleep on the porch swing. Hurrying outside, she saw no sign of him. Glancing up the street, from where she stood the whole town was in darkness.

Could he have gone to the office? That had to be where she'd find him.

Maggie hurried there, and both the office and stable were in darkness. She still checked them out with the same result: simply no sign of Cole.

Returning to the house, she rechecked his room, then thought of the only other possibility of his whereabouts. Dallas's.

Even though the saloon was closed, what if he had stayed? Maggie felt a hot blush sweeping over her at the full implication of what that would mean—Cole had spent the night with Dallas.

She felt betrayed. Foolish. Had not considered the obvious. She'd been rushing up and down the street like an outraged wife in search of a philandering husband. Obviously whatever Cole's suspicions, he didn't allow them to hinder his sexual proclivities.

Well, she mustn't let this interfere with resolving the issue of Pop's death. Her personal feelings for Cole—and his lack of them for her—could not be permitted to cloud that issue. But that didn't lessen the hurt.

Maggie left the house and climbed Boot Hill.

Night passed into day, and Maggie continued to hope for Cole's return. She preferred to have him accompany her to Timberline, but if she had to, she'd go alone.

When she felt it was a reasonable hour to pursue the issue, she bit the bullet and went to Dallas's.

Dallas and Vic were seated at a table drinking coffee and reading the morning newspaper when Maggie paused in the doorway of the saloon. Their surprise was evident.

"Maggie!" Dallas exclaimed.

Maggie felt awkward. Although Dallas Donovan was her godmother and had been a close friend to her father, because of the business the woman ran, Maggie had seen her only on rare occasions. A decision that had been made by Dallas over Mick O'Shea's protests. Nevertheless, a gift had always arrived from the proprietress on Maggie's birthday and Christmas.

Vic murmured that he had work to do and disappeared into the back room.

Dallas stood up. "Come in, dear. What can I do for you?"

The attractive blond looked stunning dressed in a green brocade dressing gown, the cost of which would probably have kept the stagecoach solvent for a year. Maggie felt awkward and dowdy in her black split skirt and plain white blouse. It was no wonder Cole was attracted to other women.

"I know this is very presumptuous of me, but I've been looking for Cole MacKenzie. Is he here?"

Dallas arched a perfect brow. "Matter of fact, he is, Maggie."

Hot with humiliation, she could feel the heat of her blush. "I thought he might be."

"He's upstairs, sleeping, but I can wake him."

"No, that won't be necessary," Maggie said hurriedly.

"Are you sure? I can't believe it's not important, or you wouldn't have come here."

"I wanted his help with something, but actually it's just as well I do it myself."

"Well, is it something I can help you with?" Dallas asked.

"No, not at all. Thank you for offering."

"Honey, you know how bad I feel about your father."

"Yes, I know. He held the same regard for you."

Now, with the seed of suspicion that Cole had planted in her mind, Maggie could only wonder if Dallas had had anything to do with Pop's death.

"And thank you for attending his funeral. I'm sorry I didn't have an opportunity to speak to you then."

"Mick O'Shea was the finest man I've ever known," Dallas said.

Maggie knew she had to get out of there before she ended up in tears. "Well, I'm sorry to have disturbed you. And please don't wake Cole. I'm sure he needs the sleep."

If ever she'd seen a brokenhearted woman, it was Maggie, Dallas reflected, as the young girl turned and left. Recalling Cole's drunken mumbling last night, she wondered what he had done to the poor girl. And why were these two young people denying the truth to each other. One look at either of them and the truth of how they felt was obvious.

Suddenly a horrifying thought occurred to Dallas. She might have given Maggie the wrong impression. She'd never told her why Cole had spent the night there.

Dallas rushed to the door. "Maggie, come back. It's not what you think."

But it was too late. The young girl was out of earshot.

* * *

Maggie's spirits had sunk to a deeper low when she saddled Vixen for the ride to Timberline. Now that she knew the truth for certain, she forced herself to put thoughts of Cole and Dallas out of her mind. What lay ahead would challenge every ounce of her endurance, and she couldn't drain herself emotionally over her un-requited love for Cole.

With the morning fog swirling above the rising peaks in the distance, Maggie rode out of Lawford.

Chapter 13

Cole slowly opened his eyes and became aware he was on a bed in a strange room. His head was throbbing, but he managed to turn it enough to discover he wasn't alone in the bed. When he recognized Keith Lawford asleep beside him, Cole groaned and closed his eyes.

Good Lord, I've died and gone to hell.

Avoiding any unnecessary shock to his head, he slipped cautiously to his feet and left the strange room. As he started down the stairway, he finally recognized where he was.

"Good morning, Texas," Dallas greeted him cheerfully.

Clutching his head, Cole said, "Please don't shout, Dallas. I have a headache."

"A fifth of barleycorn will do it every time," she said, amused.

Cole groaned. "Don't tell me I drank that much."

"You and Keith Lawford. Vic said between the two of you, you killed a whole bottle. We were lucky we could even get you two in bed. You really tied one on last night, Texas." She handed him a glass. "Drink this."

He sniffed the contents. "It smells like hell."

"Then hold your nose and drink it down. It'll help your hangover."

The liquid was foul-tasting and he almost gagged on it. "God, that's awful. I'm never going to touch another drop of whiskey."

"Sure you aren't. I can't tell you how often I've heard *that* before," Dallas said. Walking over to a table, she sat down. He joined her and cradled his aching head in his hands. "While you were sleeping, Maggie O'Shea came looking for you."

Cole raised his head. "Maggie? What did she want?"

"She said she needed your help, then changed her mind and said it was something she had to do for herself."

Now what was she up to? Whatever it was, he had a bad feeling about it. "I'd better go to the house and see what she wants. Thanks, Dallas. Sorry about last night."

The fresh air felt good, and whatever Dallas had put in that witch's brew had started to take affect.

When he entered the house, Ellie took one look at him and shook her head. "A fast night makes a slow morning."

"Don't start, Ellie. Where's Maggie?"

"Thought she'd be with you. She was real close-mouthed and looking to find you. Left here and told me not to worry about making lunch. That's why I figured you were together."

Damn! In her frame of mind Lord knows what she might do. "I hope she didn't drive that stage again to Noches."

"No call to do that. You just got back from there. And the mail don't go out till Monday," she yelled, chasing after him as he hurried out the door. "Oh, well, I'm getting used to talking to myself," Ellie grumbled, and returned to the kitchen.

Cole relaxed when he saw the stagecoach still parked in the stable. Juan was mucking out the stalls.

" 'Morning, Juan. How's your dad doing?"

"*Buenos días*, Señor Cole. *Papá* say he is good and want to come back to work."

Cole chuckled. "It would be pretty hard for him to drive a stage with a cast on his leg." He glanced at the stalls. The smile slipped from his lips, and he stiffened with foreboding. Unconsciously he began to rub the hair at the nape of his neck.

"Juan, where's Vixen?"

"Señorita Margaret she ride away."

"Did she say where she was going?"

The youngster frowned and scratched his head. "No, she not say, but she looked very sad. Juan felt very bad. She say . . . ah, she say . . ."

"What?" Cole asked, his patience near to breaking.

"Señorita Margaret say she go to face her . . . de—"

"Demons?"

"*Sí*, demons. That is the word, Señor Cole."

"Oh, my God!"

Cole rushed to the stall and saddled a horse.

* * *

Maggie stood outside the entrance to the cave, her knees trembling so badly she thought she'd collapse. Now that she was here, she regretted not swallowing her pride and asking Cole to accompany her. Whatever their differences, she had always felt safer when he was near—even in Alaska. But obviously, from Dallas's near state of undress, he had other plans for the day.

For the briefest of moments her thoughts returned to that time in Alaska. That eternity ago. Funny how her fear had never been for herself, but for Pop's safety—until Cole joined them, and she no longer was afraid.

But Cole wasn't here now. She had to do this alone.

Maggie stepped into the cave and despite the heat of the day, her trembles turned to shivers.

The demons were attacking her.

She lit the lantern and held it high like a shield against these fearsome specters of her own anxieties.

As she advanced deeper into the cave, in the eerie glow of the lantern her every movement became a sinister shadow on the granite wall. Where was the actual spot where Pop had died? She would know it when she came to it.

Suddenly she skidded on a patch of mud and dropped the lamp. She twisted an ankle as she teetered, trying to keep her balance, and then she fell to the ground. As she tried to get to her feet, she rolled off an edge and, screaming, she plummeted into black space. Her scream was choked off when her body thudded to a halt on a solid foundation that felt like mud.

For several moments Maggie lay with the breath knocked out of her from the fall. Then she sat up gingerly. Her shoulder and side had taken the brunt of the fall, and she felt them gently. As much as they hurt, she didn't think any bones were broken.

She was in pitch blackness and could feel the oozing mud around her. Shifting painfully to her knees, she began to grope cautiously along slithery walls. Maggie finally concluded that she was in a basically round hole at least six feet in diameter. She couldn't even guess how far she'd fallen. The drop had been too unexpected and frightening at the time.

She had to literally tug her hands and knees out of the mud to stand up, only to clutch her ankle and sink down again. Her whole left side from ankle to shoulder was throbbing with pain. She was helpless, in total darkness, and unable to stand.

And to her surprise, she was no longer afraid, not of the dark, not of her demons, and not of never getting out of there. All she had to do was not panic, sit quietly, and wait for Cole.

And she knew beyond a doubt, he *would* find her.

As soon as he rode up, Cole saw Vixen tethered to a tree. At least he hadn't miscalculated, but it wasn't that encouraging when there was no sign of Maggie.

The lantern was gone, and other than the little light at the entrance, the rest of the cave was in darkness. It wasn't a good sign. In daylight, there'd be no reason to take the lantern elsewhere.

"Maggie," he shouted. "Maggie, are you in here?" When there was no reply, his uneasiness escalated. "Maggie, can you hear me?"

His instincts told him she was in there. He waited

and listened, his heart thudding in his chest as he feared the worst, the fear he'd harbored on his frantic ride to get there.

In desperation he stepped outside and looked around for something with which to make a torch. He scurried around like a madman, looking for anything that would work. Picking and tossing aside limbs from trees and shrubbery, he finally found a stout enough branch. With the aid of his pocket knife and sheer strength of will he was able to crack it in half to shorten the length and trim off enough from both halves to serve his purpose.

Cole dipped the tips of the crude torches into the can of kerosene, and then he lit them.

With a torch in each hand, he moved deeper into the cave toward the one area foremost in his mind, dreading what he might encounter there.

His stomach knotted when his foot brushed against the lantern.

Dear God, don't let it be true, he prayed.

He managed to stake the torches in the mud and then checked the lantern. Most of the kerosene had spilled out, but enough remained to get it lit. Leaden with dread, he picked it up, moved to the edge of the pit, and peered into it. He saw her sitting at the bottom of the pit.

"Maggie."

She opened her eyes. "Cole! I heard you calling, and I thought I was dreaming."

"Are you hurt?"

"My left shoulder and ankle are sore."

"Can you stand at all?"

"I tried before and I couldn't. Do you want me to try again?"

"Not yet. I've got to figure out how to get you out of there."

Dammit. Why hadn't he had enough sense to bring a rope, or at least someone to help him? Instead, he'd taken off like a bat out of hell without any rescue plan in mind. He'd known about this pit, and that had been his main worry.

"Maggie, just stay calm. I'll get you out of there, but I have to leave for a moment. Don't worry. I'll be right back."

"Where are you going?" A note of panic had entered her voice.

"Just out to the horses. I'll be right back, Maggie."

Once outside, he looked around for something that might help. When he realized he was just wasting time, he stopped and analyzed the situation.

He had no rope, no ladder, and he needed to rescue a woman who could not use her left foot and most likely her left arm from a pit that was about twenty feet deep. He could hardly drag any limb into the cave that would be sturdy enough to hold their weight. The horses were of no value because the opening was too low for them to pass through, and it would be too risky to lower himself into the pit to carry her up. That could get them both down there, and then he'd be no use to either of them.

He needed a hoist and tackle. Well, he had the strength to be the hoist, hopefully, and as for the tackle . . . His glance fell on Vixen. He'd found his tackle.

Cole reached into his pocket and pulled out his pocketknife. He quickly sliced off the bridle reins and tied them together with a square knot. Then he hurried back to the pit.

"How are you doing down there?"

"I was afraid you left."

"You don't ever have to worry about that. Now, honey, you have to follow my instructions carefully." He looped the middle of the long stretch of reins around his neck and then knotted the loose ends together about a couple of feet from their ends. He dropped the ends down to her.

"Now get as close to the wall as you can." She shifted over. "You still remember how to tie a square knot from our years in Alaska, don't you?"

"How could I forget, considering how you drilled it into me. Right over left and through, left over right—"

"Yeah, you remember. Okay, tie those ends around your waist in a square knot."

"Done," she said shortly. "Oh, I see. We're tied together like mountain climbers."

"That's right. You sure the knot's firm and won't slip?"

"It's a square knot, Cole."

"Ready?"

"I'm ready."

"Now I'm going to start hoisting you. I know you've got a bad ankle, but any climbing you can do will help."

Cole grasped the reins and began to hoist her. Her mud-sodden skirt added weight, and he regretted not telling her to remove it.

It was a slow process. Despite her injured foot, Maggie was doing a creditable job of scaling the wall, but for every two feet of forward progress it seemed she'd slide back a foot. When she finally was within arm's reach, Cole shoved the excess rope behind him. Then, lowering himself onto his stomach, he peered over the rim.

"Maggie raise your right hand so I can grab it."

He leaned over and groped for her hand. He finally made contact, and just as he clamped a hand firmly around her wrist, Maggie lost her left-hand grip on the reins. Screaming, she fell backward.

Hanging by their linked hands, Maggie dangled helplessly over the open cavity. Her voice was rife with breathlessness. "How deep is this hole?"

"Don't worry about that now. I've got a good grasp on you."

"Don't let go, Cole."

"Honey, I'm not going to let go, so just remain calm."

He began to slowly lift her until he was able to rise up on his knees. The new position gave him more leverage, but now his arm was bearing the full brunt of her dangling body, and its remaining strength was being drained out of it. He could feel the strength waning from her arm, too.

"Hold on, Maggie," he encouraged her.

When her head and then her shoulders cleared the rim, he leaned across her and clutched a fistful of the waistband of her skirt. Then he hauled the rest of her body over the rim.

They were both too breathless to say anything, and for a long moment they lay on the sodden mud until they could catch their breath. Finally on hands and knees they crawled to firmer ground.

"You okay?" he asked.

"Yes." Her voice was still shaky as he slipped the knot and released the rein.

Groaning, Cole crawled back and retrieved the lantern to give them the needed light to get out of the cave without further mishap.

Once in daylight with the hazard behind them, he studied her muddied appearance. All he could think of was how close she'd come to getting killed. He couldn't yell at her, he was too grateful she was still alive. To disguise his anxiety, he tried laughter.

"Now you really look like the Maggie I remember. Your face and hands are as dirty as your clothes."

"What do you expect with you kicking mud down on my face?" she retorted. "And you don't look any better, MacKenzie."

"And you're just as spunky and sassy as you were then, Miz Trouble. Come on, there's a stream about a quarter of a mile from here where we can wash off this mud."

She tried to walk and gasped with pain. "I don't think I can make it on this ankle."

"I'll check it out as soon as we get rid of this mud." Picking her up, he lifted her onto the reinless Vixen. "Hold onto the bridle's headstall for now."

Much to the relief of both of them, the ride to the stream did not take long. It was a shallow tributary of the Pecos River and fortunately deep enough for them to submerge themselves to the waist in its water.

"Only way we'll get the mud off our clothes is to take them off. I suppose your maidenly modesty demands privacy," he said.

"It certainly does," she exclaimed.

"Okay, I'll give you ten minutes while I take care of the horses. And I promise I won't peek."

"Then hurry up and get out of here so I can get started."

"Ten minutes, Miz Margaret."

True to his word, he returned at the exact time he had threatened with the saddle blanket he'd taken off Vixen.

"You'll probably need this."

"Turn around," she ordered.

"Maggie," he said, exasperated, "I've seen you in a state of undress as much as I have dressed."

"Turn around."

Sighing, he did as ordered. "How long does it take to wrap a blanket around you?" he grumbled, after a long moment.

"All right, I'm ready."

Now wrapped in a blanket, Maggie was sitting in the sun, her face and hands devoid of mud and her hair tumbled in disarray on her shoulders. Her laundered blouse and skirt were draped over nearby shrubbery.

Cole sat down on the riverbank and pulled off his boots.

"Do you intend to disrobe in front of me?" she asked.

"If you consider removing my shirt and boots disrobing," he said, tossing aside his shirt, "I guess you could say that's my intention." He waded into the stream.

The water was cold, but the current managed to wash most of the mud off his pants as he cleaned his face and hands. Then he retrieved his shirt and boots and did the same to them.

Water ran down his face and dripped from his sodden trousers when he came out of the water and spread the shirt out next to her clothes. He went over and sat down beside her. Maggie tightened the blanket around herself, but not before he glimpsed a well-remembered satiny and very feminine shoulder.

"Let's check that ankle now."

She winced with pain when he gingerly removed the boot from her left foot.

"Looks like the cool water didn't help to bring the swelling down." He cupped her foot in his left hand and gently ran the fingers of his right hand around her ankle. "Doesn't feel broken. Can you wiggle your toes?"

"Yes," she said, demonstrating.

"Did you hurt your ankle in the fall?"

"No, I slipped in the mud and twisted it before I fell."

"Well, you won't be wearing a boot for a while."

The smile left her eyes. "So that was how Pop died, wasn't it?"

He knew what she meant. Grim-faced, he asked, "Is that what they told you?"

"Only that he fell and broke his neck."

"And you could have broken yours," he said harshly. "That was a damn fool move to come here alone, Maggie. Why didn't you ask me to come along?"

"I intended to, but . . ." She blushed hotly. "You were with Dallas, and—"

"I was *at* Dallas's, not *with* her. Matter of fact, your boyfriend and I slept it off in the same bed last night."

"Are you referring to Keith?"

"That's right."

She put a hand over her mouth to stifle her laugh. "I can't believe Keith got so drunk he had to sleep it off at Dallas's."

Cole snorted. "I can't believe it was in the same bed as me." Then, on a more serious note, he asked, "Maggie, do you know who discovered Pop's body?"

"It was Keith, Ben, Vic, and Emilio."

"How come you weren't with them? You wouldn't have known at the time that he'd been in an accident."

"When they were preparing to go and look for Pop, Ben claimed I'd only slow them up. He insisted I remain at the house."

"How did they know to look for him in that cave?"

"Ben said he'd seen Pop prowling around that area."

"What a coincidence. Unfortunately, Maggie, I don't believe in coincidence, so your Mr. Ben Lawford remains at the top of my list of suspects."

"So you still insist Pop's death wasn't an accident."

"Maggie, that pit's not much more than twenty feet deep. You fell and didn't break your neck."

"I guess I was luckier than he was," she said sadly. "I was on my knees when I rolled off the edge. And I landed on my side. Pop must have been upright, fallen backward, and landed on his head. You know, Cole, you might be so obsessed with your suspicions that you're imagining intrigue where none exists."

"That still wouldn't explain why he bought Timberline to begin with."

"Maybe he bought this land just to irritate Ben Lawford."

"Is that your opinion or Ben Lawford's?" he asked.

"I don't mean to sound disrespectful to Pop's memory, Cole, but he did dislike Ben so, and Pop wasn't above being childish at times."

He felt a rise of anger at her suggestion. "Then it must run in the family, because that's really a childish remark."

"Are you trying to start an argument?"

"Not at all. You're being naive if you think your father would bust his bank account just to become a burr in Lawford's rear end."

Maggie lowered her head. "You're right. It's unforgivable of me, but I don't have the answers." She forced a weak smile. "At least some good has come out of today. I faced my demons, so now when I ask you to sell this property, I'm doing it for practical reasons and not because I'm running away from my fears."

"Then I reckon it was worth the risk."

"Something happened to me down in that pit, Cole. You hear that in times of crisis, your whole life flashes before you, that hundreds of thoughts go through your mind when a situation looks hopeless and you believe you're about to die. None of that happened to me. I wasn't afraid of anything, Cole."

"You showed a lot of courage, Maggie."

"It wasn't that." She looked up, and her eyes glowed with trust and admiration. "I knew you would come."

He wanted to kiss her. She wanted him to. He ached to hold her and kiss her until they both were senseless. But this time it would be a mistake. A point of no return. A commitment that would carry him far beyond this moment. So he had to let the moment pass.

"I'll . . . ah . . . check on the clothes." He rushed away before he made a fool of himself.

Maggie's gaze followed his every movement as he turned the clothes over. She had often seen him shirtless in Alaska and more recently in Lawford and Noches. His physique never failed to fascinate her. Cole's broad shoulders and muscular chest and arms were a beautiful melding of flesh, muscle, and tanned skin. She wondered if he realized how handsome he actually was.

When he returned, he stretched out beside her and closed his eyes. She didn't know if he'd fallen asleep, but rather than disturb him, she chose to sit in contended silence, enjoying the feeling of just having him near.

Several hours later, when they were ready to leave, he lifted her onto his saddle and climbed on behind her. Enclosed in the circle of his arms, she leaned back against him in contentment. There was no longer any doubt in her mind. Whether he returned that love or not, she loved Cole MacKenzie with all of her heart and soul—a love that went far beyond a young girl's infatuation.

Since her father's death she had discovered a great deal about herself—her weaknesses and, surprisingly, strengths she'd never suspected she possessed.

In the process she'd done a lot of growing up—and no doubt had a lot more to do. But she no longer was afraid to confront her fears. And whatever the truth of Pop's death, she was prepared to face that, too. For whatever the future might hold, there would no longer be anything she couldn't withstand.

As long as there was Cole.

Chapter 14

When Cole carried Maggie into the house, Ellie threw up her arms and rushed over to them.

"What happened?"

"It's nothing serious, Ellie," Maggie said, trying to reassure the anxious woman. "I twisted my ankle and fell."

Ellie immediately took over. "Cole, bring her up to her room so I can get her in bed," she fired off, hurrying up the stairs ahead of him. "Then fetch Doc Stone."

"Where's his office?"

"He ain't got no office. He's the blacksmith. Send Juan. The boy knows where the doc lives."

"Ellie, you're getting too excited. I'm fine," Maggie said.

"Good thing she doesn't know where you fell," Cole murmured softly to her. Maggie laughed and rolled her eyes.

"What's that about falling?" Ellie asked.

Cole departed hurriedly, leaving Maggie to the mercy of Ellie's curiosity and tender, loving care.

As soon as he informed Juan, the boy raced down the street to find the doctor. Cole unsaddled the horses. He wanted to stay as far away from the house as he could until the doctor was gone and Ellie had settled down.

He washed down Cupid then picked up a currycomb and began to brush him. The routine task felt good. It was a long time since he'd curried a horse and had never considered until then what a relaxing task it was.

Like most things in life, there were peaks and valleys—not too many people got a free ride—but on the whole, he decided, ranching was a good life.

Granted, it'd been rough on his Grandma MacKenzie, who'd been left alone to raise three sons when his grandpa died at the Alamo. She'd grubbed out an existence on a small dirt farm while fighting Indians, outlaws, and Nature. And she'd died in the effort. But she had left behind something more significant than those few acres of land. Kathleen MacKenzie had passed on a heritage of courage, fortitude, and honor to her sons, Cole thought with pride. And today those few acres of Texas earth had grown to span almost four hundred thousand acres.

In his twenty-five years no one had been able to explain to him the mystical pull the Triple M had on his family. For no matter where they roamed—his father, his uncles, or his cousins—they had all been lured back within its boundaries.

And now he, too, felt that pull. It was time to go home.

When Juan returned, Cole thanked him for his help and sent him on his way. He continued with the task of washing and combing the remaining horses.

"You're looking good, Vixen," Cole said, with a swat to the horse's haunch when he finished the final one. The mare trotted into the stall, and Cole slid the lock in place.

He grinned. "Who but Maggie would name you horses after reindeer?" The mare stuck her head over the bar and nuzzled him. "You are a vixen, aren't you, girl?" he said, patting her neck. "Just like your mistress. You know, Vixen, she really surprised me today. That little gal's got spunk. Hurting, at the bottom of a pit, in darkness. And she was probably scared as hell even going into the cave. No telling how some other gal might have acted in the same situation. Yeah, it took a damn lot of nerve. Maggie O'Shea is quite a gal. She does Pop proud."

He walked over to the door. "Good night, deers," he called out. Grinning, he blew out the lamp and closed the door.

When he reached the house, Ellie was sitting on a rocking chair on the front porch. Cole plopped down on the top step. "How's your patient doing?"

"Doc gave her something to ease the pain. He said the ankle's sprained. Once the swelling's down, he'll be able to tell if any of the ligaments are torn."

"What about her shoulder?"

"Nothing's broken, but she'll be hurting for a while."

"Maggie's a tough little trooper, Ellie. When she was tossed head first off that stagecoach, she got up and walked away."

"You ain't telling me nothing I don't know about that gal. But she covers up a lot of hurt under that tough hide."

"Yeah, I know. She sure proved it today. Did she tell you what happened?"

Ellie nodded, then pulled up the hem of her apron and dabbed at her eyes. "When I think of what might have happened . . ."

"It didn't, Ellie, that's all that matters."

"I'm beholdin' to you, Cole MacKenzie. You brought my baby home to me."

"Ellie, there's something I have to tell you. I'm thinking about leaving soon. Going back to Texas."

"You planning on taking her with you?"

"Yes. Will you come with us?"

"Can't say. I'll have to sleep on it."

"I've got a lot to finish up here, so you've got time. It wouldn't be the same without you, Ellie, and I know you'd like the Triple M. There's plenty of help, so it won't take long to put up our own house."

"Sounds like you're talking marriage, boy."

Cole stood up. "Ellie, to tell the truth, I don't know what I'm talking. I just know I'm not leaving here without her." He leaned down and kissed the top of her head. "I'm hungry. Think I'll go in and rustle up something to eat."

"It ain't that hard. I've got some chicken and dumplings stewing on the stove. When you wash that horse smell off you, it'll be waiting for you." She returned to her rocking.

After he cleaned up, Cole peeked in on Maggie. She was sleeping soundly, so rather than disturb her, he went downstairs and ate.

* * *

The following morning Cole had to argue with Maggie to convince her that she should not attempt to go into the office.

"I am fine," she insisted. "It's not necessary for you and Ellie to treat me like an invalid."

"Maggie, the doctor said to keep you off that ankle so that the swelling can go down. So the wisest thing is to stay off it for a couple of days."

"I hope you don't think I'm going to remain in this bed all that time."

"I'll be glad to carry you downstairs, if that will make you happy, but you're not to try and hobble around. Is that clear?"

"It's senseless to argue with you, Cole. I might just as well be talking to myself. All right, take me downstairs."

He picked her up as if she were a bag of feathers. "I hate being such a burden," she fretted as he carried her down the stairs.

"You're not a burden, Maggie. Besides," he said, grinning, "I'm used to it. I had to do a lot of calf-throwing on the ranch, so if I have to hog-tie you, I will."

After depositing Maggie on the couch, he turned her over to Ellie's watchful eye and went to the stage office.

There were several unopened letters Maggie had put on the desk when they'd returned from Noches. The first one was a feed bill, and he put it aside.

The second letter was a brochure advertising a mineral spa in the southwest corner of the state. Cole recalled that in Alaska Pop had often complained about arthropathy in his joints. It must have been flaring up again.

As he started to put aside the brochure, he was struck by a staggering thought. If Pop's joints were aching and he was having trouble walking, it was feasible that he might have slipped and fallen in that cave. Maybe his deep feeling for Pop was causing him to pursue a phantom created in his own mind, when none actually existed. Don Quixote de la Mancha batting at windmills. And he'd made Maggie his Dulcinea.

Have I been that much of a damn fool?

Cole had little time to dwell on it, because the next letter caught his attention. It was addressed to him in care of Michael O'Shea in Lawford from the hotel he'd stayed at in San Francisco. Inside was another sealed letter and a note from Joe Reynolds, the hotel's desk clerk, indicating that the letter had arrived on the very day Cole had checked out.

Cole picked up the letter and immediately recognized Pop's handwriting on the envelope addressed to him. He tore it open in his haste to read it, hoping for some revelation that would make an impact on the mystery of Pop's death.

The letter was dated ten days before Pop died. He mentioned a property he intended to buy but gave no other details. In fact, most of the content involved Maggie and his concern over her growing relationship with Keith Lawford. He didn't like the difference in their ages and felt that Maggie had not had enough experience with the opposite sex to know what she was doing. He did write that he had nothing particularly against Keith Lawford other than who his father was.

Then he was so bold as to write that he'd always hoped that one day Cole and Maggie would wed. This came as a surprise. Cole had never suspected that Pop had harbored such a thought, nor had he ever hinted at it in conversation.

On the whole, the desperation voiced in the letter was that of a devoted father faced with the prospect of losing his daughter to another man. Sadly Cole folded the letter up and returned it to the envelope. Then he stuck it in his shirt pocket and went into the stable.

He found the novel on the seat where Maggie had left it.

"Juan, will you run this down to the house. Miss Margaret is waiting for it."

"*Sí*, Señor Cole. Señorita Margaret is better?"

"Much better. She just has to stay off her ankle for a couple of days." He handed the boy a quarter.

"*Gracias, señor*. Juan make much money. *Papá* will be very pleased with Juan." He pulled a dollar coin out of his pocket. "Señor Keith give to Juan."

"Why, Juan?"

"He come here and ask many questions."

"What kind of questions?"

"He ask Juan where you and Señorita Margaret go . . . how you say *ayer*?"

"Yesterday."

"*Sí*, yesterday."

"And what else did he ask you?"

"He ask if Juan and Señorita Margaret talk about him."

"And what did you tell him?"

"Juan say he told the Señorita that Señor Keith has the eye for her and Señorita Margaret say the Señor is fine *hombre*."

"Was that all of it?"

The youth grinned. "He ask what Señorita Margaret say about Señor Cole."

"Really." Cole chuckled. "I'd be curious to know the answer to that myself. What did she say about me?"

"She say Juan eat too much ice cream."

Cole was baffled. "Ice cream? What in hell does that mean?"

The boy threw his hands up in frustration. "Why you ask Juan? Juan is ten years old. Does he know about women?" He walked away, grumbling.

"Maggie, how do you feel about Juan Morales?" Cole asked later that evening as they were playing three-card monte.

She looked up from her cards. "I don't understand the question."

"Can his judgment be trusted? What with Emilio laid up probably for another month and you for a week at least, I'm going to have to depend on Juan if we're to keep the stageline operating."

"Juan is old beyond his years, Cole. He has excellent judgment. Sometimes when I'm talking to him, I forget he's only ten."

"So despite his excesses, you trust his judgment about everything."

"What excesses are you referring to?"

"You must admit he tends to eat too much ice cream."

"Ice cream! That's ludicrous, Cole. I've never seen him do anything to excess—much less overindulge in ice cream. Wherever did you get such a ridiculous idea?"

"Then you don't feel such a habit would affect his judgment."

"Of course not, even if it were true. Juan's a sensible, dependable, hardworking young man whose life has forced him to grow up before his time. I'd trust his judgment about anything or anybody."

"Glad to hear that." *Juan, you and I are going to have a long talk on the subject of ice cream—and a certain lady's opinion of me.*

"Why the silly grin, Cole?" Maggie asked.

"Do I have a silly grin?"

"You certainly do at the moment. Your deal," she said, shoving the deck at him.

A knock at the door interrupted the card game, and Cole opened the door to Keith Lawford.

"For me?" Cole said, glancing at the bouquet in the lawyer's hand. "How thoughtful."

"I thought I'd drop in to see how Margaret is feeling."

"Come in, Keith," Maggie called out. Cole stepped aside.

After much oohing and ahing over the flowers, followed by a discussion on how she felt, much to Lawford's displeasure, Cole remained. And for the next hour the three of them played cards until Keith departed.

By the following Monday Maggie was up and around, although the doctor insisted she keep the ankle wrapped and advised her to use a cane. She immediately rejected that idea.

To ease Maggie's boredom, Cole agreed to let her

ride along when he drove Gladys and Lyla back to Noches.

All week Cole had thought about the situation in Lawford, and more than ever he was determined to follow though with the decision he'd made in Noches to go back to the Triple M for a visit. It would give him the opportunity to close down the stageline permanently. He told Maggie his intention as they rode to Noches.

She balked at the idea immediately. "I understand your concern over your brother and family, but I do not intend to accompany you. I have to stay here and run the stageline."

"I'm closing down the stageline, Maggie."

"You can't do that. You promised me thirty days to turn the stageline around, and I'm holding you to that promise."

"That was before Emilio's accident. If I leave, there's no driver. Can't you understand that? And don't give me the argument that you can do the driving. It's too dangerous for a woman."

"I'll talk to Keith. Maybe he can persuade Ben to lend me one of his ranch hands until Emilio recovers."

"Maggie, use some common sense. Ben Lawford wants the stageline himself. He's not about to lend you a ranch hand to help you out. Like it or not, this is the final run—and this is my final word on the subject as well. When we get back, as soon as I wrap up the loose ends, we're leaving for the Triple M."

"I trusted you, believed in you. I'll never forgive you for this, Cole."

She didn't say another word to him for the rest of the

trip. It was just as well, Cole figured. By the time they reached Noches she would have cooled down enough to be able to discuss it more rationally. It seemed that every time their relationship took a step in the right direction, something always came up that caused a giant step backward.

But this time there'd be no compromise on his part. He had responsibilities to his family, too. This was the end of driving Dallas's "nieces" and carrying the mail back and forth between towns. He was through being a pimp and a mailman. As soon as possible, he and Maggie were taking the train to Texas, and he didn't care if she pouted all the way to the Triple M.

He whipped the reins to speed up.

After dropping off Gladys and Lyla, he drove Maggie to Josie Hallaway's for her to visit with the widow while he took care of the business at hand.

He left the horses at the livery to be watered, checked the Western Union office for a wire he was expecting, then picked up the mail. Since Mrs. Hallaway insisted Maggie remain for lunch, Cole went to the saloon.

He sat down at the remaining table in the corner. He couldn't get the problem with Maggie off his mind. He wished there could be a more agreeable solution to the problem than resorting to exerting his authority over her. If only she could see the uselessness of continuing that stageline. Actually, that damn stageline was the only real source of disagreement between them.

As he was eating a ham sandwich and drinking a glass of beer, a group of cowboys entered the barroom. Rowdy and boisterous, it was obvious they'd started their weekend early. Seeing Cole alone at a table, they walked up to him.

"We need this table, mister," one of the young cow-pokes said.

"You're welcome to it as soon as I'm through."

"You don't get it. We mean now," he said.

This wasn't a good day for Cole. The argument with Maggie that morning had set the ball in motion. And now this loudmouthed punk hassling him. Cole didn't take to shoving, particularly from loudmouthed young punks.

"Since you're in that much of a rush, sonny, I'd finish a damn sight faster if you'd get out of my face and let me eat," Cole said.

"Maybe I should help you along by pouring that drink down your throat."

"You can try, sonny."

"Yeah, sounds like it'd be interesting to watch," someone interjected.

"Wouldn't want to miss it for the world," another said.

Cole recognized the speakers' voices immediately. He jerked up his head and stared in astonishment at his cousins Zach and Josh MacKenzie.

Chapter 15

The two tall men walked over to the table, pulled out chairs, and sat down.

"Hey, whatta ya doing?" the young bigmouth said. "This is gonna be our table."

"When we're through with it," Zach said.

The rest of the cowpokes moved in closer.

"Fellas, let's not have any trouble," Josh warned them. "Our cousin has told you that when we're through, you can have the table."

"He didn't say anything about you two."

Zach, who didn't have Josh's patience, said, "Just mosey back to the bar. You're disturbing us."

"We ain't going anywhere. Maybe you ain't noticed that there's five of us to the three of you."

"Only two," Josh corrected him. "I'm getting too old to engage in bar fights. That should even the odds."

Cole had begun to feel better already. There was

nothing like the prospect of a good fight to lift a man's spirits.

"Yeah, you can count these piss-ass loudmouths as they hit the floor, Josh," Cole said.

He thrust up an arm to fend off the punch the cowboy threw at him. The man grabbed his shirtfront and yanked Cole to his feet. Cole knocked his hand away and followed through with a punch that sent the cowboy reeling backward, crashing into a table.

It was the opening bell to the free-for-all. The men at other tables grabbed their glasses as they scrambled to get out of the way when the other four cowboys broke into action.

Zach took a solid punch to the jaw but stayed on his feet and delivered a blow that knocked his attacker to the floor. By this time Cole was fighting off two of them, and Josh came to his rescue. He grabbed one of them by the back of his shirt collar and sent him sailing across the floor, busting several chairs in his path before he slammed up against the bar.

With two down and three to go, it was like shooting fish in a barrel. The MacKenzies made short work of them. Within minutes the fight was over: two of the cowboys knocked out and the other three nursing their bruises.

"Through with your lunch, cousin?" Josh asked.

Cole picked up his glass of beer, which had survived the fracas unmolested, and poured it over the young cowboy, who was stretched out cold on the floor.

"You can have the table now."

On the way out, Cole tossed some money on the bar. "This should pay for the damage, and buy those fellows a drink on me."

"God, it's good to see you guys," Cole said, after an exchange of handshakes and backslaps outside with his cousins.

"You never could stay out of trouble," Josh said good-naturedly.

"What are you doing here?"

"Waiting to catch the stage to Lawford," Josh said. "The fellow at the livery told us the driver's name was MacKenzie and we could find him in that bar."

"We figured it had to be you," Zach said.

Cole suddenly sobered. "You didn't come to bring me bad word on Jeb, did you?"

Josh shook his head. "Jake Carrington's trying to find out something through his Washington connections, and Jared Fraser's doing the same through his army ones."

"How are my folks holding up?"

"As well as can be expected," Zach said. "Your dad isn't as quick to smile and your mom's a bit sadder, but everyone's doing what they can to keep their spirits up."

"What in hell are you doing driving a stage?" Zach asked. "You'll try just about anything rather than come back to the Triple M and settle down, won't you?"

"I'm planning on heading home next week."

"That's good, Cole," Josh said. "I think you should."

"Let's find a quiet bar where we can sit down and talk." He shook his head and slapped them on the back again. "I can't believe it. It's sure good to see you guys again."

And he had never meant anything so much in his life. With just a year's difference in their ages, he, Zach, and Kitty, Josh's sister, had been inseparable playmates growing up. Josh was eight years older than the rest of his cousins and had been an older brother to all of them.

Cole had to admit that he'd always been wilder and more adventuresome than his cousins and siblings. It was Josh who always got them out of the fixes that Cole would get them into.

When Josh had joined the Texas Rangers and then the Pinkerton Agency, Zach, Kitty, and Cole had felt the loss the most. And then when Zach had been old enough to go into the Rangers, Cole had been devastated. He'd run off and ended up riding with an outlaw gang.

It'd been Zach who trailed him down and kicked his ass home before he got into more serious trouble. Trouble was, Zach then had nearly gotten himself killed when he joined up with the same gang while working undercover for the Rangers.

Now, as Cole sat across the table from them, inundated with past memories, he realized how empty his past years had really been. Josh, Zach, Kitty were all married now and settled down on the Triple M, raising their families. Jeb was missing or, God forbid, killed in the war in Cuba.

What in hell had he ever accomplished in his shallow life? Twenty-five years old and he was still wandering around like a nomad, looking for what? An ace in the hole? Every day real life was being played out on the Triple M or on a Cuban battlefield, not some damn barroom that reeked with the smell of cigarettes and stale beer.

And in his self-absorption he'd presumed to advise Maggie to grow up. Talk about not seeing the forest for the trees. No wonder she shunned his advice.

"Now, tell me what you guys are doing here," Cole asked once they were seated at a table in a less crowded saloon.

"Rose and Em came up to attend some Harvey Girl reunion in Albuquerque, so we left them there to come over here and see you."

"I've been expecting an answer to that wire I sent you."

"We figured as long as we were in New Mexico, delivering the information you asked for would be better than wiring it," Josh said. He dug in his shirt pocket and pulled out a folded paper. "It's the best we could do."

"Good thing Josh was a Pinkerton, or we'd probably never have been able to dig up that much," Zach added.

"Well, the Rangers were a big help, too. Who the hell are these people?" Josh asked.

"It's a long story." Cole gave the paper a cursory glance, then stuffed it into his shirt pocket. "I'm beginning to think I might have been barking up the wrong tree."

"Well, I'm sure glad we found you here," Zach said. "We hadn't figured on having to take a stage to reach Lawford, so this is a good break for us."

"What's with that wire you sent? Are you in any kind of trouble, Cole?" Josh asked somberly.

"Not the kind you're used to getting me out of."

Cole had no sooner uttered the words than trouble appeared before him with a pink boa wrapped around her neck.

"Well, hello, Handsome," Gladys said.

"And what do we have here?" Lyla asked from beside her. "Hello, boys."

"You mind if we join you?" Gladys said, sitting down in the chair next to Cole. Lyla followed suit and sat down between Josh and Cole.

"Fellows, this is Gladys Divine and Lyla Loving. Girls, my cousins Josh and Zach MacKenzie."

"How do, ladies," Zach acknowledged.

"Our pleasure," Josh said.

"The pleasure is all ours, Josh," Gladys replied. "Matter of fact, I can't think of a more pleasurable sight I've ever seen. You boys are sure something for these tired eyes to look at."

"You must be referring to lack of sleep, Miss Divine, 'cause those lovely eyes of yours sure wouldn't be suffering from old age," Zach spoke up. "Ouch!" he yelped, when Cole kicked him in the leg.

"Would you ladies care for something to drink?" Josh asked.

"Well, I usually don't indulge in alcohol," Lyla said, "but I'll make an exception this time." She turned her head, put two fingers to her lips, and let out a whistle. "Hey, Pete, send over a round of boilermakers."

"So you boys looking for a good time?" Gladys asked.

"They ain't boys, honey," Lyla said. "Can't you see they're *men*?"

"No, we just came in here to talk," Cole said.

"What did you do with Maggie?" she asked.

"She's having lunch with a friend."

"Male or female, honey?" Gladys asked, arching a brow.

"Female."

"The gal's crazy about you, Cole," she said.

"Did she say that?"

Zach suddenly looked interested. "Who's Maggie?"

"Margaret O'Shea. Pop's daughter."

"Aren't you her guardian?" Josh asked.

Cole nodded. "Yeah, but at the moment she's not even talking to me." He proceeded to tell them how upset Maggie was over his intention to sell the stageline and take her to the Triple M. "She said she won't come with me."

"Sounds like it would do her good," Lyla said.

"You wouldn't have to ask me more than once," Gladys spoke up.

"The trouble is that damn stageline," Cole lamented. "She just doesn't want to part with it. I'd like to set the damn coach on fire."

"Too bad you don't carry anything valuable. That way you could hope for a holdup and scare the daylights out of her," Zach said. "That might make her want to part with it."

"There's nothing that would make her want to part with it. She's obsessive about that damn stageline because it was Pop's idea. She claims it was her father's dream. I never should have agreed to let her run it."

"Wasn't he the one you panned gold with in Alaska?" Josh asked.

"Yeah, him and Maggie."

"Well, it doesn't make sense that a man who went through all the hardship of panning gold in Alaska would have a life's dream of operating a rundown stageline. I'd think he'd have higher aspirations. Your

Miss Maggie might be reading more into it than was there, or she just likes the idea of operating a stageline."

"I hadn't thought of that before, Josh, but I think you're right."

"You're just going to have to convince her of some way to get rid of the stageline," Zach said. "Burn it."

"She'd never forgive me. You know, Zach, I think your idea of scaring her might work."

Josh groaned. "Dammit, Zach, why did you put an idea like that into his head? You know he's crazy enough to try it."

Cole motioned to them to move closer and lowered his voice. "I've made up my mind. I want you two to hold up the stagecoach."

Zach and Josh exchanged glances. "Tell me he didn't say what I thought he said," Josh murmured.

"It will work, Josh," Cole said. "Zach and you can pretend to hold up the stage a couple of miles out of town. If you can act threatening enough, she should fall for it."

"I'm game," Zach said.

"You guys aren't thinking straight," Josh argued. "Zach, what if it was happening to Rose, would you think this was such a good idea?"

"Yeah, you're right. It is a dirty trick to pull, Cole."

"I'm only thinking of what's best for Maggie. There's no money, and right now there isn't even a driver, because he broke his leg. There are no passengers, and—"

"Hey, Handsome, whatta ya mean? Ain't Lyla and me passengers?"

"Free passengers, Gladys. Pop and Dallas had a business arrangement."

"You mean we've been riding free all this time?" Gladys asked, shocked.

"That's right."

"What did I always tell you, Gladys? You ain't gonna get rich giving out free rides," Lyla declared.

"I like that little Maggie gal. She's got a lot of spunk," Gladys said. "But I think Handsome there is right. She ought to give up that stageline."

Always the more prudent one, Lyla pointed out, "But if she gives it up, it'll hurt our business. How'll we get back and forth to Lawford?"

"Ben Lawford wants to buy the stageline," Cole told her. "He'll probably buy a new stage."

"Heck, if he's gonna do that, I'll set fire to the damn stage myself," Lyla remarked. "It's nothing but a pile of rotting wood and rusty springs. My butt's worn to the bone from riding in it."

"Good thing we missed the stage, cousin," Zach murmured to Josh.

"This is what we'll do," Cole said. "You two rent a couple of horses, ride out of town for a couple of miles, and then stop the stage when we show up. Just remember to sound threatening."

"Can we ride along, too?" Gladys asked. "This sounds like a lot of fun."

"If you want to walk back," Cole said.

"Riding's not my strongest talent, Handsome." Gladys winked at him. "But I do have other ones." She stood up. "Come on, Lyla. We ain't gonna get rich here."

"Good-bye, fellas." Lyla smiled complaisantly. "It's like I've always said. The handsome ones are either broke or true to their wives. We get the hog-breaths who've forgotten what the inside of a bathtub looks like."

"If they ever knew to begin with, dearie," Gladys said. She wrapped her feather boa around her neck, then slipped an arm through Lyla's. With swaying hips and linked arms, the two women walked away.

"Quite a pair, aren't they?" Josh said.

"They sure are," Zach agreed. "I see you've managed not to get bored, cousin."

"All right, let's get out of here. You fellows sure you know what you have to do?"

"Dammit, Cole, I don't like this," Josh said. "I know you have the girl's interests at heart, but this sounds too manipulative. How do you expect her to ever have any respect for you?"

"If I remember, cousin, didn't you pull all kinds of tricks to deceive Em when you met her?"

"I was a Pinkerton agent on a case. I suspected she was the thief I was tracking."

"And what about you, Zach? Didn't you deceive Rose into believing you were an outlaw?"

"You know damn well I was a Ranger then, working undercover."

"And Em and Rose ended up marrying you guys, didn't they? And what about your dad, Josh? Uncle Luke even locked up Aunt Honey in his jail before they were married to keep her from leaving. Zach, your dad forced your ma at gunpoint to marry him. Aunt Garni still laughs when she talks about how Uncle Flint broke up her wedding and forced her to marry him instead. So the way I see this, I'm doing it in the line of duty, too. I'm Maggie's guardian and I'm doing what's best for her interests."

"By scaring the hell out of her?" Josh argued.

"Trust me, Josh, it will only be temporary. Maggie's got more spunk than you can imagine."

"Uh, Cousin Cole," Zach said, "all those stories you mentioned ended up with happy endings. Are you planning on marrying this girl, too?"

"Might have to, if she doesn't shoot me first."

"Margaret, dear, you appear to be very down-hearted today. Are you ill?"

"Nothing like that, Mrs. Hallaway. Cole gave me some wretched news on the ride here today. He's my guardian, you know."

"Yes, he told me."

"I have to do what he says for three more years, and he insists we sell the stageline and I go to his parents' home in Texas."

"Why does he want to sell the stageline, Margaret?"

"It's not making money, but I can't believe it won't one day. Cole just doesn't have the patience to wait."

"Do you trust Cole on other matters, my dear?"

"Of course—with my life, if necessary. It seems Cole has always come through in a crisis when I've needed him."

Maggie was unaware how her eyes now glowed when she spoke of him. "Even in Alaska, despite how much I resented him at the time. Or now, as much as we differ on this issue of the stageline, I know his strength has helped me get through these despairing days since I lost my father. But sometimes he makes me so angry, Mrs. Hallaway, I could cry. He's the one who lacks trust. He doesn't think me capable of making my own decisions."

"How long have you been in love with him, my dear?" Josie Hallaway asked.

The question was so unexpected Maggie started to stammer. "I never said I was in love with him."

"You don't have to."

Maggie slumped in defeat. "Is it that obvious?"

"I would say so, Margaret."

"Oh, Mrs. Hallaway, I feel so miserable. He doesn't look at me as a woman but as a responsibility."

"Love can be a very rocky road to travel, Margaret. But true love is worth every step of the journey."

"Was that true with you and Mr. Hallaway?"

"Oh, my dear, you have no idea how I agonized. When we were young, our parents were neighbors, and I used to sit on my porch hoping Henry would talk to me, but it seemed he wasn't even aware I existed. It took him five years to even remember my name."

"Is it always the woman whose love goes unrequited in the beginning?"

"I'm sure that isn't always the case. But when the day comes when he finally returns that love, you realize it was all worth that agonizing you did. You must be patient, Margaret, for if it's meant to be, it will happen. You see, my dear, it's not yours or Cole's decision to make. The outcome already has been decided by a much higher power." She reached across the table and patted Maggie's hand. "Patience, my dear. You must have patience."

Maggie sighed. "And how much patience did you have to have before Henry fell in love with you?"

For the next hour Maggie listened, enthralled, to the love story of Henry and Josie Hallaway.

"He must have been a wonderful man. I wish I could

have known him," Maggie said, when Josie finished. She picked up a framed photograph of the naval officer. "And how handsome he looked in his uniform."

"Yes, indeed. He was the handsomest graduate at the naval academy," Josie said.

She went over to the umbrella stand and pulled out an ebony walking stick with an ornamental silver knob. "I've always kept this right here where he put it."

"It's very elegant," Maggie said.

"I gave it to Henry on our first wedding anniversary. Oh, my dear, he looked so dapper when we'd go out walking." She giggled lightly. "Of course, Henry only used it when he was home on leave. He said the other officers would never let him live it down if they saw him with it." She smiled at Maggie and handed her the stick.

"Here, my dear, I want you to have it. It will aid you in getting around on your sore ankle."

"Oh, no, Mrs. Hallaway, I can't accept it," Maggie said. "It's too precious to you."

"The memory is precious, my dear. That I shall always keep."

By the time Cole arrived, as encouraging as the Hallaway love story was, Maggie was still faced with the issue of Cole's insistence on closing down the stageline.

To avoid a further argument with Cole, Maggie chose to ride in the coach. It gave her a chance to think without being too distracted by Cole, sitting up on the box, whistling.

What reason did he have for being so chipper?

Chapter 16

They hadn't gone more than a couple of miles when the stagecoach came to a shuddering stop, unseating Maggie. She climbed up from the floor and stuck her head out the window.

"What's wrong?"

Cole was standing with his arms raised in the air. Two men with bandannas over their faces were on horseback.

"What are you doing?" she said, aghast.

"Quiet, lady, or you'll be sorry," one of the men threatened.

"Are you holding up the stage?"

"Somebody's got to, lady. It looks like it's about to collapse any minute."

The remark sent Cole into laughter, and she glared at him.

"You two have to be the dumbest robbers in exis-

213

tence," she said. "We aren't carrying anything valuable. All we've got is mail."

"I wouldn't say that. You're kind of cute. Get out of that coach, lady, or I'll pull you out."

"Don't you touch her," Cole warned gallantly.

"I hope you're not as stupid as you look, mister," the outlaw said to him. "If I were you, buddy, I wouldn't try anything heroic."

"Don't threaten us," Maggie declared. "And for heaven's sake, Cole, put your arms down. These two don't even have any guns."

"Neither do you, so that makes us even," the man said.

"Well, I'm not afraid of either of you. So get out of here or I'll start screaming so loud they'll hear me all the way back in Noches."

He dismounted. The man was obviously the leader of the two, because his companion hadn't said a word the whole time.

"Lady, didn't I tell you to get out of that coach?" he snarled. "I hate to hurt you, but you're asking for it."

"I'm trying to, but I have a bad ankle." Maggie picked up the walking stick to aid her.

The other man spoke up. "Let me help you, ma'am." He dismounted quickly and hurried over to the coach.

His snarling partner grabbed the door handle and yanked it so hard the door came off in his hand.

Maggie's eyes rounded, and she gaped in astonishment. "Now look what you've done, you nasty man. You broke my stagecoach." She bopped him with the walking stick.

As he backed up, clutching his head, the man

tripped and fell. Maggie continued to strike him with the walking stick until the other man succeeded in pulling it out of her hand.

"Dammit, that hurt!" the leader of the two said. He looked at his hand. "I'm bleeding. Look, Josh. I'm bleeding."

"I told you this was a stupid idea, Zach," his partner in crime declared.

"Get out of here. Do you hear me?" She snatched the walking stick away from him and began to swing it like a cudgel.

"You're crazy, lady," the injured man declared. They climbed back on their horses. "I hope you know what you're letting yourself in for," he shouted to Cole as they rode off.

"Good riddance," she declared. "I wouldn't be too concerned about his parting threat, Cole. They were really quite inept. Well, we might as well go back to Noches and see if something can be done with the door."

"Why don't we just keep going on to Lawford?"

"Cole, if you don't turn this stagecoach around, I will."

"We could end up getting stuck there overnight again, Maggie."

"I'm sure there won't be a problem getting rooms this time."

Reconsidering, Cole decided it was a good idea. Once he got Maggie secured in a room, he'd find Josh and Zach. They'd have a lot to talk over now for sure. He started grinning. He could hear Josh already.

When they reached Noches, Cole drove directly to the hotel.

"Shouldn't we report the hold-up first?" Maggie said.

"I'd rather get you settled, so you can get off that ankle. Then I'll report the robbery to the sheriff and see what can be done about the door to the coach."

"But why register first? It may not be necessary to stay overnight."

Cole had already made up his mind to spend the night. He wanted more time with his cousins. Other than a few words about Jeb, they'd barely had time to talk about his folks and the rest of the family back home. So after getting them rooms, he picked Maggie up to carry her up the stairs.

"Cole, please stop treating me as if I'm an invalid. People are staring at us."

"Let them stare. They probably think we're newly-weds."

The subject was too near and dear to her heart for Maggie to pursue.

Once in her room, Cole put her down and gave her parting instructions. "This could take a couple hours, so why don't you lie down and take a nap. When I get back, we'll go to dinner."

Maggie didn't feel like taking a nap, but by now she'd learned the wisdom of trying to challenge Cole when he was in one of his parental moods.

As soon as he left, she lay down but failed to sleep. How was she expected to when her thoughts were plagued by Cole's decision to sell the stageline? After an hour she gave up trying.

Hoping to catch a sign of Cole, she moved to the window, and sat and watched the activity outside. The steady traffic below certainly didn't compare to Law-

ford, where one could sit for hours and never see anyone pass by.

But ultimately nothing was more boring than sitting
in a strange room without anything to do, so in defiance of Cole's orders, she decided to go down to the
lobby and get a newspaper. At least reading would
help to pass the time.

Maggie was about to return to her room when who
should she encounter coming down the stairs but
Gladys and Lyla. Their familiar faces were a welcome
sight to ward off her loneliness.

"Do you girls live here?"

"No, dearie," Gladys said. "Let's just say we had
some business to attend to upstairs."

"We thought you'd be on your way back to Lawford
by now," Lyla said.

"We did leave but had to come back. The stage was
held up. Can you believe that?"

The two women exchanged glances and then broke
into laughter. Maggie joined them. "It is humorous,
isn't it?" she said when their laughter subsided. "You
should have seen the bandits' surprise when they
found out we weren't carrying anything of value."

"Well, you have to admit they were handsome
enough," Lyla commented.

"I don't know. Their faces were covered. But they
were so dumb, they tried a hold-up without even having pistols."

That set all of them to laughing again.

Maggie suddenly ceased her laughter when Lyla's
earlier statement registered in her mind. Bewildered,
she asked, "How do you know what they looked
like?"

The question cut off their laughter, and Gladys replied, "Dearie, they were only funning with you."

"You know who they are?"

"Well, kind of," Lyla said sheepishly.

"What does that mean?" Maggie asked with annoyance.

"We weren't with them long enough to *really* get to know them," Gladys said. She poked Maggie with an elbow. "If you get what I mean."

"It wouldn't have done us any good one way or another, Gladys," the more pragmatic Lyla interjected. "If *you* get what I mean."

"Well, anyway, we heard them planning to rob the stage, just to try and scare you."

"Me? Why would they want to scare me? I've never seen either of them before."

"Cole put them up to it," Lyla said.

"Cole?"

"Yeah," Gladys interjected. "He's trying to convince you to sell the stageline and figured if you were scared enough, it might help you to see the light."

At that moment a loud outburst of laughter came from the barroom connected to the lobby. Maggie's head jerked up when she recognized Cole's laugh. Eyes blazing in anger, she went over to the door, followed by Gladys and Lyla. The three women peeked into the barroom.

"There they are," Gladys whispered. "At that table over in the corner.

"Yes, I see them." She could feel the hot flush of anger consuming her body from head to toe. "Who are those men he hired to do his sneaky, dirty, work?"

"Can't you tell by looking at them?" Lyla asked.

"The eyes, that dark hair. They all look enough alike to be brothers, but they're his cousins."

"So the whole family's as sneaky as he is," Maggie said. Another loud outburst from the corner table infuriated her more. "Hmmm. Well, we'll just see who has the last laugh. Which way to the sheriff's office, girls?"

Bufford Rutherford Pike had been sheriff of Noches from the time his father, then sheriff of Noches, had been gunned down in 1878 during a bank robbery. Legend had it that Billy the Kid had delivered the fatal bullet, but others claimed it was another member of the lawless gang he rode with.

Nevertheless, Bufford Pike had been able to capitalize on his father's claim to fame, resulting in an unopposed position of sheriff for the past twenty years.

Despite this, Sheriff Pike took the responsibilities of his position seriously. He was an honest and fair lawman.

As soon as the three women came through the door of the jail, he knew he was in for trouble. Leaning back in his chair, he gave them a tolerant smile.

"Howdy, Gladys, Lyla."

"Hello, Bufford," they said in unison.

"Hope you ladies have been good."

"Why, Sheriff, there ain't any better than me and Lyla," Gladys said with a flutter of eyelashes. That brought a laugh from the deputy standing in the corner. "Harvey can vouch for that, can't you, honey?"

"Sure can, Gladys," the deputy said. "None better."

"Well, what can I do for you?" Bufford asked.

"That's our line, Sheriff," Lyla said. The two women giggled.

Maggie stepped forward. "Sheriff Pike, I'm Margaret O'Shea. I operate the stageline between Lawford and Noches."

"How do you do, Miz O'Shea? Figured you weren't one of the working gals. Sorry to hear about your pa's passing. He was a good man."

"Thank you, Sheriff. He always spoke well of you, too."

"Now, what can I do for you, Miz O'Shea?"

"I came to report a robbery. The stage was held up earlier a couple of miles out of town."

Everyone in the county knew that the O'Shea stageline never carried anything more valuable than a pouch of mail. If someone had held up that stage, they had to have been not only the most desperate men in the county, but the dumbest.

"Anyone hurt, ma'am?"

"No, thank goodness, but the stage was damaged and the incident was very frightening. I was alone and . . . and . . ." She lowered her eyes. "One of the men tried to force his attentions on me."

Sheriff Bufford Pike jumped to his feet. No man would get by with insulting a decent woman as long as he was sheriff of the county. He turned to his deputy. "There's still plenty of light to pick up their trail. Round up a posse, Harv."

"That won't be necessary, Sheriff Pike. The three men who did it are in the hotel's barroom this very minute."

"I thought there was only two," Gladys said.

Maggie looked at her. "No, Gladys, don't you remember? Three of them were involved in the crime," she said through clenched teeth.

"Did you and Lyla witness the robbery?" Bufford asked.

"No, Bufford. Me and Lyla's just offering Miz O'Shea a helping hand. Her having a sore ankle and all."

"Thought you said nobody was hurt during the hold-up, Miz O'Shea."

"My ankle was sore before the hold-up."

"You mean they attacked an injured woman?" His indignation rose. "Let's go and round up them bastards, Harv. Excuse the language, ma'am. I just get hot under the collar when I hear of a fine lady like you suffering at the hands of varmints like that." He clenched his lips together. "You said in the barroom of the hotel."

Maggie nodded. "I'll come along and point them out to you." She watched, appalled, when the sheriff went over and picked a rifle off a rack. "What are you going to do with that rifle?"

"I hope nothing."

"You aren't going to shoot them, are you?" Maggie asked, feeling a rise of panic. What had she done? She now had cause to regret her impulsiveness. Getting even was one thing, but she didn't want anybody hurt.

"Bring along an extra pair of cuffs, Harv. We'll probably need them."

The three women hurried after the sheriff and his deputy as fast as Maggie's injured ankle would allow her. When they reached the barroom, Sheriff Pike pulled Maggie aside.

"Once you point them out, I want you ladies to get out of the line of fire."

"Sir, they are not armed. I will not point them out to you unless you promise not to use any weapons."

He sighed deeply. "Miz O'Shea, you're a fine woman with a charitable heart. As long as they don't resist arrest, there'll be no violence. We promise, don't we, Harv?"

"You're the sheriff, Sheriff," Harv replied.

"And what do you intend to do with them?" Maggie asked.

"Lock 'em up for now. Tomorrow morning you can come in and sign a complaint."

"Excellent!" Maggie declared, relieved to hear her idea for revenge would not become a disaster. A night locked up in a cell would be just deserts for Cole MacKenzie and his worthless cousins. She pointed to the corner table. "It's those three men over there."

"Thank you. Now get going, ladies."

Maggie had no intention of leaving. She wanted the pleasure of seeing Cole MacKenzie and his idiot cousins hauled off to the calaboose.

"Howdy, boys," the sheriff said when he approached the table.

Seeing his badge, Cole offered his hand. "How do you do, Sheriff?

"Pike. Bufford Pike." He ignored Cole's offer of a handshake. "Don't recall seeing you boys around before. You from these parts?"

"No, Sheriff, we're just passing through," Josh said.

"I don't want any trouble, boys, but I've had a complaint about you fellas. I'm gonna have to arrest you."

"If you're referring to that fight earlier, we didn't start it, Sheriff," Cole said. "And I paid for the damage to the place."

"Ain't heard about that. Reckon I can add that to the complaint, though."

"Then what are you arresting us for?" Zach asked.

"Charge is robbery and attempted rape."

"What!" all three men exclaimed.

"Let's go. You boys can either come peaceable or at gunpoint."

"Sheriff, you've got the wrong men. We aren't carrying weapons, so there's no call for talk of guns," Josh assured him.

"Yep, that's what they all say. Get to your feet, boys, and don't try anything that would force me to hurt you."

The MacKenzies exchanged glances. "Just stay calm," Josh advised, rising to his feet. "We can straighten this out without anyone getting hurt."

"You're talking sense, boy," Pike said, cuffing him.

"The two of you are going to look like fools when you find out how wrong you are," Zach warned him as the deputy put handcuffs on his wrists.

"And the real criminals are getting away while you're wasting time arresting the wrong people," Cole added when the sheriff handcuffed his wrists behind him.

"I don't hold my job by arresting the wrong people, boy," Pike informed him. "Let's go."

"This is ridiculous," Cole complained when the cell door clanged shut behind him in the jail. "We are not criminals and can prove it."

"I checked your wallets, boys. There ain't a bit of identification in any one of them."

"My name's Josh MacKenzie. I'm from Calico, Texas," Josh informed him from his cell. "I've been a Texas Ranger and a Pinkerton agent. You can check with either of those offices to confirm it. These men are my cousins Zachary MacKenzie and Cole MacKenzie. Both have served with the Rangers. We are law-abiding citizens, Sheriff, and you've made a big mistake."

"If I have, I'll be the first to say so, boy."

"Why don't you wire Sheriff McGraw in Calico?" Zach suggested from the cell next to Cole's. "Our parents own the Triple M down there. All our fathers were even Texas Rangers."

"And mine was also a sheriff in California," Cole added.

"So you boys are from the Triple M," Pike said.

"Yes, have you heard of it?" Cole asked.

"Heard of the ranch, but so have a lot of folks here. That ain't proof that you are who you say."

"If you don't believe us, send a wire to my father, Luke MacKenzie, in Calico. He'll confirm what we're saying," Josh said.

"Well, I ain't ever been accused of not being fair." Pike sat down and wrote out a message. "Harv, take this over to the telegraph office and send it off."

As soon as the deputy left, Pike said, "Why don't you boys just relax and settle down for the night? It's likely we won't hear anything back till morning."

"I know someone who can prove who I am," Cole said. "She's right here in town."

"I ain't taking the word of any whore, boy."

"You don't have to. I'm her legal guardian. Her name is Margaret O'Shea. She owns the stageline and is registered at the hotel right now."

"Zat so?" Pike said. "She's your witness, huh?"

"Yes, I've been driving the stage for her."

"Zat so? Well, boy, I've been a sheriff for nigh onto twenty years now, and I ain't heard such bullshit in my life. Emilio Morales is the driver of the O'Shea stage, and Miz Margaret O'Shea is the gal who's filing the complaint against you. 'Night, boys."

With that, Sheriff Bufford Rutherford Pike blew out the lamp in the cellblock and returned to his office.

Chapter 17

⌒⌒◯◯⌒⌒

The morning haze hovering above the peaks of the Sangre de Cristo shrouded the mountain range in a quilt of white fluff.

Sleepy-eyed and grumbling, Ephraim Pearl, Noches stationmaster, stepped out on the platform, his sleep having been disturbed when the freight train of the Rocky Mountain Central Railroad, which usually raced through with a whistle blast every morning at six on the dot, came to an unexpected grinding halt at the depot.

What was even more of interest to him were the three men who stepped out of the caboose. With a short whistle blast, the train rolled on. The whole thing hadn't taken more than thirty seconds, and had he not gotten up to pee, he might have slept right through it.

The three men were tall, and despite aging, carried themselves with an air that the innocent could not help

but admire, the guilty, fear. And their lined faces chron-
icled the history of Texas. He'd bet a full month's
wages they were Rangers or had been.

" 'Morning," he said.

" 'Morning," one responded. The other two men
nodded and walked on by. "Which way to the jail?"

"Two blocks straight down the street."

"Thanks."

"Yep, Rangers all right," Ephraim mumbled as he
stepped inside. "Somebody's in for a heap of trouble."

Sheriff Pike had set up a table outside Cole MacKenzie's cell, and the two men were playing chess. Bufford
loved to play chess. Trouble was in his line of work it
was difficult to meet a man who could play it. So neither man had slept much during the night, because
Bufford had to take advantage of the opportunity
when it presented itself.

Cole MacKenzie was not pleased with the arrangement, but he hoped it would keep the sheriff in good
enough spirits to listen to reason whenever that deceiving, lying, trouble-making Maggie O'Shea showed up.

When the bell above the outside door tinkled, Bufford got up from his chair. "Now, who the hell is that at
this time of the morning?" he grumbled, "Don't make
your move until I come back," he said, and thumped
out of the cellblock.

Cole stood up and stretched. Trying to play chess
with his arms through the bars of a cell wasn't the most
comfortable activity. He glanced around at the dingy
jail and saw that Zach was sound asleep in the other
cell. Josh had begun to stir.

How in hell did he get himself and his cousins into

such a mess? It was only meant to make her see reason. He couldn't wait to get his hands around Maggie's throat. This time she'd gone too far.

The cellblock door clanged open, and, yawning, Cole sat down, prepared to resume the game. He jumped to his feet at the sight of the man who entered. "Uncle Luke!"

"Cole," Luke MacKenzie replied, nodding at his nephew.

Josh bolted to his feet and grinned sheepishly at his father. "Hi, Dad."

The voices were enough to wake Zach. He shook his head to make sure he was awake. "Am I dreaming?"

"You damn better hope you are," Flint MacKenzie replied to his son. "What are you doing behind bars?"

But Cole's attention was on the third man who entered. "Hi, Dad."

"Hello, son," Cleve MacKenzie replied.

For a long moment Cole just stared at his father. Pride, love, understanding were all wrapped up in the way his father said the simple, three-letter word "son." Cole had felt this from the time he was born. Do grown men cry? He wanted to. How he loved this man. And it had been so long since he'd seen him. The thought wrenched at his heart. He could tell by the look in his father's eyes that he was having the same emotional reaction.

"Dad, I can explain."

"Later. I'm just glad to see you, son, even if you are behind bars. We got here as soon as we could. Dave Kincaid arranged for us to be picked up by one of their freight trains coming through."

"It's good to have cousins who own railroads," Cole

said, trying to sound lighter than he felt. "How's Mom doing, Dad?"

"Worried sick about both of her sons," Cleve said.

"Any more word about Jeb?"

"Not yet."

After Josh had made an explanation to his father and uncles, Luke spoke to the sheriff.

"Sheriff Pike, do you really think it's necessary to keep these boys behind bars?"

"Got no choice, Mr. MacKenzie. Robbery and rape are pretty serious charges."

"Rape?" all three fathers shouted in disbelief.

"You've got the wrong men, Sheriff," Flint declared with indisputable certainty.

When all of the men started protesting at the same time, Cleve MacKenzie gave a loud whistle. They all stopped shouting and stared at him. "Quiet!" Cleve said. "Sheriff Pike, why don't we all settle down and discuss this calmly and quietly? There's obviously been a big mistake, and I'm certain it can be all cleared up."

" 'Fraid not, Mr. MacKenzie. Your son appears to be a fine young man. Friendly, even-tempered, and a fine chess player to boot. But the little gal made a positive identification."

Flint always had a shorter fuse than his brothers. Now near to bursting, he shouted, "Little gal? You ain't expecting us to believe they raped a child."

"She's not a girl, Uncle Flint. She's a woman," Cole said.

"And she's lethal, Dad," Zach added.

"Sheriff, neither my son nor my nephews are rapists," Luke said. "I'd like to speak to the young lady who made that charge. She is obviously confused."

"What now?" the sheriff declared, when the bell tinkled again. "You'd swear it was high noon, and the sun's just rose." He strode out.

"The girl's Maggie O'Shea, Dad. Just because we faked a robbery, Maggie had us arrested to get even. I swear that's the truth."

"I believe you, Cole. O'Shea? Isn't that the girl in Lawford you wrote us about?"

"Yes. The one whose father died."

"And made you her guardian."

Cole nodded.

"What's this rape charge all about?" Flint asked.

"That's bullshit, Uncle Flint. She probably added that just to make the charges worse."

"Worse then a stage robbery?" Luke asked, disgusted. "I want to talk to this girl."

At that moment Bufford Pike returned to the cellblock accompanied by the woman in question. All six MacKenzies stared at her, until Zach said, "Run for cover, Dad. At least we're safe behind these bars."

"Maggie, don't you think this has gone far enough?" Cole said. "Thanks to you, we've been locked up in these cells all night."

"Young lady, I don't understand this whole thing," Luke said sternly. "You've made some serious charges against these men."

"They did hold up the stage," Maggie said in her own defense.

"But we didn't use any guns, Dad," Josh spoke up.

Luke was beginning to lose his patience as much as Flint had done already. He gave his son a sharp look. "It was a stupid thing to do, Josh."

"Tell that to Cole," Josh replied.

Cole jumped in to defend himself, and within seconds the three cousins were shouting and adding opinions while Maggie tried to state her case to their fathers.

Once again they all began to talk at once: Maggie and Cole spatting with each other, Flint and Luke reprimanding Josh and Zach, Cleve trying to reason with Bufford, and Bufford trying to quiet them all down.

Suddenly another shrill whistle split the air, but it hadn't come from Cleve. Lyla stood in the open doorway of the cellblock. "Hey, what's all the noise about in here?"

"We heard you all the way outside," Gladys added, pushing in behind her.

The cellblock was now filled solidly, with no room to move around.

"This ain't no Elks' convention, ladies," Pike said. "So I'd appreciate you getting out of here."

"No, let them stay, Sheriff Pike," Cole said. "They're our witnesses. They heard us plan the robbery as a joke."

Bufford Pike regarded Lyla and Gladys with a critical eye. "Is that true, ladies?"

"Sure is, Sheriff. We heard it all."

"They were just funning," Lyla added.

"Well, I didn't think it was so funny," Maggie sputtered.

Still trying to resolve the whole thing, the sheriff asked Maggie, "What did they steal?"

"Nothing. There *was* nothing to steal or they would have," Maggie said.

Cole would not hear of it. "We knew that before we even planned it."

"Pretty hard to make a case, ma'am, when no

weapons were used in a holdup where nothing was stolen."

"She was the one with the weapon," Zach shouted. "And I've got the bruises to prove it."

"Son, don't tell me you let a little gal like that beat you up," Flint said.

"What was I supposed to do? Hit her back?"

Maggie was in a snit. "I wouldn't have hit you if you hadn't broken my stagecoach."

"I didn't break that pile of rubbish," Zach shouted. "The damn door fell off when I opened it."

"To assist you out, I might add," Josh piped up, in defense of his cousin.

"Good Lord, Sheriff," Zach insisted, "if Josh hadn't intervened, that crazy girl would have beaten me to death."

The sheriff looked dubious. "You expect me to believe that little gal beat you up?"

"She was pounding me with a walking stick with a metal top. What do you think?"

"Sounds to me like she's the one who should be behind bars, Sheriff," Luke said, tongue in cheek. "Attempted murder is a serious crime."

"I'd say she had good cause," Lyla spoke up in defense of Maggie.

"Gotta agree, Bufford," Gladys said. "As handsome as these fellas are, it was a dirty trick to pull on the little gal."

"Didn't I tell you, ladies, you've got no call here?"

"We're witnesses, Bufford," Gladys said with a dramatic sweep of her feather boa.

Bufford shoved away the feathered end of it that landed across his face and peered at Maggie. "From what I can tell, Miz O'Shea, it weren't no robbery if nothing was stolen. Now what about your charge of rape?"

"Rape?" Maggie asked, perplexed. "I didn't say anything about rape."

"What did I tell you, Sheriff?" Cole shouted victoriously.

"You told me that boy forced his attentions on you."

"He did—has—I mean does," Maggie said. "From the time I've known him, he's been giving me orders and telling me what I should do and shouldn't do."

"Some gals have all the luck," Gladys murmured to Lyla.

"Maggie, I'm your guardian. That's my responsibility," Cole declared.

"Well, I'm fed up with it, and I'm not standing for any more. Do you hear me, Cole MacKenzie?" she screeched.

"Dammit, Maggie, will you drop those stupid charges so we can get out of here?" Cole said.

Once again everyone started talking at once. Accusations of hysterical girls, immature boys, and even a crooked sheriff ricocheted off the walls like stray bullets.

Bufford cast his eyes heavenward and reached for the key to the cells.

The entourage shifted en masse to the outer office. "I ain't gonna put any cuffs on you boys, but you're not free to go," Bufford said. "I'm gonna let Judge Gardner decide what to do with you."

"I know the judge," Maggie said.

"You been arrested before, Miz O'Shea?" Bufford asked, with a leery eye in her direction.

"No, of course not. I've met him socially. Judge Gardner is the godfather of a close friend, Keith Lawford." She smirked at Cole. "He's Ben Lawford's closest friend and has been a mentor to Keith. You can be certain his judgment will be fair."

"Oh, that's great. The deck's already stacked against us, boys," Cole complained.

Amidst the rumble of grumbling from most of them and the nonstop squabbling between Maggie and Cole, the crowd followed the sheriff to the courthouse.

Court was in session when they entered, and the judge's gavel pounded repeatedly, calling for order, as they shuffled in. He looked sternly down at them from the height of his bench.

"What's going on, Sheriff Pike?"

"Excuse me, Your Honor, but I have a problem here and I need your advice."

"Very well, but quiet those people, or I'll have them ejected from the courtroom."

"Ejected, hell," Cole mumbled. "I'll gladly leave willingly." The remark brought murmurs of agreement from the other MacKenzies.

"I said quiet!" Judge Gardner declared, reinforcing the command with another forceful bang of the gavel.

As soon as he finished with the case in progress, the judge waved them to come forward.

"Sheriff, will you explain what this is all about? I don't have any other case scheduled."

"No, Judge, I ain't got no signed complaint."

"Then what are you doing in my court?"

"Miz O'Shea here claims three of these men robbed her stagecoach."

"Well, did they or didn't they?"

"That's the question, Judge. Nothing was stolen, and they didn't carry weapons."

"She did, Judge," Zach piped up.

"Young man, refrain from any comments unless I speak directly to you. It's a pleasure to see you again, Miss O'Shea. How's my godson?"

"Very well, Your Honor."

"You and him talking marriage yet?" he asked.

"Well, sir, my father died recently, and I have not had time to think about marriage," Maggie said.

"Sorry to hear about your father. But when the time comes, I hope I get an invitation to the wedding."

"When the time comes, Your Honor," Maggie answered diplomatically.

"Your Honor, I object," Cole said.

"Are you the defense attorney?"

"No, but I object on the grounds that you'd be prejudiced, Judge, since you know the plaintiff and the godfather of the man who hopes to marry her."

Judge Gardner leaned on his arms and peered down at Cole. "You're walking on thin ice, boy, so tread lightly."

"Your Honor, I'm one of the defendants, but I'm also the legal guardian of the plaintiff and the trustee of her assets, one of which is the stageline. At the time of the robbery, I was actually the driver of the stage. No robbery occurred. As a matter of fact, the other defendants are my cousins. Miss O'Shea resents my authority and is spitefully making the accusation when she knows there actually was no criminal intent."

The judge looked at Sheriff Pike. "Who are these defendants?"

"I'm Cole MacKenzie, Your Honor."

Cleve stepped forward. "And I'm his father, Cleve MacKenzie."

"Andrew Zachary MacKenzie, Your Honor," Zach said.

"My son. Flint MacKenzie's the name."

Josh stepped up next to his cousins and uncles. "Josh MacKenzie, Judge Gardner."

"And I'm his father, Luke MacKenzie."

"Are you the same MacKenzies from the Triple M down in Texas?" he asked Luke.

"Yes, we are," Luke said.

"I've been a judge too long not to recognize the names of Luke, Flint, and Cleve MacKenzie, gentlemen." He glared at the sheriff. "Dammit, Bufford, you ought to know better. These three men have distinguished themselves as Texas Rangers."

"As have our three sons who stand before you accused of robbery, Your Honor," Luke said.

"And our accuser is the woman your godson intends to marry," Cole reminded him.

"I understand," the judge said grimly. "Tell me, son, did you and your cousins hold up that stage?"

"It was a joke, Your Honor. There was no actual hold-up. It was like jumping out and saying boo."

"Uh-huh. Like saying boo," the judge said, nodding slowly.

"That's right, sir."

The judge turned to Gladys. "Nice to see you again, Miss Divine."

"Thank you, Judge," Gladys said.

"And you, too, Miss Loving."

"The same to you, Your Honor," Lyla replied.

"Haven't seen you ladies before the court for some time. What have you got to do with this case?"

"We're witnesses, Judge," Gladys said. This time Sheriff Pike sidestepped away and avoided the boa as it whipped past his face.

"Witnesses to what?"

The question set up a maelstrom of explanations, with everyone trying to talk over the others. The clap of the judge's gavel reverberated like thunder in the courtroom, silencing the voices.

"All of you go and sit down while I come to a decision," he ordered.

Bufford stepped forward. "Uh, Judge, may I speak to you for a moment?"

The judge stood up and leaned over the bench, and Bufford whispered in his ear and then returned to his seat.

"I understand there's still another charge," Judge Gardner said.

Cole jumped to his feet. "Judge, it was proven there was no rape. Miss O'Shea said the sheriff misunderstood her."

"Rape? First I heard of that."

Maggie spoke up. "Your Honor, I assure you that was a misunderstanding."

"And was it a misunderstanding when you boys busted up the Bonanza? Miss O'Shea and Mr. MacKenzie, sit down."

"I just want to say, Your Honor, that I was the victim there," Cole said. "I was sitting alone eating lunch and minding my own business when these five drunken cowboys started a fight with me. It was a blessing my cousins showed up, or who knows what might have happened to me."

"I'd hate to think," the judge said dryly.

"Even though it wasn't our fault, Judge, I paid for the damage just the same."

"Mr. MacKenzie, didn't I tell you to sit down and be quiet? Frankly I have a problem visualizing you as a victim. Now sit down, or I'll charge you with contempt of court."

Cole sat down, and they all remained quiet, staring at the lone man on the bench. Finally the judge cleared his throat and motioned for them to come forward.

"From what I can tell, we've got two crimes here."

"Judge, even Maggie admits there was no rape attempt," Cole said.

Gardner banged his gavel and then shook it at Cole. "I'm not telling you again, young man, to wait and speak when you're spoken to."

"Yes, sir," Cole said.

"Now, as I was saying, as far as I can tell, there's been two crimes committed.

"As to the charge of robbery, I find you three men guilty. Just because there was no actual robbery does not change the fact that you made a mockery of what is considered a serious crime.

"And as for you, young lady," he said, addressing Maggie, "even though I'm looking forward to the wedding, I have to find you guilty of deliberately lying to and misleading an officer of the law just to satisfy a whim. That, too, is making a mockery of the law." He pulled out a pocket watch and studied it.

"According to my watch, it's 9:25. The southbound train pulls in at 1:15. I figure most of you can clear out of town on it. The rest can start walking, 'cause any of you still in town after that will be locked up. That means any of you—plantiffs, defendants, and their relatives."

"But that might be impossible, Your Honor. We're having the stagecoach repaired. It may not be ready by then."

"You always have this trouble listening to orders, boy? You just better hope it'll be ready."

"Judge, what about witnesses? Lyla and me live here," Gladys said. "Do we have to leave, too?"

"I'll make an exception of you and Miss Loving, but the rest of you I want out of Noches. Now get out of my court before I charge you all with disturbing the peace."

Judge Frank Gardner fortified the declaration with a final bang of the gavel.

Chapter 18

❦

Cole checked to make sure the stagecoach would be completed on time, then he and Maggie joined the MacKenzies at the diner. Whatever grievance they might have had with her had long been put behind them. Even Cole no longer seemed angry with her. And surrounded by these tall Texans, Maggie had never felt so protected in her life.

Too soon it became time to depart, and she and Cole accompanied them to the depot. A whistle sounded, heralding the arrival of the train, and while the cousins were exchanging the usual handshakes and backslapping, Luke and Flint came over and said good-bye to Maggie.

"The gates of the Triple M will always be open to you, Maggie," Luke said.

"Even if you have to shoot our nephew, we'll understand," the laconic Flint MacKenzie added.

When they left, Maggie stepped back and watched Cole's farewell to them. She could see how much he wanted to be with them. Her heart went out to him. He'd been thrust into a situation that was not of his choosing and appeared to hate it more each day. Yet his loyalty to Pop's dying wish prevented him from joining his family.

She wished that at the times they had their clashes she remembered that loyalty to her father was why Cole remained in Lawford. But unfortunately she always allowed her feelings for Cole to cloud the issue. She never saw his objections as proper and logical but rather as a betrayal by the man she loved.

As she waited, she saw two men disembark from the train. Their eastern three-piece suits and derby hats looked ludicrous amid the tall, western-clad MacKenzies, who had begun boarding.

Zach came over to her and offered his hand. "No hard feelings?" he said with an engaging grin.

"No, of course not." Maggie smiled sheepishly. "I'm sorry for hitting you the way I did. I really thought you were a desperado."

"I had it coming. I hope we'll see you on the Triple M soon. I know my wife, Rose, will want to meet you as soon as I tell her this whole story. I reckon more than once she probably had a mind to whack me with something harder than a walking stick." He offered a boyish grin. "We're expecting another child in a few months."

"That's wonderful, Zach."

"I'm sure we'll see you before then. Good-bye, Maggie, and don't let that cousin of mine ride roughshod over you. His intentions are good. Trouble is, he just doesn't understand women." Then, laughing, he kissed her on the cheek and departed.

No sooner had Zach left than Josh came over to her. "Until we meet again, Maggie. And I hope that will be soon."

"I suspect it might be, Josh, if Cole has his way."

"No matter how you may feel now, I think you'll like the Triple M, Maggie. My wife was raised in the East, but she took to ranch life as if she'd been born to it. You couldn't blast her off the ranch now if you tried. We're expecting another child in a couple months."

"My goodness, Zach just told me the same thing about himself. Is there a scheduled breeding time on the Triple M?"

She covered her mouth in embarrassment. Such an indelicate statement would never have passed the lips of Miss Margaret. Would have shocked the ears of Keith Lawford. But they sounded natural coming from the mouth of Maggie O'Shea. And she was beginning to see that Maggie O'Shea was a much more comfortable person to be around. At least to Josh MacKenzie, because it appeared he wasn't shocked in the least, but chuckled in amusement.

"My wife and Zach's wife are real close. They were Harvey Girls together. It would really be something if their babies were born around the same time."

"Well, I hope everything goes well for both of them."

"Maggie, I can't leave without apologizing for my part in that hoax we tried to play on you. But I gotta give you credit, you turned the tables on us."

"It all seems ridiculous now, doesn't it?"

"It *was* ridiculous, but we're kind of a crazy family." He grinned. "But I reckon you've already figured that out for yourself." Josh enveloped her in a hug. "Take care, Maggie, and we'll see you soon."

Cleve MacKenzie came over and gently grasped her by the shoulders. Looking up into his eyes was like looking into Cole's. He had the same warm sapphire gaze. "Good-bye for now, Maggie."

"I hope you'll hear some good news soon about your missing son, Mr. MacKenzie," Maggie said.

"I have to believe we will. I know that one day both of my sons will be home. And I'm looking forward to your coming. You'll be a fine addition to the family, Maggie O'Shea. I can't wait until Adee meets you. She's been so anxious to see Cole settle down."

"I don't think I'll have anything to do with that."

When his dark eyes glowed with warmth, she saw his age was no consideration. He was an incredibly handsome man. What kind of woman had won the heart of Cleve MacKenzie? She would have to be quite extraordinary.

"I think you will, Maggie O'Shea. I think you'll have *everything* to do with it. I've sensed a change in Cole that his mother and I have been waiting to see. He may not be aware of it, but it has happened. In matters of the heart, women are much smarter than men. Isn't that right?" he said with a wise smile.

Maggie's cheeks burned in a blush. "If you expect me to admit I'm in love with your son, Mr. MacKenzie, you're . . ." She intended to deny it, but the perception in his eyes would see through the weak lie. "You're right. But I'm afraid it's hopeless, sir. You see, I've been in love with Cole since I was sixteen, and he just isn't interested in me."

"Have you told him how you feel, Maggie?"

"Heavens, no! He'd only laugh." She forced a smile. "But for your sake and your wife's, I hope one day he does meet a woman he can love." She dropped her eyes to disguise her heartache.

Cleve tucked a finger under her chin and tipped it up, forcing her to meet his gaze filled with the wisdom that age and experience had brought to him. "He has already, my dear."

Kissing her on the cheek, he hurried away as the train whistle sounded its warning blast for departure.

As if tempted to chase after it, for a long moment Cole remained on the platform and watched the train puff away. Then he turned around and came over to her.

"Well, we'd better get started back to Lawford."

Maggie could see how much saying good-bye to his family had affected Cole, so she opted to ride back in the coach. If it hadn't been for her, he'd probably have been back on the Triple M right now. With such a caring family, she couldn't understand why he'd ever left it to begin with. Nothing on earth would ever have lured her away from them were she as fortunate to have had such a family.

Cole was just pulling out when the two men she remembered seeing at the depot rushed up to the stage. After a short conversation with Cole and an exchange of money, they climbed into the coach, tipped their hats to her, and then settled back on the opposite seat.

Although she had purchased a novel to help pass the time, Maggie could not concentrate on the printed words. Her thoughts wandered back to these last few hours spent with the MacKenzies.

What an incredible family! Throughout the meal she

had garnered bits and pieces about the family's history. Despite their joking and teasing with one another, the loyalty, love, and honor among them was apparent. Being an only child and raised motherless, the thought of being nurtured in the loving bosom of uncles, aunts, and cousins sounded like paradise to Maggie. She envied Cole. Then she chastised herself. She'd had Pop.

The men were mulling over drawings and speaking in low tones. Maggie tried to avoid listening to their conversation, but her curiosity was piqued enough to wonder why they'd be on their way to Lawford. Had they taken the wrong coach?

"Excuse me, gentlemen, do you have business in Lawford?"

"Yes, we do, madam." They went back to their muted conversation.

Well, so much for sticking your nose where it doesn't belong, Maggie. She went back to trying to solve her own problem, her continual running battle with Cole—saving the stageline.

In an effort to resume reading, she turned again to the novel. The rocking motion soon lulled her into drowsiness, so she leaned her head back and closed her eyes. It felt pleasant and restful after yesterday's hectic activity.

The men continued speaking in low tones and occasionally she'd overhear a word or two as she slipped into a light sleep.

Suddenly her eyes popped open. Had she been dreaming, or had she heard the word "Timberline." She sat up straight again. Surely she'd been dreaming.

The men rolled up their drawings, and in a short time their light snores filled the coach. Sighing, Maggie opened the novel again. Why hadn't she ridden up front in the box?

Upon arriving, Cole saw men draping bunting on the buildings.

"What's going on?" he asked Maggie as soon as the two men got their luggage and went into the hotel.

"Oh, I forgot. Tomorrow's the Founder's Day celebration."

She was more concerned about what she'd overheard on the stagecoach and immediately told him about it.

"Are you sure you weren't sleeping, Maggie?"

"No, I'm not. That's the problem."

"I'd like to get a look at those drawings. That would help," he said. "Maybe Pop set all this up and they came to meet with him. So if it's something to do with Timberline, they're sure to try and contact you. Why didn't you tell them who you were?"

"I tried to find out why they were coming to Lawford, but they cut me off. Then later, I didn't know if I'd heard right, and it would have been very embarrassing if I'd been wrong and was caught as an eavesdropper. Didn't they give you an indication of what their business is here in Lawford?" she asked.

"Nope, they paid for their fare and that was it."

"That's what I mean. They weren't too friendly."

He dug into his pocket and handed her some money. "Well, at least the stageline finally earned something today."

"I'd like to discuss that very issue with you, Cole."

"We've had our last discussion on that issue, Maggie." He climbed up again and drove the horses to the stable.

Maggie could tell that this time there'd be no changing Cole's mind. "I'm going to need some divine intervention, Lord," she murmured.

"Well, there you are, gal," Ellie said as soon as Maggie walked through the door. "You sit down and tell me what's going on here. That telegram you sent only told me enough to whet my appetite."

Ellie poured them each a cup of coffee and then sat and listened while Maggie told her the whole story of what had ensued when Cole and two of his cousins faked a robbery to persuade her to go along with his decision to sell the stageline.

"And you had them arrested for that?" Ellie declared, when Maggie finished. "Shame on you, gal."

"Well, I didn't think we'd all end up before the judge or I wouldn't have done it. And the last thing I expected to happen was that Cole's father and uncles would show up."

"What are they like?"

Her smile widened in remembrance. "Ellie, they are really nice. I think I could learn to worship his father. And his two uncles are wonderful, so are his cousins for that matter, even if they were part of that hoax. All of the men have served in the Texas Rangers at one time or another. And did you know that Cole's grandfather died at the Alamo and his grandmother raised her three sons alone?"

Maggie's eyes filled with sadness. "But, Ellie, it's so sad. She and Luke's wife, he's the eldest of the three brothers, were murdered during a Comanchero attack on the ranch while the sons were at war. When Luke came back, he had to track down his son, Josh, who was only two years old at the time of the attack, all the way into Mexico. He became a lawman in California and remarried when Josh was six years old. A soft smile tipped the corners of her mouth. "Josh is the eldest of the cousins. He's so nice, Ellie. He married a Harvey Girl, whom he'd been hired to find. Oh, I forgot to tell you Josh was a Pinkerton agent then. Anyway, she was a rich girl from out East who had run away from home, and when he tracked her down, they fell in love with each other." She reached across and covered Ellie's hand. "Isn't that romantic?"

"It don't get no romanticker than that," Ellie said, amused.

"Now, Uncle Flint is the second brother. He's the most reticent of the three. Kind of grumpy on the outside, but you can sense that inside he's as soft as a marshmallow." Her eyes rounded with excitement. "Ellie, you won't believe how he met his wife."

"I bet I'm about to find out," Ellie replied.

"Uncle Flint saved her when the wagon train she was traveling with was destroyed by a Comanche attack. Isn't that incredible? Zach is Flint's son." Maggie grinned. "He's got a lot of mischief in him, you can tell. And guess what, he married a Harvey Girl, too. He met her when he was working undercover as an outlaw. She thought he was a no-good drifter but fell in love with him anyway. That just goes to prove that there's no telling whom you'll fall in love with. But this is the unbelievable part; she's the best friend of the Harvey Girl who Josh married. And she never knew Zach and Josh were cousins. You see, Zach couldn't reveal his true identity to her because he had infiltrated this outlaw gang.

"And I can't say enough about his father, Cleve MacKenzie. Ellie, he's handsome—of course, they all are—and he's soft-spoken, kind, and very caring."

Once again her eyes clouded with sadness. "Right now, his youngest son is missing in action in Cuba."

"So Cole's mother is Cuban? That explains why he has that good-looking coloring."

"No, his mother's actually of Spanish descent but born and raised in Texas. Her name is Adrianna. Isn't that a beautiful name? Mr. MacKenzie's eyes glow with love every time he mentions her."

"Sounds to me like you're gonna like living among these MacKenzies."

"Cole said that as soon as he wraps up the loose ends here we're going to live on the Triple M whether I want to or not."

"My guess is now that you've met a few of 'em, the thought don't seem as bad to you as it once did."

Maggie grasped her hand. "Only if you come with us, Ellie. I won't go there without you."

"Cole already talked to me about it, honey. He said I'm welcome to come."

"You will, won't you, Ellie?" Maggie pleaded. "I couldn't bear it without you."

"Darlin', I'm getting on in years to be thinking of getting uprooted."

"Ellie, you've given the O'Sheas your love and care practically your whole life. It's time now to let me do the same for you. Promise me, Ellie, you'll come. Cole won't let me stay here. In three years, I'll be free, and then we can come back."

"'Course I'm coming with you. You don't think I'd let you go off alone, do you?"

Maggie got up and threw her arms around the woman. "I love you, Ellie."

"I love you, too, darlin'. Now get out and let me get to making these pies for tomorrow's celebration."

"Do you know that with all that's been on my mind, I entirely forgot about Founder's Day. I'd better get to the bank, since it'll be closed tomorrow for the celebration."

Before departing, Maggie sat down and removed the bandage from her ankle. She'd had enough of it. She tested her weight on it, and the ankle felt fine.

Satisfied, she hurried to the bank to deposit the money Cole had given her from the two ticket sales and find out how much money remained in the account.

Both Keith and Cole had told her the balance was low when Pop died, and since then, what with feed bills and a new wheel for the coach, she hoped the account was still solvent.

"Howdy, Margaret," Ben Lawford's young nephew greeted her when she entered. "What can I do for you today?"

"I'd like to make a deposit, Jimmy. And will you tell me the balance in the account?"

"Sure will. How have you been doing since your pa died, Margaret?"

"I'm getting along. Thank goodness I have friends like Ellie and Keith. And Cole MacKenzie's been a big help, too."

"Yeah, I figured as much when he came in and deposited money in the account."

This was news to Maggie. "I didn't realize he'd done that. How much did he deposit?"

Jim opened a ledger book to the O'Shea account and

showed it to her. "It was this two-hundred-dollar deposit, Maggie. Ain't been a deposit made that large from the time Mick opened the account."

"Thank you, Jimmy."

"Here's your receipt for today's deposit," he said.

"Yes, thank you," Maggie said, dazed. Still stunned by the revelation that Cole had deposited his own money, because she had begged him to keep the stageline operating.

To keep a dream alive she had blinded herself to the obvious.

She left the bank, and as hard as it would be, Maggie realized there was only one course open to her.

Chapter 19

From the window of the stage office Cole saw the two men come out of the hotel carrying the rolled drawings. Ever since Maggie had told him about their conversation in the stagecoach, he had been mildly curious about them and now decided to follow them and see what they were up to.

After a block, they entered Keith Lawford's office. Logically, they could have gone in there for a dozen reasons. Lawford could be remodeling his office or even building one elsewhere. Maybe he was going to build a house in town.

What now bothered Cole was whether Maggie had been awake or dreaming when she thought she heard them mention Timberline.

His curiosity went beyond being merely mild when Ben Lawford rode into town with several of the Lazy L riders. He went into Keith's office. Cole's instincts told him Maggie hadn't been asleep. This had something to do with Timberline—and Pop's death.

For a short while Maggie had him thinking that Pop had died accidentally, that he was batting at windmills to think otherwise. But there was no closing his eyes again. Something about this smelled to high heaven.

Cole decided to see if he could find out anything about the men from their hotel rooms. Since they were the only guests registered, it wouldn't be too difficult to get into the rooms.

He went to the side steps leading up to the balcony. From what he remembered of the hotel's layout when he'd been registered there, the windows of the four front rooms opened onto the balcony, and logically those were the ones rented first.

Cole smiled in satisfaction when he found two of those windows opened. At least he was still thinking like a Ranger.

Climbing into the first room, he recognized the traveling bag. Cole riffled through it quickly, but there was nothing in it to give a clue as to who the men were or where they came from. The same was true of the bag in the other room. Somehow he'd have to get a look at those drawings.

At least he could get their names from that smart-assed desk clerk. He climbed out of the window and this time entered the hotel through the lobby.

"Howdy, Mr. MacKenzie," the clerk said. "You looking for a room? Ellie and Maggie kick you out, did they?"

"No, Joey. I brought a couple of guys in today on the stage."

"You mean that Mr. Romberg and Mr. Kern?"

"That's the two. Where are those fellows from?"

"Register says Albuquerque."

"Did they say what business they're in?"

"Nope. Just asked how to get to Keith Lawford's office. They left with a bunch of prints and drawings. Looked real important." He grinned widely. "Maybe the Lawfords are gonna redevelop the town."

"Why mess with perfection? Whoever comes here anyway?"

"You did, didn't ya?" Joe said smugly. "Now these two fellas. Other than them two whores that come here on weekends, that's more people than we had all last year except for the Founder's Day celebration."

"What in hell is Founder's Day?"

"Didn't Maggie tell ya? It's tomorrow. Uncle Ben throws a big celebration to honor the founder of the town. Folks come out for miles 'cause there's free food and drink."

"Who founded the town?"

"Uncle Ben did."

"So he gives a celebration honoring himself." Cole shook his head. "That figures. And because of that, he keeps this hotel operating?" Cole asked.

Joey shrugged. "It's his money. You don't hear me complaining, do ya? It keeps me working. And according to Uncle Ben, you close down the hotel, you're closing down the town."

"Joe, the town is already closed down," Cole said on his way out.

A short time later he saw the two men return to the hotel. They no longer had the drawings with them.

* * *

As usual Ellie was hard at work in the kitchen when Cole entered the house.

"Heard you spent a night in the calaboose," she teased.

"Thanks to Maggie."

"Heard tell you kind of asked for it."

"And I think the party you 'heard tell' this from was being pretty one-sided in the heard telling. Ellie, there are ways of getting even without having people locked up in jail overnight. Good thing my dad and uncles showed up, or my cousins and I would probably still be in that jail."

"Maggie told me she never would have signed a complaint."

"She didn't have to. That sheriff brought us up before the judge without one."

"I sure miss all the fun."

"Well, if you'd ever get out from in front of that stove, maybe you wouldn't. Once I get you to Texas, you're going to take it easier."

"Never said I was going, did I?"

He slipped his arms around her waist and nuzzled her. "You wouldn't let us go without you, now, would you, Ellie?"

"Try that sweet talk on Maggie, Cole MacKenzie, maybe it will get you farther than it does with me."

"I don't think it would help. I'm a dirty word in her book."

"Your family sure isn't. 'Pears like they made a good impression on her. Even those cousins of yours, who must have as much devilment in them as you do."

"They come close. They were on their way here

when we met them in Noches. Say, that reminds me of something." He dug into his shirt pocket and pulled out the paper Josh had given him.

Cole sat down and read the information he'd asked his cousins to check for him. The report was startling.

"Ellie, where's Maggie?"

"She went upstairs. She was in good spirits when she left, but I could tell she wasn't too perky when she came back. Thought maybe you two had gotten into a squabble again."

"No, I haven't talked to her since we've been back."

Cole went upstairs and tapped on her door. "Maggie, may I come in?"

"Just a minute."

When she opened the door, he could tell she'd been crying. "What's wrong, Maggie?"

"Oh, I've just been feeling a little sorry for myself." She walked to the window and gazed out. "I tell myself I'm not going to, but invariably I end up doing it."

"I wish I could help. I don't like us always being at odds."

"You aren't to blame, Cole. I may act like you are, but there are things that happen in life that's nobody's fault."

"Well, I'm back to believing Pop's death wasn't one of them."

She turned around, surprised. "Please don't start that again, Cole."

"Maggie, while we were in Noches last week, I wired Josh and asked him to find out whatever he could about Dallas and Vic. That's why he and Zach showed up in Noches. They thought they should bring the information rather than wire it." He handed her the paper. "Read this."

"I don't understand," Maggie said when she finished and handed it back to him.

"Don't you see the connection?" Cole asked. "Dallas C. Riley married John Donovan in 1871. She had a brother, Joseph V. Riley, who was accused of killing a man ten years later. This Joseph Riley claimed he was innocent, but the Rangers arrested him. He escaped, and no one's seen or heard from him since."

"What has all that got to do with Pop's death?"

"Maggie, I'm willing to bet that stagecoach that Joseph V—as in Victor—Riley and Dallas C—as in Chance—Donovan are none other than Dallas and Vic. They're sister and brother. All this time I thought the connection between them might have been romantic, and Vic might have killed Pop out of jealousy."

"Well, now that you suspect they're related, it destroys that theory completely. Vic would have no reason to kill Pop out of jealousy."

"What if Pop found out who Vic really is?"

Maggie sank down in a chair. "So you think Vic's the killer."

"I'm not sure. If Pop found out the truth, someone like Ben could have found out, too, then threaten to expose Vic if he didn't get rid of Pop. You can bet Vic's not the only one involved here."

"You mean Dallas?"

"Naturally she must know the truth."

"Then why not confront her?"

"Before I confront anyone, I want to see those drawings. I think the answer involves Timberline some way.

So there's no sense in going off half-cocked until I have something to back up my suspicions. I've already searched Romberg's and Kern's hotel rooms. They've apparently given the drawings to either Ben or Keith. I saw them go into your boyfriend's office with them, and they came out empty-handed, and Ben was there at the time. I've got to get a look at those damn drawings."

"What about tomorrow during the celebration? If Ben takes the drawings to his ranch, there'll be no one at his house. His crew comes to the celebration, and all the businesses in town close up."

"That's a good idea. I'll check out Lawford's office tonight. If the drawings aren't there, tomorrow I'll ride out to the ranch."

"Whatever you're thinking, Keith is not involved in this, Cole."

"He may be involved by knowing what happened but keeping quiet to protect his father. Regardless, we won't say anything to Dallas and Vic until we know more. And certainly not a word to your boyfriend. Agreed?"

"Yes, I agree," she said reluctantly.

"Good girl. I've got to send a telegram. See you later."

Maggie felt as if she were in a nightmare. Everything in her life was in shambles. Vic a murderer. Dallas involved. Could she be wrong about Keith, too? Maybe it *was* time to leave Lawford. Get a fresh start on the Triple M.

Oh, yes, Maggie, that will be just fine, especially when Cole brings back a wife to meet you.

Well, that would just be another bridge to cross.

First things first, she decided. And that was to sell the stageline.

Figuring Cole had gone back to the office, Maggie went there to find him. Juan was alone, sweeping the office floor.

"Is Cole here, Juan?"

"No, Señorita Margaret."

"What are you doing here so late, Juan? You should be home with your father."

"Juan is almost through sweeping the floor. Then he will leave."

"I won't be back, so be sure and put out the lantern and lock the doors."

"*Sí, señorita.*"

I won't be back. The words sounded like a portent of what was to come. Soon the office would belong to someone else.

Maggie wished she could have discussed her intention with Cole—not that he'd object to selling the stageline. But she had to act on her decision immediately before she lost her courage and changed her mind. If Ben had left, she'd have Keith draw up a sales contract.

As she walked to Keith's office, the street was busier than usual. A couple of the Lazy L riders were tacking up bunting on the front of buildings in preparation for tomorrow's celebration, while several others were erecting a rostrum for Ben to make his annual speech.

Maggie was about to knock on the door when she heard the raised voices of Ben and Keith from within. The two men were in a heated argument. With all the mystery surrounding the two arrivals in town, she didn't hesitate to listen.

"I wish you had told me what you were up to sooner," Keith said. "Timberline is a valuable piece of property, and I won't stand by and let you mislead Margaret."

"This is business, boy. You think I built the Lazy L by sidestepping the manure piles? You step in the horse-shit even if it dirties up your boots."

"What you've done and are planning is uncon-scionable, Father. I won't close my eyes and be a party to it."

"You listen, boy, and you listen good. If you expect the Lazy L to be yours one day, you best start showing me you're man enough to run it. This is my town, boy, I own everyone in it. So you best decide if you're with me or against me. And if you're against me, you can start packing, 'cause the town's not big enough for the two of us."

"Is that why you're so against Cole MacKenzie?"

"You're damn right!"

"Because you can't buy him the same as you couldn't Mick O'Shea."

"I ain't gonna bother to try, boy. Like I told him, I got an ace in the hole—O'Shea's daughter. So you do what you have to do, and I'll take care of my end."

"I will not make Margaret a pawn in your game, Fa-ther. Did you ever stop to consider you could serve your purpose a damn sight better with MacKenzie's cooperation?"

"What ain't getting through to you, boy? *I* built the Lazy L. *I* built the town. I did and I'll continue doing whatever I have to in order to get the job done. I don't need the help of Cole MacKenzie or you for that matter. Time you realize that. You're with me or against me, but you ain't stopping me."

It was a relief for Maggie to hear that Keith wasn't a part of whatever was going on. But considering what she had just overheard, it appeared that Cole's suspicions were justified. She had to tell him this latest.

Maggie was about to leave when the door was flung open and Ben Lawford slammed into her. His quick grab kept Maggie from being knocked off her feet.

"Uh, sorry, Margaret," he said, stooping down to pick up the rolled plans he had dropped.

"Mr. Lawford, you're just the man I want to see," she said hastily, hoping he wouldn't suspect she'd overheard any of the conversation.

Keith came rushing over and took her arm. "Margaret, come in. Are you okay?" Ben followed her back in and closed the door.

"I'm fine, Keith." He pulled up a chair for her to sit down. "I came to have you draw up an agreement between your father and me for the sale of the stageline." She smiled at Ben Lawford. "That is, if your offer to buy it still stands, Mr. Lawford."

"Of course it does, Margaret."

Keith frowned. "I thought you wanted to hold onto the line, Margaret."

"I do, but Cole MacKenzie insists I sell it. I guess he's right. I just don't have the financial resources to keep the line operating." She looked at Ben to emphasize her point. "In truth, Ben, there are few customers to make it profitable."

"That'll be my problem, Margaret," he replied.

"If you're certain this is what you want, Margaret, I'll draw up a bill of sale relinquishing all assets and rights to my father," Keith said.

"Yes, my mind's made up."

"What do you want for it?" Ben asked.

"I hadn't thought about it."

"What is it worth to you, Father? Often the value of an item lies in how badly it is desired," Keith said meaningfully.

Ben glared at his son. "The coach is falling apart. I'll have to replace it."

"Yes, but there's six horses that are used to pulling a coach."

"You getting a commission on this sale, son?" Ben asked, clearly irritated.

"I'm merely looking out for Margaret's interests."

"Ain't that MacKenzie's job?"

"Cole doesn't know I'm here, but I know he won't object."

"Just the same, I think you should advise him, Margaret, since he will have to sign the agreement," Keith said.

"I'll offer a thousand dollars," Ben declared. "That ought to be a fair price for six old horses and a run-down stable."

"The stable is in excellent condition, Mr. Lawford. And the horses are still very stouthearted."

"Well, that's my offer, and it's a fair one."

"It's acceptable to me, Keith. You can write it up, and I'll see that Cole signs it."

"What about Timberline, Margaret?" Ben suddenly asked.

Maggie glanced up to see Keith give his father a glaring look.

"I haven't decided what I want to do about Timberline, Mr. Lawford."

"Why would you want to hold on to that piece of land, girl? You can't ranch it unless you want to run a herd of mountain goats."

"I have no intention of ranching it, Mr. Lawford. I'm just not ready to sell it as yet. Pop must have thought a lot of it to have bought it, though. I have to think about it longer."

"Makes no sense in just sitting on a piece of land, especially when you need money." It was obvious he was working himself up into anger again. "I agreed to give you more than that stagecoach line is worth. You ought to show some compromise here, girl."

"Mr. Lawford, all I can say is that if and when I decide to sell Timberline, I'll let you make the first offer."

"It'll be the only offer. Who else would want it?"

"My father obviously did."

Ben picked up the rolled drawings and stormed out.

"You'll have to excuse my father's manners, Margaret," Keith said.

"I'm sorry if I upset him, Keith."

"Don't blame yourself. He's easily annoyed when things don't go his way. No one knows that better than I do."

Maggie stood to leave. "I'll have the papers ready for you in the morning. It's a fair offer, Margaret."

"Thanks to you, Keith."

He walked her to the door and then kissed her on the cheek and said good-bye.

As she started down the street to the stable, hoping to find Cole, she saw a dark cloud of smoke in the vicinity of the stageline office.

She smelled it just as the shout of *Fire!* rang out.

Chapter 20

Maggie's heart was thudding in her breast by the time she reached the office. She stared in horror at the bright glow that filtered through the smoke billowing out of the door.

From within the adjoining stable she could hear the frantic whinnies of the horses trapped in stalls. With no thought to her own safety, Maggie dashed into the stable. The smoke that had sifted through from the office closed in around her, stinging her eyes and making breathing difficult.

As yet the flames had not spread to the stable, but the horses were kicking and neighing in their panic to get out.

Maggie managed to get a rope around Cupid's neck, but the horse fought the restraint, and she didn't have the strength to control him.

Suddenly Cole appeared along with several of the

Lazy L riders. He snatched the rope out of her hand.

"Get out of here, Maggie." He began to cough from the smoke he'd sucked into his throat. She staggered outside and watched helplessly as the men managed to get the horses out and tethered to hitching posts on the opposite side of the street.

Pandemonium reigned outside. The air was becoming thick with fiery sparks and black smoke. The bucket brigade that had formed had already emptied the horse trough in front of the stable and was shouting for more water. There were men pouring buckets of water on the rooftops of the hotel and bank in the hope of saving the buildings if the fire jumped the street. Ben and Joey Lawford were running out of the bank with sacks of money and records.

Amid screams and shouts people ducked and scattered when the office window burst from the heat, showering shards of glass on the street. The stage office had become a solid wall of flames and smoke, so people ceased to attempt to put out that fire and began to concentrate on trying to save the adjacent buildings.

Maggie watched, sickened, as the roof of the walls and ceiling of the office crashed down in a blazing inferno. The flames consumed the door and leaped into the stable, gorging on the straw and dry wood.

Emilio Morales, his leg in a heavy cast of plaster of paris, limped up beside her and stared, appalled, at the burning building. "Have you seen, Juan, Señorita Margaret?"

"Isn't he with you?"

"No. I haven't seen him since he left to come and clean the stable."

"I saw him then and—" The words froze in her

throat when she was struck by the possibility that Juan
might still be inside. *Oh, dear God, don't let it be!* Horrified, she glanced around desperately, looking for Cole.
She finally spied him with Keith. The two men were
helping Dallas and Vic wet down the saloon.

Maggie raced up to him. Breathless, she said, "Cole,
Juan is missing. The last time I saw him, he was sweeping out the stable."

"Oh, my God!" Cole said. He and Keith ran back to
the burning building."

"I'm going in," Cole said.

"But you don't know if he's even in there," Keith
said.

"If he wasn't, he'd be out here, and you know it."

Cole pulled off his bandanna and soaked it in a
trough and then tied it around his nose and mouth.
Keith and Maggie dumped several buckets of water
over his head to wet down his clothing.

Emilio limped awkwardly up to them, the anguish
and desperation in his eyes saying so much more than
words could ever express.

"If he's in there, Emilio, I'll get him out," Cole said.

Maggie's heart was wrenched and tears streaked her
cheeks. They all knew it would take a miracle for Cole
to survive in that blazing building, and she wanted to
tell him not to do it, but she knew he would as long as
there was an element of hope.

At such a moment all wanted to find words to say to
him—Keith with his college degree, Maggie with the
love she felt for him, and Emilio with the heartache of a
father handicapped and unable to go to the rescue of
his own son—but there was no time for words.

Cole nodded and entered the stable. When he disappeared through the door, Emilio murmured softly, *"Vaya usted con Dios, Señor Cole."*

The smoke was so thick that there was no visibility, and the heat was intense. Within seconds his breathing became labored. Cole knew there had been no sign of Juan in the stalls when they got the horses out, so he got down on his hands and knees and crawled among the bales of hay. A rafter near the inside wall collapsed in a burning heap, and he ducked his head to protect his eyes from the flaming cinders flying around. Hot sparks bit at his bare arms as he continued the search.

He groped around the floor, the smoke and bales preventing him from seeing anything. When he'd gone as far as he could, he knew his search was hopeless.

The smoke had become denser with every passing moment, his breathing more shallow. A portion of the roof caved in, narrowly missing him. A stream of black smoke spiraled skyward through the gaping hole.

Cole could feel himself starting to become disoriented, and he had to force himself to concentrate. There was only one other place he hadn't checked—the horse trough.

Praying he was headed in the right direction, he crawled toward the rear wall and slammed into the trough with his head. Unable to see, he groped in the receptacle. It was empty of water, but he made contact with a wet body on the bottom. He knew it was Juan. The boy's clothes must have absorbed whatever water had remained in the trough, because they were soaked. It took all of his waning strength to lift Juan out of the trough, and as he headed for the door, he thought his lungs would burst in the few seconds it took to reach it.

When he appeared in the doorway, a cheer rose from

the small crowd that had become aware of the drama being enacted. Cole staggered outside, gasped some much-needed air into his burning lungs, and then sank to his knees and began coughing.

The doctor was bent over Juan, and helping hands carried the boy away as Maggie knelt at Cole's side. She didn't attempt to talk to him but remained in silence beside him. When his coughing finally ceased, she helped him to his feet.

"Juan?" he asked hoarsely. His throat felt raw when he tried to speak.

"He's alive," she said, "The doctor said he'll know more about Juan's condition as soon as he examines him further. He thought the body signs appeared encouraging."

"Thank God."

"Cole, let's get you to the doctor, too."

"I'll be fine as soon as I can drag some fresh air into my lungs. Let's get away from this heat and smoke."

They hurried away just as the remaining part of the roof collapsed.

Tears glistened in Maggie's eyes, and he slid his arm around her shoulders as they stood in silence and watched the final wall topple and burn to ashes.

Keith Lawford returned from the doctor's office and joined them.

"How's Juan?" Cole asked.

"Coughing up a storm right now, but the doctor said it was good he passed out, because it slowed down his breathing, thus reducing his smoke inhalation."

"Does Juan have any idea how the fire started?" Maggie asked.

"Yes. He said it was his fault. When he was leaving

the office, he dropped the lantern, and it started the office on fire. He tried to put it out with buckets of water from the stable's horse trough, but the fire spread rapidly, and when his pants caught on fire, he ran to the trough and climbed in to put it out. All he remembers is the smoke. I guess he got dizzy and passed out, because he said that's the last thing he can remember before waking up in the doctor's office. I'd say he's a very lucky little boy. He probably inhaled less smoke than you did, Cole."

"I should go to him," Maggie said.

"Ellie and Emilio are with him right now. Doc wants to keep Juan under observation overnight, and there'll be no blasting Emilio away from his bedside."

"It's a blessing he wasn't hurt more," Maggie said.

"Are *you* okay, Margaret?" Keith asked. Cole could see how sensitive Keith Lawford was to Maggie's loss.

"I'm fine, Keith. Thank you. I'm just relieved no one was hurt more seriously," she said.

"Well, I'd better go and check to see how my father fared through all this," Keith said. He grasped Maggie's hand and brought it to his lips. "I'll talk to you later, Margaret."

After he left, Maggie turned again and gazed sorrowfully at the ruins. In the midst of the smoldering ashes stood the charred skeleton of the stagecoach—a symbolic embodiment of her father's dream. Cole wanted to weep with her. He knew how much her heart was aching, and he couldn't stand to ignore her suffering. He took her in his arms and without thought lowered his head.

His lips claimed hers with a gentleness he hadn't believed he possessed. The kiss was meant to comfort, to console. But from the first contact with her soft lips somehow the kiss took on a meaning of its own. And Lord, it felt good.

He drew her tighter into his arms, cradling the warmth of her against his body. That felt even better. They became isolated in a shared moment of a sensation that let them forget the inferno surrounding them—the sheer pleasure a mere joining of the lips can create between a man and a woman.

His shortness of breath cut off the kiss sooner than he wanted to, and for a long moment they stared at each other, one as stunned as the other.

He cupped her face between his hands. "Maggie, I'm sorry."

She stepped away. "I understand, Cole. You were just feeling sorry for me."

That may have been his original motive, but there was no accounting for how the kiss affected him. He didn't understand that himself.

Dallas Donovan came over to them, and upon seeing Maggie's devastation, she tucked her arm through Maggie's.

"Honey, I think you could use a drink right about now. It's for damn sure you can, Texas."

Maggie was too numb to argue and allowed Dallas to lead her into the saloon. There were no customers. They sat down at a table.

"Vic, bring the special bottle and some glasses," Dallas said.

"Make mine a glass of water," Cole said. "Straight up," he added.

Vic came over with a tray in hand and sat down with them. "That was a decent thing you did for that kid, MacKenzie."

"I didn't do anything that any one of you wouldn't have done in my place."

Dallas snorted. "Maybe so, but I'd say that's what they mean by being in the wrong place at the wrong time."

She poured them each a drink. "Now, honey," she said to Maggie, "this will sting a little going down, but it'll do you good right now."

"I'll stick with my water," Cole said.

"I think we all know what that stageline meant to Mick O'Shea," Dallas said. "It was kind of a lasting memory of him to the town." She raised her glass in the air. "You may be gone, Mick, but you'll never be forgotten."

"Here, here," Vic and Cole joined in.

Dallas downed her drink in a gulp, and Vic followed suit. Cole sipped his water slowly, trying to flush out his throat.

Maggie followed Dallas's example and swallowed the drink in a single gulp. Her eyes popped open as the astringent whiskey burned her throat. Cole grinned and handed her his water. She gulped it down, draining the glass.

"First shot of whiskey, huh?" Dallas asked.

Maggie nodded. "Why didn't you warn me?"

"The second one goes down easier," Dallas offered in consolation.

"You know, strangely enough, the alcohol does seem to have a bracing effect on me," Maggie conceded. "But I find the taste abominable. I don't understand how anyone can develop a liking for it." Nevertheless, she offered up her glass for another drink. While Vic got Cole a pitcher of water, Dallas refilled the rest of their glasses.

"Take this one a little slower, honey," she advised.

Maggie took a sip of the drink and then turned up her nose. "Oh, my! It tastes even worse when you drink it slowly."

"Make her next drink a glass of sassafras, Vic," Dallas ordered. "This gal's got no appreciation for good whiskey."

The four of them continued to sit and talk. Maggie had switched her drink to sassafras. Cole stayed with water, and Dallas and Vic with the whiskey.

Maggie had to admit that the two drinks she'd had did help to steady her nerves. As she listened to Dallas and Vic speak fondly of past times with Pop, she saw that they related these times with fondness. Since her father's death, she had inadvertently attached a sadness to the past memories of Pop, but Dallas and Vic, along with Cole adding some of his stories, soon had her smiling, even laughing at times, as they described their memories in a celebration of Pop's life, not death.

She found it harder and harder to believe that regardless of what Josh's investigation implied, either Dallas or Vic could have had anything to do with Pop's death.

When Ben and Keith came in, Dallas invited the two men to join them. They pulled up chairs and sat down.

"Well, Ben, did you carry all my money back into the bank?" Dallas teased.

"It's back where it belongs, but I had your interests

at heart when I toted it out of there, Dallas. I'd rather be safe than sorry," he said good-naturedly. "Especially when it comes to your money, Dallas."

This was the first time Cole had had a chance to see Ben Lawford interacting with any of the people in the town. Ben and Dallas were obviously comfortable with each other—but then again, Dallas seemed to have that affability with everyone. How much was genuine and how much put on? He'd know more when he got an answer to the telegram he'd sent Josh earlier that afternoon.

"At least the only thing lost was the stable," Ben said. "I'll take the horses back to the Lazy L. There's no place in town to board them."

"Thank you, Mr. Lawford, that's very good of you," Maggie said.

"Keith tells me you went into that burning stable to find that Morales kid. Took a lot of courage, MacKenzie."

Cole arched a brow. "But not too much intelligence."

Ben burst into loud laughter. "I could grow to like you, boy, if I wasn't looking forward to your leaving my town. You're my kind of man, MacKenzie." He looked in disgust at his son. "Kind of a dying breed. You kind of remind me of myself when I was younger."

"I'm sure there's an intended compliment somewhere in that," Cole replied.

"We were talking about Mick O'Shea, Ben," Dallas said. "It made us sad to see the stageline burn down."

"It didn't make me sad. The damn thing was an eyesore. That kid did the town a favor when he burned it down." He glanced around at the disapproving glares from the people seated at the table.

"Judging from the looks I'm getting, it's a good thing the kid fessed up to it, or you'd all be blaming me for the fire."

"Father, you're being inexcusably insensitive to Margaret's feelings."

"If I am, I'm sorry, Margaret. But there ain't one person at this table who deep down don't agree with me. It wasn't bad enough how it looked. The stage wasn't even safe to ride in."

He leaned toward Cole. "Don't hear you saying anything to the contrary, MacKenzie. Or are you trying to spare Margaret's feelings, too?"

"Maggie knows how I feel about the stageline. I don't intend to air my opinion to you."

"While we're on that subject, I made you an offer on Timberline. Figure you've had time to consider it."

"Don't recall asking for any offer, Lawford, but you sure have been quick to make them."

Ben offered a weak grin. "Just hoping to see the end of you, MacKenzie."

"Sorry to hear that, Lawford, because until I get to the bottom of Pop's death, get used to seeing me, because I'm going to be around."

Dallas and Vic exchanged a meaningful look, and Ben gulped down his drink, then shoved back his chair and stood up.

"Well, if we gotta drive them horses back to the ranch, I better get the boys moving. You coming?" he asked Keith.

Keith stood up. "I'll have those papers ready in the morning, Margaret."

"What papers?" Cole asked as soon as the two men disappeared through the door.

"I'll explain later," Maggie said. "I want to go and say good-bye to the team."

"Thanks for the drink, Dallas," Cole said, and hurried out after her. She had some explaining to do.

Chapter 21

~~~~~~

Since they would need transportation, Cole insisted they keep Cupid and Vixen in town, so Ben left them saddles and bridles. Cole stood back and watched as Maggie said good-bye to the rest of the team, promising to ride out to see them as soon as she could. She adored those horses, and he had to admit he had begun to get attached to Vixen. The mare had always seemed glad to see him—probably the only person or thing in town that was.

While Maggie lingered over her farewell to the horses, Cole went over and checked the ashes. The site was still a hot bed with pockets of smoke still rising from the ruins. He figured it would bear watching in the event a wind came up during the night.

As soon as the Lazy L crew rode away, Cole walked over to where Maggie was talking to Keith. "Thought you were leaving with your father."

Keith shook his head. "I changed my mind and decided to clear up my desk before Founder's Day tomorrow."

"What's all this about a paper Maggie has to sign?"

"I was on my way to the office to discuss that with you, Cole, when the fire broke out," Maggie said.

"Well, I'm here now, so let's discuss it."

She gave him an irritated look. "I prefer to wait until we get home," she said with icy deliberation.

That could only mean she anticipated an argument. Well, he didn't care if she'd given the stageline to Lawford, he was that relieved to see the end of the damn thing. What rankled him was the possibility that Ben Lawford thought he'd outsmarted him.

"Just remember, Keith, I'm the one who has to approve and sign those papers. If I don't like the arrangement, whatever Maggie agreed to will be off."

"Considering the office and stable have since burned down, my father's offer is more than generous, Cole."

Keith's attention was suddenly drawn to a buggy that had halted across the street to view the remains of the fire. "For heaven sakes, it's the Bennetts! Will you excuse me?" He hurried over to them.

"How much did Lawford offer you?" Cole asked, after a cursory glance at the older couple and younger woman who occupied it.

"A thousand dollars."

Cole shrugged. "That's a pretty good offer."

"You can thank Keith for that."

"I'm glad to see you've come to your senses about selling that line. I just wish you would have told me your intentions so that I could have handled it."

"If I'd done that, you and Ben would still be arguing over the price."

"What caused you to make up your mind so quickly? You sure were against the idea this morning."

"I'll tell you exactly what made me change my mind, Cole MacKenzie. It was *you*. Why didn't you tell me you had put your own money into the bank to keep the stageline operating? I had to find that out from that supercilious Jimmy Lawford. How do you think I felt?"

"I guess I didn't stop to consider that," Cole admitted.

"I wanted to legitimately prove to you that I could make a go of the stageline without your help, but you didn't trust me or give me the chance to do that. From the moment Pop's will was read, you haven't trusted me to make one decision for myself."

"I suppose I am taking my responsibility as your guardian too seriously."

"That's putting it mildly. You're suffocating me, Cole. When is it going to end?"

"I guess in three years or whenever you get married."

"No, I'll tell you when it's ending: *right now*. Do you understand? I'll decide what I'll do with *my* life. You just worry about your own, and you and I will get along just fine." She spun on her heel and strode away.

Cole couldn't help grinning as he watched her march over to the buggy. He didn't know if it was the two whiskies talking or Maggie. Her gown was soot-covered, her hair was disheveled, and he knew her heart was breaking from losing the stable and the team, but her shoulders were squared and her head unbowed.

Maggie O'Shea was some woman all right. At first it looked like she was going to wallow in self-pity, but she had fooled him. Had shown real mettle. Damn right! Spunk and grit to spare. She rolled with the punch—and nobody got the better of her.

Cole's grin broadened. Her having him and his cousins arrested in Noches was an example.

So why would Pop figure I'd ever want to marry a little hellion like Maggie?

"Margaret, you remember Mr. and Mrs. Bennett, don't you?" Keith asked.

"I'm afraid not. It was so long ago," Maggie said. "And I was pretty young at the time. I know you lived next to us."

"Margaret, we can't tell you how bad we feel about your father's death," the older woman said.

"Thank you, Mrs. Bennett."

"Please call me Aunt Jane. That's what you used to do when you were a very little girl. You used to toddle over from next door whenever you smelled me baking cookies."

"Don't know if you ever heard, but Mick and I were neighbors when we were kids, too," Harry Bennett said. "I sure missed him when he left Lawford to prospect for gold."

"And when he came back two years ago, we had left Lawford already. There was just no longer a need for a schoolteacher here."

"But we always come back for Founder's Day," Jane Bennett said.

"And this is their daughter, Caroline," Keith said.

"I know you don't remember me," Caroline said.

"But I remember you so well. You were such a darling little girl, but now you're beautiful. I feel so terrible about your father, Margaret, and Keith has just told us about the fire today. How strong you are. I admire your fortitude."

Maggie didn't remember the woman at all, but she liked her on sight. If anyone was beautiful, it was Caroline Bennett. She figured Caroline was probably in her late twenties or possibly even older, with blond hair and clear blue eyes, but her real beauty lay in the soothing serenity she emanated.

When Cole came over, Keith introduced the Bennetts to him, and Harry reacted at once.

"Cole MacKenzie? Didn't you pan gold in Alaska with Mick?"

"Yes, for two years."

"I always visualized you as being an older man," Mrs. Bennett said. "My goodness, you don't appear to be much older than Margaret."

"He's seven years older," Maggie said quickly.

"Looking back, I guess I was pretty young," Cole said. "Maggie certainly was then. All I know is that I feel a darn sight older right now."

"I'm sure after such a harrowing day you both do," Caroline said.

This struck up a line of light banter about being as old as you feel. Caroline Bennett was so lovely and feminine that Maggie felt filthy and awkward in her soot-laden clothing. She had to freshen herself up.

"Will you be staying with us, Aunt Jane?" Maggie asked.

"We usually do, but if it's not convenient, we can stay at the hotel."

"Why don't we all go back to the house? I'm sure Ellie is anxious to see you, and I'd like to get out of these dirty clothes. I imagine you would, too, Cole."

"And then I insist you all join me for dinner," Keith said.

"Well, you and Cole squeeze in, and we'll drive you," Harry Bennett offered.

Maggie declined the offer. "I'm too dirty. It's just a block. You go on and I'll catch up with you."

"The same here," Cole said.

Keith climbed in and sat down next to Caroline. "We'll see you at the house," Maggie said as the buggy rolled away.

"My goodness, Caroline's quite lovely, isn't she?" Maggie said, as they walked back to the house.

"She certainly is."

"It's surprising she hasn't married. She's so pleasant and even-tempered. I can't believe she hasn't been asked."

"At least by the man she prefers."

Coming from Cole, the remark was too ambiguous to simply be intended as casual conversation. "What do you mean by that?"

"You aren't very observant, Maggie. I think your boyfriend missed the boat there."

"You believe she cares for Keith?"

"If you didn't notice, you're as blind as he is."

They reached the house and he hopped up on the porch. "All right, ladies first. The bathroom's yours, but don't use all the hot water."

After a quick inquiry into Juan's condition, Maggie went upstairs and took a quick bath. She would have liked to wash the smoke smell out of her hair but knew

it would take too long to dry. By the time she had
dressed and hurried back downstairs, they all were
seated around the kitchen table, drinking coffee. She
noticed Cole was still drinking water, and it crossed
her mind that his throat must still be bothering him.
She felt a pang of regret that she'd been so relieved
about Juan that she hadn't given his condition much
concern. That nobody really had.

Cole excused himself and went upstairs to bathe. He
closed the door and leaned back against it. The scent of
jasmine lingered in the room, and for a long moment he
stood and breathed in the sweet fragrance of Maggie.

After drawing his bath, he sank gratefully into the
tub of hot water. He soaped the smell of smoke out of
his hair, then leaned back and closed his eyes. The
memory of his frantic search for Juan, the hellish
smoke and fire, played through his mind like a nightmare. He regretted he hadn't told the others to go on to
dinner without him. He had no desire for company. He
wanted to be alone and to thank God for just being
alive.

When he joined the others, the elder Bennetts had
decided they were too tired to go out to dinner. Since
he intended to keep an eye on the smoldering ashes,
Cole offered them his bedroom for the night, and Maggie and Caroline were going to double up in her room.

As much as he enjoyed the company at dinner, he
couldn't shake the mood he had slipped into, and listened, rather than contributed, to the conversation.
Maggie was unusually quiet, too. As he watched her
listening and hanging onto every word Caroline said,
Cole realized how much Maggie was starved for female companionship. It reinforced his determination

to take her to the Triple M, where she'd have the company of women near her own age.

"I heard about your heroism today, Cole," Caroline said. "It must take a lot of courage to go into a burning building to save a life."

"It was more of a reaction than a calculated risk on my part, Caroline."

"You must be very proud to have a hero for a guardian, Margaret."

"I'm very proud and grateful for what Cole did, but I really don't feel I need a guardian."

"The role's kind of new to me, too," Cole added.

"It was a provision in Mick O'Shea's will," Keith offered by way of explanation.

"That's very interesting," Caroline said. "He must have had a purpose in selecting such a young man to be her guardian. Why wouldn't he select Ellie or even you, Keith?"

Caroline had raised an interesting point that Cole hadn't considered before: purpose, not motive. Could there have been more purpose than motive behind Pop's choice? Since his arrival in Lawford he'd been so suspicious of Keith Lawford that he'd figured Pop didn't trust the man either, but why wouldn't he have trusted Ellie? He would have to read that letter from Pop again.

With Cole withdrawing from the conversation, Keith preened in the attention of both women. In Cole's opinion, it was a sad state of affairs when two women as beautiful as Maggie and Caroline were desperate enough to fawn over a pri—, ah, man, like Lawford. Cole was convinced more than ever that he had a responsibility to get Maggie as far away from Lawford, New Mexico, as he could.

The smell of smoke still lingered in the air when they left the diner. Cole halted when they reached the site of the fire.

"Go on, I think I'll hang around and kind of keep an eye on things."

"Cole, it's going to get chilly," Maggie said.

"If it does, I'll come and get a blanket."

Keith took Maggie's arm. "Come on, Margaret. Cole knows what he's doing."

As Keith led her away, Maggie turned her head and looked back. Cole was staring desolately at them.

Caroline and Maggie had sat up in her bedroom and talked for over an hour before they finally went to bed. It didn't take long for Caroline to fall asleep, but Maggie couldn't. She was concerned about Cole. It just wasn't like him to be so quiet.

When she heard the clock strike two, Maggie got out of bed and walked to the window. Where was he? What was he doing out there?

Then she saw him below in the backyard. As she watched, he covered Cupid with the blanket the horse had shaken off. Then he murmured a few words to Vixen and walked back up the street like a sentinel, guarding a town he didn't even care about.

Maggie put on her robe and slippers and went downstairs. Grabbing the afghan from the couch, she slipped out the door and went in search of him. She found him sitting across the street from the burned-out stable, leaning back against the telegraph station.

"Maggie, what are doing up at this hour?" Cole asked.

Maggie spread out the afghan and sat down beside him. "I came out to tell you to come back and lie down to get some sleep. The fire's out, Cole, and it's a calm night. There's nothing to worry about."

"I'm not tired, Maggie."

"How can you not be? You spent last night in jail. I don't imagine you got much sleep there either. What's bothering you, Cole? Is it something I've done?"

"No, Maggie. I've just got a lot on my mind."

"Are you sure it's not because I spoke to Ben Lawford about selling the stageline?"

"Nothing like that, believe me. I guess I'm having a reaction to the fire. I never thought much about life or death before. Until the fire, I hadn't realized what a frail grasp we actually hold on life. In a moment's passing it can slip through our fingers. Snuffed out easier than putting out a candle. I guess the lesson to be learned is don't squander your life. I sure as hell have wasted mine up until now."

"You've got a chance to change it, Cole. We all do. You said you have a lot on your mind. What else is bothering you?"

"Pop's death. I'm hoping I'm wrong about Dallas and Vic being involved."

"I can't believe they are, any more than Keith is."

"And if you find out he is, do you love him that much, Maggie?"

"I know he's not, Cole. I overheard him and Ben arguing right before the fire broke out. He told Ben he wouldn't be a party to whatever Ben was planning or let him make me a pawn in his game."

"What is Ben planning?"

"I don't know. I didn't hear. All I know is that Keith told him you couldn't be bought any more than Pop could. It was a really heated argument, Cole. Ben as much as told Keith if he wasn't with him on this to get out of town."

"Well, with any luck I should have an answer to the telegram I sent within the next couple of days."

"And if they aren't involved, that would narrow your suspicions down to Ben then, wouldn't it?"

"Well, we'll know more about his plans after I see those drawings. Something else is bothering me, too: Caroline's comment about Pop's motive in making me your guardian. Did you ever discuss marrying Keith with Pop?"

Maggie thought for a moment and then nodded. "Yes, about a week or so before he died. He told me Keith said he wanted to marry me."

"Could the conversation have been about ten days before Pop died?"

"I guess so. Yes, that would be about right."

"What did you tell him?"

"That I was aware of Keith's feelings and that ultimately I probably would."

"And how did he react to that?"

"Like it was the end of the world. He really was upset. I'd never seen Pop that upset before."

"Maggie, I never told you, but last week I got a letter forwarded to me that Pop had written ten days before he died. He said how concerned he was over your growing relationship with Keith Lawford. According to the date of Pop's will, that's the same time he wrote the letter to me. If we assume that when he drew up the will he didn't expect to die so soon after, it almost looks like the desperation he related to in his letter and telegram to me could have been related to your relationship with Keith."

Cole was not about to mention Pop's statement that he hoped one day Cole and Maggie would wed. "This whole thing is getting more confusing by the minute, but I think we'll have some of the answers by tomorrow."

Maggie yawned. "I'll be glad when it's over."

"Come on. I'll walk you back to the house so you can go back to bed."

"I'll stay here with you, Cole," she said drowsily. "And besides, I'm too sleepy to walk back." She leaned against him, and he slipped his arm around her shoulders and hugged her to his side. She fell asleep in his arms, her head against his chest.

And as the night grew longer, eventually Cole slept, too.

Chapter 22

Dawn streaked the horizon when Maggie opened her eyes and found herself cuddled in the warm cocoon of Cole's arms. She couldn't think of a better way to start a day, and for a long moment she remained still, enjoying the pleasant sensation.

She realized she'd better get back to the house before the town started stirring. It would be the basis of a lot of gossip if she were found asleep in Cole's arms—in her nightgown and robe to boot.

Trying not to disturb him, she slipped out of his arms and got to her feet. For several seconds she was unable to move away from the sleeping figure. He looked so boyish and vulnerable in slumber.

I love you, Cole MacKenzie. It seems like I've loved you forever.

Maggie walked across the street and looked at the ruins of the stable. There no longer appeared to be any hot spots. As soon as she was dressed, she'd go through the rubble and see if there was anything of value that had been spared. From what she could see, it was very unlikely.

Well, Maggie, you asked for divine intervention. Looks like you got it.

Funny that after such a disaster she could view the ruins of something that had once been the driving force of her existence, that had been the cause of constant quarrels with Cole, and feel so objective about its loss. It was a sign she was ready to get on with her life.

Ellie came up to her and slipped an arm around her waist. "I figured I'd find you here. This is the first time I've seen it. Couldn't bring myself to look at it sooner."

"It's all gone, Ellie. At least we won't be leaving it behind when we leave."

"Think we best wake that boy before the town gets moving?"

"Let him be, Ellie. He needs the sleep. I'll get dressed and come back and wake him then."

Arm in arm they walked back to the house.

When they arrived at the house, Caroline was awake and bubbling over with anticipation of the day's activities. When Maggie announced she was going to wash her hair to get rid of the smoke smell, Caroline immediately volunteered to do it for her.

Laughing like schoolgirls, the two women then proceeded to dress for the day. While they were eating breakfast, Cole came in, carrying the afghan, and by the time he had shaved and changed his clothes, Ellie and Jane Bennett had begun to pack up the pies Ellie had baked for the Founder's Day celebration.

Gradually the town began to take on a new personality as people began to arrive for the celebration. The charred remains of the stable drew everybody's attention.

As soon as the Lazy L rode in, Cole pulled Maggie aside.

"I'll get back as soon as I can. You're going to have to cover for me if Lawford starts asking questions."

"Be careful, Cole," Maggie said.

"Don't worry. When I was in the Rangers, I did a lot of undercover work."

"Undercover or under the covers," she teased.

"That, too," he said, grinning. Then he faded into the crowd.

Cole had no problem following the well-worn road leading to the Lazy L's ranch house. He moved off the trail and concealed himself in the trees, where he could observe the house. When he didn't see any movement for fifteen minutes, he dismounted, tethered Cupid, and headed down the hill, cautiously approaching in the event that some riders had remained behind.

The next problem to overcome was the possibility of someone being in the house. When he saw a harnessed chuckwagon parked in front of a side door, he knew that was probably the case. After trying several windows, he found an unlocked one near the front of the house and peeked in. Seeing the room was empty, he opened the window and climbed in.

Not bad, he thought, looking around at what appeared to be a comfortably appointed parlor. The question now was where had Ben put the drawings?

Cole started to cross the room, then froze when he heard approaching footsteps. He hurriedly hunched down behind a leather couch just as an oriental man came into the room. The man made several trips loading prepared food into the chuckwagon, and then finally, to Cole's relief, he climbed up on the box of the wagon and drove away, obviously headed for town.

Now Cole was able to move freely around the house, and after checking out several rooms, he found the drawings in a rear room that appeared to be Ben's study. Sitting down at the desk, he spread out one of the drawings.

He was no expert at reading drawings, but it appeared to be more of a map than anything else. The usual legend indicating the directional symbols was drawn on one corner, and a line marked the boundary between the Lazy L and Timberline. Another line indicated the Pecos River. There were several intersecting circles marked with latitude and longitude as well as elevation, and even one indicating the location of the cave.

What he found interesting was that all of these markings appeared on the Timberline side of the boundary. He might have been wrong about some things, but at least one hunch was right: Ben Lawford's interest in Timberline was due to a lot more than the scenery. He found the other two drawings were merely duplications of the one he'd just viewed.

What in hell did those marked spots mean? Could they possibly be gold deposits? It would certainly explain why Ben was so anxious to get his hands on Timberline.

Cole rummaged through the desk until he found a piece of paper and a pencil, then he made a rough copy of the map, replaced everything as he'd found it, and got out of there.

His curiosity was piqued beyond ignoring. Being this close to Timberline, he decided to take a look. Without the proper equipment, it would be impossible to locate those markings on the map. He didn't even have a compass. But he sure as hell knew north from south.

Cole returned to the cave and wondered why that spot was marked, since it was considerably distant from the other markings. Somehow there had to be an obvious clue there that he was overlooking. He decided to take a closer look at the rear of it.

Cole lit the lantern and entered, cautiously stepping past the muddy pitfall. He carefully examined the rear wall, looking for a vein or spot that might indicate some kind of distinguishing mark. There was nothing he could see, but the clue had to be right before his eyes. Frustrated, he started to go back, tracing his fingertips along the cold granite wall.

Upon reaching the mud patch, he stepped carefully across it, avoiding the dangerous edge of the pit. In so doing, he splattered mud on the bottom of his trousers. Disgusted, he pulled the bandanna from around his neck to wipe off the mud and attempted to wet it in the thin trickle of water leaking through a crack in the wall.

He stopped and ran his fingers along the crack. The water was warm to the touch. That didn't make sense. The cave was cool, the water in the Pecos and all the streams was cool. But this water was warm.

And then it all became clear to him. The reason why Pop bought Timberline, why he was convinced he could save the town. The source of the water was a hot spring.

That explained the brochure Pop had received in the

mail. He hadn't intended to visit a hot spring. He was planning on opening one.

This was a craze among easterners. They flocked to these sites for therapeutic reasons: to soak in the healing waters or drink the mineral water. And they'd have to come through Lawford to reach Timberline.

Bless his heart, Cole thought with affection, *that was how Pop figured on saving the town.*

And that bastard Lawford had somehow gotten wise to it. Cole climbed on Cupid and headed back to town.

Shortly after Cole's departure Keith Lawford had joined Maggie and Caroline. He tagged along with them as the crowd assembled in front of the bank awaiting the speech of the host—and guest of honor—Ben Lawford. It wasn't until Ben got up on the rostrum that Keith asked where Cole was.

"I think he went back to the house to sleep. He was awake most of the night to make sure the fire didn't flare up again." Maggie didn't have to say more because Ben began to speak.

Ben gave his usual dissertation on the history of Lawford, describing how he had settled there with a wife and infant son. In his blunderbuss fashion he described how he'd protected the town by fighting off the Indians and any riffraff who tried to destroy it. He got a loud round of applause when he expressed his sorrow over the loss of one of Lawford's most beloved citizens, Mick O'Shea. And in conclusion he intended to resurrect the demolished stageline so that the good citizens of Lawford would not become isolated from the rest of the country.

The crowd let out a cheer when the Lazy L's chuck-wagon arrived. Maggie and Caroline took Juan and Emilio each a plate of food. Both father and son were doing well and in good spirits, and after a short visit, the two girls returned to the celebration and sat down in the shade while Keith went to get them plates of food.

"I don't remember seeing you at the celebration last year, Caroline, or even the year before," Maggie said.

"No, we didn't come back for it. When we left Lawford five years ago, we moved to Chicago. Father thought there was a greater need for schoolteachers in a larger city. It was just too far to come back for the celebration. He retired this summer and is considering returning to Lawford."

"How would you feel about coming back here to live?"

Caroline glanced over to where Keith was getting their food. "I've always loved Lawford."

"I don't," Maggie said. "I'm looking forward to leaving."

"Where are you going?"

"Cole is taking me to his parents' ranch in Texas. Ellie is going with us."

"I'm sorry to hear that, and I know my mother will be, too. She and Ellie are such good friends."

"I don't remember much of any childhood I spent here, and with Pop gone, there's really nothing in Lawford to hold me."

"I have the impression you and Keith are very close," Caroline said guardedly.

"Yes, we are. We're very good friends." Maggie didn't

feel this was the time to mention that's all she wanted
them to be.

"I would have thought Keith would have married
by now. We expected to hear a long time ago that he
had finally married."

"Well, let's face it, Caroline, the pickings are pretty
poor here in Lawford."

"He seems pretty attentive to you." Caroline
sounded very wistful, and it crossed Maggie's mind
that maybe Cole was right about Caroline's feelings for
Keith.

"He is to you, too. He's such a gentleman."

"I noticed Cole MacKenzie is very attentive to you
also."

"He's not attentive, he's autocratic."

"Maybe so, but he's a handsome autocrat."

"Oh, you noticed that, too," Maggie said. They both
broke out in giggles.

Maggie told Caroline about the incident in Noches
when she had Cole and his cousins arrested. Their eyes
were watering from laughing by the time she finished
describing the confusion in the jail and court.

"I wish you could have seen it, Caroline. The judge
actually ordered us all out of the city. Lord knows what
he'll do if we ever show up there again."

"Show up where?" Keith asked, putting down
plates heaped high with food.

"Noches," Maggie said. "I was just telling Caroline
about the judge ordering us all out of the city."

"Judge Gardner?" Keith asked.

"Yes."

"He's my godfather. My mentor."

Maggie nodded. "He did mention your name." She

avoided saying it was in relation to them getting married. "Keith, did you draw up that paper to be signed?"

"Yes, whenever Cole is ready."

"Why don't I go and see if I can find him," Maggie said. "You and Caroline enjoy yourselves."

Maggie hurried away before they could suggest coming with her. She saw Ben Lawford talking to Romberg and Kern, and when he walked away, Maggie approached them. With luck, maybe she could find out something that might be helpful.

"I hope you gentlemen are enjoying the celebration. It's an important day for Ben."

"It is nice," Romberg said.

"But we have other business to attend to," Kern complained. "With no stagecoach, we had to remain this day."

"Well, sir, no one planned the fire." These unpleasant men were so self-absorbed they hadn't even expressed sympathy to her over the loss of the coach and stable. "Did you complete your business with Ben successfully?" she asked, hoping to give them the impression she knew what that business was all about.

"Yes," Romberg said. "He is providing us the use of his buggy tomorrow to get us back to where we can catch a train."

"Will you be returning to Lawford?"

"Of course," Kern said, "With Mr. Munson."

"Mr. Munson?"

"The geologist."

"Oh, of course. Mr. Munson, the geologist," Maggie said. "And when will that be?"

"In two weeks. Come, Karl," Romberg said. "There is pie. I hope it is apple."

So there was a geologist involved in whatever Ben was up to. Maggie was sure Cole would find that interesting.

Once back at the house she began pacing the floor. What was keeping Cole? She couldn't stall much longer. Surely he'd had plenty of time by now to get there and back. What if he'd been caught? If so, Ben would have been informed, so she ruled that out. What if something had happened to him? What if he was lying hurt? Helpless? She couldn't visualize Cole being helpless about anything.

She was building herself into a panic. Cole was fine. Cole could take care of himself in any emergency. Cole was . . . *"unsaddling Cupid right now!"* she cried, peering out of the window.

Maggie rushed out the door. "Thank God, you're back. I've been worried to death. What took you so long?"

"Maggie, you're not going to believe what I found out. I think I've figured out what's behind this, but I don't know for sure who's involved besides Ben Lawford." He grabbed her hand. "Let's get to the telegraph office and hope Josh came through, then I'll tell you all about it."

"Well, I've been doing some investigative work, too," she said, practically at a run to keep up with his long strides.

The telegraph operator was standing in the doorway of the Western Union office, chomping on a piece of pie.

"Did a telegram come for me?" Cole asked.

"Sure did, Mr. MacKenzie. Been looking for you."

He frowned. "Who's this Joseph Riley? Friend of yours?"

Cole gave him an impassive look and held out his hand. "The wire, please."

The operator dug the telegram out of his pocket and handed it to Cole, then went back to chewing on the pie.

"Where can we go for some privacy?"

"Back to the house, I guess," Maggie said.

On the way there Cole read the message from Josh, and as soon as they reached the house, he handed it to Maggie.

She read it swiftly and then looked at him, confused.

"According to that wire, the real killer confessed to the crime five years ago, so Joseph Riley is no longer wanted for the murder," Cole said.

"Well, if that's true, and Joseph Riley was cleared of the crime, Vic has nothing to hide."

"Unless he doesn't know he's been cleared. He's been in hiding all these years. If he'd known the truth, I doubt he would have continued to use a false identity."

"At least we have the facts now. I think the time has come to confront Dallas and Vic with them."

"Were you able to get in and read the drawings?" Maggie asked. "Cole, I found out from that unpleasant Mr. Romberg and Mr. Kern that they'll be coming back to Lawford with a geologist. What's going on?"

Cole told her what he'd discovered at the Lazy L and his return to the cave. "I figure Pop discovered the hot spring and intended to build a spa."

"Cole, that still doesn't mean that Ben killed him."

"No, but it does offer a good motive, doesn't it? All I've heard from the people in this town is that no one would have any reason to kill Pop. I'm going to talk to Dallas now. It's clear she knows more than she's saying."

"Well, I'm coming with you," Maggie declared.

When they reached the bar, it was empty except for Dallas. With free food and beer outside, no one was about to spend their own money.

"Dallas, it's time we have a long talk," Cole said, sitting down at a table.

"I figured you'd get around to it sooner or later, Texas."

"Dallas, we know you and Vic are sister and brother."

"Then you probably know why we aren't admitting it," she said.

"Yes."

"I didn't murder that man, Cole," Vic said from the doorway of the supply room.

"I know that." Cole pulled the telegram out of his pocket and handed it to Dallas. She read it and looked at her brother, tears filling her eyes. Vic came over and read the wire. He lowered his head in silence.

"I hope to God you weren't involved in Pop's murder," Cole said.

"Pop wasn't murdered, Cole," Vic said.

"Yeah, so I've heard since I came to town. I think differently. I figure Ben found out why Pop bought Timberline and killed him to get the property."

"Well, you're wrong, Texas, because I was there and saw what happened."

Maggie gasped. "You were there—and you never said anything."

"Because it *was* an accident, and nothing would have been gained by bringing Ben's name into it. We'd gone into the cave to get out of the rain. Mick was there. Ben discovered the water seeping through the wall was hot. He put two and two together and figured the source was a hot spring. Mick told him he was going to put up a spa to bring people into the town. You know how Ben loves this town, honey. He told Mick he'd put up the money for part ownership of the spa, Mick agreed, and they shook hands. When they started to leave, Mick slipped and broke his neck in the fall. I swear to you, Ben was nowhere near Mick at the time."

"And you left him there," Maggie said, appalled. "I thought he was your friend."

"We got a rope and Ben climbed down. Mick was dead. You could tell that by just looking at him. We didn't know what to do. Everyone in town knew how Mick and Ben argued, so we decided to keep Ben's name out of it. The next day, Ben formed a search party and recovered the body."

"Why wouldn't you just tell the truth instead of pretending you didn't know? You let Pop lie out there, knowing the truth."

"Ben asked me not to. He said there'd always be some people who wouldn't believe him."

"And why should we believe you," Maggie cried. "You lied about Vic all these years."

"Vic is my brother. He was accused of a murder he hadn't committed. Wouldn't you have done the same, Maggie?" Dallas said sadly. "Honey, your father was dead. We couldn't do anything for him. I loved him as much as I did my own brother."

"But why would you go along with Ben's wishes?" Maggie asked. "If you backed up his story, people would believe it."

Cole had listened in silence throughout Dallas's confession. "Because she's in love with Ben."

"That's right, Texas. Ben and I have been having an affair for the past fifteen years."

For a long moment Maggie sat speechless. She finally found her voice. "Does Keith know the truth about my father's death?"

"No. Ben, Vic, and myself are the only ones."

"Did Keith know about the hot springs on Timberline?" Cole asked.

"Not until yesterday. Ben told me Keith was furious when he found out his father was trying to cheat Maggie."

Maggie still struggled with accepting the explanation. "I don't see why I should believe anything you've said, Dallas. From what I can tell, you've done nothing but deceive us for years."

"I guess you have no reason to trust me, honey, but I'm telling you the truth."

"Yes, she is, Maggie," Cole said.

"How do you know?"

"Because she has nothing to gain by lying."

"She's just admitted she's in love with Ben."

"Maggie, you've got no reason to trust me either, but I know she's not lying, same as Cole does," Vic said.

"I don't know what to believe anymore. I have to get out of here." She ran out of the saloon.

"Dallas, do you know why Pop sent me a telegram saying he was desperate and to come at once?"

Dallas wiped away her tears and smiled. "I told him to."

"I don't get it."

"He was crying in his beer one night because he was worried that Maggie would agree to marry Keith. Whether you know it or not, he always hoped that you and Maggie would hitch up. So I told him the quickest way to get you here is to tell you he's desperate and needs your help. It worked, didn't it?" She became somber. "What are you going to do, Cole?"

"Well, like you said, Dallas, nothing can be done to help Pop any more." He got to his feet. "I'd better go after Maggie and make sure she's all right. The poor kid's taken a lot of punches these past few weeks."

Vic shook his hand. "Thanks for everything."

"Yeah, I'm happy for you, pal. By the way, why were you following me when I first showed up?"

"I was hiding from the law, and you've got Ranger stamped across your forehead, MacKenzie."

Cole stopped in the doorway. "And, Dallas, tell Lawford for me he's gonna give Maggie a damn sight more than five thousand dollars if he wants Timberline."

Returning to the house, Cole found Maggie sitting on the front porch. "You okay about all this, Maggie?"

"Yes. It's all shocking to me, but I'm relieved to know Pop's death was an accident."

"How about you and I riding out to Timberline tomorrow to try and find that spring? You can ask Caroline to join us, if you want to."

"Caroline and her folks just left with the Calhouns. Peggy Calhoun is Mrs. Bennett's sister, and they'll be visiting there for a couple of days."

"I'm sorry I didn't get to say good-bye to them."

"Caroline said they'll stop back here to say good-bye before going back to Chicago."

"I'm hoping we'll be the ones saying good-bye as we leave for Texas. I've had all I want of your town, Maggie."

"You know, Cole, I have, too," Maggie said.

"Well, since I've only had a couple of hours sleep in the past two nights, I don't know about you, but I'm going to bed. Good night, Maggie."

"Good night, Cole."

Maggie sat on the porch and looked up at the sky. She suddenly felt very good. She had been surrounded by disaster for weeks, and she felt like she had finally weathered the worst storm of her life.

Tomorrow was a new beginning.

Chapter 23

Cole had already eaten when Maggie came downstairs the next morning. Ellie greeted her with a bowl of oatmeal and a slice of freshly baked bread. "Cole said not to expect the two of you for dinner or supper."

"That's right. Did he tell you about Timberline?"

"Yeah, ain't that something! If what he says is true, pretty soon there'll be a lot of them snooty easterners passing through Lawford. You still planning on leaving?"

"I haven't changed my mind, and I don't think Cole will change his. He wants out of here."

"He says the place can make a lot of money."

"I don't care about money, Ellie. I just want a stable life, marriage, and children."

"Heard tell you can have all that right here in Lawford," she said with a sly grin."

"Lawford doesn't hold too many pleasant memories for me. If you've changed your mind about leaving, Ellie, I'll understand. Lawford's always been your home, and the thought of being uprooted is probably disturbing to you."

"I ain't gave it a never no mind," Ellie said. "Home is where the heart is, gal, and my heart's where you are."

Maggie got up and hugged her. "I don't know how I'd ever get along without you, Ellie."

Preening in the affection, Ellie said, "I've packed you a lunch. That young fella said the two of you are going to try and find that hot spring. Lord only knows how long that'll take."

"Where is Cole?"

"He's out saddling the horses. You best get out there before he rides off without you."

" 'Bye, darling," Maggie called on her way out.

Once they were on their way, Cole explained that he figured if there was a spring, it must be pretty well concealed, or it would probably have been discovered a long time ago.

"Well, where is the logical site for a hot spring?"

"Usually, a flat area, but there are none that I've seen on Timberline. That map they made has a couple of spots marked. They must be possibilities. I'm told that the springs were formed from volcanic activity centuries ago. That's about all I know about hot springs."

"How hot is hot, Cole?"

"I guess the water's a little over a hundred degrees."

"Well, that means all we have to do is find a spring that was formed a few million years ago, and we'll be able to take a hot bath."

"That's about it, babe," he said lightly.

For hours and hours they rode through the area, not actually knowing what they were looking for. They finally stopped and ate the lunch, then resumed the search again.

It was nearing dusk when they stopped again to rest.

"Cole, I think this is hopeless. It will soon be too dark to see. We don't even know what we're looking for. Let's leave it for the geologists. They have the knowledge and proper equipment."

"I suppose you're right."

"What difference does it make anyway? I don't want Timberline, Cole."

"I guess it's ego on my part. I kind of wanted to wrap up all the loose ends before we left, that's all."

"Just to show Ben how smart you are, right?" she teased.

"You know, Miz Margaret, you've really got my number, haven't you?"

"I always had your number, MacKenzie, since I was fourteen."

"Is that right?" She backed up when he began to stalk her. "Since you were fourteen, huh?"

"That's right."

"Well, since you're so smart, what has Miz Margaret figured out I'm about to do to Maggie?" he said, continuing to stalk her. "Wring her neck, or give her the spanking Pop should have done a long time ago?"

"You'd have to catch her first, MacKenzie." She turned and started to run, and he chased after her.

Laughing, she dodged from tree to tree, always managing to keep out of his reach. "I always could outrun you, even in Alaska."

"It's not going to do you any good, because I'll catch you eventually."

She ducked into a copse, and he followed her.

"You've kind of backed yourself into a corner in here, Miz Margaret."

Maggie backed up and tripped over a fallen log, and as she started to fall backward Cole grabbed her. Clutched together, they fell—into a pool of hot water.

"Maggie, this is it! We've found it, baby. We've found it!"

Gleeful with joy, they began to splash and romp like children in the water.

Finally, exhausted, they climbed out and pulled off their wet boots and stockings. When Cole began to shed his wet clothing, Maggie stepped behind a bush for concealment and removed her blouse and riding skirt. She figured she'd at least get rid of her wet underclothing and put the skirt and blouse back on. She had stripped down to just her drawers when she felt the familiar awareness of his nearness. Her heart began to hammer in her breast, and she turned slowly. He stood not more than a few footsteps away, shirtless and barefoot, his opened jeans hanging loosely on his hips. Drops of water glistened like shards of glass in the dark hair on his chest and the rumpled strands that clung to his forehead.

He looked dark, disheveled, and deadly.

She made no attempt to cover herself when her bare breasts fell under the perusal of his hungry gaze, their dusky puckered tips hardened to pointed peaks.

Her feminine instinct told her this was it. It was finally going to happen. The magnetism between them had drawn them to this inevitable moment, and when he lifted his gaze to meet hers, the passion in his sapphire eyes promised her all that she had yearned for . . . dreamed . . . fantasized . . . from the moment she fell in love with him. The prolonged anticipation became too great to bear. She stepped forward.

He pulled her against him. Sweet sensation swirled through her body from the erotic feel of heated flesh on heated flesh. His tongue circled her parted lips and he began to gently tug at them. The sensation became so tantalizing that she sought a greater contact. Reaching up, she grasped his face between her hands and captured his mouth with her own.

His response was instant and ardent—and he took control.

Lowering his head, he claimed her parted lips, increasing the pressure as the kiss grew hungrier. Her head began to whirl from the erotic feel of her bare breasts crushed against the solid, heated wall of his chest.

Sliding his tongue between her lips, he laved the moist chamber of her mouth in hot, tantalizing sweeps. No other man had ever kissed her like this before, and her body trembled from the thrill of it. He kissed her again and again—drugging kisses, tantalizing in their potency, each one deepening until they both were intoxicated by the divine excitement of their aroused passion.

She felt bereft when he broke the contact until his warm, moist breath stirred the hair at her ear. "I've thought about this from the time I saw you in Lawford's office."

"That's not as long as I've wanted you to," she murmured in response, and gasped from the feel of the incredible sensual slide of his hand to her breast.

"Maggie, are you sure this is what you want?"

"I've never wanted anything so much in my life."

To prove the urgency of her words, she moved out of his arms and released her drawers. They dropped to the ground, and she stepped out of them, then boldly raised her head and met the inflamed passion in his eyes.

Darker and more deadly-looking.

"My God, Maggie, you're so beautiful."

The awe in his voice heightened her desire to an overpowering urgency. In a quick movement, he slipped his pants down his long legs and kicked them aside. He was not wearing drawers.

Other than that glimpse of him in Noches, Maggie had never seen a man completely naked before. Her eyes widened in alarm at the sight of his male arousal. Instinctively she backed away.

As if sensing her rising panic, he reached out and grasped her hands. "I'll try not to hurt you, Maggie."

"Cole, I've never—"

"Hush, love, I know. I understand," he murmured. "It's not too late to stop."

"No!" she cried in panic. "Don't stop. Please don't stop."

He slowly slid his hands along the length of her arms, gently pulling her into his embrace. When he lowered his mouth to hers, she parted her lips.

The kiss began gently, but within seconds the pressure increased as he filled his hands with her breasts and skimmed his thumbs across the turgid peaks. She broke the kiss with an ecstatic sob, moaning his name over and over.

The sound drove him wild. His loins flooded with hot blood. Reclaiming her mouth with hot sweeps of his tongue, he lowered her to the ground. Now, powered by lust, he had to taste more of her. Restraint was no longer an option. Cupping the underside of one of her breasts, he brought it to his mouth and like a nursing babe he suckled the firm globe. She arched her back reflexively, and he shifted his mouth to the other breast. She responded with low, blissful moans that drove him to even greater heights of passion. His hands caressed her, his mouth tasted her—laving, nipping, tugging, and suckling as she thrashed beneath him, her breath coming in ragged gasps when he drew ever nearer to the core of her passion.

She stiffened slightly when he parted her thighs and palmed the heated center, and then he began to massage her there with the same fervor his mouth feasted on her breasts. She began to writhe mindlessly, her responsive body convulsing with spasmodic tremors.

"Oh, God, Cole! Oh, dear God!" she cried out in ecstasy until her breath became too precious to waste on words.

Then and only then did he mount her, his kiss swallowing her sob of pain when he pierced the thin membrane that veiled her virginity.

Blood pounded at his temple, his brain, his loins as he inched deeper inside. She tightened around him, and the tempo of his thrusts increased—faster and faster, deeper and deeper until his body shuddered in the ecstatic bliss of a climax.

He rolled off her, and they lay side by side, the sound of their raspy breathing breaking the silence.

After a long moment Maggie opened her eyes.

Cole lay on his side, gazing down at her, his arm propped up with his head cradled in his hand. He smiled and, blushing, she lowered her gaze.

"Now that's a Miss Margaret blush if I ever saw one. What's wrong?" he asked, tucking a few errant strands of hair behind her ear.

His touch was warm and so incredibly gentle that, if she had not been in the afterglow of their lovemaking, she'd probably have started crying.

"I can't believe what we just did," she murmured.

"Regrets, Maggie?" He lay back, whatever he was thinking veiled behind his lowered eyelids.

"Heavens, no! Nothing like that." She leaned across him. "It was the most incredible sensation I've ever felt." She kissed him lightly on his lips, and then, smiling with contentment, she laid her head on his chest and idly caressed the dark hair on it. The sound of his warm chuckle broadened her smile. "What?" she asked, raising her head.

"Miss Margaret would show greater reserve."

"I suppose she would. Should. But I'll always be Maggie to you, won't I, Cole? You'll never admit I'm no longer that sixteen-year-old."

"Not anymore. You've convinced me. You're all woman, Maggie O'Shea." *And what a woman!*

She leaned forward, her face so near he could feel the warmth of her breath. "Did you enjoy it as much as I did?"

"Oh, yeah."

"Let's do it again."

"Maggie, you're outrageous." He started to warn her they never should have done it the first time, but she shifted on top of him, stifling his words with the pressure of her lips. Then it became too late for any warning. The darting forays of her tongue, the sensuous slide of her bare flesh against his, the exquisite stabbing of the peaks of her breasts became an assault on his reflexes. His arousal was instantaneous. His loins felt on fire as his heated blood washed through him again in a floodtide of lust.

He'd been having sex since he was in his teens and had always been in command, but the touch of her mouth and hands was testing his control to the limit. And it felt so good that he closed his eyes and let his senses enjoy it, curious to know how far her incredible passion would carry her.

She had learned the lesson well.

The more she continued, the bolder she became: stroking, caressing, tasting whatever fell under her hands and mouth. His slightest gasp, jerk of a nerve, shift of a muscle would cause her to re-examine the sensitive spot, and he groaned aloud from the erotic exploration like a virgin schoolboy at the hands of a dominatrix.

It was torture. It was ecstasy.

The cords of his neck and arms were taut, perspiration dotted his brow, and his loins were on fire, his organ throbbing and so hard he thought he'd burst. With an uncontrollable growl of lust, he rolled over and saw she was as far gone as he. Her lips were parted, her breath coming in gasps, and her eyes were so dark with passion they gleamed like emeralds. When he parted her legs, she was moist and waiting.

Gorging on the deliciousness of her breasts, he drove into her, savoring the mindless ecstasy of each one of their combined shuddering tremors of release.

When his breathing returned to normal, Cole felt coated with perspiration. He had to rinse off, but he was too sapped to move. Turning his head, he glanced at the spring. Was it always that far away? He'd look like a fool if he crawled to it on his hands and knees. So, biting the bullet, he got to his feet, walked the few yards, and waded in.

The sun had set, and moonlight glistened on the small pool set in its protective grove of trees and granite rock. The warm water was relaxing and washed away the salty sweat. What he needed more was the shock of cool water. Unfortunately the Pecos was too far to even consider it.

Climbing out of the water, he hustled around until he located his jeans, pulled them on over his damp body, and then walked over to Maggie.

She had fallen asleep. For a long moment he gazed down at her. She looked so damn innocent and childlike that he started to feel like a lecher again. But she sure as hell was no child. She was all woman. And she put all her energy and passion into making love, much as she did into anything she undertook.

Just looking at her and recalling their lovemaking began to arouse him again. All he would have to do was go over there, kiss her, and she'd roll over and drive him to wildness. God, what a feeling! No woman had ever raised him to such heights that he lost control. All these past ten years he'd never suspected what he really had been missing. And it was too good to turn away from.

He stepped toward her and then halted. If he dived in again, there'd be no ending. Not if it was up to that little temptress with that delicious, squirming, responsive body of hers. Lord, he could still taste it and was hungry for more.

But the onus of stopping was on his shoulders.

He went over and shook her gently. "Maggie, wake up."

She opened her eyes and smiled at him. "I guess I fell asleep." Her eyes widened in surprise. "You're all dressed."

"Yeah, and time for you to get dressed, too. We best get moving."

"Do we have to?" She grabbed his hand and pulled him down. "Oh, you're wet."

"I rinsed off in the spring." He stood up and grasped her hand, pulling her to her feet.

She pursed her lips together, pretending to pout. He wanted to devour them until she begged him to stop. "You're no fun. You should have wakened me. We could have done it together."

We'd have done it together, all right.

His loins knotted in response to the thought as he watched her trip lightly to the spring, like an alluring wood nymph in the moonlight—a beautiful, seductive maiden whose touch could drive a man to madness.

His own lips suddenly felt dry, and he moistened them with his tongue. He was hot for her again. And he'd never had sex in a hot spring before. It would be a first. The more he thought of it, the more appealing the idea became until his head prevailed over an aching groin. Hadn't there been enough other firsts tonight already?

Get over it, MacKenzie. Tonight wasn't your first roll in the hay. So don't let your loins do your thinking.

He quickly put his shirt on, then sat down and pulled on his stockings and boots before he changed his mind.

Cole was aware when Maggie came out of the water, but not trusting the temptation, he purposely avoided looking at her. He busied himself by gathering up their wet underclothes, wringing them out, then stuffing them into the saddlebags. Then he tightened the cinches on the horses and waited until she finally came over.

"All set?"

Maggie nodded. "I still don't know why we have to go back to town," she said as he helped her to mount.

"It's the wisest thing to do." He swung up into the saddle and they moved off.

"What difference would it have made?"

"Maggie, you know if we stayed, we'd have made love again."

"I would hope so."

"Well, we have to stop. It was a mistake."

"A mistake? Why? How can you say that?"

"The obvious reason is that you could get pregnant."

"Would that be so bad, Cole?" A note of rising resentment now overshadowed her previous puzzlement.

"Yes, it would. The thought of it scares the hell out of me."

"Then maybe you should have considered that before, not after."

"Maggie, I'm to blame for what happened. And as much as I care for you, I'm not ready to make a commitment to you or anyone right now."

"Did I ask for one?" She goaded her horse and passed him.

Cole caught up with her. "No, you didn't, Maggie, but a baby would. That would be an indisputable commitment. I'm sorry you don't understand, but if I *were* ready to settle down, I'd—"

"Be willing to *settle* for me. Is that what you're trying to say, Cole?"

"I'm trying to tell you I took your virginity, and if you get pregnant as a result, I wouldn't hesitate to accept my responsibility."

"Even if you don't want to. How noble of you, Cole. But let me make one thing perfectly clear. You didn't *take* my virginity; I *gave* it to you."

"What's the difference?"

"It means you have no responsibility. So you don't owe me anything, Cole. Nothing at all. No responsibility. No love. And no need to give up your worthless, shallow lifestyle to marry me, because I wouldn't marry you even if you fathered a dozen babies with me. You've always said it's time for me to grow up. That means forgetting a bastard like you ever existed. So get out of my life, Cole. Now. And this time don't come back. I never want to see or hear from you again."

Maggie goaded her mount to a full gallop and rode ahead of him. This time he didn't try to catch up with her. When they reached the house, she dismounted and went inside.

She didn't look back.

Maggie willed herself not to cry as she removed her clothes and pulled the nightgown over her head. Tears would reflect self-pity. And she had no cause for self-pity. Self-pity debilitated one's fortitude; betrayal energized it.

And she had been betrayed . . . deceived . . . deflowered.

And bewildered as well, for how was it possible that loving a man as much as she loved Cole, he couldn't help but love her back?

But she wouldn't cry.

Maggie picked up a brush and began to apply vigorous strokes to her hair. She had meant what she'd said to Cole: she'd been a willing participant in their intimacy. More than willing, she conceded. Reflecting on the evening, she'd given as much as she'd taken. But unlike him, she had not been deceitful. She'd been in love with him. His motive had merely been lust.

Putting aside the brush, she climbed into bed. No, indeed. She did not feel sorry for herself. If anything, she pitied Cole MacKenzie. Some day he'd have to answer to a power greater than himself—and he'd have a lot of explaining to do.

With the satisfaction of that conviction, Maggie closed her eyes—and cried herself to sleep.

When she awoke the next morning, Maggie's resolve was stronger than ever. Cole MacKenzie would never love her, and the time had come to put that foolish dream behind her once and for all. She had tried honesty and trickery with him, and neither had worked. And nothing ever would.

If I got pregnant, he'd do me the favor of marrying me. Indeed! Well, no thanks, Cole MacKenzie. If you can't do me the favor of loving me, I'm not asking for any others.

There was someone who did love her—and it was time she accepted reality. Dreams were for naive girls such as she once had been. Now she was seeing life the way it really was. And that was the sad but true reality that Cole MacKenzie would never love her. The time had come to get him out of her life once and for all.

She dressed and left the house.

Chapter 24

"**W**here is she, Ellie?" Cole asked, when Maggie was not at the breakfast table.

"She said she had an errand to run and not to hold breakfast."

"Did she say where?"

"Young Lawford's office."

He was curious. What was so important that Maggie had gone to Keith Lawford's office this early in the morning? She'd been in a dangerous mood last night when she left him, and they had a lot to talk over and settle between them.

He'd handled the whole thing wrong last night. Said all the wrong things. He'd known what he was doing, but she was an innocent with no idea of what she was letting herself in for. He'd only been trying to let her know that he was to blame, that she shouldn't feel any guilt. But from past experience he knew she was controlled by her emotions and had little rein on her responses. He knew—and he'd let it happen.

Cole was still at the breakfast table when Maggie returned and joined him.

"I'm glad you both are here," she said with a cheery smile. "I have some wonderful news to tell you. Keith and I are getting married." Her announcement was greeted with silence. "Well, isn't anyone going to say anything?"

"Every time I give you credit for showing some common sense, Maggie, you manage to convince me how wrong I am." He got up and left.

The trouble with walking out as he had done was that he had no place to go. If he went to his room, he'd soon feel so cooped up that he'd probably end up putting his fist through the wall. The stable and office were no longer an option, since they'd been destroyed in the fire. And he was in no mood to go to Dallas's. He needed to be alone.

Cole saddled Cupid and rode out of town. With no intent in mind, he ended up at Timberline. Dismounting, he sat down near the edge of the spring in the same spot where he'd made love to Maggie.

Now would be as good a time as any to leave—clear out. Adiós, Lawford. So long, it's been good to know you. I've no reason to remain. The circumstances of Pop's death are resolved. I'll remain Maggie's guardian for three more years. But if she marries Keith Lawford, the responsibility for her welfare will rest on her husband's shoulders. And I'd be leaving her in good hands. Keith Lawford's intelligent, he's rich, and he loves her.

But sure as God made little green apples, I know that Maggie doesn't love Keith Lawford.

*   *   *

Maggie stood at her bedroom window and watched Cole ride away. The situation was going to be very awkward until he left Lawford for good. The sooner he did that, the sooner she could get on with her life.

She went back to the dresser and put some finishing touches to her hair, and then she went downstairs to await Keith's arrival. He had insisted they ride out to the Lazy L to tell his father the good news. Maggie knew why Ben would be pleased—Timberline. And as far as she was concerned, Ben Lawford could have it. She never wanted to set foot on Timberline again. Not only had her father died there, but also it would always be a constant reminder of what she and Cole had shared at the pool.

As always, Keith arrived promptly, and Maggie let him do most of the talking on the way to the Lazy L. As she expected, Ben was ecstatic when he heard the news. Short of salivating and rubbing his hands together gleefully, Ben looked like a glutton with fork and knife viewing the plump roasted fowl set before him.

Trouble is, *she* was that cooked goose.

Ben insisted the wedding be held as soon as possible, and Maggie listened listlessly as he and Keith began to make plans for the prenuptial party to be held the coming Saturday, with the wedding to follow the day after.

Maggie agreed to whatever they suggested. The sooner she married, the sooner Cole would leave.

Before returning to town, she went over to the corral and visited with the team. At least they'd soon be back together again, she thought desolately, with a backward glance at the horses.

Maggie was relieved there was no sign of Cole when she got back from the Lazy L. Before she had a chance to discuss the wedding arrangements with Ellie, the Bennetts drove up, and Maggie hurried out to greet Caroline.

After an exchange of hugs and kisses, she put on a bright smile. "Caroline, I'm getting married."

Caroline glowed with pleasure. "Oh, I'm so happy for you, Margaret. So Cole finally proposed."

"Cole?" Maggie said. "I'm marrying Keith."

Caroline's smile faded into a look of shock. She turned away momentarily, and when she turned back, her face was wreathed in a smile. "That's wonderful news."

"Caroline, please stay for the wedding. I want you to be my maid of honor."

"Well, I don't know . . ."

"We're getting married in less than a week, and I've got so much to do. And since these will be my final days of maidenhood, I'd love to spend them with you. Will you, Caroline?"

"All right, Margaret. I'd like that, too."

"Oh, that's wonderful." Maggie threw her arms around her, and they hugged again. "It'll mean so much to me to have you here."

"How ever are you going to prepare for a wedding in less than a week?" Caroline said as they hurried up to Maggie's room.

"It's going to be held at the Lazy L. Ben's handling all those arrangements. My problem is what to wear." Maggie riffled through the few gowns in the closet. "These dresses are so old. I really don't have a nice enough gown for a bridal dress."

"Why don't we make you one?"

She looked hopefully at Caroline. "Do we have the time?"

"Of course. My mother will help. She's an excellent seamstress. She makes all my dresses."

"Let's check at the general store and see what bolts of material they have."

They rushed out of the house and hurried to the store. The selection was limited and disappointing. The choice consisted of red and white checked gingham and black muslin.

The two women looked at each other. "Noches," Maggie said.

"Definitely Noches," Caroline agreed.

"Oh, no!" Maggie groaned. "How will we get there? No stagecoach, remember?"

"I can drive my parents' buggy."

When they returned to the house, Ellie and Jane came down the stairs carrying armfuls of clothing and plants.

"What's going on?" Maggie asked.

"I'm moving back to my own bed," Ellie declared.

"What about Cole?"

"He's moved out. He said with the Bennetts here and all, it would be more convenient if he stayed at the hotel until he leaves for Texas."

"He's very thoughtful," Caroline said.

"Did he say what day he'll be leaving, Ellie?" Maggie asked.

"Not to me."

"Well, thank goodness Cole's agreed to my getting married. It would have been just like him to interfere."

"Margaret, I think you do him an injustice," Caroline said. "I find Cole to be a very nice man and very considerate of others."

"You don't know him as well as we do. Right, Ellie?"

"Cole MacKenzie's a fine young man," Ellie declared. "If I were his mother, I'd be proud to call him son." She stomped away.

"Wedding jitters," Maggie said, by way of explanation for Ellie's disgruntlement.

At dinner that night, despite Cole's absence, there was still a tension in the air, especially between Maggie and Ellie. Even Caroline's soothing efforts failed to lessen it.

When Keith stopped in later to say good night, Caroline rushed to greet him. "Congratulations, Keith. I'm so happy for the both of you."

"Thank you, Caroline."

"The Bennetts are remaining in Lawford for the wedding," Maggie said. "Caroline has agreed to be my maid of honor."

"That's very nice of you," he said to her.

"I'm flattered to have been asked," Caroline replied.

The whole conversation sounded forced to Maggie. Was everybody but her suffering from wedding jitters?

"Have you decided on your best man, Keith?" Jane Bennett asked.

"I haven't thought about it, Mrs. Bennett."

"Why not Cole MacKenzie?" Caroline suggested.

"No!" Maggie hadn't realized she'd shouted it out until she saw them all staring at her in surprise. "That is, I know Cole is anxious to return to Texas. He intends to leave Lawford this week."

"I can't believe he wouldn't delay his departure if you ask him," Caroline said.

Keith intervened to help her out. "I'm not particularly close to any of the ranch hands, but I could ask Vic."

"He'd be an excellent choice," Maggie agreed.

"Well, I just dropped in to say good night, but I thought you'd be interested, Maggie, in knowing Cole signed the paper for the sale of the stageline. We transferred the funds into your bank account."

So it was final. That chapter of her life closed. On with the next one. She walked out onto the porch with Keith.

"You know this week is going to be very hectic, Keith. I think everyone's nerves will be on edge."

"We'll get through it, dear, don't worry."

He kissed her and left.

Maggie watched him walk away. *I swear, Keith, I'll do everything possible to be a good wife to you.*

When she went back inside, she discovered the rest of the household had retired. Caroline was brushing out her hair when Maggie entered the bedroom.

"Did you tell Keith we were going to Noches tomorrow?" Caroline asked.

"Oh, my! I forgot," Maggie said. She undressed quickly and pulled on her nightgown.

"Shame on you, Margaret. He might have wanted to join us. I would have thought you'd want him to. It's such an exciting time. I'd want to share it with the man I love."

"You're right. He's staying in town tonight. I'll ask him first thing in the morning."

Later, as they lay in bed, Maggie asked, "Caroline, why did you think Cole would ask me to marry him?"

The question had nagged at her since Caroline first mentioned it.

"I don't know. The two of you seemed so close—as if you belonged together."

"Funny, that's how you and Keith appear to me."

Caroline blushed. "Keith and I. Goodness, Margaret, you are really mistaken. Keith and I have always just been good friends."

"Well, that's more than Cole and I have been. We don't even like each other," Maggie said, climbing into bed.

They lay in bed and chatted for another hour before finally falling asleep.

When Maggie went downstairs the next morning, Ellie was alone in the kitchen. She went up behind her and slipped her arms around Ellie's waist.

"Are you still mad at me, Ellie?"

"'Course not. I don't go to bed mad at the people I love. That don't mean I ain't got an opinion, though."

"That's what I love about you, Ellie." She kissed her on the cheek then headed for the door.

"Where are you going now?"

"I'll be right back."

Feeling the need for fresh air, Cole climbed out onto the balcony. From where he stood, he saw Maggie hurrying up the street to Keith's office. She tapped on the door, and when it opened, Cole saw the lawyer's smile of pleasure. Unconsciously Cole's hands clenched into fists when Keith reached for Maggie and kissed her. Then, after a brief conversation, Keith locked his office, and hand in hand the couple went back to the house.

Get out, MacKenzie. Walk away and don't look back.

Cole climbed back into his room, his stomach tied in a knot.

On the ride to Noches the three of them sang songs, but Maggie noticed Keith was never quite able to get into the spirit as vigorously as she remembered Cole doing. Nevertheless, the miles passed swiftly as they laughed and sang and spoke of old times.

On several occasions Maggie caught Keith's lingering glance at Caroline, or her wistful look at him. And it made her wonder how close they had once been.

As soon as they reached Noches, they shooed Keith away so they could pick out the material and accessories for Maggie's wedding gown. Keith decided to visit his godfather, Judge Gardner, and then meet them for lunch.

The first purchase was a pattern for the gown. They found one that pleased them both. It had a dropped round neckline with a ruffled collar and cap sleeves. The full skirt dropped in elegant folds to the floor with an overskirt of two panels divided at the waist and flowing stylishly down the sides and across the back.

"This will be beautiful on you, Margaret, and compliment your lovely neck and shoulders," said Caroline.

Maggie hadn't been aware she had a lovely neck and shoulders. No one had ever mentioned it to her before.

The next major task was to find the right material. They selected a white satin for the gown, matching white satin brocaded with roses for the side panels, and silk tulle dotted with tiny pearls for the veil.

"Why don't we run the same pearls along the scalloped edges and hem of the panels?" Caroline suggested.

"Won't that take a lot of time? We only have three days to make this gown, Caroline."

"We can do it. There are four of us. And are you forgetting my mother was a seamstress before she met my father? She'll know exactly what to do."

Caroline was a woman on a mission for the rest of the morning. They purchased white satin pumps, elbow-length gloves, and white hose. When she was satisfied they had all the accessories they needed, she took Maggie into a lingerie shop and bought a yellow silk nightgown and negligee.

"This is my wedding gift to you, Margaret."

"Oh, Caroline, it's beautiful. I've never owned anything so lovely."

"It will look gorgeous with your auburn hair," she said.

"Where did you learn all this?" Maggie inquired. "I didn't realize how ignorant I am."

"Darling, have you forgotten I've lived in Chicago for the past five years? I work in a mercantile store. You learn quickly."

"I don't know what I'd have done without you. You're the most unselfish person I've ever known."

"Nonsense. I'm just trying to be helpful to two people who mean very much to me. And besides, we aren't through yet. We still have to make the gown."

When they joined Keith at the appointed time, he couldn't believe the stack of boxes and packages they had.

"I can see that marriage is going to be an expensive proposition," he joked.

"Wait until Cole finds out how much I've spent to-day. He'll probably raise the roof."

"I don't think he'll mind, Margaret, as long as you didn't spend it on the stageline," Keith said.

On the ride back to Lawford Maggie insisted upon riding in the rear seat with the piled-up packages. It had been an exhausting day, and she sat relaxing as Keith and Caroline talked quietly together. And every time her thoughts strayed to Cole, Maggie willed herself to think of her forthcoming wedding.

For the next three days all four of the women devoted all their time to making the wedding gown. Time and time again Maggie had to put it on to be fitted and then take it off to be sewn.

But through it all, she and Caroline grew closer and closer. Maggie suspected Caroline was in love with Keith, but she couldn't bring herself to ask her friend. No one knew better than Maggie the heartache of unrequited love—or how hopeless that love could be. Maggie would willingly step aside if she believed Keith held the same feeling for Caroline. But it appeared that he regarded Caroline as merely a good friend.

And if Maggie's suspicions were correct, no one worked more tirelessly than Caroline did toward making a wedding gown for the future bride of the man she loved.

They sewed, stitched, tucked, trimmed, and hemmed until Maggie didn't want to even look at a pair of scissors or threaded needle again. Finally by Friday all that remained to be done was the veil.

No one could agree on the proper length. Maggie preferred it shorter, Caroline and her mother thought it should be worn longer. Since they were more knowledgeable on the subject, she bowed to their judgment.

And in the three days that passed, Maggie never once saw a sign of Cole. When she finally broke down and asked if he had gone back to Texas, Ellie told her he was leaving Lawford the day of the wedding.

That night, long after Caroline had fallen asleep, Maggie lay awake. She tried to force herself not to think of never seeing Cole again, but Ellie's words kept going through her mind. Finally, unable to sleep, she got out of bed.

Maggie walked outside and sat down on the porch. Upon hearing one of the horses neigh, she got up to go and check them. As she rounded the corner of the house, she stopped and stepped back into the shadows.

Cole was with the horses, talking to Vixen. The mare nuzzled him as he cooed to her and patted her head. Did every female, no matter what the species, fall under his charm? Ellie, Dallas, Caroline seemed to adore him, those two prostitutes, Gladys and Lyla, literally drooled over him, as did the ones in Alaska, and now even a mare found him irresistible. Was she the only female who could cut through his charm and recognize that the real Cole MacKenzie was a self-absorbed bastard who put his own interests above anyone else?

That isn't true, Maggie, and you know it. Look how he loved Pop. Look how he stayed up all night when the stable burned down. Don't pass judgment on him because of what happened between the two of you. You know you were as responsible for that as he was. If you're really sincere about getting over him, stop trying to convince yourself he's a scoundrel. You know Cole MacKenzie will always be there for you if you need him. Accept the reality that he's just not interested in making a commitment. He was honest about that from the beginning. You were the one who lied about your true feelings. When you can face him without resentment, you will be over him. So stop trying to brand him guilty because of your deceit—or is it conceit? Cole MacKenzie is a good man, Maggie. Have the character to face him and tell him so.

But she couldn't. She couldn't face him and tell him because he knew she didn't love Keith but was going to marry him despite that. When he walked past, she slunk back deeper into the shadows.

When Maggie was sure he was gone, she went over to the horses. Nuzzling the mare's cheek, she whispered, "You're a female, Vixen. I wish you could tell me what to do. I could use some horse sense right now."

Ellie was sitting in the rocking chair when Maggie returned to the porch.

"What's bothering you, darlin'?"

"Oh, Ellie, I don't know what's wrong with me." She sat down and laid her head on Ellie's lap. "I'm about to marry one of the nicest and kindest people in the world, and I'm not sure I'm doing the right thing."

"Don't you love him?"

"I love Keith. He's fine and good. And I know he'll always be good to me."

"Then what's the problem, child?" Ellie began to stroke her head gently.

"You know what it is, Ellie. I don't have to say it." She looked up into Ellie's troubled gaze. "What if I can't forget him, Ellie? What if I let it destroy Keith's happiness? I tell myself I'll be the best wife he could ever hope for. But what if I fail?"

"I believe you can do anything you set your heart to, darlin'."

"But that's some of the problem. It's not only Cole. Am I just thinking of myself? Putting my interests above others?"

"I don't understand."

"Ellie, you've known both Keith and Caroline for a long time, haven't you?"

"Their whole lives."

"Were they ever interested in each other?"

"At one time folks thought they'd get hitched. But then the Bennetts moved away, and that seemed to end it."

"So they could still be in love."

"Could be, but if he loved her, honey, wouldn't he have married her by now?"

"But what about Caroline? Ellie, she loves him. Maybe she came back to tell him so, and I've spoiled it for them."

"Maggie, if it was meant to be, it would have been. You can't blame yourself when two people don't have the sense to do something about it when they love each other." She paused and said suggestively, "Any two people, no matter who they are."

"Well, sometimes love is just one-sided. Then you can't do anything about it."

"Then it just ain't meant to be. But, darlin', I've knowed you too long not to believe you'll do the right thing. Now get yourself upstairs and get your beauty rest. You don't want black circles under them pretty eyes of yours at the party tomorrow, do you?"

Maggie returned to her room, and as she lay in bed,

she thought of Ellie's words. *You'll do the right thing.*

But what was the right thing to do?

The morning of the party dawned clear and sunny. As the day progressed, everyone but Maggie grew more excited about the party and tried to find things to do to pass the time until leaving for the Lazy L. Caroline and her parents decided to go to the Calhouns for the day and meet Maggie and Ellie at the party.

Once again Maggie put on her wedding gown, so Ellie could put some finishing tucks to it. Before they could complete the task, Ellie ran out of white thread.

"Just stay as you are, darlin', I'll go to the general store and get a spool."

While she was gone, Maggie picked up the veil and put it on again. She still felt it hung too long in back. Hearing footsteps below, she decided to get Ellie's opinion and hurried down to the kitchen.

"Ellie, don't you think this veil's too . . ." The words froze in her throat. Cole turned around and stared at her, transfixed.

"Oh, I thought you were Ellie returning."

He didn't say anything but continued to stare. She thought he was still angry with her, so she started to leave.

"You'll make a beautiful bride, Maggie."

"Thank you."

"Did I ever tell you the story of how my mother and father met?"

"No." She turned around and faced him.

"It seems my dad owned this casino in Fort Worth, and on the day she was scheduled to get married, my mother ran out on the wedding my grandfather had arranged for her. Dad said he looked up and saw this heavenly vision, dressed in a wedding gown, standing in the doorway. He'd never seen her before, but he knew he'd marry her one day."

"Is that what you're hoping for, Cole? To suddenly look up and see her standing there and know that one day you'll marry her?"

His gaze never left her face, but she knew that under the circumstances a simple answer of yes or no would be too definite for him.

"Doesn't every man, Maggie?"

This time he made the move to leave. He got as far as the door when she called to him.

"Cole, wait. I want to thank you for not interfering with the wedding."

He paused with his hand on the doorknob. "Why would I interfere, Maggie, if that's what you really want. It is what you want, isn't it?"

"Yes. It's what I want, Cole."

"Then you've got it, baby," he said gently.

The door slammed behind him.

Chapter 25

Maggie felt numb. She had no recollection of climbing the stairway or removing the veil and gown. By rote she began to dress for the party, and by the time Ellie returned, she had finished except for her hair.

"What are you doing, girl. I thought . . ." Ellie's words trailed off when she saw Maggie's stricken face. "What happened, darlin'?"

"Cole was here while you were gone."

"So the two of you had another fight."

"No, we didn't argue. I wish we had. I can handle his anger—not his kindness."

"What about finishing the dress?"

"It's fine the way it is, Ellie. You'd better get ready to go to the party. The buggy will be here soon."

"Did Cole say he'd be at the party?" Ellie asked.

Bemused, Maggie said, "I really don't know."

By the time she had finished pinning her hair up and adding a touch of color to her cheeks, the buggy arrived to transport them to the Lazy L.

Keith greeted her when she arrived, and they passed among the guests, accepting congratulations and best wishes for happiness. As soon as Ben saw Maggie, he took her arm and led her and Keith to a rostrum. Calling for quiet, he spoke of how much tomorrow's nuptials meant to him and how one day his grandchildren would be riding the range of the Lazy L.

Maggie looked helplessly at Keith and then forced a smile as the guests clapped and cheered. Her gaze sought out certain faces among them: the worried frown of Ellie, the pensive gaze of Dallas, Caroline's stricken expression. A quick glance at Keith revealed his somber look. These faces seemed to express the reality of the occasion more than any of Ben Lawford's fatuous words.

Then her gaze found the one person she sought. Cole was standing away from the throng, leaning back against a wall of the house.

He was too distant to see his expression, but she knew it would reveal the same disillusionment as the other four, for whatever their reasons.

Much to Maggie's relief, Ben finally finished his welcoming speech, ending it with a collective toast to the future bride and groom. Mercifully Keith led her off the rostrum.

Once again they were swamped by well-wishers. She tried to keep an eye on Cole, but he disappeared before she could speak to him. When Keith was pulled away by Ben, Maggie slipped away, but could not find Cole. Desolate, she sought a quiet spot in the darkened shadows of the garden where she could be alone.

You'll do the right thing. The litany continued to weigh on her conscience.

"I wanted to say good-bye."

Startled, she jerked her head up. Cole stood a short distance away.

She lifted her chin and forced a smile. "You mean good night. Good-byes sound so final, Cole."

"I mean good-bye, Maggie."

"I don't understand. Aren't you coming to the wedding tomorrow?"

"No. I decided it would be better if I didn't. I told Ben I'd meet him in the morning before the wedding and sign the bill of sale for Timberline. Then I'll be leaving."

"Going back to the Triple M," she said with a brave smile.

"Yeah."

"I guess now I'll never get to meet the rest of the MacKenzies."

"The gate will always be open." Her heart quickened when he said, "Are you sure this is what you want to do, Maggie?"

"I don't know; I hope I'm doing the right thing."

"I'll get you the best price I can out of Ben, Maggie, if you're positive you want to sell it to him. You know, you could keep it. He'd put up the cash to develop Timberline and split the profits with you the same way he intended to do with Pop."

Good God, he thought she meant Timberline. "I don't want to have anything more to do with Timberline, Cole. And I don't want to talk about it anymore. There's so much else I have to say to you."

"Honey, I think we've both said enough." He stepped closer and cupped her cheeks in his hands. "I wish you happiness, Miz Margaret. Lawford's a good man. I know he'll take good care of you."

"Cole, I'm sorry for the nasty things I said to you. I didn't mean them. I'd never have made it through Pop's death without you."

"Yes, you would. Don't sell yourself so short." She felt the tears sliding down her cheeks, and he brushed them aside with his thumbs. "You've got incredible strength, Maggie O'Shea. You do Pop proud. I'll never forget you, baby."

She thought her heart would burst as she watched the tall figure walk away. She wanted to call out to him to stop. To stay. To take command. To tell her what to do. To kiss her. To make love to her just once more.

But she didn't, because she knew if he had wanted to, he would have.

Maggie needed time to compose herself, so she remained in the shadows. Going into that crowd at this time would be unbearable, but if she left now, it would be an embarrassment to Keith.

When she finally felt she was ready to venture out of hiding, a couple approached and sat down on a nearby bench. She couldn't leave without passing them, so rather than embarrass herself by suddenly popping out of the darkness, she welcomed the excuse to remain in the shadows.

Maggie recognized the speaker's voice the instant

340 ANA LEIGH

she heard it. "I hadn't realized how much I missed you, Caroline, until you came back. Whatever happened to us?"

"When you didn't write, Keith, I assumed you no longer cared."

"But I did send you a letter. You never answered it. So I assumed the same about you."

"I never received a letter. I swear it."

"Oh, God, Caroline, we've wasted five years. And now it's too late. I won't hurt Margaret. She's suffered too much already."

"I know. And I wouldn't let you. She's very dear to me."

"If only—"

"Please don't say anything more," Caroline said. "It's too late for regrets." Sobbing, she rushed away.

For a long moment Keith remained on the bench, then, shoulders slumped, he got up and followed.

Maggie stepped out of the shadows. She felt surprised but not shaken by what she'd just overhead. Hadn't she suspected as much?

Sadly, they were three miserably unhappy people trying not to hurt one another but headed on a course that could ruin all three of their lives.

You'll do the right thing.

"Damn right, I will, Ellie."

Maggie sought out Caroline and found her talking to several people. She took her hand. "Please excuse me, but I must speak to Caroline."

"What is it, Margaret?" Caroline asked, as Maggie strode purposefully through the crowd in search of Keith.

"Where is he?"

"Where is who, Margaret?" Caroline asked, clearly puzzled by Maggie's actions.

"Keith. Do you know where he is?"

"I have no idea. Why are you asking me?"

Maggie glanced askance at her. "Now, why do you think? Oh, there he is," Maggie said, spying Keith with his father.

Towing Caroline, Maggie marched up to them. "Excuse me, Ben, but I have to speak to Keith at once."

"Well, I hope you can talk some sense into him, gal, 'cause I can't. Sounds like he's getting cold feet."

"That's exactly what I intend to do." She clasped Keith with her other hand as Caroline and Keith exchanged perplexed looks.

"Margaret, what is this all about?" Keith asked when she led them back to the secluded garden.

"Now, sit down and listen to me. It's time the three of us had a long talk. I happened to have overheard the two of you when you were just here."

"Oh, God, Margaret, I'm so sorry," Keith said.

Caroline was desolate. "Margaret, neither of us meant to hurt you. You must believe me."

"Of course I do. But if either of you loves me as much as you say, you should have been honest about your feelings for each other." That coming from her lips was ludicrous.

"Don't blame Caroline. It's not her fault."

"Keith, it's both of your faults. Just like Ellie said last night: if two people are in love they have to have the common sense to do something about it. Well, since the two of you don't appear to have that common sense, I guess I'll have to come up with a solution. Keith, do you love, Caroline?"

"I love both of you, Margaret."

"I realize that. But are you *in love* with Caroline."

"Desperately."

"And Caroline, do you love Keith?"

"With all my heart."

"Then don't you think it's about time the two of you got married?"

"But, Margaret, it would publicly embarrass you."

"Keith, I have a confession to make. I love you dearly, but I am not in love with you either. I was going to marry you just the same. If we care about each other, why would we commit something so disastrous to one another? As for publicly embarrassing me, I'm leaving Lawford anyway."

"Are you going to Texas?" Keith asked.

Maggie sobered. "No. Cole and I have had a serious falling out, so I haven't decided exactly where I'm going. I just want out of Lawford. And I can't let him know, or he'll take me to Texas with him." A sudden inspiration flashed through her mind. "I have the solution. We'll elope."

"Margaret, now you've got me thoroughly confused," Keith said.

"We'll elope tonight. The three of us will get out of here. We'll leave word that you and I have eloped and Caroline accompanied us to return home. No one will suspect that it's really you and Caroline who will get married. And Cole won't try to stop it, because he just wants to see me safely wed and off his hands."

"You know, it might work," Keith reflected.

"Of course it will work. I've been outsmarting Cole MacKenzie since I was fourteen."

"But what about Ben? He might try and stop us," Caroline said.

"We'll get to Noches before he finds out, and I'll get my Uncle Frank to marry us right away. Whether my father likes it or not isn't the issue, sweetheart. It's our lives."

"Besides, Caroline," Maggie added, "Ben just wants Timberline. That's the only reason he was insistent Keith marry me. Well, I'm still going to sell it to him, so he's getting what he wants."

"What about Ellie and my parents?" Caroline asked. "They should be told the truth."

"You're right. We do need someone whom we can trust to tell them after we're safely gone."

"I know who I would trust," Keith said. "Dallas. She knows how to keep her mouth shut."

"Keith, are you aware that Dallas and your father have been carrying on for fifteen years?"

"Of course, but I've never discussed it with him. They're certainly old enough to know what they're doing. I doubt anybody else knows about them except Vic. They've been remarkably discreet. Which proves how close-mouthed Dallas is, Margaret."

"Well, I suppose she is the most likely. If we tell Ellie or the Bennetts, they might let it slip accidentally. So let's get out of here. Caroline, you and I will go back to the house and pack whatever we need. What about transportation? We need a buggy or wagon."

"I can get us a buggy," Keith said. "And I have extra clothes in my bedroom at the office. I'll leave now and hitch up the buggy. You ladies meet me down at the corral. I'm going to tell my father that Caroline isn't feeling well and we're taking her back to the house."

"While you do that, I'll tell Dallas what we're up to," Maggie said.

"Do you think it will get her in trouble with Ben?" Caroline asked solicitously.

"Not after fifteen years," Maggie replied, with her newly acquired wisdom on the subject of love. She and Caroline went to hunt down Dallas.

As soon as they told Dallas of Keith's and Caroline's elopement plans, she hugged Caroline. "Good for you, honey. I never understood why you and Keith didn't marry a long time ago."

"Dallas, you have to hold off saying anything as long as you can. We need as much of a head start as we can get," Maggie said. "Just in case we're followed."

"You afraid Cole MacKenzie will come after you, Maggie?"

"I know he will, if he thinks I'm not getting married. He doesn't trust me to be on my own."

Dallas smiled judiciously. "I don't think that's the only reason, but good luck to all of you. I'll be rooting for you. Shame you're cheating the town out of a wedding, though."

"Celebrate it without us," Maggie said. She kissed Dallas on the cheek. "I wish I'd taken the time to get to know you better, Dallas. You've been a good friend all these years."

Dallas hugged her. "Get out of here, Maggie, before you have me in tears."

As soon as they were in town, Keith dropped the

women off at the house and went on to his office to pack.

"I hope we're doing the right thing," Caroline said as she and Maggie shoved their clothing into traveling bags.

"You want to marry Keith, don't you?"

"Yes, but I don't like disappointing my parents."

"I'm sure they'll get over it when they see how happy you are. I'll explain everything thoroughly to them when I come back to Lawford in a couple of days."

"But what will you have accomplished if Cole is still here? He'll make you go back to Texas with him."

"He won't still be here. He said he was leaving tomorrow morning right after he and Ben finish their business."

"Our disappearance could delay that."

"Caroline, the sky could fall tomorrow and Ben would still go through with acquiring Timberline."

"But maybe Cole wouldn't. What if he tries to follow us?"

"Why would he? He's approved of Keith and me getting married. I don't think he much cares if we do it in Lawford, New Mexico, or Timbuktu."

Before extinguishing the lamp, Maggie took a backward glance at her bridal gown and veil hanging on the closet door.

Who knows? Maybe some day I'll have occasion to wear it.

Ten minutes later the conspirators were on the road to Noches, and several hours later Keith knocked on the door of the residence of Frank and Ethel Gardner.

Sleepy-eyed, the judge opened the door. "Keith! Come in. Come in. What are you doing here at this hour? Is something wrong?"

"Uncle Frank, I have a favor to ask of you," Keith said.

Chapter 26

❧ ◌◌ ❧

Dallas waited for an hour before executing her strategy. She quietly pulled Ellie and the Bennetts aside and told them the truth about the elopement. She saved Ben for the last. Once they were alone, Dallas told him what had happened, and as soon as he started his outburst, she told him to shut up.

"Why would you be upset that your son is marrying the woman he loves instead of the one you want him to marry? Do you ever think of anyone besides yourself, Ben Lawford?"

"Dammit, Dallas, this is business."

"If you're thinking about Timberline, Maggie said Cole's signing the papers tomorrow morning, so you'll get what you want anyway."

"Just the same, you should have told me sooner. We're in love, ain't we? People in love don't keep secrets like this from each other."

"I heard people in love get married, too. That doesn't seem to have influenced your thinking."

"Dammit, Dallas, you know I love ya."

"So you've been telling me for fifteen years. Well, I'm tired of waiting for you to ask, Ben. Maggie had the right idea. When the time comes that you know you're butting your head against a stone wall, it's time to move on."

"You saying we're through?"

"That's right, Ben. I'm tired of pushing drinks across a bar and then sneaking off to meet you. And since you're in a buying mood, how about buying my half of Dallas's? I'm getting out of this town, too."

"You can't do that."

"Well, you just watch me, Ben Lawford."

"I won't let you."

"I don't see how you figure you can stop me."

"I'll marry you first before I'll let you go."

She put her hands on her hips and faced him boldly. "When, in another fifteen years?"

"Dammit, Dallas, you drive a hard bargain." Then he broke out in a wide grin. "Reckon that's why I love you, sweetheart. This here town's expecting a wedding tomorrow, and we'll give it one."

He pulled her into his arms and kissed her.

Seeing no sign of Cole, Dallas then put the second part of her strategy into action. She went back to the saloon, which had been closed for the party, and lit every lamp available. She wanted a blaze of light to attract attention.

It worked. Within minutes Cole strolled in. "Party over already?"

"Afraid so," Dallas said, pouring him a drink. "The guests of honor ran out on it."

With a negligent shrug that he didn't quite carry off successfully, Cole said, "That's to be expected. They're probably getting a head start on the honeymoon."

"That's not what I meant. They eloped."

"What? Why would they do that when the wedding's tomorrow?"

"Well, like you said, Texas, maybe they couldn't wait to start the honeymoon." She saw his hand tighten around the glass. "You know, I've spent a lot of years behind this bar, figuring people out. Gotta admit I was wrong about you. Guess I was hoping, just like Mick, that you'd be the one who married Maggie."

"I did her a favor. I sure as hell would make a lousy husband."

"What makes you think so? You sure as hell love her. That's fifty percent of what makes a marriage work."

"Who said I love her?"

"Maybe you can fool yourself, Texas, but you can't fool me."

"Is that right? Well, what's the other fifty percent?"

"That she loves you."

"If she loves me so much, how come she ran off to marry Lawford?"

"How come you let her? I always heard you MacKenzies were men of action. You telling me you're gonna just stand by and let another man steal your woman from you?"

"It's for her own good, Dallas."

"Dammit, Texas, nothing sours my stomach more

than listening to a stupid man who thinks he's being noble." She raised her glass in a toast. "Well, here's to the bride and groom. May they have a long life together."

"How long ago did they leave?"

"About an hour or so ago. A fast horse could most likely catch them."

Cole slammed down his glass. "Hold that toast, Dallas, 'cause it hasn't happened yet." He rushed out.

Vic came over to her side. "Why didn't you tell him the truth like you did the others?"

With a pleased smile, Dallas slipped her arm around her brother's waist. "Sometimes it's smarter to go in the back door instead of charging through the front one. Besides, I always liked reading stories where the hero rides to the rescue of the woman he loves."

Vic grinned and slipped an arm around her shoulders. "I think you just like happy endings, sis."

Cole had saddled Cupid and was about to ride away when Ellie arrived home.

"Did you hear about the elopement?" she asked.

"Yes, Dallas told me all about it," he said. "I'm on my way to Noches right now." He dismounted and followed her into the house. "Maybe Maggie left a note that will tell us more."

While Ellie checked her bedroom and kitchen, Cole went upstairs to Maggie's room. Seeing the wedding dress hanging there was like a punch to the gut—a symbol of the mistake he'd made. For some reason that he couldn't explain even to himself, he stuffed it into a bag and took it with him.

Ellie came hurrying out of the kitchen when he came downstairs. "Did you find a note?"

"No," he said, as he ran out the door.

"What have you got in that bag, Cole?" she called to him.

"Her wedding dress," he yelled back.

"What does she need that for?" Ellie said, chasing after him. "Maggie's not the one getting married."

But he had already galloped away.

Cole figured he must have scattered every jackrabbit and rattlesnake from New Mexico to Texas as he galloped through the darkness. He felt he couldn't be too far behind them, since he doubted Keith would drive a buggy through the night at any great speed. But at the same time, he couldn't run poor old Cupid to death and often had to slow his pace.

When he rode into Noches, most of the commercial businesses were closed except for the saloons and the hotel. The hotel desk clerk was leaning on his hands, fighting sleep.

"Hi, Pete, remember me?" Cole asked.

"Oh, yeah, you and that scroungy kid that was with you came in a couple weeks ago."

"That's right. The weekend of that horse auction."

"You ever find a room?"

"Yes, thanks to you, at Mrs. Hallaway's, just as you suggested.

"Well, we've got plenty of rooms tonight." He shoved the registration book at Cole. "Three dollars a night in advance."

"Do you have a Miss Margaret O'Shea registered?"

"Auburn hair and green eyes?"

"Yes, that's her. What room is she in?"

"She ain't. I remember she was in here about a week or so ago."

Cole frowned. Where else would they have gone but here? "Did you have any late trains out of here tonight?"

"Nope. The last train came through two hours ago."

"Do you have a Keith Lawford registered?"

"Mr. and Mrs. Lawford. Newlyweds. Married just tonight." Pete smirked. "They're in the bridal suite."

"You have a bridal suite here?"

"We call it the governor's suite when he's in town and uses it."

"What's the room number?"

"Top floor. Only room on that floor. For privacy you know. Hey, where're you going?" Pete asked.

"Upstairs to congratulate the happy couple." Cole took the stairs two at a time to the third floor and pounded on the door.

Dressed in a belted robe, Keith opened the door. "Cole!"

"Where is she?"

"Where is who?" Keith asked.

"You know damn well who I mean." Cole shoved past Keith and strode into the suite.

"For God's sake, Cole, what do you think you're doing?"

"All right, get out of that bed. You're getting out of here," he demanded, bursting into the bedroom.

Caroline poked her head out from under the sheet.

"Satisfied?" Keith said, pushing him out of the bedroom. "Now get out of here."

"What the hell's going on?" Cole demanded.

"Caroline and I were married tonight. As you might have observed, this is our wedding night. So I'd appreciate you getting the hell out of here, and don't ever pull a stunt like this again. I'll tolerate it once but never again."

"I'm sorry. I thought Maggie and you were getting married."

"Even if we had, you're still out of line."

"Where's Maggie, Keith?"

"I have no idea. I'm not her guardian. You are."

"She came with you, didn't she?"

"I'm not saying. Maggie doesn't want to see you, Cole."

"She's spending the night at a Mrs. Hallaway's," Caroline said, joining them.

"Thank you, Caroline. And I'm sorry for breaking in like this."

"And congratulations, Lawford." He shook Keith's hand.

"Cole, why can't you let her be? Margaret wants to start a new life."

"That's exactly what I have in mind for her. As I said, congratulations, Lawford," he said on his way out.

Keith closed and locked the door behind him. "Poor Margaret. She'll never get away from him. Caroline, I thought you were Margaret's friend. Why did you tell him where he could find her?"

"Because I didn't want to see them waste five years, as we did."

"I don't understand."

"Oh, Keith," Caroline said, "if you had done what Cole is doing, we would have married five years ago."

Keith swooped her up in his arms. "Then I think we shouldn't waste any more time, should we, my love."

Maggie sat down, hugged her knees, and tucked them under her chin as she gazed into the fireplace. She was so happy for Keith and Caroline. She smiled, recalling Judge Gardner's confusion at the ceremony when he told Maggie to take her place beside Keith, only to be told she wasn't the bride. Keith had to explain to the perplexed man why he wasn't marrying Maggie tomorrow as planned but rather Caroline now.

But all ended well, and with her and the judge's wife as witnesses, Judge Gardner finally pronounced Keith and Caroline man and wife.

All in all it was an exciting evening. Her face sobered, but what now lay ahead for her?

For certain she would not remain in Lawford. That would be the same as being buried alive. Perhaps she should move to St. Louis. There would be plenty of opportunities for employment in the city, but it would take a lot of persuading to convince Ellie to move there.

Well, that decision didn't have to be made tonight. The smile returned to her face, and she glanced up at the portrait of Henry Hallaway hanging above the fireplace. "At least Keith and Caroline were married, Captain Hallaway."

Maggie ran a hand over the smooth satin of the yellow nightgown Caroline had given her. She'd purposely brought it along to give the garment back to Caroline for her own wedding night, but her friend wouldn't hear of it and had insisted Maggie keep it.

Sighing, she stood up to go to bed when suddenly

the door burst open. She was too surprised to do more than stare at Cole MacKenzie, who stood in the doorway.

Maggie felt a warm glow as his sapphire gaze boldly raked the length of her, the sensuous gown clinging to her curves.

"Expecting company, Miz Margaret?"

"It's Mrs. Lawford."

"And where is Mr. Lawford?" he asked mockingly. "Building up his courage?"

"He had to step out for a moment, so I advise you to get out of here before he returns."

"Now, why doesn't that scare me?" Cole said.

"How did you know where to find me?"

"Wasn't hard to figure out."

"What are you doing?" she cried when he closed the door and turned the key in the lock.

"Don't like uninvited guests dropping in."

"What do you want, Cole?"

He tossed a bag on the chair. "You forgot your wedding gown."

Her pulses began pounding erratically as he slowly approached her. "Stay away from me, Cole. I'm a married woman."

She backed away until she found herself pressed against a wall, and he leaned into her, his arms imprisoning her on each side of her head.

"You gonna stop me, Maggie?"

To her disgust she found the gleam in his eyes as exciting as it was frightening. "Don't do this, Cole."

"I want you, Maggie," he murmured, so close that his breath mingled with hers. "And you want me. Why try to deny it?"

His mouth closed over hers. Hot blood surged through her and like quicksilver raised her desire to an intensified degree that aroused her passion. But she had to resist him.

When they broke apart, she was too breathless to move. Drained of resistance, she sagged against him and rested her cheek against his chest. He slipped a finger under her chin and tipped up her head. She saw his dark eyes were suffused with desire, but whatever he saw in her eyes made him drop his hands and step back.

"What makes you think you can barge in here and make love to me as if I belonged to you?"

"Because you do." At her angry glare, he added, "The way I belong to you." She moved away, and he didn't try to stop her.

"This is no laughing matter, Cole. Don't you see that if you don't let me go, I'll never be able to build a life for myself?"

"I hope that's true, because you're the one who should be laughing, Maggie. I want you to build that life with me." He came over to her and turned her to face him, cupping her cheeks between his hands. "Ah, honey, I thought I had all the answers. No strings. No commitments. I didn't need anything other than a few bucks in my pocket. So I thought I could let you go. But I can't, Maggie. I can't go on wondering where you are. What you're doing. If you're happy. Who's kissing you now."

Emotionally she was being torn apart, but she attempted to be flippant. "I promise to write you regularly. Will that make you happy?"

"I'm trying to tell you that I love you, baby. You

opened my heart to love, and now I can't think of going on without you. I need you more than anything or anyone in my life."

"Is this some trick to get me to go back to Lawford with you?"

"It's not a trick, Maggie. I don't know when I fell in love with you. I had no idea what love really was. I'd never been in love before, so I thought it would happen as it did for my dad. One look and you're in love. And maybe that's how it was, Maggie, from the beginning with us. Maybe my skull was just too thick to let it sink through. But it has now, and I know I love you. I'll always love you. I couldn't let you marry Lawford without telling you, anymore than I can let you leave now without admitting how wrong I've been. Can't we give it another try? Forget everything in the past and start all over again. I swear, if you're not happy, if it doesn't work, I'll let you go. But let's try, baby."

"You'd never let me go, Cole."

"I promise I will."

She shook her head. "No, you wouldn't, because I wouldn't let you." Tears glistened in her eyes. "I was so right."

"Yes, you were right. I'm everything you accused me of being. I shouldn't expect you to forgive me, much less love me."

"That's not what I mean. I was right about this room. Don't you see, Cole, it's everything I believed it to be. It's enchanted. Felicitous. Just as I said. I love you, Cole MacKenzie. I love you so much."

"Will you marry me, Maggie? I promise I'll do everything I can to make you happy. And if you don't want to live on the Triple M, we won't."

"But I do want to live on the Triple M. I can't think of anything that would make me happier."

"Oh, baby, I love you!" He picked her up and swung her around in a circle, and then kissed her over and over again, covering her face, her eyes, her lips with quick, moist kisses.

When he finally put her down, they were both breathless. "Now, I advise you to put some clothes on, or we'll end up in that bed."

"More of your promises, MacKenzie."

She smiled seductively, then slowly slipped the straps of the gown off her shoulders. The satin gown slid down her body, hugging her curves as hungrily as his eyes were.

Groaning, he said hoarsely, "Maggie, you know this will delay our wedding considerably, but a man has to live up to his promises, doesn't he?"

His mouth reclaimed hers. Slipping his tongue between her lips, he explored the honeyed chamber of her mouth with heated probes, filling her with hot, arousing sensation that incited her to want more. She knew she was putty in his hands—but what better hands to mold her?

He pulled her tighter into the curve of his hips, and she gasped when his hardened arousal pressed against her, flooding her with hot, tantalizing sensation. Her passion soared.

Bombarded by the remembrance of their previous intimacy, she knew they had already reached the point of no return.

He pulled off his shirt, and when he lifted her as if she were weightless, she slipped her arms around his neck. Closing her eyes, she savored the strength of the firm, muscled wall of his chest and the tantalizing feel of the corded muscles of his shoulders under her fingertips as he carried her to the bed.

He divested himself of the rest of his clothes quickly and then stretched out the unyielding length of his long body over hers, painting a trail of tantalizing kisses down the column of her neck. The erotic heat of his mouth closed around a taut peak of a breast, drawing it into his mouth as the warmth of his hand closed over the core of her femininity. She writhed in response, her head and body flooded with such sensation that she lost track of time or place.

At times she moaned, gasped, pleaded, as he brought her body to one tremor after another, filling her senses with the scent of him, the feel of him, the touch of his wondrous hands and mouth, and the incredible sensation they created. And through it all, her ears were deafened by his groans provoked by her hands and mouth as they carried themselves to that sublime pinnacle that only true lovers can reach.

For a long time after, they lay side by side, drawing much-needed breath into heaving lungs, and then he rolled over and cradled his head on his propped arm.

Brushing some strands of hair off her cheek, he asked, "What time did you say your husband was due back, Mrs. Lawford?"

"You're not going to let me forget that, are you? You know I never would have married Keith in the end."

"Any more than I'd have let you." He got out of bed. "Come on, honey, no more distractions, you little minx. We're getting married."

"At this hour? Don't be ridiculous. Come back to bed, Cole."

He lifted her out of bed. "The next time I make love to you, Maggie O'Shea, you're going to be Mrs. Cole MacKenzie."

And as he spun her around, he looked up at the portrait hanging over the fireplace.

Cole winked. "Right, Henry?"

Chapter 27

Keith broke the kiss and raised his head. "No! Not again. He wouldn't, not even MacKenzie."

The loud banging at the door continued. "Come on, Lawford, open the door."

"You'd better see what he wants, Keith, before he wakes up the whole hotel," Caroline murmured.

Grumbling, Keith got out of the bed, belted his robe, and went to the door. "What now, MacKenzie?" he snarled, flinging the door open. Then he gaped in surprise to see Margaret with him, dressed in a wedding gown.

"Lawford, we need your help," Cole said.

"With what?"

"Maggie and I want to get married, and we need you to get your judge friend to do it."

"Is this what you want, Margaret, or did he bully you into it?"

"No, Keith. I want to marry him."

"All right, I'll talk to Judge Gardner in the morning. Good night."

Cole's hand shot up to prevent Keith from closing the door. "We want to get married *now*."

"Do you have any idea what time it is?"

"Not in the least," Cole said.

"It's midnight. I've already disturbed the judge once tonight."

"He'll understand. He's your godfather, isn't he?"

Caroline came out of the bedroom. "Really, Cole, it's much too late for this . . . Maggie! What are you doing in that bridal gown?"

"Cole and I are getting married. He wanted me to wear it."

"Married? Oh, that's wonderful." She hugged her. "I'm so happy for you."

"Is anyone happy for me?" Cole said.

"How about being happy after the sun comes up," Keith grumbled.

"Just what are you doing here at this hour, Cole?" Caroline asked.

"Caroline, do you believe they want to get married now?" Keith said.

Caroline's eyes rounded. "At this hour?"

"Why not?" Cole asked.

She looked at Maggie skeptically. "And you, Maggie?"

"Oh, yes. With all my heart. And we want you and Keith as witnesses."

Giggling, Caroline turned to her husband. "Let's get dressed, darling. We're going to a wedding."

A short time later Judge Gardner opened his door to an insistent knocking.

"Uncle Frank, I need a favor from you."

The judge looked at the newlywed couple, then at Cole, and finally at Maggie dressed in a bridal gown.

"Didn't I order the two of you out of town?"

"That was all a misunderstanding, Judge Gardner," Maggie said, with a sweet smile.

He shook his head. "I knew you were trouble the moment I laid eyes on you." Sighing, the good judge called to his wife, "Ma, bring me the Bible."

The next morning the two newlywed couples rode back to Lawford, Keith and Caroline to pack for an extended honeymoon, Cole and Maggie to finalize all the legal transactions before leaving for Texas. They arrived just in time to attend the surprise nuptials of Ben and Dallas.

The bride glowed with happiness. Maggie had never seen Dallas looking so beautiful. And observing Ben with an objective eye, she had to admit he was rather a handsome man.

Of course, being Ben, he didn't take Keith's elopement graciously, but that was to be expected. And since it didn't bother Keith, Maggie saw no reason why it mattered. Ben needed a put-down from his autocratic behavior, and the sweet disposition of Caroline would soon have the rancher eating out of her hand. She smiled. Dallas would see to that.

Maggie walked up to the new bride and, smiling through their tears, the two women hugged and kissed.

"If only Pop could be here to see this day. I know he'd be so happy for both of us, Dallas."

"What makes you think he isn't here, honey?" Dallas said.

Caroline came over and linked her arm with Maggie's. The three women glanced over to where Cole was following Ben Lawford into Keith's office.

"I'd sure like to be a mouse and listen to what's going on in there," Dallas said.

"Cole told me as soon as it's all settled, we'll be leaving."

"We'll miss you, Margaret, and Ellie, too, when she follows you," Caroline said.

"I suspect that once Ben starts developing Timberline, there'll be a lot of changes and new faces in town."

"It still won't be the same without you and Ellie," Dallas declared. She pulled each of them to her side. "But just think, girls, yesterday we were all spinsters, and today we're married matrons."

"You're right," Caroline agreed.

"Speak for yourselves, ladies," Maggie declared. "I'm only eighteen. I don't feel like any matron. I don't even feel married yet."

"I wouldn't advise you to let Cole hear you say that," Caroline said, laughing.

"Speaking of Cole, I should go and get my clothes packed."

"I'll help you," Caroline said.

"And I better go and mingle with my other guests. Do you believe it, girls? Dallas Donovan, the first lady of Lawford."

"Dallas Donovan Lawford," Maggie corrected her.
They broke into laughter.

Inside Keith's office Ben's temper had flared. "I've got no use for the O'Shea house. Why should that be part of the bargain?"

"Father, Cole is right. Ellie's bedroom could be converted into the stageline office, then all you'd have to do is add on a stable."

Ben glared at his son. "Whose side are you on, boy? I ain't forgetting that you ran off and got married instead of getting it done right here in Lawford."

"You two can fight that out later. Let's get back to business," Cole said. "Emilio and Juan can live in the rest of the house. For the manager of the stageline it would be very convenient."

"That's another thing, MacKenzie. I should be able to choose who I want to manage the stageline, not you."

"Can you think of a better choice? Emilio has a good head on his shoulders and he's honest. An honest man working for you is the best investment you can make. And as long as he remains honest, a condition of the sale is that he remains the manager."

"I was going to offer him the job anyway, MacKenzie, so you ain't making me do anything I hadn't planned. I just don't like you telling me what I have to do."

"Well, just think, Ben, the whole package is only twenty thousand dollars. That's cheap at half the cost."

"Only twenty thousand dollars! You know how

many cattle I had to run to make that kind of money? Your wife's walking away with it, and she hasn't lifted a hand. If you ask me, that's a damn lopsided arrangement."

"You'll earn that back and more the first year that spa opens," Keith assured him. "Let's face it, Father, not only will you make money from the spa, but every business you own here in Lawford will profit from it: the hotel, the diner, the general store, and the stageline, just to name a few."

"Why shouldn't I profit from them? This is my town, ain't it? I built it, didn't I? And this is a hell of a time for you to be running off on a honeymoon when I need you the most."

"Father, Caroline and I will be back before they turn over the first shovel of dirt."

"And just to show you what a fair person I am, I'll even let you know where the hot spring is," Cole said.

Ben's eyes bulged. "You mean you found it?"

Cole nodded. "Yeah. And if there's one, there's probably others."

"All right, Keith. Get them papers written up so we can get this over with. I don't want to keep MacKenzie here from leaving."

"I'll have them ready within the hour," Keith said.

Ben headed for the doorway. "Now, if you gentlemen will excuse me, I'd like to go and join my bride."

Cole and Keith exchanged glances. "Wouldn't we all?" Cole said.

"You two ain't the only ones who's got a honeymoon ahead of him," Ben reminded them.

He paused in the doorway. "And don't think you got the better of me, MacKenzie. I figured it would cost

me twenty-five thousand before it was all settled."
Chortling with pleasure, he departed.

Later, after all the papers were signed and Maggie
had packed up her clothes, Cole loaded the bags in the
buggy while she went up Boot Hill for a final visit
with Pop.

Dallas and Vic came over to say good-bye. Cole gave
Dallas a big hug and kiss. "I owe you more than I can
ever pay, Dallas. If there is ever anything you need, you
know where to find me."

"Just be good to her, Texas. That'll be payment
enough."

"You gave me Maggie as a wedding gift, Dallas." He
handed her a paper. "Here's my gift to you. It's
nowhere near as worthy, but I've signed over my share
of Dallas's to you."

She laughed lightly and whispered, "You should
have held off and made Ben buy you out. He says he
wants me home with him, so I'm giving Dallas's to
Vic."

"Good for you, sweetheart."

He and Vic shook hands. "I owe you a lot, Cole, and
it's a damn sight more than just the saloon. A plain
thank-you don't cover it," Vic said.

"Vic, it's been a pleasure. And I'm glad it all worked
out for you."

"If you're ever up this way again, MacKenzie, the
drinks are on the house."

"Who knows, some day I might take you up on
that."

Keith came over, and the two men shook hands.
"Well, we've had our share of ups and downs, Cole,

but all in all, I guess we both had Maggie's interests at heart. It's been a pleasure knowing you."

"The same here, Keith. And since I'm taking two of the town's residents with me, it'll be up to you and Caroline to replace them."

"We're working on it," he said, grinning. "And it'll be a damn sight easier knowing you won't be around to interrupt us."

"You'll see that Ellie gets off okay?"

"Of course. Take care of Maggie, Cole."

"With my life," Cole pledged.

Emilio and Juan Morales had stood back during the good-byes. They now stepped forward.

"Señor Lawford has told me what you have done for me and my son," Emilio said. "We are grateful to you, Señor Cole, and wish you and Señorita—Señora Margaret much happiness."

"Juan knows you will have much happiness, Señor Cole," Juan interjected.

"Emilio and Juan, the two of you are one of the few pleasant memories I'll take back to Texas with me. And, Juan, if you ever decide you want to try ranching, just write to me at the Triple M Ranch, Calico, Texas."

"Juan thinks that one day, like Señor Cole, he will try many jobs before he returns to what he did in the beginning."

"You know, kid, I figure with your wisdom some day you're going to be governor of this state. And when you run for president, you've got my vote."

"*Vaya con Dios*, Señor Cole," Emilio said.

"*Y Usted, mi amigo*," Cole replied.

Cole said a temporary good-bye to Ellie until she

could pack up the house and join them. Then he walked over to the buggy to wait for Maggie.

Ben came over and joined him.

"Well, you're a real horse trader, MacKenzie. I'll give you credit for that. You sure you don't want a pound of my flesh before you pull out?"

"The pleasure's been all mine, Ben. And thank you for the use of the buggy. I'll leave it at the livery in Noches."

"It was the only way to make sure you'd get out of town," he said. "And I hope this means you're clearing out of my town once and for all."

"As far as I'm concerned, the town's all yours, Ben. But you make sure you treat that woman right, or you haven't seen the last of me."

"I won't have to trouble my mind with that threat, MacKenzie. I know when I've struck gold." He grinned. "And I didn't have to go all the way to Alaska to do it."

Cole glanced over to see Maggie coming down Boot Hill. "Well, Ben, as they say, gold is where you find it. I reckon we both hit a bonanza."

For the first time since they had met, Ben Lawford broke into a genuine smile. "I reckon we did, son." The rancher offered his hand, and the two antagonists shook hands.

"Ready, honey?" Cole asked, when Maggie came up to the buggy.

She turned her head and took a final look around her and then, smiling through her tears, she clasped the hand of her future.

"I'm ready, my love."

* * *

"Where are we going?" Maggie asked, when Cole veered the buggy off the road.

"I thought we'd take a final look at Timberline."

In a short time he reined up and they climbed out. Hand in hand they walked to the pool.

"This place is really beautiful. It's a shame part of it's going to be disturbed," Cole said.

"Well, I'll always remember it as it is now. Pristine. Peaceful. And the spot where you first made love to me."

"Our special spot."

"Cole, what are you doing?" she asked, when he knelt down and began to remove her shoes and hose.

"This place deserves a proper good-bye."

"Cole, this is madness." But she made no attempt to stop him.

He unbuttoned her gown and slipped it off her shoulders, then pulled her chemise over her head and kissed the tip of each of her breasts as he lowered her drawers.

Maggie shivered with anticipation as she helped him shed his clothing.

"You know, we're trespassing," she said, slipping her arms around his neck when he picked her up.

"That should make my fantasy even more enjoyable."

"What fantasy is that?" she asked, as he lowered her into the water of the heated pool.

"Making love to you in a hot spring," he murmured just before he kissed her, before he touched her, before he entered the incredible ecstasy of her.

Epilogue

 ◦◦◦

Christmas Eve
1898

Maggie glanced around with awe. This was her first Christmas Eve on the Triple M, and this year Cleve and Adee were the hosts.

The celebration had begun early with the arrival of the Carringtons, Kincaids, and Giffords, who were on their way to Colorado to celebrate Christmas day on the Roundhouse.

This was Maggie's first opportunity to meet Cole's three female cousins and their families. They welcomed her into the family clan as warmly as all the MacKenzies on the Triple M had done.

The house overflowed with all shapes and sizes of MacKenzies gathered together to celebrate the occasion. The tantalizing smell of ham and turkey roasting in the oven blended with the scent of pine and candles.

Everyone there, whether alone or held in the arms of a parent, hung an ornament on the ceiling-high pine tree that stood in the corner.

The day wore on as they all laughed and tried to talk over one another to be heard. Maggie had never experienced such an outpouring of love and fellowship.

Honey MacKenzie sat down at the piano, and they gathered around it and sang Christmas carols, while Luke and Flint cradled their newborn grandsons in their arms.

When all the carols were exhausted, they changed to popular songs, and Beth, Cynthia, Angie, and Honey blended their lovely voices into a quartet.

When they finished one of the selections, Emily and Rose pulled Maggie up with them and held a whispered conference with the other women. When it was over, Honey pounded out several attention-getting chords.

"Ladies and gentlemen," Flint's wife, Garnet, announced. "In honor of our newest bride and groom, and with our apologies to the composer, James Thorton, we ladies wish to serenade the groom with a song.

"Oh, Lord," Cole mumbled.

"You better brace yourself, cousin," Josh teased, beside him.

"Ready, ladies?" Garnet said.

Honey struck a chord, and they all began to sing directly to Cole.

"She loved you as she never loved before, when first she saw you on the Alaskan shore. Come to her, or her dream of love is o'er—"

Then Maggie sang out in a clear soprano to him, "I loved you as I loved you—"

Then they all joined together to finish it off. "When she was sweet, when she was swee-e-e-et sixteen."

The song was met with hoots, whistles, applause—and a groan from Cole.

As the laughter continued, Adee slipped out of the room and went into the deserted kitchen. Cleve followed and found her dabbing at her eyes.

He put his arms around her. "I know it's hard, Angel."

"I can't stop believing he'll come back to us, Cleve."

"He will, sweetheart. At least Cole is back to stay. Now wipe your eyes and let's return to our guests."

"You go back. I need a minute to compose myself."

"I love you, Angel." He lowered his head and kissed her.

The lone figure, watching through the window, wiped away the tears that misted his eyes. Then Jeb MacKenzie opened the door and stepped into the room.

"Merry Christmas, Mom and Dad."

Cleve and Adrianna MacKenzie raised their heads and turned around.

As they walked back to their house later that night, Ellie scurried ahead of Maggie and Cole to get out of the cold.

"What a wonderful night this has been," Maggie said. "I'm so happy for your father and mother."

Cole slipped his arm around her shoulders and hugged her to his side. "Yeah, it's good to see them this happy again. And Jeb looks good, considering what he's gone through."

"And think of what your family went through trying to find out what happened to him, when all this time he was in a hospital in Cuba."

"Trouble was, he had amnesia from the head wound he sustained. Jeb said he was wounded last July at the Battle of Santiago and didn't get his memory back until a week ago. When they found him, he had been stripped of all his clothing and identification, so that's why he couldn't be identified. Because of his coloring, no one even knew whether he was American, Spanish, or Cuban until he finally came out of the coma and spoke English. But since he had amnesia, they still didn't know who he was.

"Well, he's home now," Maggie said. "And I'm sure your mother will enjoy helping him recuperate completely from the ordeal."

A burst of wind caused her to hunch closer against him, and his arm tightened reflexively around her. Smiling, she glanced up at him. The collar of his jacket was turned up around his neck, and he'd shoved his Stetson up on his forehead. He was so handsome it gave her pleasure just to look at him. Never had she seen him so relaxed as he was here on the Triple M. This was his natural element. He and this place were a part of each other. And she prayed that their unborn child would grow up to be just like him.

Now that she was certain she was pregnant, she'd been saving the news to tell him when they were alone tonight as a special Christmas gift.

When they reached their house, rather than enter, he continued on. "Where are we going?"

"To the stable. It's Christmas Eve, isn't it?"

"So I've been told," she said, laughing.

"Well, tell me, honey, who comes on Christmas Eve to visit all good little boys and girls?"

"Santa Claus!" she exclaimed.

"And how does he get here?"

"In a miniature sleigh with eight tiny reindeer, or something like that," she giggled.

"Well, would you settle for six reindeer?"

He opened the stable door. Her eyes rounded with surprise and joy at the sight of the six horses in the stalls. With a cry of joy, she ran from stall to stall, hugging and patting each one as she called them by name.

Tearfully, she turned back to Cole. "How did you ever get them from Ben?"

"I threatened to go back to Lawford if he didn't sell them to me."

"Oh, Cole, thank you. It's the best Christmas gift I could ever hope for."

She walked into his outstretched arms.

"Merry Christmas, baby," he murmured.

Maggie looked up into his incredible sapphire eyes and, smiling through her tears, exclaimed, "Merry Christmas, my beloved. And I have something to tell you. Do I have a Christmas gift for you!"

Avon Romances—
the best in exceptional authors
and unforgettable novels!

Have you ever dreamed of writing a romance?

*And have you ever wanted
to get a romance published?*

Perhaps you have always wondered how to
become an Avon romance writer?
We are now seeking the best and brightest undiscovered
voices. We invite you to send us your query letter to
avonromance@harpercollins.com

What do you need to do?

Please send no more than two pages telling us
about your book. We'd like to know its setting—is it
contemporary or historical—and a bit about the hero,
heroine, and what happens to them.

Then, if it is right for Avon we'll ask to see part of the
manuscript. Remember, it's important that you have
material to send, in case we want to see your story quickly.

Of course, there are no guarantees of publication,
but you never know unless you try!

*We know there is new talent just waiting
to be found! Don't hesitate . . . send us
your query letter today.*

The Editors
Avon Romance

MSR 0302